OXFORD WORLD'S

THE STORY OF AN A

OLIVE SCHREINER (1855–1920) was the major South African novelist to emerge in the late nineteenth century. She was the ninth of twelve children born to a German father and an English mother, and was raised as a strict Calvinist on a mission station. However, her religious faith wavered when she was still a young child. After her father was declared insolvent in 1866, she had to part from her parents. Between the ages of 15 and 26 she held a succession of posts as a governess. Her spare time was devoted to writing stories, reading the major Victorian intellectuals, and developing her own distinctive brand of free-thought. Over a period of 8 years, Schreiner saved for her passage to Britain to find a publisher for *The Story of An African Farm* and to train in medicine.

Greeted with enthusiasm in 1883, *African Farm* enabled Schreiner to forge a successful career as a polemical writer. During the 1880s she formed close friendships with some of the most progressive intellectuals of the day, including Eleanor Marx, Edward Carpenter, and members of the Men and Women's Club. Deeply involved in Cape politics during the 1890s, she was passionately opposed to the second Anglo-Boer War (1899–1902). *Trooper Peter Halket of Mashonaland* (1897), the longest of her many allegories, is a swingeing attack on the expansionist policies of Cecil Rhodes. Her highly popular *Dreams* (1891) were an inspiration to the suffrage movement. Similarly, *Woman and Labour* (1911) provided a powerful analysis of sexual inequality, influencing many interwar feminists such as Vera Brittain.

Continually troubled by asthma, Schreiner's life was split between periods of convalescence and intense political campaigning. In 1894 she entered into an intermittently happy marriage to S. C. Cronwright, an ostrich farmer. She died of heart-failure on 10 December 1920. Much of her work was published posthumously, including two novels started in the 1870s, *From Man to Man* (1926) and *Undine* (1929).

JOSEPH BRISTOW is Professor of English at the University of California, Los Angeles, where he edits the Journal *Nineteenth-Century Literature*. His recent books include *Effeminate England: Homoerotic Writing after 1885* (1995) and *Sexuality* (1997). He is completing a full-length study of Victorian poems, gender, and desire.

OXFORD WORLD'S CLASSICS

*For over 100 years Oxford World's Classics have brought
readers closer to the world's great literature. Now with over 700
titles—from the 4,000-year-old myths of Mesopotamia to the
twentieth century's greatest novels—the series makes available
lesser-known as well as celebrated writing.*

*The pocket-sized hardbacks of the early years contained
introductions by Virginia Woolf, T. S. Eliot, Graham Greene,
and other literary figures which enriched the experience of reading.
Today the series is recognized for its fine scholarship and
reliability in texts that span world literature, drama and poetry,
religion, philosophy and politics. Each edition includes perceptive
commentary and essential background information to meet the
changing needs of readers.*

OXFORD WORLD'S CLASSICS

OLIVE SCHREINER
'RALPH IRON'

The Story of an
African Farm

Edited with an Introduction and Notes by
JOSEPH BRISTOW

OXFORD
UNIVERSITY PRESS

OXFORD
UNIVERSITY PRESS

Great Clarendon Street, Oxford OX2 6DP

Oxford University Press is a department of the University of Oxford.
It furthers the University's objective of excellence in research, scholarship,
and education by publishing worldwide in

Oxford New York

Auckland Bangkok Buenos Aires Cape Town Chennai
Dar es Salaam Delhi Hong Kong Istanbul Karachi Kolkata
Kuala Lumpur Madrid Melbourne Mexico City Mumbai Nairobi
São Paulo Shanghai Singapore Taipei Tokyo Toronto

Oxford is a registered trade mark of Oxford University Press
in the UK and in certain other countries

Published in the United States
by Oxford University Press Inc., New York

Editorial material © Joseph Bristow 1992

The moral rights of the author have been asserted

Database right Oxford University Press (maker)

First published as World's Classics paperback 1992
Reissued as an Oxford World's Classics paperback 1998

British Library Cataloguing in Publication Data

Data available

Library of Congress Cataloging in Publication Data

Schreiner, Olive, 1855–1920.
The story of an African farm / Olive Schreiner: edited with an
introduction / by Joseph Bristow.
p. cm.—(Oxford world's classics)
Includes bibliographical references.
I. Title. II. Series.
PR9369.2.S37S7 1992 823—dc20 91–47609

ISBN 0–19–283664–1

5 7 9 10 8 6

Printed in Great Britain by
Clays Ltd., St Ives plc

CONTENTS

ACKNOWLEDGEMENTS

Acknowledgements must be made to the many people who have greatly assisted me in obtaining all the necessary materials for preparing this edition: the librarians of the Mary Badland Library, Sheffield City Polytechnic; my colleagues, Jan Berry, Frances Dann, and Alison Oram; the staffs of the London Library and Sheffield University Library; and Kim Scott Walwyn and Judith Luna, both of Oxford University Press. Druuske Hawkridge and David Hawkridge kindly advised me on English translations of several Dutch and Taal words. Laura Chrisman introduced me to Schreiner's writings. My thanks to them.

J.E.B.

Sheffield
August 1991

INTRODUCTION

I

The modest title gives no clue to the contents. It is the story of the growth of the human mind cut off from all but the most commonplace influences, facing its own doubts, crushing its own and others' deceits, and at last beating out a music which is not very melodious, but which is thoroughly honest. On the solitary 'Kopje', in the growth of the little Dutch Waldo, there come up for solution one after another the simple questions of human nature and human action that the world has labelled with many big names; and this young lady historian of Boer life—if the above surmise is correct—faces them as they rise with refreshing temerity, and what is still more surprising and refreshing, she has the right word to say about almost all. Orthodox Christianity, Unitarian Christianity, woman suffrage, marriage, Malthusianism, immortality—they all arise over the horizon of this African farm.[1]

These words of high praise come from the pen of Henry Norman, a little-known critic, in his expansive review of 'Theories and Practice of Modern Fiction' published in the liberal *Fortnightly Review*. His generous comments produced a huge amount of interest in Schreiner's exceptionally innovative novel. Appearing under the pseudonym Ralph Iron, *The Story of An African Farm* presented itself as a man's work. But reviewers were quick to see through this rather thin and implausible disguise. Behind the so-called man of iron was a woman of twenty-eight, recently arrived from the Cape, and soon to be involved with some of the most progressive of the burgeoning socialist and feminist movements in Britain. One of the book's greatest admirers was the Marxist activist Edward Aveling, who championed its 'bold out-speaking' and

[1] Henry Norman, 'Theories and Practice of Modern Fiction', *Fortnightly Review*, NS 34 (1883), 882. The *Athenaeum* was also impressed by *African Farm*, commenting on its 'considerable power': No. 2888 (3 Mar. 1883), 276.

'irreligious standpoint'.[2] He felt that Schreiner's fiction, if in some respects deficient in form and clumsy in technique, was none the less 'pointing the eyes' of her 'readers in the direction of the great socialistic revolution' that to him seemed imminent. It was this polemical aspect of her compelling story set on the High Karoo that aroused so much excitement among many other political radicals, including Eleanor Marx (who, not without coincidence, would later live as Aveling's common-law wife). The homosexual emancipationist, Edward Carpenter, frequently recommended her novel to his comrades. She met him through the Fellowship of the New Life, a group propagating the ideas of the American visionaries, Henry Thoreau and Walt Whitman, and from which the influential Fabian Society would develop.

Brought out in two volumes in January 1883, *African Farm* turned into an instant commercial success. Its strongly philosophical and political themes, all the ones Norman lists, fed into some of the most troubled areas of late Victorian thought. Deeply informed by the political economy of John Stuart Mill, the social Darwinism of Herbert Spencer, and the Transcendentalism of Ralph Waldo Emerson, Schreiner's strongly intellectual novel courageously faced up to the increasing agnosticism of her age, its growing doubts about the sanctity of marriage, and the violence incurred by imperialist expansion. It is now also recognized as the first distinctly 'feminist' fiction in English (campaigners for women's rights had begun to own the label 'feminist' by this time), and this is because Lyndall—one of the two orphans on the farm—embodies a sexual type which would subsequently cause great controversy in the press. She stood out as the rebellious female who, within a matter of years, became known as the 'New Woman'. Revered by radicals and reviled by reactionaries, the forthright 'New Woman', with her desire for 'free union', not marriage, and for reformed dress, not frilly frocks, appalled the pages of *Punch* and animated the columns of *Progress*. Schreiner's story prepared the way for a host of 'New Woman' novelists

[2] Edward B. Aveling, 'A Notable Book', *Progress: A Monthly Magazine of Annotated Thought*, 1 (1883), 162.

publishing in the late 1880s and 1890s—Mona Caird, Sarah Grand, and George Egerton counting as the most prominent among them.

Set in the 1860s, *African Farm* tells a quite straightforward tale. Its strengths derive, not so much from its stark setting and jolting sequence of events, but more from the manner in which Schreiner handles her disquieting story. Although the novel contains several long passages of polemic (such as Lyndall's passionate claims for independent womanhood in Part II), and although two long sections take the form of mystical allegories (which adopt, if only to subvert, the diction of a biblical parable), most of the narrative comprises a series of loosely connected episodes about the residents of the farm. Employing frequent lapses of time between chapters, Schreiner's narrator adumbrates only the most pertinent details of each character, and relies much more on *showing* the actions, thoughts, and moods of these isolated people, rather than *telling* us exactly how they function. Several critics have expressed dissatisfaction with Schreiner's narrative technique, finding it variously 'artless', 'vague', and 'diffuse'. But its rather fragmentary structure, I would argue, is part of its modernity. Readers of this haunting novel will find that they are often obliged to infer the key links between each incident. Crucial pieces of evidence—such as the precise details of Lyndall's extra-marital relationship—are left to our own imagining. Oblique references such as this should not be misread as either coy discretion on Schreiner's part or, more crudely, her inability to handle sensitive subject-matter. Since her novel is altogether more daring in its views on sexuality than perhaps any other fiction of its time, Schreiner's chosen narrative method, which depends on leaving occasional clues, muted signs, and gentle hints at the deeper significance of what is happening, ensures that none of its potentially explosive elements is made sensational. And so in obviating the excitability of many conventional stories of unrequited love, Schreiner accomplishes a poignant and disturbing tone in her writing—which is lingeringly elegiac, strangely discordant, and, since the notes it strikes are so unusual, more sustained in its power to shock.

Throughout its twenty-six and highly varied chapters, *African Farm* takes many opportunities to reveal its awareness of the limitations to orthodox kinds of narrative. Otto Farber, the ingenuous German overseer, is absorbed by far-fetched romances (they are 'as real and as important to himself as the matters of his own life' (p. 61)); Em, the domesticated young girl who will inherit the farm, likes only 'nice' stories, not the copy of Mill's *Political Economy* that features so regularly in the central chapters (p. 75); Tant' Sannie, the avaricious Boer woman who rules the children's lives with a somewhat hypo-critical hand, believes that any stories other than those in the Bible are the Devil's work ('Polity-gollity-gominy' is her amus-ingly garbled name for Mill's treatise (p. 81)); and, in Part II, when Waldo sets out to work near the diamond fields, he meets a boy who champions shilling shockers such as the '"Black-eyed Creole" . . . where the fellow takes the nigger-girl by the arm, and the other fellow cuts off' (p. 219). Like so many of the violent and weak-willed types Waldo encounters, this careless young man is responsible for knackering Waldo's horse.

Indeed, nearly all the characters in the novel have their lives, if not destinies, shaped by a particular structure of storytelling. Bonaparte Blenkins, the Irish confidence-trickster who ruins nearly everyone on the farm, makes a dastardly life out of his tall tales. Claiming spurious affiliations with the Duke of Wellington, the Duke of Sutherland, and no one less than Napoleon himself, Blenkins presents himself as a veteran adventurer. Tant' Sannie and Otto are completely taken in by his far-fetched yarns. Only Lyndall dares to enquire: 'how do we know that the story is true?' (p. 28). Lyndall, who admires the historical Bonaparte, his indomitable will, and his power to lead and conquer, is saddened by the way the Emperor's life concluded in obscure tragedy: 'it is only the made-up stories that end nicely; the true ones all end so' (p. 14). Even at the age of twelve, she recognizes that her strong desire to vanquish the many obstacles that necessarily lie in her path will not, ultimately, be fulfilled. Distrusting the enchantments of romance, Lyndall is the only one who understands how fiction can manipulate illusions to make the world seem a much more comfortable place.

Schreiner's demonstrably high level of consciousness about what may and may not be achieved by various narrative conventions alerts us to the unchartered ground she is trying to break in fiction. This is not a novel that reaches predictable conclusions. Instead, it is replete with unjust outcomes, forestalled ambitions, and, like Napoleon Bonaparte's fate on St Helena, utter bathos. The articulate Lyndall, who espouses a precocious feminist politics, finally wastes away after the death of her three-hour-old child; Em, longing for a good marriage, thinks herself ugly, grows fat, and eventually settles with a man she had earlier rejected; Otto, the kindly German farmer, is cruelly sent to his death by the unscrupulous newcomer Blenkins; and his self-reliant son Waldo, who bravely advances to an agnostic position, having been denied God's revelation on earth, dies prematurely. But Tant' Sannie, who has no hesitation in marrying for purely economic reasons, and whom we may expect to suffer some reversal of fortune, never ceases to prosper; and Blenkins, who perpetrates appalling crimes of brutality against Otto and Waldo, never feels the sting of the whip on his own hide.

There is a clear point to this marked imbalance of justice. The characters with the greatest moral strengths are the ones who enjoy the least material gain. Yet their respective fates are perhaps not so surprising, given the fact that ethical principles—of fairness, equity, and compassion—are so far removed from the bitter reality of life on the farm. In the midst of the High Karoo, raising sheep and ostriches, relations between them are essentially based on property and contracted labour. The farm, its structure of ownership, and the day-to-day work that must go on there have brought this disparate group of mismatched people together. Familial ties are altogether less important than those of economic necessity. Only the disempowered among this group forge any links of affection. And they are, in the main, the losers.

Two of the three children, Lyndall and Waldo, concentrate the attention of the narrative more than any of the other figures. They serve to mediate Schreiner's principal agnostic and feminist concerns. Although these young people are complete opposites—he is practical, she is intellectual; he is

short of speech, she is eloquent—they importantly comple-
ment one another. Like a twin brother and sister, their bond
is the strongest in the book, reaching spiritual proportions.
And it would seem that they have, for all their differences, a
connection that says much about the most progressive elements
of the species. Schreiner, it must be stressed, saw particular
human types as manifesting the most advanced state of human
nature, and her social Darwinism is in evidence on many pages
of the book. For Lyndall, at least, her close friendship with
Waldo transcends gender; it stands above and beyond the
sexual. And for Waldo, after Lyndall's untimely death, his life
can only have meaning with the thought of being reunited with
her. In some respects, their love parallels the childhood passion
of Tom and Maggie Tulliver in George Eliot's *The Mill on the
Floss* (1860). (Eliot's novel has also been claimed as one of the
main prototypes of 'feminist' fiction in English. Schreiner
informed the sexologist Havelock Ellis that she had read it as a
young woman, and 'not cared for' Eliot's writing.[3] But its
presence can certainly be felt.)

The unfortunate Lyndall and Waldo, however, unlike the
charming Tullivers, are not related by blood. Victorian novels
are generally very specific about family genealogies. One only
has to think of the generational obsessiveness of Emily Brontë's
Wuthering Heights (1847) to see how this is the case. Yet precise
details about Lyndall's parentage are never revealed. Her only
family connection is with Em, her cousin. Em, whose origins
are equally obscured from view, enjoys prospects altogether
better than Lyndall's. Before they come of age, Em and
Lyndall are in the care of Tant' Sannie, who married Em's
father when he knew he was going to die. Tant' Sannie is
reluctant to remarry, since the farm would pass out of her
hands. As soon as Em reaches sixteen in Part II, and so
succeeds to her property, Tant' Sannie's future is luckily
secured. The Boer woman weds one of her distant relatives,
little Piet Vander Walt, a nineteen-year-old albino widower,
the most inappropriate husband imaginable for a woman in her

---

[3] Havelock Ellis, 'Notes on Olive Schreiner' (1884) repr. in Cherry
Clayton (ed.) *Olive Schreiner* (Johannesburg: McGraw-Hill, 1983), 41.

thirties who has been married twice already. Throughout *African Farm*, the bonds between individuals, even in marriage, often have a striking incongruity, absurdity, and precariousness about them. Even Lyndall and Waldo cannot form a lasting partnership. Instead, this young man and woman recognize in one another what it means to be unable to fit into a society based on institutions, such as Christianity, that cannot serve them adequately.

Waldo, first seen as a surly lad of fourteen, is one of Tant' Sannie's most badly treated employees. Like his large-hearted father Otto, Waldo's days are spent looking after the sheep and pigs. But he is deeply unhappy with his parent's blind faith. It fails to explain everything he sees around him. Given pride of place in the earliest chapter, he is shown listening with fear to the ticking of a watch. Every second that goes by sends a shuddering note of death through his tortured frame. What is it that should cause such terror? Waldo has learned through rudimentary books on science that each movement on the clockface signals the passing away of another human life. Countless bodies are discharged to the grave as he tries to enumerate the seconds inexorably measured out by the watch. It makes Waldo think of all the civilizations that have vanished, one after another—Ancient Greece, Rome, the dynasties of India and China. It is as if the boy had read, like Schreiner, W. H. Lecky's *History of European Morals* (1869) and Edward Gibbon's *Decline and Fall of the Roman Empire* (1776–88). Such a view of history—implying the comparative brevity and futility of human endeavours—terrifies him.

Schreiner has good reason for beginning her story with this eerie episode. Not only does Waldo's peculiar awe at the evanescence of human life represent a characteristically anguished response to developments in Victorian scientific and historical thought; by focusing on a watch, it also takes a sidelong glance at one of the most influential tracts on 'revealed religion' in the early nineteenth century. The work to which Schreiner implicitly alludes is William Paley's *Natural Theology* (1802), and it is her task to indicate how such a view of divine ordinance in the world can no longer adequately account for human life. For many years Paley's book was compulsory reading on university syllabuses, and it opens with the memorable image of a timepiece. Paley argues that should he have been out walking and his foot struck upon a stone, he would be wise to think that this obstacle had lain there for ever. But were he to have found a watch along his path, then he would learn that such a complex object, with its intricate component parts, had been put there for a purpose. This, Paley claims, is a suggestive metaphor for God's design in the world. Such theology, then, involves interpreting God's presence from the intentional organization of the natural environment. But for Waldo the watch suggests, not God's presence, but his inexistence. How can life have any meaning if it is reduced to infinitesimal units of time? What divine hand could order the universe thus? So the world for him seems chaotic, inhumane, statistical. Desperate for godly revelation so he may assuage his restless spirit, Waldo re-enacts the Old Testament scene where Cain attempts to propitiate the Lord. He touchingly offers a lamb chop as a sacrifice, asking the Almighty to come down and burn his dinner-meat. And when the holy fire fails to appear, he sinks into despair.

These early sections of *African Farm* obviously present a world where all the old religious and political certainties are collapsing. During one of the Sunday services, Waldo echoes the scepticism emanating from the Higher Critics of the Bible. Following D. F. Strauss's and Ernest Renan's *Lives* of Jesus (translated in 1846 and 1863 respectively), paralleling the South African Bishop Colenso's penetrating analysis of the Pentateuch (1862–3), and extending the liberal debate conducted by the Oxonian authors of *Essays and Reviews* (1860)—these were the main volumes that served to undermine much orthodox Christian teaching—Waldo is led to ask 'mockingly strange, trivial questions' about the inconsistencies between the Gospels: 'Why did the women in Mark see only *one* angel and the women in Luke *two*?' (p. 33).[4] Such 'adder-like thoughts' plague him. Just as the relentless ticking of the

[4] For discussion of these religious controversies, see Bernard M. G. Reardon, *Religious Thought in the Victorian Age: A Survey from Coleridge to Gore* (London: Longman, 1980), particularly pp. 321–59.

watch has a levelling effect on human aspirations, so too does Waldo's knowledge of prehistory cast his understanding of the farm and its arid outlying reaches into an expressly modern and troublingly alienated vision. A school book on physical geography has taught him that the landscape he inhabits was once the bottom of a lake. The fixed parameters of biblical time, therefore, have been broken by the boundless, transformative vision of Victorian science. Africa, so often claimed by imperialists to be a god-forsaken continent without a recorded past, has a store of cave-paintings whose meaning, if confounding Western forms of knowledge at this time, has a strange allure for Waldo. Taken together, these particular elements of Schreiner's novel certainly accentuate a disjunction between dominant Victorian precepts about history, religion, and culture and the never-ending world of the Karoo where the stark 'primitive' farmlands and its seemingly 'civilized' European inhabitants do not cohere. Stretching out towards the horizon, Africa exceeds the explanations offered by the world-view brought by those invaders who have settled there.

Yet Waldo, who senses that the rocks and stones surrounding the farm somehow 'speak' to him, is not completely at a loss in this world. The solitary Karoo is, after all, the only home he has known. He understands that the age-old inscriptions and drawings in the caves must have been 'beautiful' to the 'Bushmen' who created them (p. 16), and that they served some purpose. In this way, Schreiner's novel absorbs many of the findings of comparative anthropology, a discipline that came into its own in the 1870s, and makes us see for the first time in English fiction how 'art' could be understood in the 'primitive cultures' analysed by Edward Tylor and his contemporaries. In a sense, Waldo has 'primitive' qualities, although it is the task of the narrative to question the relative merits of 'civilized' and 'primitive' values. Somewhat later in the story, in his clumsy manner, he carves a wooden grave-post for his deceased father. The mysterious stranger who accidentally meets him near the farm, and narrates the inspiring allegory of 'The Hunter', wishes to purchase Waldo's craft-work from him. Money, the unnamed stranger reckons, would be a generous exchange for so worthless an object. But Waldo

refuses to part with his unwieldly sculpture. As the stranger
can see only too clearly, Waldo is trying to express some truth
about his own life through this ham-fisted piece of carving,
and it arouses this gentleman's pity.

Waldo, however, need not be pitied. His course in life is to
come to terms with 'a striving, and a striving, and an ending
in nothing' (p. 74), to reach the limits of his capabilities,
succeed in what few things life has been able to offer him, and
not to give up on his dreams. The crucial central chapter
entitled 'Times and Seasons'—which draws on the biblical
wisdom in Ecclesiastes only to abandon it—provides a sum-
mary of social and sexual development that may be read as a
parallel to the remarkable changes Waldo painfully experi-
ences. Unable to find God, the boy plunges himself into
building a sheep-shearing machine. But his mechanical cre-
ation is also fated. Blenkins, the sadistic con-man whose
capitalist mind sees the boy in search of making his fortune
through a successful patent, ruthlessly crushes Waldo's efforts
with his foot.

Eager to dominate any rivals for his crown, this ironically
named 'Bonaparte' takes his vindictive impulses out on the
weakest members of the farm community. Otto loses his life to
him. The gentle overseer is too naïve to realize that Blenkins is
disposing of the old man's sheep in an attempt to control the
farm. Blenkins's meretricious behaviour charms Tant' Sannie,
who is humoured by the Irishman's spiteful attitude towards
the diffident Waldo, turning the boy head-over-heels in the
pig-sty, and tying him to a whipping-post. Suspicious of any
writings he does not understand, Blenkins has already hurled
Mill's *Political Economy*, which Waldo finds thoroughly
engrossing, at the poor boy's head. Mill's book would have
informed the knowledge-hungry Waldo that capitalism often
thrives on fraud: that is why Mill is led to enquire into
alternative structures for living—Fourierism, Communism, St
Simonism. It is not so surprising, then, that the exploitative
and half-educated Blenkins should commit Mill's *magnum opus*
to the flames. Likewise, when he delivers a rousing hell-fire
sermon at one of the Sunday gatherings, Blenkins asks the
members of his small congregation to search their souls in

answer to the question: 'What is a liar?' (p. 36). This bitingly satirical moment exposes the rhetoric of the pulpit as little more than a confidence-trick.

Plotting his route to success by as many deceitful means as possible, Blenkins informs the Boer woman that Otto is conniving to marry her. This, he thinks, will be his master-stroke. The outraged Tant' Sannie consequently dismisses Otto, a man who has done no harm whatsoever. Having packed his bags to leave, Otto dies—presumably of heart-failure. And Blenkins arranges the burial of the old German before Waldo has learned of his father's death. It is only with the arrival of Tant' Sannie's niece that the Irish opportunist wrecks his chances. At fifteen, Trana intends to marry as soon as she can. Her father has £2000, a thriving farm, and 500 sheep. Tant' Sannie boasts, and Blenkins can clearly see, that Trana will be an excellent prospect for a future husband. So he makes a pass at the young woman, oblivious to Tant' Sannie who, having scrambled upstairs into her commodious loft, watches them embrace from above. Blenkins then flees her wrath. And Part I of the novel concludes with the Irishman cowering in the grounds of the farm, pleading with Waldo for something to eat. Finding Blenkins both food and money, Waldo displays extraordinary tolerance towards his former persecutor. His humanity is greater by far than those who hold power over him.

Only Lyndall comes close enough to Waldo to appreciate his considerable depth of character. Lyndall, who has the least personal security on the farm, is the most determined figure in the book. It is she, for example, who summons up the courage to unlock Waldo from the outhouse where Blenkins has brutally held him captive. From the outset, she expresses a serious turn of mind, with a clear sense of right and wrong. When Blenkins takes over as the children's inept schoolmaster, she leaves his class in disgust when he insists that Copernicus was a tyrannical Roman Emperor, not a Renaissance scholar who revolutionized his contemporaries' understanding of the spheres. Ostensibly God-fearing but actually frightened of 'spooks', Tant' Sannie generally complies with the young Lyndall's wishes, lest she disturb the spirits of the orphan's parents. Much later we discover that during the hiatus of four years that separates Parts I and II, Lyndall obtained a place for herself at a girls' boarding-school, and that Tant' Sannie agreed to her going. This intervening period marks a mysterious lacuna in the story, and it takes some time before we can comprehend what preceded her return to the farm.

Embittered and exhausted in Part II, Lyndall makes long speeches to Waldo about woman's social deposition. Inspired by the tracts of women's rights composed by Schreiner's most admired thinkers—especially Mill in *On The Subjection of Women* (1869)—Lyndall espouses views that struck readers in the 1880s with greater force than any other aspect of the novel. So momentous are Lyndall's beliefs that they threaten to overwhelm her; it is as if she is physically unable to withstand the intellectual magnitude of her vision: 'I am so pressed in upon by new things that, lest they should trip one another up, I have to keep forcing them back. My head swings sometimes. But this one thought stands, never goes—if I might but be one of those born in the future; then, perhaps, to be born a woman will not be to be born branded' (p. 153). Acknowledging that she holds opinions about independent womanhood that are well ahead of her time, Lyndall admits that she has little choice in the world as it stands: 'A woman must march with her regiment. In the end she must be trodden down or go with it; and if she is wise she goes' (p. 155). Women, in other words, are inevitably compromised. But, there again, they are significantly imagined as a 'regiment'—taking up the banner of the vilified 'monstrous regiment' of women that so outraged the Protestant Reformer, John Knox, who notoriously attacked all forms of female authority in 1558. Gradually moving forward, this gathering mass of women will one day overcome. Admiring military strength, Lyndall impresses Waldo with these thoughts: 'Do you think if Napoleon had been born a woman that he would have been contented to give small tea-parties and talk small scandal? He would have risen; but the world would not have heard of him as it hears of him now—a man, great and kingly, with all his sins' (p. 157). For Lyndall, the feminist future should be one of heroic endeavour. (Schreiner would praise such 'virile' womanhood at length in *Woman and*

Labour (1911). But Schreiner's heart was firmly set against warmongering.) In the meantime, this young woman of seventeen, whom we later discover to be pregnant outside marriage, must resign herself to making 'kapjes' (sun-bonnets) and 'sasarties' (kebabs). She refuses to marry her stranger because, she tells him, he would crush her. In addition, Lyndall makes the astonishing admission that her sexual desire for this man was based on her fear of him. Her unbending feminist principles would seem, in part, to be counteracting her acknowledged masochism. Here, in its unusual examination of sexual fears and fantasies, the novel is displaying a prescient understanding of the contradictory drives that would become known by the turn of the century as the psychoanalytical unconscious.

Lyndall's defiant resistance to a marriage based on her subordination created some misapprehensions among readers—or so Schreiner thought:

One thing I always find difficult to understand is how people gather from any of my writings that I think lightly of marriage. I think it to be the most holy, the most organic, the most important sacrament in life, and how men and women can enter into it with the lighthearted indifference they do, has always been, and is, a matter of endless wonder to me.

Because poor little Lyndall *who died when she was* A CHILD OF SEVENTEEN, found out she had made a mistake in her relation with that man, and saved herself from turning it into a life-long fornication, and prostitution—therefore people seem to suppose I am opposed to life-long and deathless marriage between the man and woman!![5]

This statement may encourage us to read Lyndall's death as an act of self-sacrifice, like those of Antigone and Lucretia in classical legend. Her dismal plight certainly contrasts sharply with the life celebrated by the ebullient Tant' Sannie, who in the penultimate chapter proudly holds up her healthy new baby and exclaims to Em: 'marriage is the finest thing in the world. I've been at it three times, and if it pleased God to take

[5] 'To the Rev. J. T. Lloyd', undated fragment (1895), in *Olive Schreiner: Letters*, i, *1871–1899*, ed. Richard Rive (Oxford: Oxford University Press, 1988), 259–60.

this husband from me I should have another. There's nothing like it, my child; nothing' (p. 261). *African Farm*, then, points to the impossibility of total equality in a longstanding partnership for a woman with demands as great as Lyndall's. But the outlook of the novel is not entirely bleak. Schreiner's flat refusal to provide a utopian ending to her story forcefully points to the need to equalize relations between men and women.

Like many late-Victorian radicals, Schreiner projected sexual change, not outside, but within the limiting categories of gender. Just as Lyndall wishes to emulate manly virtues, Gregory Nazianzen Rose, the gentleman-farmer who arrives in Part II, seeks the opposite. Like so many of the names in the novel, his is particularly significant. St Gregory Nazianzen as Bishop of Constantinople was instrumental in establishing the orthodox Christian faith on the basis of the Nicene creed, defending the Church from Arianism. Legend has it that St Gregory was unsure about his vocation as a priest. Similarly heralding a new age, saint-like in his zeal, and also displaying much uncertainty about his proper role in life, Schreiner's Gregory leads the novel towards its most complex analysis of sexual relations—one that may strike readers as completely out of keeping with the rest of the book. His oddness, however, serves to amplify the deficiencies of so many of Schreiner's feeble men.

In their authoritative history of the gendering of modern literature, Sandra M. Gilbert and Susan Gubar observe that *African Farm*, when juxtaposed to earlier Victorian fictions, reveals 'a startling decline in masculine potency'.[6] The novel is populated with male characters who, if not genetically weakened by the life on the Karoo (like Tant' Sannie's albino widower), reveal the Cape as a dumping-ground for second-rate types who have not managed to survive as the fittest in their home countries. Rose in fact hails from the English yeomanry but, like Blenkins, has aristocratic pretensions,

[6] Sandra M. Gilbert and Susan Gubar, *No Man's Land: The Place of the Woman Writer in the Twentieth Century*, ii, *Sexchanges* (New Haven, Conn.: Yale University Press, 1989), 57.

writing on notepaper lavishly bearing his family crest. Rose, however, is in every other way different from the Irish trickster since he exudes a sweet-smelling feminine sensibility, gazing narcissistically at his 'unmanly' features, and confiding about his 'fine nature' to his sister (pp. 139–40). He is certainly not the kind of man to punish others just for the sake of it. Lyndall, who possesses the sharpest awareness of sexual differences, finds some amusement in this 'man–woman', and jokes with Waldo: 'How happy he would be sewing frills into his little girl's frocks, and pretty he would look sitting in a parlour, with a rough man making love to him!' (p. 163). There is more than a hint of homosexuality in this daring description. With the passing in Britain of the 1885 Criminal Law Amendment Bill two years after the appearance of *African Farm*, acts of 'gross indecency' between males were prohibited. This law was promptly exported to the colonies. Schreiner's fiction, then, shows an exceptional responsiveness to changing perceptions of late Victorian masculinity. Although the novel does not take the truly scandalous risk of allowing Gregory Rose to fall in love with another man, it permits a near equivalent. For during Lyndall's final and pitiful illness, he tends his beloved in the disguise of a female nurse.

A new breed of man, desiring to transgress his allotted sexual place, Rose finally falls in love with Lyndall's 'Napoleonic' virtues, as well as being drawn to her elfin beauty. Her high-minded and dismissive attitude towards him magnetically pulls on his subservient instincts. Although he first becomes engaged to Em (whose 'idea of love' is also 'only service' (p. 145)), his affections quickly change. The engagement is broken off, Lyndall disappears with her stranger, and Rose traces her over several months to a boarding-house in Bloemfontein. Deluded after the death of her new-born baby, unable to eat, Lyndall is finally carried away in her male nursemaid's arms, dying on her final journey back to the farm. Later, he wears around his neck a piece of cloth containing the only letter Lyndall ever wrote him; it contains four simple words: 'You must marry Em' (p. 262). He duly complies.

Shortly afterwards, Waldo returns from the tough world of the diamond-fields, and completes a long letter to the absent

Lyndall before Em reveals that her cousin is dead. Just as his
father's death occurred outside his knowledge, so too do
Lyndall's and, fittingly enough, his own. For Waldo, whose
fears and desires put the novel in parenthesis, is finally seen
resting in the sunshine of the Karoo at its most lush: 'beauty
and growth had crept even into the beds of the sandy furrows
and lined them with weeds' (p. 260). This fecund landscape
provides a positive note on which to end. Having fallen asleep,
he gradually loses consciousness, coalescing with the natural
world that had for so long been a source of bewilderment to
him. First seen desperately failing in his religious faith, and
then momentarily turning atheist (Lyndall thinks him 'mad'
for doing so (p. 69)), Waldo has eventually become agnostic
after reading the book handed to him by his stranger in Part I.
Schreiner informed Ellis that this was 'intended to be Spencer's
First Principles' (1862).[7] Spencer's agnostic emphasis on the
relativistic conditions of knowledge was a formative influence
on Schreiner. Absorbed by the stranger's powerful allegory of
'The Hunter' (which Schreiner felt important enough to
reprint in *Dreams* (1891)), Waldo comes to see that the search
for truth can never be complete—one only may enjoy oblique
glances at it. But that does not mean he should abandon his
pursuit. The stranger informs Waldo that he 'believes nothing,
hopes nothing, fears nothing' (p. 122), and such freedom from
prescriptive creeds fills the boy with admiration. In Part II,
this man of the world, who carries a 'bright French novel'
(p. 136) along with Spencer's work of social Darwinism,
fleetingly reappears to Waldo in a city park. Well-dressed, in
the company of attractive women, this man, like Lyndall's
unnamed lover, remains an obscure object of desire—enjoying
a life far more sophisticated than those who inhabit the
demoralized acres of the farm.

   Waldo, then, is left to dream of things of greater magnitude
than the life he can enjoy on this earth. And such dreaming,
according to Schreiner's aesthetics, should be seen as a gift.
Like many radical visionaries of her time (one thinks of
William Morris and Edward Bellamy), Schreiner believed that

   [7] 'To Havelock Ellis', 28 Mar. 1884, in *Lettters*, ed. Rive, 36.

dreams provided an alternative state of consciousness where altogether better worlds might be imagined. Indeed, Schreiner's whole narrative may be viewed as an exploratory dreamvision that tests the limits of her own intellectual preoccupations, with Lyndall and Waldo embodying the chief of them. Even if neither can coexist in the present world, there is at least the hope that they may combine in the nebulous 'Hereafter'. Shortly before he dies, Waldo vividly dreams of Lyndall placing her hand against his heart. The ensuing pain is so 'real' it abruptly awakens him (p. 254). Startling dreams of this kind, Schreiner argues, can anticipate the shape of the revolutionary 'new time' signalled most clearly in 'Times and Seasons'. They will, implicitly, imagine a compassionate place where young minds are no longer disturbed by social and sexual inequalities. Waldo, like Lyndall, has his freedom, but not on earth. The novel reaches its close by insisting that their idealism is not misguided but necessary: 'So age succeeds age, and dream succeeds dream . . . Our fathers had their dreams; we have ours; the generation that follows will have its own. Without dreams and phantoms man cannot exist' (p. 295). Taking her lead from Darwin, Schreiner insists that social evolution depends on each and every generation creating its own myths for survival.

II

African Farm brought into the open conscience-wracking issues. Receiving hundreds of letters from readers, Schreiner turned into something of a celebrity—even her local chemist in London refused to take money from the admired author. (Her slim volume of *Dreams* would generate even more correspondence and bigger sales—some twenty-five editions amounting to no less than 80,000 copies in forty years.) But Schreiner never went to press with another substantial work of fiction in her lifetime, although others were promised. She wrote to the popular journalist W. T. Stead in 1894: 'Neither on the subject of Christianity nor of sex have I gone from the standpoint of *An African Farm*, as people will understand if ever I publish one of my larger books.'[8] There were several long manuscripts in process, the lengthiest and most unwieldy of them being *From Man to Man*, which probably originates from the same time as *African Farm*, and on which she worked intensively during the 1880s. Her husband, S. C. Cronwright-Schreiner, undertook to edit this unfinished novel, and it finally appeared in 1926.

Most of Schreiner's writings take their bearings from the solid intellectual work she carried out—sometimes at up to ten hours a day—when composing *African Farm*. And it might be argued that her most accomplished fiction, such as the stunning childhood portrait in the 'Prelude' to *From Man to Man*, is that which refers back to life in the Cape where she grew up. (Schreiner's depictions of London, by contrast, display little of this power.) Many of the names in both novels also have a special personal resonance for Schreiner. It is not insignificant that her own first names—Olive Emilie Albertina—were adopted from her three brothers who died before she was born. Called 'Emilie' until she was twelve, she demanded to be known as 'Olive' thereafter. It was at this point in her life, when she realized that she could no longer depend on her parents' support, that she, like Lyndall, precociously converted to freethought—a highly inclusive term for those who claimed a variety of pantheistic and agnostic beliefs. Perhaps Em in *African Farm* may be thought of as a spectre of Schreiner's old self? Schreiner's use of 'Lyndall' would seem to repossess the maiden name of her disciplinarian mother, Rebecca, who kept all her children in careful check. And it is just possible to see how 'Otto' is encrypted in 'Gottlob', Schreiner's well-meaning but debt-ridden German father. But if revealing the intimate relations between Schreiner's novel and her own traumatic adolescence, these speculations, like any that draw freely on scraps of biographical information, have their limitations.

To be sure, Schreiner has been unevenly served by her

[8] 'To W. T. Stead', Feb. 1894, in *The Letters of Olive Schreiner 1876–1920*, ed. S. C. Cronwright-Schreiner (London: T. Fisher Unwin, 1924), 213.

biographers, and this has led to some severe estimations of her work. From Cronwright-Schreiner in his *Life* of 1924 onwards, successive biographers have together built up a picture of her as a restless asthmatic whose respiratory debility was a symptom of unfulfilled or thwarted sexual passions. Endlessly deliberating over *From Man to Man*, she was also unable to conclude the so-called 'sex-book' planned and drafted during the 1890s (the manuscript eventually perished when her home was ransacked by British soldiers during the 1899–1902 war). A briefer version of it was written from scratch and emerged as *Woman and Labour*. For some reason, her introduction to the writings of Mary Wollstonecraft commissioned by Havelock Ellis—a work that, had it come to fruition, may have clarified her connections with earlier developments within feminism—was never finished. (The fragments of the inchoate fifteen-page manuscript are now located in the Settler's Museum at Grahamstown.) On many occasions, Schreiner's critics have consequently been tempted to view her writings as a sequence of abortive attempts at over-ambitious projects. *African Farm*, after all, was originally to have been called *Mirage*, followed by the cheerless motto: 'Life is a Series of Abortions.' The desire of many biographers to attribute a sense of incompleteness and abandonment to her life—a life that made the journey of six thousand miles between continents no less than five times—casts a remarkably long and misleading shadow over her large body of work.

For Schreiner's writings, despite all her ill-health, unhappy liaisons with men, and seeming indecision in remaining in one place or another, none the less amount to a total of six major volumes during the sixty-five years of her life, among them the powerful analysis of female 'sex parasitism' salvaged from her aborted 'sex book'. Boldly contending against the sexist biases of the social evolutionists, *Woman and Labour* turned their steadfastly Darwinian rhetoric inside-out to make far-sighted feminist connections between intellectual and manual labour, and that other—and often forgotten—'labour' of bearing children. Distinguished for its rhetorical gusto, this work would become one of the touchstones of the suffrage movement. Besides these achievements, Schreiner produced many influential papers on social and political subjects, from ripostes to Cecil Rhodes's despicable policy of annexation to disquisitions on the hotly debated 'woman question'. Many of these, together with a number of polemical allegories, were collected in posthumous editions.

Although vehemently opposed to the dominant order of the day, Schreiner's life and work have sometimes not lived up to modern critical expectations, and any serious consideration of *African Farm* must examine these sometimes harsh judgements closely. Having turned to Schreiner's story as the first notable work of feminist fiction, Elaine Showalter's appraisal smacks of disappointment. Instead of raising each and every woman character to a level of dignity, Schreiner, argues Showalter, exhibits an insistently patronizing attitude towards Tant' Sannie and Em. In other words, Schreiner is guilty of presenting unsympathetic stereotypes: 'Reduced to their sexual functions, women in Schreiner's novels seem monstrous, swollen, destructive.' Furthermore, the novel, with its anticlimactic ending, witnessing Lyndall's gradual demise, seems 'depressing and claustrophobic',[9] hardly a triumphant tale of militant feminism. Showalter is not alone in her objections. Earlier feminist readers also found fault with Schreiner's work. Her interlarding of political thoughts in the gaps between sections of her story proved somewhat distracting. A vocal campaigner for the suffrage, Arabella Shore, although praising Schreiner's 'daring . . . speculations' and 'recklessly unconventional . . . morality', observed that 'the reveries and rhapsodies' were 'not always readable and sometimes singularly out of place'.[10] And the assertive young Rebecca West, writing in *The Freewoman* for 1912, rather bluntly commented that Schreiner was 'less a woman than a geographical fact'—so synonymous had the author become with her country of birth. *African Farm*, West thought, was 'good' but unfortunately 'spoilt by an illicit attempt to improve the reader's morals'. Despite Schreiner's

[9] Elaine Showalter, *A Literature of Their Own: British Women Novelists from Brontë to Lessing*, new rev. ed. (London: Virago Press, 1982), 196, 203.

[10] Arabella Shore, 'Modern English Novels', *Westminster Review*, 134 (1890), 149.

'warm, attractive, aggressive personality', her writing—including *Dreams* and *Woman and Labour*—remained sadly 'far inferior to her'.[11] Politics and poetics here, as elsewhere in literary history, seem not to have made a satisfying match.

Equally dismaying has been Schreiner's evident insensitivity to native life and ethnic differences. Carol Barash, for one, remarks that Schreiner's thought, despite all its feminist strong-mindedness, is hardly free from racial prejudice.[12] The anti-Semitism of *From Man to Man* is a glaring example— although it has to be quickly added that Schreiner's *Letter on the Jew* expressed her outrage against the pogroms led by the Russians in 1906. Similarly, the derisory representation of Tant' Sannie may appear to be poking unwarranted fun at the Boers. (There again, Boer women are depicted much more favourably in the short story 'Eighteen-Ninety-Nine', and an essay published in the *Fortnightly Review* for 1896.) But perhaps the most disconcerting issue here is how *African Farm* mistreats the marginalized black Africans as entirely inferior species. Even if Schreiner dared to challenge Spencer's social Darwinism on the ground of gender, she was far less decisive on the question of race. Lyndall, sounding as if she had taken a leaf out one of Francis Galton's early studies of eugenics, condescendingly muses, with no detectable irony, on the Darwinian future of an African herdsman and his kin: 'Will his race melt away in the heat of a collision with a higher?' (p. 194). This is one of the few glimpses we see of the black workers who enable the farm to function. J. M. Coetzee, comparing Schreiner's novel with Pauline Smith's *The Little Karoo* (1925), comments on these white writers' 'Silence about the place of black labour', and believes that that this 'repres-

[11] Rebecca West, 'So Simple', *The Freewoman*, 12 Oct. 1912, repr. in *The Young Rebecca: Writings of Rebecca West 1911–1917*, ed. Jane Marcus (London: Macmillan, 1982), 73.

[12] Carol Barash, 'Introduction' to *An Olive Schreiner Reader: Writings on Women and South Africa* (London: Pandora Press, 1987), 19. Joyce Avrech Berkman provides a richly detailed analysis of Schreiner's racial attitudes in *The Healing Imagination of Olive Schreiner: Beyond South African Colonialism* (Amherst, Mass.: University of Massachusetts Press, 1989), 83–90.

ents a failure of imagination before the problem of how to integrate the dispossessed black man' into a landscape that has witnessed the devastation of native peoples.[13] Although we occasionally catch sight of the 'Hottentot' (Khoi) maid crushing corn-meal, Schreiner's farm is, by and large, a slow-moving place, where work slumps into the background—its monotony is so implicit it is near-invisible. It would take Sol. T. Plaatje's *Native Life in South Africa* (1916) to bring the voice of the disenfranchised blacks into print.

Yet these failures in Schreiner's fiction—if we choose to call them that—surely indicate the historical limits within which she made her political and aesthetic choices. Virginia Woolf, who read Schreiner's works intently, and whose *Three Guineas* (1938) follows in the pacifist tradition of *Trooper Peter Halket of Mashonaland* (1897), could not help but praise the 'brilliance and power' of *African Farm*. As Jane Marcus has demonstrated, aspects of Schreiner's first novel leave their impression on Woolf's *The Years* (1937).[14] But Woolf, like many other commentators, felt Schreiner ultimately stood as 'one half of a great writer; a diamond marked by a flaw'.[15] It is perhaps the case that Schreiner, well into her middle age by the turn of the century, had not the advantages of Woolf's own time to shine as brilliantly as she might have done. Women's suffrage, after all, had been won in 1918, two years before Schreiner's death. Over a century after the publication of *African Farm*—a period which has witnessed the successful rise of the women's movement, together with the sustained brutalities of apartheid—the discernible weaknesses of Schreiner's first book may threaten to occlude the extraordinary and long-lasting impact it made in 1883. It was at least a decade, if not more, in advance of its contemporaries. In 1894, for example, a whole essay in the left-leaning *Westminster Review* meticulously analysed Schrei-

---

[13] J. M. Coetzee, *White Writing: On the Culture of Letters in South Africa* (New Haven, Conn.: Yale University Press, (1988), 71–2.

[14] Jane Marcus, *Virginia Woolf and the Languages of Patriarchy* (Bloomington, Ind.: Indiana University Press, 1987), 63.

[15] Virginia Woolf, 'Review of *The Letters of Olive Schreiner*', *New Public*, 18 Mar. 1925, repr. in *Women and Writing*, ed. Michèle Barrett (London: The Women's Press, 1979), 181, 183.

ner's undaunted presentation of some of the most pressing concerns of the anxious *fin-de-siècle*.[16] Her vision proved vital for those urging a decisive break with the Victorians' most dearly held pieties. In so many ways, Schreiner's avant-garde dreams would enable a whole generation to imagine how and why sexual and religious changes had to become real.

[16] Thomas F. Husband, '*The Story of an African Farm*: A Reflection', *Westminster Review*, 141 (1894), 631–42.

NOTE ON THE TEXT

The Story of an African Farm was first published in two volumes by Chapman and Hall in January 1883. The present text is based on a reprint of the second edition which appeared in one volume, with corrections, in July of that year.

SELECT BIBLIOGRAPHY

MAIN WORKS: *The Story of an African Farm* (London: Chapman and Hall, 1883); *Dreams* (London: T. Fisher Unwin, 1893); with S. C. Cronwright-Schreiner, *The Political Situation* (London: T. Fisher Unwin, 1896); *Trooper Peter Halket of Mashonaland* (London: T. Fisher Unwin, 1897); *An English South African's View of the Situation* (London: T. Fisher Unwin, 1911); *Thoughts on South Africa* (London: T. Fisher Unwin, 1923); *Stories, Dreams and Allegories* (London: T. Fisher Unwin, 1923); *From Man to Man; or, Perhaps Only . . .* (London: T. Fisher Unwin, 1926); and *Undine* (London: Benn, 1929).

BIOGRAPHY: Several biographies have appeared since Schreiner's death in 1920. Most draw on the somewhat tendentious narrative outlined by S. C. Cronwright-Schreiner in *The Life of Olive Schreiner* (London: T. Fisher Unwin, 1924). See Vera Buchanan-Gould, *Not without Honour: The Life and Writings of Olive Schreiner* (London: Hutchinson, 1955); D. L. Hobman, *Olive Schreiner: Her Friends and Times* (London: Watts, 1955); and Johannes Meintjes, *Olive Schreiner: Portrait of a South African Woman* (Johannesburg: Keartland, 1965). These have been superseded by Ruth First and Ann Scott, *Olive Schreiner: A Biography* (London: André Deutsch, 1980, repr. with an introduction by Nadine Gordimer, London: The Women's Press, 1989). Problems in accounts of Schreiner's life are explored by Liz Stanley, 'How Olive Schreiner Vanished, Leaving Behind Only Her Asthmatic Personality', in *Feminism and Friendship: Two Essays on Olive Schreiner*, Studies in Sexual Politics No. 8 (Manchester: Department of Sociology, University of Manchester, 1986), 47–79. Schreiner's close friendship with Havelock Ellis is detailed in Phyllis Grosskurth, *Havelock Ellis: A Biography* (London: Allen Lane, 1980), 72–92.

LETTERS: *The Letters of Olive Schreiner 1870–1920*. ed. S. C. Cronwright-Schreiner (London: T. Fisher Unwin, 1924); *Letters, 1871–1899*, ed. Richard Rive (Oxford: Oxford University Press, 1988); *My Other Self: The Letters of Olive Schreiner and Havelock Ellis*, ed. Yaffa Claire Draznin (New York: Peter Lang, 1992).

CRITICISM: The most substantial critical study of Schreiner is Joyce Avrech Berman, *The Healing Imagination of Olive Schreiner: Beyond South African Colonialism* (Amherst, Mass.: University of Massachusetts, 1989). Two wide-ranging collections of criticism are

Cherry Clayton (ed.), *Olive Schreiner* (Johannesburg: McGraw Hill, 1983), and Malvern Van Wyk Smith and Don MacLennan (eds.), *Olive Schreiner and After: Essays and Southern African Literature in Honour of Guy Butler* (Cape Town: David Philip, 1983). Recent feminist explorations of Schreiner's work include Berkman, *Olive Schreiner: Feminism on the Frontier* (St Alban's, Vt.: Eden Press, 1979); Jane Marcus, 'Olive Schreiner: Cartographer of the Spirit', *The Minnesota Review*, 12 (1979), 58–66; Kathleen Blake, *Love and the Woman Question: The Art of Self-Postponement* (Brighton: Harvester, 1982), 202–27; Rachel Blau Du Plessis, *Writing beyond the Ending* (Bloomington, Ind.: Indiana University Press, 1985), 20–30; Carol Barash, 'Virile Womanhood: Olive Schreiner's Narratives of a Master Race', *Women's Studies International Forum* 9 (1986), 33–40, repr. in Elaine Showalter (ed.), *Speaking of Gender* (New York: Routledge, 1989), 269–81, and 'Introduction' to *An Olive Schreiner Reader: Writings on Women and South Africa* (London: Pandora Press, 1987), 1–20; Sandra M. Gilbert and Susan Gubar, *No Man's Land: The Place of the Woman Writer in the Twentieth Century*, ii, *Sexchanges* (New Haven, Conn.: Yale University Press, 1989), 50–71; Nancy L. Paxton, '*The Story of an African Farm* and the Dynamics of Woman-to-Woman Influence', *Texas Studies in Language and Literature*, 30/4 (1988), 562–82; Laura Chrisman, 'Allegory, Feminist Thought, and the *Dream* of Olive Schreiner', *Prose Studies*, 13/1 (1990), 126–50; Ruth Brandon, *The New Women and the Old Men: Love, Sex and the Woman Question* (London: Secker and Warburg, 1990), 1–94; and Elaine Showalter, *Sexual Anarchy: Gender and Culture in the Fin-de-Siècle* (London: Bloomsbury, 1991), 53–8. Gerald Monsman places *African Farm* in relation to contemporaneous Victorian works in 'Olive Schreiner: Literature and the Politics of Power', *Texas Studies in Language and Literature*, 30/4 (1988), 583–611. Schreiner's involvement in the experimental 'Men and Women's Club' convened by the free-thinking Karl Pearson is explained in Judith R. Walkowitz, 'Science, Feminism and Romance: The Men and Women's Club 1885–1889', *History Workshop Journal*, 21 (1986), 37–59. Links with 'decadent' writers such as Arthur Symons and Ernest Dowson are investigated in Linda Dowling, 'The Decadent and the New Woman in the 1890s', *Nineteenth-Century Fiction*, 33/4 (1979) 434–53. The South African context of her writing is examined in J. M. Coetzee, *White Writing: On the Culture of Letters in South Africa* (New Haven, Conn.: Yale University Press), 63–72. An important recent feminist and post-colonial inquiry into Schreiner's works is Susan R. Horton, *Difficult Women, Artful Lives: Olive Schreiner and Isak Dinesen, In and Out of Africa* (Baltimore, MD: The Johns Hopkins University Press, 1995).

A CHRONOLOGY OF
OLIVE SCHREINER

1855 24 March: born at Wittebergen, Basutoland. Christened Olive Emilie Albertina, the ninth child of Gottlob Schreiner and Rebecca Schreiner née Lyndall, missionaries first sponsored in South Africa by the London Missionary Society.

1866 Gottlob Schreiner declared insolvent. Family disperses.

1867 Joins older brother Theo and attends his school at Cradock.

1870 Works for cousin at Lily Hope, Avoca, in first position as a governess.

1871 Meets free-thinking Willie Bertram at Hermon mission station. Reads his copy of Herbert Spencer's *First Principles* which confirms her agnosticism. Her asthma attacks begin at around this time. Schreiner announces that she is to be called 'Olive', not 'Emilie' any more.

1872 Briefly engaged to Julius Gau, a representative of a Swiss insurance company, whom Schreiner met through the Robinsons' network of free-thinkers. Joins her older brother Theo and older sister Ettie at the diamond-fields at New Rush (later known as Kimberley). Teaches children of local diggers. Starts *Undine* and short stories.

1874 Begins succession of posts as a governess in the Cape. Works on early drafts of *Undine*, *From Man to Man*, and *The Story of an African Farm*.

1873 Meets Mary Brown and John Brown. They devise the 'English plan' to enable Schreiner to train in medicine in 1881.

1874 Purchases Ralph Waldo Emerson's *Essays*.

1875 *Undine* nearly completed. Reading John Stuart Mill's *Logic*. Teaching at the Fouches at Klein Ganna Hoek farm near Cradock.

1876 Father dies. Based at Ratel Hoek near Tarkastad. Reading Goethe and Montaigne.

1879 Works for the Cawoods at Ganna Hoek. Early version of *African Farm* complete.

1880 Sends manuscript of *African Farm*, to the Browns in England.
      Publisher turns it down. Works on suggested revisions.

1881 Travels to England. Enrols as a nurse at Edinburgh Royal
      Infirmary but has to give up after several days because of ill-
      health. Seeks publisher for *African Farm*.

1883 Chapman and Hall accept *African Farm* on the recommendation
      of a reader's report by the eminent novelist, George Meredith.
      Published in two volumes in January, the novel proves an
      immediate success, and a second edition quickly follows. Fifteen
      editions will appear in Schreiner's lifetime.

1884 Meets the sexologist Havelock Ellis and forms very close friend-
      ship with him.

1885 Participates in the radical Men and Women's Club convened by
      the free-thinking Karl Pearson, to whom Schreiner is strongly
      drawn. Meets the radical socialist and homosexual emancipation-
      ist Edward Carpenter through the Fellowship of the New Life.
      George Moore, Irish exponent of naturalism in the novel,
      proposes to her; Schreiner declines him.

1886 Intellectual relationship with Pearson breaks down. Suffers
      mental and physical collapse. Leaves England for Europe. Still
      working on *From Man to Man*. Bryan Donkin, physician to
      many radical intellectuals, proposes to her; Schreiner declines
      him.

1887 Seeks publisher for her collection of allegorical and visionary
      writings.

1889 Meets the 'decadent' and 'symbolist' poet and critic Arthur
      Symons. Returns to South Africa in October.

1890 Begins series of periodical essays on South Africa (collected
      posthumously in 1923). Meets Cecil Rhodes in Cape Town.
      Settles in Matjesfontein.

1891 *Dreams* published.

1892 Meets Samuel 'Cron' Cronwright, an ostrich farmer. Working
      on further allegories, including 'The Buddhist Priest's Wife'.

1893 Visits friends and family in England. *Dream Life and Real Life*
      published.

1894 Marries Cronwright. He, unusually, takes her name. Asthma
      attacks severe during summer months, forcing the newly-weds
      to leave for the better climate of Kimberley.

1895 Baby dies shortly after birth. No less than six miscarriages will follow.

1896 Publishes (with Cronwright-Schreiner) *The Political Situation*.

1897 Travels to England to publish fictional attack on Rhodes, *Trooper Peter Halket of Mashonaland*.

1898 Moves to Johannesburg.

1899 Outbreak of second Anglo-Boer War. Publishes her pro-Boer anti-war tract, *An English South African's View of the Situation*, causing offence to her brother Will, Prime Minister of the Cape Colony.

1900 Prominent in the women's protest movement in the Cape. Living under martial law in Hanover.

1902 Working on *Woman and Labour*, *From Man to Man*, and several stories, including 'Eighteen-Ninety-Nine'.

1903 Mother, a Roman Catholic convert, dies.

1906 Publishes pamphlet, *Letter on the Jew*.

1908 Supports South African federation. Letter on women's suffrage appears in *Cape Times*.

1909 Publishes *Closer Union* in London. Supports Mahatma Gandhi's *satyagraha* movement.

1911 Publishes *Woman and Labour* in London.

1913 Vice-President of Women's Enfranchisement League at Kalk Bay. Resigns because the League wants vote for white women only. Sails for England.

1914 Schreiner travelling in Germany at the outbreak of the First World War. Goes to London. Begins work on pacifist tract, *The Dawn of Civilization* (fragments published posthumously in *Stories, Dreams, and Allegories*).

1916 Publishes pacifist propaganda in *Labour Leader*.

1919 Suffering from depression.

1920 Cronwright-Schreiner travels to England after separation of five years. Returns to South Africa. Dies of heart-failure on 10 December at Wynberg.

1923 *Stories, Dreams and Allegories* and *Thoughts on South Africa* published.

1924 Cronwright-Schreiner edits *The Life of Olive Schreiner* and *The Letters of Olive Schreiner 1870–1920.*

1926 *From Man to Man* published.

1929 *Undine* published.

The Story of an African Farm

PREFACE

I HAVE to thank cordially the public and my critics for the reception they have given this little book.

Dealing with a subject that is far removed from the round of English daily life, it of necessity lacks the charm that hangs about the ideal representation of familiar things, and its reception has therefore been the more kindly.

A word of explanation is necessary. Two strangers appear on the scene, and some have fancied that in the second they have again the first, who returns in a new guise. Why this should be we cannot tell; unless there is a feeling that a man should not appear upon the scene, and then disappear, leaving behind him no more substantial trace than a mere book; that he should return later on as husband or lover, to fill some more important part than that of the mere stimulator of thought.

Human life may be painted according to two methods. There is the stage method. According to that each character is duly marshalled at first, and ticketed; we know with an immutable certainty that at the right crises each one will reappear and act his part, and, when the curtain falls, all will stand before it bowing. There is a sense of satisfaction in this, and of completeness. But there is another method—the method of the life we all lead. Here nothing can be prophesied. There is a strange coming and going of feet. Men appear, act and re-act upon each other, and pass away. When the crisis comes the man who would fit it does not return. When the curtain falls no one is ready. When the footlights are brightest they are blown out; and what the name of the play is no one knows. If there sits a spectator who knows, he sits so high that the players in the gaslight cannot hear his breathing. Life may be painted according to either method; but the methods are different. The canons of criticism that bear upon the one cut cruelly upon the other.

It has been suggested by a kind critic that he would better have liked the little book if it had been a history of wild adventure; of cattle driven into inaccessible 'kranzes' by Bush-men; 'of encounters with ravening lions, and hair-breadth escapes.' This could not be. Such works are best written in Piccadilly or in the Strand: there the gifts of the creative imagination, untrammelled by contact with any fact, may spread their wings.

But, should one sit down to paint the scenes among which he has grown, he will find that the facts creep in upon him. Those brilliant phases and shapes which the imagination sees in far-off lands are not for him to portray. Sadly he must squeeze the colour from his brush, and dip it into the grey pigments around him. He must paint what lies before him.

R. IRON

GLOSSARY

Several Dutch and Colonial words occurring in this work, the subjoined Glossary is given, explaining the principal.

Benaauwdheit	Indigestion.
Brakje	A little cur of low degree.
Bultong	Dried meat.
In-span	To harness.
Kappje	A sun-bonnet.
Karroo	The wide sandy plains in some parts of South Africa.
Karroo-bushes	The bushes that take the place of grass on these plains.
Kartel	The wooden-bed fastened in an ox-waggon.
Kopje	A small hillock, or 'little head.'
Kraal	The space surrounded by a stone wall or hedged with thorn branches, into which sheep or cattle are driven at night.
Mealies	Indian corn.
Meerkat	A small weasel-like animal.
Meiboss	Preserved and dried apricots.
Nachtmaal	The Lord's Supper.
Out-span	To unharness, or a place in the field where one unharnesses.
Predikant	Parson.
Reim	Leather rope.
Schlecht	Bad.
Sloot	A dry watercourse.
Spook	A ghost.
Stamp-block	A wooden block, hollowed out, in which mealies are placed to be pounded before being cooked.
Upsitting	In Boer courtship the man and girl are supposed to sit up together the whole night.
Velschoen	Shoes of undressed leather.

We must see the first images which the external world casts upon the dark mirror of his mind; or must hear the first words which awaken the sleeping powers of thought, and stand by his earliest efforts, if we would understand the prejudices, the habits, and the passions that will rule his life. The entire man is, so to speak, to be found in the cradle of the child.

ALEXIS DE TOCQUEVILLE*

CONTENTS

PART I

PART II

PART I

CHAPTER I
Shadows from Child-life

The Watch

THE full African moon poured down its light from the blue sky into the wide, lonely plain. The dry, sandy earth, with its coating of stunted 'karroo'* bushes a few inches high, the low hills that skirted the plain, the milk-bushes with their long, finger-like leaves, all were touched by a weird and an almost oppressive beauty as they lay in the white light.

In one spot only was the solemn monotony of the plain broken. Near the centre a small, solitary 'kopje'* rose. Alone it lay there, a heap of round iron-stones piled one upon another, as over some giant's grave. Here and there a few tufts of grass or small succulent plants had sprung up among its stones, and on the very summit a clump of prickly-pears lifted their thorny arms, and reflected, as from mirrors, the moon-light on their broad, fleshy leaves. At the foot of the 'kopje' lay the homestead. First, the stone-walled 'sheep kraals'* and Kaffir* huts; beyond them the dwelling-house—a square red-brick building with thatched roof. Even on its bare red walls, and the wooden ladder that led up to the loft, the moonlight cast a kind of dreamy beauty, and quite etherealized the low brick wall that ran before the house, and which enclosed a bare patch of sand and two straggling sunflowers. On the zinc roof of the great open waggon-house, on the roofs of the outbuild-ings that jutted from its side, the moonlight glinted with a quite peculiar brightness, till it seemed that every rib in the metal was of burnished silver.

Sleep ruled everywhere, and the homestead was not less quiet than the solitary plain.

In the farm-house, on her great wooden bedstead, Tant' Sannie, the Boer-woman,* rolled heavily in her sleep.

She had gone to bed, as she always did, in her clothes; and the night was warm and the room close, and she dreamed bad dreams. Not of the ghosts and devils that so haunted her waking thoughts; not of her second husband, the consumptive Englishman, whose grave lay away beyond the ostrich-camps; nor of her first, the young Boer; but only of the sheep's trotters she had eaten for supper that night. She dreamed that one stuck fast in her throat, and she rolled her huge form from side to side, and snorted horribly.

In the next room, where the maid had forgotten to close the shutter, the white moonlight fell in in a flood, and made it light as day. There were two small beds against the wall. In one lay a yellow-haired child, with a low forehead and a face of freckles; but the loving moonlight hid defects here as elsewhere, and showed only the innocent face of a child in its first sweet sleep.

The figure in the companion bed belonged of right to the moonlight, for it was of quite elfin-like beauty. The child had dropped her cover on the floor, and the moonlight looked in at the naked little limbs. Presently she opened her eyes and looked at the moonlight that was bathing them.

'Em!' she called to the sleeper in the other bed; but received no answer. Then she drew the cover from the floor, turned her pillow, and pulling the sheet over her head, went to sleep again.

Only in one of the outbuildings that jutted from the waggon-house there was someone who was not asleep. The room was dark; door and shutter were closed; not a ray of light entered anywhere. The German overseer, to whom the room belonged, lay sleeping soundly on his bed in the corner, his great arms folded, and his bushy grey-and-black beard rising and falling on his breast. But one in the room was not asleep. Two large eyes looked about in the darkness, and two small hands were smoothing the patchwork quilt. The boy, who slept on a box under the window, had just awakened from his first sleep. He drew the quilt up to his chin, so that little peered above it but a great head of silky black curls and the two black eyes. He stared about in the darkness. Nothing was visible, not even the outline of one worm-eaten rafter, nor of the deal table, on which lay the Bible from which his father had read before they went to bed. No one could tell where the tool-box was, and where the fireplace. There was something very impressive to the child in the complete darkness.

At the head of his father's bed hung a great silver hunting watch. It ticked loudly. The boy listened to it, and began mechanically to count. Tick—tick—tick! one, two, three, four! He lost count presently, and only listened. Tick—tick—tick—tick!

It never waited; it went on exorably; and every time it ticked *a man died!* He raised himself a little on his elbow and listened. He wished it would leave off.

How many times had it ticked since he came to lie down? A thousand times, a million times, perhaps.

He tried to count again, and sat up to listen better.

'Dying, dying, dying!' said the watch; 'dying, dying, dying!'

He heard it distinctly. Where were they going to, all those people?

He lay down quickly, and pulled the cover up over his head; but presently the silky curls reappeared.

'Dying, dying, dying!' said the watch; 'dying, dying, dying!'

He thought of the words his father had read that evening— *'For wide is the gate, and broad is the way, that leadeth to destruction, and many there be which go in thereat.'*

'Many, many, many!' said the watch.

'Because strait is the gate and narrow is the way, that leadeth unto life, and few there be that find it.'★

'Few, few, few!' said the watch.

The boy lay with his eyes wide open. He saw before him a long stream of people, a great dark multitude, that moved in one direction; then they came to the dark edge of the world, and went over. He saw them passing on before him, and there was nothing that could stop them. He thought of how that stream had rolled on through all the long ages of the past— how the old Greeks and Romans had gone over; the countless millions of China and India, they were going over now. Since he had come to bed, how many had gone?

And the watch said, 'Eternity, eternity, eternity!'

'Stop them! stop them!' cried the child.

And all the while the watch kept ticking on; just like God's will, that never changes or alters, you may do what you please.

Great beads of perspiration stood on the boy's forehead. He climbed out of bed and lay with his face turned to the mud floor.

'Oh, God, God! save them!' he cried in agony. 'Only some; only a few! Only for each moment I am praying here one!' He folded his little hands upon his head. 'God! God! save them!'

He grovelled on the floor.

Oh, the long, long ages of the past, in which they had gone over! Oh, the long, long future, in which they would pass away! Oh, God! the long, long, long eternity, which has no end!

The child wept, and crept closer to the ground.

The Sacrifice

THE farm by daylight was not as the farm by moonlight. The plain was a weary flat of loose red sand, sparsely covered by dry karroo bushes, that cracked beneath the tread like tinder, and showed the red earth everywhere. Here and there a milk-bush lifted its pale-coloured rods, and in every direction the ants and beetles ran about in the blazing sand. The red walls of the farmhouse, the zinc roofs of the outbuildings, the stone walls of the 'kraals,' all reflected the fierce sunlight, till the eye ached and blenched. No tree or shrub was to be seen far or near. The two sunflowers that stood before the door, out-stared by the sun, drooped their brazen faces to the sand; and the little cicada-like insects cried aloud among the stones of the 'kopje.'

The Boer-woman, seen by daylight, was even less lovely than when, in bed, she rolled and dreamed. She sat on a chair in the great front room, with her feet on a wooden stove, and wiped her flat face with the corner of her apron, and drank coffee, and in Cape Dutch swore that the beloved weather was damned. Less lovely, too, by daylight was the dead English-man's child, her little step-daughter, upon whose freckles and low, wrinkled forehead the sunlight had no mercy.

'Lyndall,' the child said to her little orphan cousin, who sat with her on the floor threading beads, 'how is it your beads never fall off your needle?'

'I try,' said the little one gravely, moistening her tiny finger. 'That is why.'

The overseer, seen by daylight, was a huge German, wearing a shabby suit, and with a childish habit of rubbing his hands and nodding his head prodigiously when pleased at anything. He stood out at the kraals in the blazing sun, explaining to two Kaffir boys the approaching end of the world. The boys, as they cut the cakes of dung, winked at each other, and worked as slowly as they possibly could; but the German never saw it.

Away, beyond the 'kopje,' Waldo his son herded the ewes and lambs—a small and dusty herd—powdered all over from head to foot with red sand, wearing a ragged coat, and shoes of undressed leather, through whose holes the toes looked out. His hat was too large, and had sunk down to his eyes, concealing completely the silky black curls. It was a curious, small figure. His flock gave him little trouble. It was too hot for them to move far; they gathered round every little milk-bush as though they hoped to find shade, and stood there motionless in clumps. He himself crept under a shelving rock that lay at the foot of the 'kopje,' stretched himself on his stomach, and waved his dilapidated little shoes in the air.

Soon, from the blue bag where he kept his dinner, he produced a fragment of slate, an arithmetic, and a pencil. Proceeding to put down a sum with solemn and earnest demeanour, he began to add it up aloud: 'Six and two is eight—and four is twelve—and two is fourteen—and four is eighteen.' Here he paused. 'And four is eighteen—and—four—is—eighteen.' The last was very much drawled. Slowly the pencil slipped from his fingers, and the slate followed it into the sand. For a while he lay motionless, then began muttering to himself, folded his little arms, laid his head down upon them, and might have been asleep but for a muttering sound that from time to time proceeded from him. A curious old ewe came to sniff at him; but it was long before he raised his head. When he did, he looked at the far-off hills with his heavy eyes.

'Ye shall receive—*ye shall receive—shall, shall, shall,*' he muttered.

He sat up then. Slowly the dulness and heaviness melted from his face; it became radiant. Mid-day had come now, and the sun's rays were poured down vertically; the earth throbbed before the eye.

The boy stood up quickly, and cleared a small space from the bushes which covered it. Looking carefully, he found twelve small stones of somewhat the same size; kneeling down, he arranged them carefully on the cleared space in a square pile, in shape like an altar. Then he walked to the bag where his dinner was kept; in it was a mutton chop and a large slice of brown bread. The boy took them out and turned the bread over in his hand, deeply considering it. Finally he threw it away and walked to the altar with the meat, and laid it down on the stones. Close by in the red sand he knelt down. Sure, never since the beginning of the world was there so ragged and so small a priest. He took off his great hat and placed it solemnly on the ground, then closed his eyes and folded his hands. He prayed aloud.

'Oh, God, my Father, I have made Thee a sacrifice. I have only twopence, so I cannot buy a lamb. If the lambs were mine I would give Thee one; but now I have only this meat; it is my dinner-meat. Please, my Father, send fire down from heaven to burn it. Thou hast said, Whosoever shall say unto this mountain, Be thou cast into the sea, nothing doubting, it shall be done. I ask for the sake of Jesus Christ. Amen.'

He knelt down with his face upon the ground, and he folded his hands upon his curls. The fierce sun poured down its heat upon his head and upon his altar. When he looked up he knew what he should see—the glory of God! For fear his very heart stood still, his breath came heavily; he was half suffocated. He dared not look up. Then at last he raised himself. Above him was the quiet, blue sky, about him the red earth; there were the clumps of silent ewes and his altar—that was all.

He looked up—nothing broke the intense stillness of the

blue overhead. He looked round in astonishment, then he bowed again, and this time longer than before.

When he raised himself the second time all was unaltered. Only the sun had melted the fat of the little mutton-chop, and it ran down upon the stones.

Then, the third time he bowed himself. When at last he looked up, some ants had come to the meat on the altar. He stood up and drove them away. Then he put his hat on his hot curls, and sat in the shade. He clasped his hands about his knees. He sat to watch what would come to pass. The glory of the Lord God Almighty! He knew he should see it.

'My dear God is trying me,' he said; and he sat there through the fierce heat of the afternoon. Still he watched and waited when the sun began to slope; and when it neared the horizon and the sheep began to cast long shadows across the karroo, he still sat there. He hoped when the first rays touched the hills till the sun dipped behind them and was gone. Then he called his ewes together, and broke down the altar, and threw the meat far, far away into the field.

He walked home behind his flock. His heart was heavy. He reasoned so: 'God cannot lie. I had faith. No fire came. I am like Cain—*I am not His. He will not hear my prayer. God hates me.'

The boy's heart was heavy. When he reached the 'kraal' gate the two girls met him.

'Come,' said the yellow-haired Em, 'let us play "coop."* There is still time before it gets quite dark. You, Waldo, go and hide on the 'kopje;' Lyndall and I will shut eyes here, and we will not look.'

The girls hid their faces in the stone wall of the sheep-kraal, and the boy clambered half way up the 'kopje.' He crouched down between two stones and gave the call. Just then the milk-herd came walking out of the cow-kraal with two pails. He was an ill-looking Kaffir.

'Ah!' thought the boy, 'perhaps he will die to-night, and go to hell! I must pray for him, I must pray!'

Then he thought—'Where am *I* going to?' and he prayed desperately.

'Ah! this is not right at all,' little Em said, peeping between the stones, and finding him in a very curious posture. 'What *are* you doing, Waldo? It is not the play, you know. You should run out when we come to the white stone. Ah, you do not play nicely.'

'I—I will play nicely now,' said the boy, coming out and standing sheepishly before them; 'I—I only forgot; I will play now.'

'He has been to sleep,' said freckled Em.

'No,' said beautiful little Lyndall, looking curiously at him; 'he has been crying.'

She never made a mistake.

The Confession

ONE night, two years after, the boy sat alone on the 'kopje.' He had crept softly from his father's room and come there. He often did, because, when he prayed or cried aloud, his father might awake and hear him; and none knew his great sorrow, and none knew his grief, but he himself, and he buried them deep in his heart.

He turned up the brim of his great hat and looked at the moon, but most at the leaves of the prickly-pear that grew just before him. They glinted, and glinted, and glinted, just like his own heart—cold, so hard, and very wicked. His physical heart had pain also; it seemed full of little bits of glass, that hurt. He had sat there for half an hour, and he dared not go back to the close house.

He felt horribly lonely. There was not one thing so wicked as he in all the world, and he knew it. He folded his arms and began to cry—not aloud; he sobbed without making any sound, and his tears left scorched marks where they fell. He could not pray; he had prayed night and day for so many months; and to-night he could not pray. When he left off crying, he held his aching head with his brown hands. If one might have gone up to him, and touched him kindly; poor, ugly little thing! Perhaps his heart was almost broken.

With his swollen eyes he sat there on a flat stone at the very top of the 'kopje;' and the tree, with every one of its wicked leaves, blinked, and blinked, and blinked at him. Presently he began to cry again, and then stopped his crying to look at it. He was quiet for a long while, then he knelt up slowly and bent forward. There was a secret he had carried in his heart for a year. He had not dared to look at it; he had not whispered it to himself; but for a year he had carried it. 'I hate God!' he said. The wind took the words and ran away with them, among the stones, and through the leaves of the prickly-pear. He thought it died away half down the 'kopje.' He had told it now!

'I love Jesus Christ, but I hate God.'

The wind carried away that sound as it had done the first. Then he got up and buttoned his old coat about him. He knew he was certainly lost now; he did not care. If half the world were to be lost, why not he too? He would not pray for mercy any more. Better so—better to know certainly. It was ended now. Better so.

He began scrambling down the sides of the 'kopje' to go home.

Better so!—But oh, the loneliness, the agonized pain! for that night, and for nights on nights to come! The anguish that sleeps all day on the heart like a heavy worm, and wakes up at night to feed!

There are some of us who in after years say to Fate, 'Now deal us your hardest blow, give us what you will; but let us never again suffer as we suffered when we were children.'

The barb in the arrow of childhood's suffering is this:—its intense loneliness, its intense ignorance.

CHAPTER II
Plans and Bushman-paintings

AT last came the year of the great drought, the year of 1862.
From end to end of the land the earth cried for water. Man
and beast turned their eyes to the pitiless sky, that like the roof
of some brazen oven arched overhead. On the farm, day after
day, month after month, the water in the damns fell lower and
lower; the sheep died in the fields; the cattle, scarcely able to
crawl, tottered as they moved from spot to spot in search of
food. Week after week, month after month, the sun looked
down from the cloudless sky, till the karroo-bushes were
leafless sticks, broken into the earth, and the earth itself was
naked and bare; and only the milk-bushes, like old hags,
pointed their shrivelled fingers heavenwards, praying for the
rain that never came.

It was on an afternoon of a long day in that thirsty summer,
that on the side of the 'kopje' furthest from the homestead the
two girls sat. They were somewhat grown since the days when
they played hide-and-seek there, but they were mere children
still.

Their dress was of dark, coarse stuff; their common blue
pinafores reached to their ankles, and on their feet they wore
home-made 'vel-schoen.'*

They sat under a shelving rock, on the surface of which
were still visible some old Bushman-paintings, their red and
black pigments having been preserved through long years from
wind and rain by the overhanging ledge: grotesque oxen,
elephants, rhinoceroses, and a one-horned beast, such as no
man ever has seen or ever shall.

The girls sat with their backs to the paintings. In their laps
were a few fern and ice-plant leaves, which by dint of much
searching they had gathered under the rocks.

Em took off her big brown kappje★ and began vigorously to fan her red face with it; but her companion bent low over the leaves in her lap, and at last took up an ice-plant leaf and fastened it on to the front of her blue pinafore with a pin.

'Diamonds must look as these drops do,' she said, carefully bending over the leaf, and crushing one crystal drop with her delicate little nail. 'When I,' she said, 'am grown up, I shall wear real diamonds, exactly like these, in my hair.'

Her companion opened her eyes and wrinkled her low forehead.

'Where will you find them, Lyndall? The stones are only crystals that we picked up yesterday. Old Otto says so.'

'And you think that I am going to stay *here* always?'

The lip trembled scornfully.

'Ah, no,' said her companion. 'I suppose some day we shall go somewhere; but now we are only twelve, and we cannot marry till we are seventeen. Four years, five—that is a long time to wait. And we might not have diamonds if we did marry.'

'And you think that I am going to stay here till then?'

'Well, where *are* you going?' asked her companion.

The girl crushed an ice-plant leaf between her fingers.

'Tant' Sannie is a miserable old woman,' she said. 'Your father married her when he was dying, because he thought she would take better care of the farm, and of us, than an Englishwoman. He said we should be taught and sent to school. Now she saves every farthing for herself, buys us not even one old book. She does not ill-use us—why? Because she is afraid of your father's ghost. Only this morning she told her Hottentot★ that she would have beaten you for breaking the plate, but that three nights ago she heard a rustling and a grunting behind the pantry door, and knew it was your father coming to "spook" her. She is a miserable old woman,' said the girl, throwing the leaf from her; 'but I intend to go to school.'

'And if she won't let you?'

'I shall make her.'

'How?'

The child took not the slightest notice of the last question, and folded her small arms across her knees.

'But why do you want to go, Lyndall?'

'There is nothing helps in this world,' said the child slowly, 'but to be very wise, and to know everything—to be clever.'

'But I should not like to go to school!' persisted the small, freckled face.

'And you do not need to. When you are seventeen this Boer-woman will go; you will have this farm and everything that is upon it for your own; but I,' said Lyndall, 'will have nothing. I must learn.'

'Oh, Lyndall! *I* will give you some of my sheep,' said Em, with a sudden burst of pitying genosity.

'I do not want your sheep,' said the girl slowly; 'I want things of my own. When I am grown up,' she added, the flush on her delicate features deepening at every word, 'there will be nothing that I do not know. I shall be rich, very rich; and I shall wear not only for best, but every day, a pure white silk, and little rose-buds, like the lady in Tant' Sannie's bed-room, and my petticoats will be embroidered, not only at the bottom, but all through.'

The lady in Tant' Sannie's bedroom was a gorgeous creature from a fashion-sheet, which the Boer-woman, somewhere obtaining, had pasted up at the foot of her bed, to be profoundly admired by the children.

'It would be very nice,' said Em; but it seemed a dream of quite too transcendent a glory ever to be realized.

At this instant there appeared at the foot of the 'kopje' two figures—the one, a dog, white and sleek, one yellow ear hanging down over his left eye; the other, his master, a lad of fourteen, and no other than the boy Waldo, grown into a heavy, slouching youth of fourteen. The dog mounted the 'kopje' quickly, his master followed slowly. He wore an aged jacket much too large for him, and rolled up at the wrists, and, as of old, a pair of dilapidated 'vel-shoens' and a felt hat. He stood before the two girls at last.

'What have you been doing to-day?' asked Lyndal, lifting her eyes to his face.

'Looking after ewes and lambs below the dam. Here!' he said, holding out his hand awkwardly, 'I brought them for you.'

There were a few green blades of tender grass.

'Where did you find them?'

'On the dam wall.'

She fastened them beside the leaf on her blue pinafore.

'They look nice there,' said the boy, awkwardly rubbing his great hands and watching her.

'Yes; but the pinafore spoils it all; it is not pretty.'

He looked at it closely.

'Yes, the squares are ugly; but it looks nice upon you—beautiful.'

He now stood silent before them, his great hands hanging loosely at either side.

'Someone has come to-day,' he mumbled out suddenly, when the idea struck him.

'Who?' asked both girls.

'An Englishman on foot.'

'What does he look like?' asked Em.

'I did not notice; but he has a very large nose,' said the boy, slowly. 'He asked the way to the house.'

'Didn't he tell you his name?'

'Yes—Bonaparte Blenkins.'

'Bonaparte!' said Em, 'why that is like the reel Hottentot Hans plays on the violin—

> '"Bonaparte, Bonaparte, my wife is sick;
> In the middle of the week, but Sundays not,
> I give her rice and beans for soup"——

It is a funny name.'

'There was a living man called Bonaparte once,' said she of the great eyes.

'Ah, yes, I know,' said Em—'the poor prophet whom the lions ate. I am always so sorry for him.'

Her companion cast a quiet glance upon her.

'He was the greatest man who ever lived,' she said, 'the man I like best.'

'And what did he do?' asked Em, conscious that she had made a mistake, and that her prophet was not the man.

'He was one man, only one,' said her little companion slowly, 'yet all the people in the world feared him. He was not born great, he was common as we are; yet he was master of the world at last. Once he was only a little child, then he was a lieutenant, then he was a general, then he was an emperor. When he said a thing to himself he never forgot it. He waited, and waited, and waited, and it came at last.'

'He must have been very happy,' said Em.

'I do not know,' said Lyndall; 'but he had what he said he would have, and that is better than being happy. He was their master, and all the people were white with fear of him. They joined together to fight him. He was one and they were many, and they got him down at last. They were like the wild cats when their teeth are fast in a great dog, like cowardly wild cats,' said the child, 'they would not let him go. They were many; he was only *one*. They sent him to an island in the sea, a lonely island, and kept him there fast. He was one man, and they were many, and they were terrified at him. It was glorious!' said the child.

'And what then?' said Em.

'Then he was alone there in that island, with men to watch him always,' said her companion, slowly and quietly, 'and in the long, lonely nights he used to lie awake and think of the things he had done in the old days, and the things he would do if they let him go again. In the day when he walked near the shore it seemed to him that the sea all around him was a cold chain about his body pressing him to death.'

'And then?' said Em, much interested.

'He died there in that island; he never got away.'

'It is rather a nice story,' said Em; 'but the end is sad.'

'It is a terrible, hateful ending,' said the little teller of the story, leaning forward on her folded arms; 'and the worst is, it is true. I have noticed,' added the child very deliberately, 'that it is only the made-up stories that end nicely; the true ones all end so.'

As she spoke the boy's dark, heavy eyes rested on her face.

'You have read it, have you not?'

He nodded. 'Yes; but the brown history tells only what he did, not what he thought.'

'It was in the brown history that I read of him,' said the girl; 'but I *know* what he thought. Books do not tell everything.'

'No,' said the boy, slowly drawing nearer to her and sitting down at her feet. 'What you want to know they never tell.'

Then the children fell into silence, till Doss, the dog, growing uneasy at its long continuance, sniffed at one and the other, and his master broke forth suddenly—

'If *they* could talk, if *they* could tell us now!' he said, moving his hand out over the surrounding objects—'then we would know something. This "kopje," if it could tell us how it came here! The "Physical Geography" says,' he went on most rapidly and confusedly, 'that what are dry lands now were once lakes; and what I think is this—these low hills were once the shores of a lake; this "kopje" is some of the stones that were at the bottom, rolled together by the water. But there is this—how did the water come to make one heap here alone, in the centre of the plain?' It was a ponderous question; no one volunteered an answer. 'When I was little,' said the boy, 'I always looked at it and wondered, and I thought a great giant was buried under it. Now I know the water must have done it; but how? It is very wonderful. Did one little stone come first, and stopped the others as they rolled?' said the boy, with earnestness, in a low voice, more as speaking to himself than to them.

'Oh, Waldo, God put the little "kopje" here,' said Em with solemnity.

'But how did he put it here?'

'By wanting.'

'But how did the wanting bring it here?'

'Because it did.'

The last words were uttered with the air of one who produces a clinching argument. What effect it had on the questioner was not evident, for he made no reply, and turned away from her.

Drawing closer to Lyndall's feet, he said, after a while, in a low voice,

'Lyndall, has it never seemed to you that the stones *were* talking to you? Sometimes,' he added, in a yet lower tone, 'I lie under there with my sheep, and it seems that the stones are really speaking—speaking of the old things, of the time when the strange fishes and animals lived that are turned into stone now, and the lakes were here; and then of the time when the little Bushmen lived here, so small and so ugly, and used to

sleep in the wild dog holes, and in the "sloots",* and eat
snakes, and shot the bucks with their poisoned arrows. It was
one of them, one of these old wild Bushmen, that painted
those,' said the boy, nodding towards the pictures—'one who
was different from the rest. He did not know why, but he
wanted to make something, so he made these. He worked
hard, very hard, to find the juice to make the paint; and then
he found this place where the rocks hang over, and he painted
them. To us they are only strange things, that make us laugh;
but to him they were very beautiful.'

The children had turned round and looked at the pictures.

'He used to kneel here naked, painting, painting, painting;
and he wondered at the things he made himself,' said the boy,
rising and moving his hand in deep excitement. 'Now the
Boers have shot them all, so that we never see a little yellow
face peeping out among the stones.' He paused, a dreamy look
coming over his face. 'And the wild bucks have gone, and
those days, and we are here. But we will be gone soon, and
only the stones will lie on here, looking at everything like they
look now. I know that it is I who am thinking,' the fellow
added slowly, 'but it seems as though it were they who are
talking. Has it never seemed so to you, Lyndall?'

'No, it never seems so to me,' she answered.

The sun had dipped now below the hills, and the boy
suddenly remembering the ewes and lambs, started to his feet.

'Let us also go to the house and see who has come,' said
Em, as the boy shuffled away to rejoin his flock, while Doss
ran at his heels, snapping at the ends of the torn trousers as
they fluttered in the wind.

CHAPTER III
I was a Stranger, and Ye Took Me in*

As the two girls rounded the side of the 'kopje,' an unusual scene presented itself. A large group was gathered at the back door of the homestead.

On the door-step stood the Boer-woman, a hand on each hip, her face red and fiery, her head nodding fiercely. At her feet sat the yellow Hottentot maid, her satellite, and around stood the black Kaffir maids, with blankets twisted round their half-naked figures. Two, who stamped mealies* in a wooden block, held the great stampers in their hands, and stared stupidly at the object of attraction. It certainly was not to look at the old German overseer, who stood in the centre of the group, that they had all gathered together. His salt-and-pepper suit, grizzly black beard, and grey eyes were as familiar to everyone on the farm as the red gables at the homestead itself; but beside him stood the stranger, and on him all eyes were fixed. Ever and anon the new-comer cast a glance over his pendulous red nose to the spot where the Boer-woman stood, and smiled faintly.

'I'm not a child,' cried the Boer-woman, in low Cape Dutch, 'and I wasn't born yesterday. No, by the Lord, no! You can't take *me* in! My mother didn't wean me on Monday. One wink of my eye and I see the whole thing. I'll have no tramps sleeping on my farm,' cried Tant' Sannie blowing. 'No, by the Devil, no! not though he had sixty-times-six red noses.'

There the German overseer mildly interposed that the man was not a tramp, but a highly respectable individual, whose horse had died by an accident three days before.

'Don't tell me,' cried the Boer-woman; 'the man isn't born that can take *me* in. If he'd had money, wouldn't he have bought a horse? Men who walk are thieves, liars, murderers, Rome's priests, seducers! I see the Devil in his nose!' cried Tant' Sannie, shaking her fist at him; 'and to come walking into the house of this Boer's child, and shaking hands as though he came on horseback! Oh, no, no!'

The stranger took off his hat, a tall battered chimney-pot, and disclosed a bald head, at the back of which was a little fringe of curled white hair; and he bowed to Tant' Sannie.

'What does she remark, my friend?' he inquired, turning his cross-wise looking eyes on the old German.

'Ah—well—ah—the—Dutch—you know—do not like people who walk—in this country—ah!'

'My dear friend,' said the stranger, laying his hand on the German's arm, 'I should have bought myself another horse, but crossing, five days ago, a full river, I lost my purse—a purse with five hundred pounds in it. I spent five days on the bank of the river trying to find it—couldn't. Paid a Kaffir nine pounds to go in and look for it at the risk of his life—couldn't find it.'

The German would have translated this information, but the Boer-woman gave no ear.

'No, no; he goes to-night. See how he looks at me—a poor, unprotected female! If he wrongs me, who is to do me right?' cried Tant' Sannie.

'I think,' said the German in an undertone, 'if you didn't look at her quite so much it might be advisable. She—ah—she—might—imagine that you liked her too well,—in fact—ah—'

'Certainly, my dear friend, certainly,' said the stranger, 'I shall not look at her.'

Saying this, he turned his nose full upon a small Kaffir of two years old. That small naked son of Ham became instantly so terrified that he fled to his mother's blanket for protection, howling horribly.

Upon this the new-comer fixed his eyes pensively on the stamp-block, folding his hands on the head of his cane. His boots were broken, but he still had the cane of a gentleman.

'You vaggabonds se Engelschman!' said Tant' Sannie, looking straight at him.

This was a near approach to plain English; but the man contemplated the block abstractedly, wholly unconscious that any antagonism was being displayed towards him.

'You might not be a Scotchman or anything of that kind, might you?' suggested the German. 'It is the English that she hates.'

'My dear friend,' said the stranger, 'I am Irish every inch of me—father Irish, mother Irish. I've not a drop of English blood in my veins.'

'And you might not be married, might you?' persisted the German. 'If you had a wife and children, now? Dutch people do not like those who are not married.'

'Ah,' said the stranger, looking tenderly at the block, 'I have a dear wife and three sweet little children—two lovely girls and a noble boy.'

This information having been conveyed to the Boer-woman, she, after some further conversation, appeared slightly mollified; but remained firm to her conviction that the man's designs were evil.

'For, dear Lord!' she cried; 'all Englishmen are ugly; but was there ever such a red-rag-nosed thing with broken boots and crooked eyes before? Take him to your room,' she cried to the German; 'but all the sin he does I lay at your door.'

The German having told him how matters were arranged, the stranger made a profound bow to Tant' Sannie, and followed his host, who led the way to his own little room.

'I thought she would come to her better self soon,' the German said joyously. 'Tant' Sannie is not wholly bad, far from it, far.' Then seeing his companion cast a furtive glance at him, which, he mistook for one of surprise, he added quickly, 'Ah, yes, yes; we are all a primitive people here—not very lofty. We deal not in titles. Everyone is Tanta and Oom—aunt and uncle. This may be my room,' he said, opening the door. 'It is rough, the room is rough; not a palace—not quite. But it may be better than the fields, a little better!' he said, glancing round at his companion. 'Come in, come in. There is something to eat—a mouthful: not the fare of emperors or kings; but we do not starve, not yet,' he said, rubbing his hands together and looking round with a pleased, half-nervous smile on his old face.

'My friend, my dear friend,' said the stranger, seizing him by the hand, 'may the Lord bless you, the Lord bless and reward you—the God of the fatherless and the stranger. But for you I would this night have slept in the fields, with the dews of heaven upon my head.'

Late that evening Lyndall came down to the cabin with the German's rations. Through the tiny square window the light streamed forth, and without knocking she raised the latch and entered. There was a fire burning on the hearth, and it cast its ruddy glow over the little room, with its worm-eaten rafters and mud floor, and broken white-washed walls. A curious little place, filled with all manner of articles. Next to the fire was a great tool-box; beyond that the little bookshelf with its well-worn books; beyond that, in the corner, a heap of filled and empty grain-bags. From the rafters hung down straps, 'reims,'* old boots, bits of harness, and a string of onions. The bed was in another corner, covered by a patchwork quilt of faded red lions, and divided from the rest of the room by a blue curtain, now drawn back. On the mantelshelf was an endless assortment of little bags and stones; and on the wall hung a map of South Germany, with a red line drawn through it to show where the German had wandered. This place was the one home the girls had known for many a year. The house where Tant' Sannie lived and ruled was a place to sleep in, to eat in, not to be happy in. It was in vain she told them they were grown too old to go there; every morning and evening found them there. Were there not too many golden memories hanging about the old place for them to leave it?

Long winter nights, when they had sat round the fire and roasted potatoes, and asked riddles, and the old man had told of the little German village, where, fifty years before, a little German boy had played at snowballs, and had carried home the knitted stockings of a little girl who afterwards became Waldo's mother; did they not seem to see the German peasant girls walking about with their wooden shoes and yellow, braided hair, and the little children eating their suppers out of little wooden bowls when the good mothers called them in to have their milk and potatoes?

And were there not yet better times than these? Moonlight nights, when they romped about the door, with the old man, yet more a child than any of them, and laughed, till the old roof of the waggon-house rang?

Or, best of all, were there not warm, dark, starlight nights, when they sat together on the doorstep, holding each other's hands, singing German hymns, their voices rising clear in the still night air—till the German would draw away his hand suddenly to wipe quickly a tear the children might not see? Would they not sit looking up at the stars and talking of them—of the dear Southern Cross; red, fiery Mars; Orion, with his belt; and the Seven Mysterious Sisters—and fall to speculating over them? How old are they? Who dwelt in them? And the old German would say that perhaps the souls we loved lived in them; *there*, in that little twinkling point was perhaps the little girl whose stockings he had carried home; and the children would look up at it lovingly, and called it 'Uncle Otto's star.' Then they would fall to deeper speculations—of the times and seasons wherein the heavens shall be rolled together as a scroll, and the stars shall fall as a fig-tree casteth her untimely figs, and there shall be time no longer; 'when the Son of man shall come in His glory, and all His holy angels with Him.' In lower and lower tones they would talk, till at last they fell into whispers; then they would wish good-night softly, and walk home hushed and quiet.

To-night, when Lyndall looked in, Waldo sat before the fire watching a pot which simmered there, with his slate and pencil in his hand; his father sat at the table buried in the columns of a three-weeks-old newspaper; and the stranger lay stretched on the bed in the corner, fast asleep, his mouth open, his great limbs stretched out loosely, betokening much weariness. The girl put the rations down upon the table, snuffed the candle, and stood looking at the figure on the bed.

'Uncle Otto,' she said presently, laying her hand down on the newspaper, and causing the old German to look up over his glasses, 'how long did that man say he had been walking?'

'Since this morning, poor fellow! A gentleman—not accustomed to walking—horse died—poor fellow!' said the German, pushing out his lip and glancing commiseratingly over his spectacles in the direction of the bed where the stranger lay, with his flabby double chin, and broken boots, through which the flesh shone.

'And do you believe him, Uncle Otto?'

'Believe him? why, of course I do. He himself told me the story three times *distinctly*.'

'If,' said the girl slowly, 'he had walked for only one day his boots would not have looked so; and if——'

'*If!*' said the German, starting up in his chair, irritated that anyone should doubt such irrefragable evidence—'*if!* Why, he told me *himself!* Look how he lies there,' added the German pathetically, 'worn out—poor fellow! We have something for him though,' pointing with his forefinger over his shoulder to the saucepan that stood on the fire. 'We are not cooks—not French cooks, not quite; but it's drinkable, drinkable, I think; better than nothing, I think,' he added, nodding his head in a jocund manner, that evinced his high estimation of the contents of the saucepan and his profound satisfaction therein. 'Bish! bish! my chicken,' he said, as Lyndall tapped her little foot up and down upon the floor. 'Bish! bish! my chicken, you will wake him.'

He moved the candle so that his own head might intervene between it and the sleeper's face; and, smoothing his newspaper, he adjusted his spectacles to read.

The child's grey-black eyes rested on the figure on the bed, then turned to the German, then rested on the figure again.

'*I* think he is a liar. Good-night, Uncle Otto' she said slowly, turning to the door.

Long after she had gone the German folded his paper up methodically, and put it in his pocket.

The stranger had not awakened to partake of the soup, and his son had fallen asleep on the ground. Taking two white sheep-skins from the heap of sacks in the corner, the old man doubled them up, and lifting the boy's head gently from the slate, on which it rested, placed the skins beneath it.

'Poor lambie, poor lambie!' he said, tenderly patting the great rough bear-like head; 'tired, is he!'

He threw an overcoat across the boy's feet, and lifted the saucepan from the fire. There was no place where the old man could comfortably lie down himself, so he resumed his seat.

Opening a much-worn Bible, he began to read, and as he read pleasant thoughts and visions thronged on him.

'I was a stranger, and ye took me in,' he read.

He turned again to the bed where the sleeper lay.

'I was a stranger.'

Very tenderly the old man looked at him. He saw not the bloated body nor the evil face of the man; but, as it were, under deep disguise and fleshly concealment, the form that long years of dreaming had made very real to him. 'Jesus, lover, and is it given to us, weak and sinful, frail and erring, to serve *Thee*, to take *Thee* in!' he said softly, as he rose from his seat. Full of joy, he began to pace the little room. Now and again as he walked he sang the lines of a German hymn, or muttered broken words of prayer. The little room was full of light. It appeared to the German that Christ was very near him, and that at almost any moment the thin mist of earthly darkness that clouded his human eyes might be withdrawn, and that made manifest of which the friends at Emmaus* beholding it, said, 'It is the Lord!'

Again, and yet again, through the long hours of that night, as the old man walked, he looked up to the roof of his little room, with its blackened rafters, and yet saw them not. His rough bearded face was illuminated with a radiant gladness; and the night was not shorter to the dreaming sleepers than to him whose waking dreams brought heaven near.

So quickly the night fled, that he looked up with surprise when at four o'clock the first grey streaks of summer dawn showed themselves through the little window. Then the old man turned to rake together the few coals that lay under the ashes, and his son, turning on the sheep-skins, muttered sleepily to know if it were time to rise.

'Lie still, lie still! I would only make a fire,' said the old man.

'Have you been up all night?' asked the boy.

'Yes; but it has been short, very short. Sleep again, my chicken; it is yet early.'

And he went out to fetch more fuel.

CHAPTER IV

Blessed is He that Believeth

BONAPARTE BLENKINS sat on the side of the bed. He had wonderfully revived since the day before, held his head high, talked in a full sonorous voice, and ate greedily of all the viands offered him. At his side was a basin of soup, from which he took a deep draught now and again as he watched the fingers of the German, who sat on the mud floor before him mending the bottom of a chair.

Presently he looked out, where, in the afternoon sunshine, a few half-grown ostriches might be seen wandering listlessly about, and then he looked in again at the little white-washed room, and at Lyndall, who sat in the doorway looking at a book. Then he raised his chin and tried to adjust an imaginary shirt-collar. Finding none, he smoothed the little grey fringe at the back of his head, and began—

'You are a student of history, I perceive, my friend, from the study of these volumes that lie scattered about this apartment; this fact has been made evident to me.'

'Well—a little—perhaps—it may be,' said the German meekly.

'Being a student of history then,' said Bonaparte, raising himself loftily, 'you will doubtless have heard of my great, of my celebrated kinsman, Napoleon Bonaparte?'

'Yes, yes,' said the German, looking up.

'I, sir,' said Bonaparte, 'was born at this hour, on an April afternoon, three-and-fifty years ago. The nurse, sir—she was the same who attended when the Duke of Sutherland was born—brought me to my mother. "There is only one name for this child," she said: "he has the nose of his great kinsman;" and so Bonaparte Blenkins became my name—Bonaparte Blenkins. Yes, sir' said Bonaparte, 'there is a stream on *my* maternal side that connects me with a stream on *his* maternal side.'

The German made a sound of astonishment.

'The connection,' said Bonaparte, 'is one which could not be easily comprehended by one unaccustomed to the study of aristocratic pedigrees; but the connection is close.'

'Is it possible!' said the German, pausing in his work with much interest and astonishment. 'Napoleon an Irishman!'

'Yes,' said Bonaparte, 'on the mother's side, and that is how we are related. There wasn't a man to beat him,' said Bonaparte, stretching himself—'not a man except the Duke of Wellington. And it's a strange coincidence,' added Bonaparte, bending forward, 'but *he* was a connection of mine. His nephew, the Duke of Wellington's nephew, married a cousin of mine. *She* was a woman! See her at one of the court balls— amber satin—daisies in her hair. Worth going a hundred miles to look at her! Often seen her there myself, sir!'

The German moved the leather thongs in and out, and thought of the strange vicissitudes of human life, which might bring the kindsman of dukes and emperors to his humble room.

Bonaparte appeared lost among old memories.

'Ah, that Duke of Wellington's nephew!' he broke forth suddenly; 'many's the joke I've had with him. Often came to visit me at Bonaparte Hall. Grand place I had then—park, conservatory, servants. He had only one fault, that Duke of Wellington's nephew,' said Bonaparte, observing that the German was deeply interested in every word: 'he was a coward—what you might call a coward. You've never been in Russia, I suppose?' said Bonaparte, fixing his cross-wise look-ing eyes on the German's face.

'No, no,' said the old man humbly. 'France, England, Germany, a little in this country; it is all I have travelled.'

'*I*, my friend,' said Bonaparte, 'have been in every country in the world, and speak every civilized language, excepting only Dutch and German. I wrote a book of my travels— noteworthy incidents. Publisher got it—cheated me out of it. Great rascals those publishers! Upon one occasion the Duke of Wellington's nephew and I were travelling in Russia. All of a sudden one of the horses dropped down dead as a door-nail. There we were—cold night—snow four feet thick—great forest—one horse not being able to move sledge—night coming on—wolves.

'"Spree!" says the Duke of Wellington's nephew.

'"Spree, do you call it?" says I. "Look out."

'There, sticking out under a bush, was nothing less than the nose of a bear. The Duke of Wellington's nephew was up a tree like a shot; I stood quietly on the ground, as cool as I am at this moment, loaded my gun, and climbed up the tree. There was only one bough.

'"Bon," said the Duke of Wellington's nephew, "you'd better sit in front."

'"All right," said I; "but keep your gun ready. There are more coming." He'd got his face buried in my back.

'"How many are there?" said he.

'"Four," said I.

'"How many are there now?" said he.

'"Ten," said I.

'"Ten! ten!" said he; and down goes his gun.

'"Wallie," I said, "what have you done? We're dead men now."

'"Bon, my old fellow," said he, "I couldn't help it; my hands trembled so!"

'"Wall," I said, turning round and seizing his hands, "Wallie, my dear lad, good-bye. I'm not afraid to die. My legs are long—they hang down—the first bear that comes and I don't hit him, off goes my foot. When he takes it I shall give you my gun and go. You may yet be saved; but tell, oh, tell Mary Ann that I thought of her, that I prayed for her!"

'"Good-bye, old fellow!" said he.

'"God bless you!" said I.

'By this time the bears were sitting in a circle all round the tree. Yes,' said Bonaparte impressively, fixing his eyes on the German, 'a regular, exact circle. The marks of their tails were left in the snow, and I measured it afterwards; a drawing-master couldn't have done it better. It was that saved me. If they'd rushed on me at once, poor old Bon would never have been here to tell this story. But they came on, sir, *systematically*, one by one. All the rest sat on their tails and waited. The first fellow came up, and I shot him; the second fellow—I shot him; the third—I shot him. At last the tenth came; he was the biggest of all—the leader, you may say.

'"Wall," I said, "give me your hand. My fingers are stiff with the cold; there is only one bullet left. I shall miss him. While he is eating me you get down and take your gun; and live, dear friend, live to remember the man who gave his life for you!" By that time the bear was at me. I felt his paw on my trousers.

'"Oh, Bonnie! Bonnie!" said the Duke of Wellington's nephew. But I just took my gun, and put the muzzle to the bear's ear—over he fell—dead!'

Bonaparte Blenkins waited to observe what effect his story had made. Then he took out a dirty white handkerchief, and stroked his forehead, and more especially his eyes.

'It always affects me to relate that adventure,' he remarked, returning the handkerchief to his pocket. 'Ingratitude—base, vile ingratitude—is recalled by it! That man, that man, who but for me would have perished in the pathless wilds of Russia, that man in the hour of my adversity forsook me.' The German looked up. 'Yes,' said Bonaparte, 'I had money, I had lands, I said to my wife, "There is Africa, a struggling country; they want capital; they want men of talent; they want men of ability to open up that land. Let us go."

'I bought eight thousand pounds worth of machinery—winnowing, ploughing, reaping machines; I loaded a ship with them. Next steamer I came out—wife, children, all. Got to the Cape. Where is the ship with the things? Lost—gone to the bottom! And the box with the money? Lost—nothing saved!

'My wife wrote to the Duke of Wellington's nephew; I didn't wish her to; she did it without my knowledge.

'What did the man whose life I saved do? Did he send me thirty thousand pounds? say, "Bonaparte, my brother, here is a crumb?" No; he sent me nothing.

'My wife said, "Write." I said, "Mary Ann, NO. While these hands have power to work, NO. While this frame has power to endure, NO. Never shall it be said that Bonaparte Blenkins asked of any man."'

The man's noble independence touched the German.

ase is hard; yes, that *is* hard,' said the German,
his head.

parte took another draught of the soup, leaned back
t the pillows, and sighed deeply.

think,' he said after a while, rousing himself, 'I shall now wander in the benign air, and taste the gentle cool of evening. The stiffness hovers over me yet; exercise is beneficial.'

So saying, he adjusted his hat carefully on the bald crown of his head, and moved to the door. After he had gone the German sighed again over his work—

'Ah, Lord! So it is! Ah!'

He thought of the ingratitude of the world.

'Uncle Otto,' said the child in the doorway, 'did you ever hear of ten bears sitting on their tails in a circle?'

'Well, not of ten, exactly; but bears do attack travellers every day. It is nothing unheard of,' said the German. 'A man of such courage too! Terrible experience that!'

'And how do we know that the story is true, Uncle Otto?'

The German's ire was roused.

'That is what I do hate!' he cried. 'Know that is true! How do you know that anything is true? Because you are told so. If we begin to question everything—proof, proof, proof, what will we have to believe left? How do you know the angel opened the prison door for Peter,* except that Peter said so? How do you know that God talked to Moses, except that Moses wrote it? That is what I hate!'

The girl knit her brows. Perhaps her thoughts made a longer journey than the German dreamed of; for, mark you, the old dream little how their words and lives are texts and studies to the generation that shall succeed them. Not what we are taught, but what we see, makes us, and the child gathers the food on which the adult feeds to the end.

When the German looked up next there was a look of supreme satisfaction in the little mouth and the beautiful eyes.

'What dost see, chicken?' he asked.

The child said nothing, and an agonizing shriek was borne on the afternoon breeze.

'Oh, God! my God! I am killed!' cried the voice of Bonaparte, as he, with wide open mouth and shaking flesh, fell into

the room, followed by a half-grown ostrich, who put its head
in at the door, opened its beak at him, and went away.

'Shut the door! shut the door! As you value my life, shut the
door!' cried Bonaparte, sinking into a chair, his face blue and
white, with a greenishness about the mouth. 'Ah, my friend,'
he said tremulously, 'eternity has looked me in the face! My
life's thread hung upon a cord! The valley of the shadow of
death!' said Bonaparte, seizing the German's arm.

'Dear, dear, dear!' said the German, who had closed the
lower half of the door, and stood much concerned beside the
stranger, 'you have had a fright. I never knew so young a bird
to chase before; but they will take dislikes to certain people. I
sent a boy away once because a bird would chase him. Ah,
dear, dear!'

'When I looked round,' said Bonaparte, 'the red and yawning cavity was above me, and the reprehensible paw raised to
strike me. My nerves,' said Bonaparte, suddenly growing faint,
'always delicate—highly strung—are broken—broken! You
could not give a little wine, a little brandy, my friend?'

The old German hurried away to the bookshelf, and took
from behind the books a small bottle, half of whose contents
he poured into a cup. Bonaparte drained it eagerly.

'How do you feel now?' asked the German, looking at him
with much sympathy.

'A little, *slightly* better.'

The German went out to pick up the battered chimney-pot
which had fallen before the door.

'I am sorry you got the fright. The birds are bad things till
you know them,' he said sympathetically, as he put the hat
down.

'My friend,' said Bonaparte, holding out his hand, 'I forgive
you; do not be disturbed. Whatever the consequences, I
forgive you. I know, I believe, it was with no ill-intent that
you allowed me to go out. Give me your hand. I have no ill-
feeling; none!'

'You are very kind,' said the German, taking the extended
hand, and feeling suddenly convinced that he was receiving
magnanimous forgiveness for some great injury, 'you are very
kind.'

'Don't mention it,' said Bonaparte.

He knocked out the crown of his caved-in old hat, placed it on the table before him, leaned his elbows on the table and his face in his hands, and contemplated it.

'Ah, my old friend,' he thus apostrophized the hat, 'you have served me long, you have served me faithfully, but the last day has come. Never more shall you be borne upon the head of your master. Never more shall you protect his brow from the burning rays of summer or the cutting winds of winter. Henceforth bare-headed must your master go. Good-bye, good-bye, old hat!'

At the end of this affecting appeal the German rose. He went to the box at the foot of his bed; out of it he took a black hat, which had evidently been seldom worn and carefully preserved.

'It's not exactly what you may have been accustomed to,' he said nervously, putting it down beside the battered chimney-pot, 'but it might be of some use—a protection to the head, you know.'

'My friend,' said Bonaparte, 'you are not following my advice; you are allowing yourself to be reproached on my account. Do not make yourself unhappy. No; I shall go bare-headed.'

'No, no, no!' cried the German energetically. 'I have no use for the hat, none at all. It is shut up in the box.'

'Then I will take it, my friend. It is a comfort to one's own mind when you have unintentionally injured anyone to make reparation. I know the feeling. The hat may not be of that refined cut of which the old one was, but it will serve, yes, it will serve. Thank you,' said Bonaparte, adjusting it on his head, and then replacing it on the table. 'I shall lie down now and take a little repose,' he added; 'I much fear my appetite for supper will be lost.'

'I hope not, I hope not,' said the German, reseating himself at his work, and looking much concerned as Bonaparte stretched himself on the bed and turned the end of the patchwork quilt over his feet.

'You must not think to make your departure, not for many

days,' said the German presently. 'Tant' Sannie gives her consent, and——'

'My friend,' said Bonaparte, closing his eyes sadly, 'you are kind; but were it not that to-morrow is the Sabbath, weak and trembling as I lie here, I would proceed on my way. I must seek work; idleness but for the day is painful. *Work, labour*—that is the secret of all true happiness!'

He doubled the pillow under his head, and watched how the German drew the leather thongs in and out.

After a while Lyndall silently put her book on the shelf and went home, and the German stood up and began to mix some water and meal for roaster-cakes. As he stirred them with his hands he said,

'I make always a double supply on Saturday night; the hands are then free as the thoughts for Sunday.'

'The blessed Sabbath!' said Bonaparte.

There was a pause. Bonaparte twisted his eyes without moving his head, to see if supper were already on the fire.

'You must sorely miss the administration of the Lord's word in this desolate spot,' added Bonaparte. 'Oh, how love I thine house, and the place where Thine honour dwelleth!'

'Well, we do; yes,' said the German; 'but we do our best. We meet together, and I—well, I say a few words, and perhaps they are not wholly lost, not quite.'

'Strange coincidence,' said Bonaparte; 'my plan always was the same. Was in the Free State once—solitary farm—one neighbour. Every Sunday I called together friend and neighbour, child and servant, and said, "Rejoice with me, that we may serve the Lord," and then I addressed them. Ah, those were blessed times,' said Bonaparte; 'would they might return.'

The German stirred at the cakes, and stirred, and stirred, and stirred. He could give the stranger his bed, and he could give the stranger his hat, and he could give the stranger his brandy; but his Sunday service!

After a good while he said,

'I might speak to Tant' Sannie; I might arrange; you might take the service in my place, if it——'

'My friend,' said Bonaparte, 'it would give me the profoundest felicity, the most unbounded satisfaction; but in these worn-out habiliments, in these deteriorated garments, it would not be possible, it would not be fitting that I should officiate in service of One, whom, for respect, we shall not name. No, my friend, I will remain here; and, while you are assembling yourselves together in the presence of the Lord, I, in my solitude, will think of and pray for you. No; I will remain here!'

It was a touching picture—the solitary man there praying for them. The German cleared his hands from the meal, and went to the chest from which he had taken the black hat. After a little careful feeling about, he produced a black cloth coat, trousers, and waistcoat, which he laid on the table, smiling knowingly. They were of new shining cloth, worn twice a year, when he went to the town to 'nachtmaal.'* He looked with great pride at the coat as he unfolded it and held it up.

'It's not the latest fashion, perhaps, not a West End cut, not exactly; but it might do; it might serve at a push. Try it on, try it on!' he said, his old grey eyes twinkling with pride.

Bonaparte stood up and tried on the coat. It fitted admirably; the waistcoat could be made to button by ripping up the back, and the trousers were perfect; but below were the ragged boots. The German was not disconcerted. Going to the beam where a pair of top-boots hung, he took them off, dusted them carefully, and put them down before Bonaparte. The old eyes now fairly brimmed over with sparkling enjoyment.

'I have only worn them once. They might serve; they might be endured.'

Bonaparte drew them on and stood upright, his head almost touching the beams. The German looked at him with profound admiration. It was wonderful what a difference feathers made in the bird.

CHAPTER V
Sunday Services

Service No. I

THE boy Waldo kissed the pages of his book and looked up. Far over the flat lay the 'kopje,' a mere speck; the sheep wandered quietly from bush to bush; the stillness of the early Sunday rested everywhere, and the air was fresh.

He looked down at his book. On its page a black insect crept. He lifted it off with his finger. Then he leaned on his elbow, watching its quivering antennae and strange movements, smiling.

'Even you,' he whispered, 'shall not die. Even you He loves. Even you He will fold in His arms when He takes everything and makes it perfect and happy.'

When the thing had gone he smoothed the leaves of his Bible somewhat caressingly. The leaves of that book had dropped blood for him once; they had taken the brightness out of his childhood; from between them had sprung the visions that had clung about him and made night horrible. Adder-like thoughts had lifted their heads, had shot out forked tongues at him, asking mockingly strange, trivial questions that he could not answer, miserable child—

Why did the women in Mark see only one angel and the women in Luke two? Could a story be told in opposite ways and both ways be true? Could it? could it? Then again:—Is there nothing always right, and nothing always wrong? Could Jael the wife of Heber the Kenite* 'put her hand to the nail, and her right hand to the workman's hammer?' and could the Spirit of the Lord chant pæans over her, loud pæans, high pæans, set in the book of the Lord, and no voice cry out it was a mean and dastardly sin to lie, and kill the trusting in their sleep? Could the friend of God marry his own sister, and be beloved, and the man who does it to-day goes to hell, to hell? Was there nothing always right or always wrong?*

Those leaves had dropped blood for him once: they had made his heart heavy and cold; they had robbed his childhood of its gladness; now his fingers moved over them caressingly.

'My Father God knows, my Father knows,' he said; 'we cannot understand; He knows.' After a while he whispered smiling—'I heard your voice this morning when my eyes were not yet open, I felt you near me, my Father. Why do you love me so?' His face was illuminated. 'In the last four months the old question has gone from me. I know you are good; I know you love everything; I know, I know, I know! I could not have borne it any more, not any more.' He laughed softly. 'And all the while I was so miserable you were looking at me and loving me, and I never knew it. But I know it now, I feel it,' said the boy, and he laughed low; 'I feel it!' he laughed.

After a while he began partly to sing, partly to chant the disconnected verses of hymns, those which spoke his gladness, many times over. The sheep with their senseless eyes turned to look at him as he sang.

At last he lapsed into quiet. Then as the boy lay there staring at bush and sand, he saw a vision.

He had crossed the river of Death, and walked on the other bank in the Lord's land of Beulah.* His feet sank into the dark grass, and he walked alone. Then, far over the fields, he saw a figure coming across the dark green grass. At first he thought it must be one of the angels; but as it came nearer he began to feel what it was. And it came closer, closer to him, and then the voice said, 'Come,' and he knew surely Who it was. He ran to the dear feet and touched them with his hands; yes, he held them fast! He lay down beside them. When he looked up the face was over him, and the glorious eyes were loving him; and they two were there alone together.

He laughed a deep laugh; then started up like one suddenly awakened from sleep.

'Oh, God!' he cried, 'I cannot wait; I cannot wait! I want to die; I want to see Him; I want to touch Him. Let me die!' He folded his hands, trembling. 'How can I wait so long—for long, long years perhaps? I want to die—to see Him. I will die any death. Oh, let me come!'

Weeping he bowed himself, and quivered from head to foot. After a long while he lifted his head.

'Yes; I will wait; I will wait. But not long; do not let it be very long, Jesus King. I want you; oh I want you,—soon, soon!' He sat still, staring across the plain with his tearful eyes.

Service No. II

IN the front room of the farm-house sat Tant' Sannie in her elbow-chair. In her hand was her great brass-clasped hymn-book, round her neck was a clean white handkerchief, under her feet was a wooden stove. There, too, sat Em and Lyndall, in clean pinafores and new shoes. There, too, was the spruce Hottentot in a starched white 'cappje,' and her husband on the other side of the door, with his wool oiled and very much combed out, and staring at his new leather boots. The Kaffir servants were not there, because Tant' Sannie held they were descended from apes, and needed no salvation. But the rest were gathered for the Sunday service, and waited the officiator.

Meanwhile Bonaparte and the German approached arm-in-arm—Bonaparte resplendent in the black cloth clothes, a spotless shirt, and a spotless collar; the German in the old salt-and-pepper, casting shy glances of admiration at his companion.

At the front door Bonaparte removed his hat with much dignity, raised his shirt collar, and entered. To the centre table he walked, put his hat solemnly down by the big Bible, and bowed his head over it in silent prayer.

The Boer-woman looked at the Hottentot, and the Hottentot looked at the Boer-woman.

There was one thing on earth for which Tant' Sannie had a profound reverence, which exercised a subduing influence over her, which made her for the time a better woman—that thing was new, shining black cloth. It made her think of the 'predikant;'* it made her think of the elders, who sat in the top pew of the church on Sundays, with the hair so nicely oiled, so holy and respectable, with their little swallow-tailed coats; it made her think of heaven, where everything was so holy and respectable, and nobody wore tan-cord, and the littlest angel had a black tail-coat. She wished she hadn't called him a thief and a Roman Catholic. She hoped the German hadn't told him. She wondered where those clothes were when he came in rags to her door. There was no doubt, he was a very respectable man, a gentleman.

The German began to read a hymn. At the end of each line Bonaparte groaned, and twice at the end of every verse.

The Boer-woman had often heard of persons groaning during prayers, to add a certain poignancy and finish to them; old Jan Vanderlinde, her mother's brother, always did it after he was converted; and she would have looked upon it as no especial sign of grace in anyone; but to groan at hymn-time! She was startled. She wondered if he remembered that she shook her fist in his face. This was a man of God. They knelt down to pray. The Boer-woman weighed two hundred and fifty pounds, and could not kneel. She sat in her chair, and peeped between her crossed fingers at the stranger's back. She could not understand what he said; but he was in earnest. He shook the chair by the back rail till it made quite a little dust on the mud floor.

When they rose from their knees Bonaparte solemnly seated himself in the chair and opened the Bible. He blew his nose, pulled up his shirt-collar, smoothed the leaves, stroked down his capacious waistcoat, blew his nose again, looked solemnly round the room, then began,——

'All liars shall have their part in the lake which burneth with fire and brimstone, which is the second death.'

Having read this portion of Scripture, Bonaparte paused impressively, and looked all round the room.

'I shall not, my dear friends,' he said, 'long detain you. Much of our precious time has already fled blissfully from us in the voice of thanksgiving and the tongue of praise. A few, a very few words are all I shall address to you, and may they be as a rod of iron dividing the bones from the marrow, and the marrow from the bones.

'In the first place: What is a liar?'

The question was put so pointedly and followed by a pause so profound, that even the Hottentot man left off looking at his boots and opened his eyes, though he understood not a word.

'I repeat,' said Bonaparte, 'what is a liar?'

The sensation was intense; the attention of the audience was riveted.

'Have you any of you ever seen a liar, my dear friends?' There was a still longer pause. 'I hope not; I truly hope not. But I will tell you what a liar is. I knew a liar once—a little boy who lived in Cape Town, in Short Market Street. His mother and I sat together one day, discoursing about our souls.

'"Here, Sampson," said his mother, "go and buy sixpence of 'meiboss'* from the Malay round the corner."

'When he came back she said, "How much have you got?"

'"Five," he said.

'He was afraid if he said six and a half she'd ask for some. And, my friends, that was a *lie*. The half of a "meiboss" stuck in his throat, and he died, and was buried. And where did the soul of that little liar go to, my friends? It went to the lake of fire and brimstone. This brings me to the second point of my discourse.

'What is a lake of fire and brimstone? I will tell you, my friends,' said Bonaparte condescendingly. 'The imagination unaided cannot conceive it: but by the help of the Lord I will put it before your mind's eye.

'I was travelling in Italy once on a time; I came to a city called Rome, a vast city, and near it is a mountain which spits forth fire. Its name is Etna. Now, there was a man in that city of Rome who had not the fear of God before his eyes, and he loved a woman. The woman died, and he walked up that mountain spitting fire, and when he got to the top he threw himself in at the hole that is there. The next day I went up. I was not afraid; the Lord preserves His servants. And in their hands shall they bear thee up, lest at any time thou fall into a volcano. It was dark night when I got there, but in the fear of the Lord I walked to the edge of the yawning abyss, and looked in. That sight—that sight, my friends, is impressed upon my most indelible memory. I looked down into the lurid depths upon an incandescent lake, a melted fire, a seething sea; the billows rolled from side to side, and on their fiery crests tossed the white skeleton of the suicide. The heat had burnt the flesh from off the bones; they lay as a light cork upon the melted fiery waves. One skeleton hand was raised upwards, the finger pointing to heaven; the other, with outstretched finger, pointing downwards, as though it would say: "I go below, but you, Bonaparte, may soar above." I gazed; I stood entranced. At that instant there was a crack in the lurid lake; it swelled, expanded, and the skeleton of the suicide disappeared, to be seen no more by mortal eye.'

Here again Bonaparte rested, and then continued—

'The lake of melted stone rose in the crater, it swelled higher and higher at the side, it streamed forth at the top. I had presence of mind; near me was a rock; I stood upon it, The fiery torrent was vomited out, and streamed on either side of me. And through that long and terrible night I stood there alone upon that rock, the glowing fiery lava on every hand—a monument of the long-suffering and tender providence of the Lord, who spared me that I might this day testify in your ears of Him.

'Now, my dear friends, let us deduce the lessons that are to be learnt from this narrative.

'Firstly: let us never commit suicide. That man is a fool, my friends, that man is insane, my friends, who would leave this earth, my friends. Here are joys innumerable, such as it hath not entered into the heart of man to understand, my friends. Here are clothes, my friends; here are beds, my friends; here is delicious food, my friends. Our precious bodies were given us to love, to cherish. Oh, let us do so! Oh, let us never hurt them; but care for and love them, my friends!'

Everyone was impressed, and Bonaparte proceeded.

'Secondly: let us not love too much. If that young man had not loved that young woman, he would not have jumped into Mount Etna. The good men of old never did so. Was Jeremiah ever in love, or Ezekiel, or Hosea,* or even any of the minor prophets? No. Then why should we be? Thousands are rolling in that lake at this moment who would say, "It was love that brought us here." Oh, let us think always of our own souls first.

> "'A charge to keep I have,
> A God to glorify;
> A never-dying soul to save,
> And fit it for the sky.'"*

'Oh, beloved friends, remember the little boy and the "meiboss"; remember the young girl and the young man; remember the lake, the fire, and the brimstone; remember the suicide's skeleton on the pitchy billows of Mount Etna; remember the voice of warning that has this day sounded in your ears; and what I say to you I say to all—watch! May the Lord add His blessing!'

Here the Bible closed with a tremendous thud. Tant' Sannie loosened the white handkerchief about her neck and wiped her eyes, and the coloured girl, seeing her do so, sniffled. They did not understand the discourse, which made it the more affecting. There hung over it that inscrutable charm which hovers for ever for the human intellect over the incomprehensible and shadowy. When the last hymn was sung the German conducted the officiator to Tant' Sannie, who graciously extended her hand, and offered coffee and a seat on the sofa. Leaving him there, the German hurried away to see how the little plum-pudding he had left at home was advancing; and Tant' Sannie remarked that it was a hot day. Bonaparte gathered her meaning as she fanned herself with the end of her apron. He bowed low in acquiescence. A long silence followed. Tant' Sannie spoke again. Bonaparte gave her no ear; his eye was fixed on a small miniature on the opposite wall, which represented Tant' Sannie as she had appeared on the day before her confirmation, fifteen years before, attired in green muslin. Suddenly he started to his feet, walked up to the picture, and took his stand before it. Long and wistfully he gazed into its features; it was easy to see that he was deeply moved. With a sudden movement, as though no longer able to restrain himself, he seized the picture, loosened it from its nail, and held it close to his eyes. At length, turning to the Boer-woman, he said, in a voice of deep emotion,—

'You will, I trust, dear madam, excuse this exhibition of my feelings; but this—this little picture recalls to me my first and best beloved, my dear departed wife, who is now a saint in heaven.'

Tant' Sannie could not understand; but the Hottentot maid, who had taken her seat on the floor beside her mistress, translated the English into Dutch as far as she was able.

'Ah, my first, my beloved!' he added, looking tenderly down at the picture. 'Oh, the beloved, the beautiful lineaments! My angel wife! This is surely a sister of yours, madame?' he added, fixing his eyes on Tant' Sannie.

The Dutchwoman blushed, shook her head, and pointed to herself.

Carefully, intently, Bonaparte looked from the picture in his hand to Tant' Sannie's features, and from the features back to the picture. Then slowly a light broke over his countenance; he looked up, it became a smile; he looked back at the miniature, his whole countenance was effulgent.

'Ah, yes; I see it now,' he cried, turning his delighted gaze on to the Boer-woman; 'eyes, mouth, nose, chin, the very expression!' he cried. 'How is it possible I did not notice it before?'

'Take another cup of coffee,' said Tant' Sannie. 'Put some sugar in.'

Bonaparte hung the picture tenderly up, and was turning to take the cup from her hand, when the German reappeared, to say that the pudding was ready and the meat on the table.

'He's a God-fearing man, and one who knows how to behave himself,' said the Boer-woman as he went out at the door. 'If he is ugly, did not the Lord make him? And are we to laugh at the Lord's handiwork? It is better to be ugly and good than pretty and bad; though of course it's nice when one is both,' said Tant' Sannie, looking complacently at the picture on the wall.

In the afternoon the German and Bonaparte sat before the door of the cabin. Both smoked in complete silence—Bonaparte with a book in his hands and his eyes half closed; the German puffing vigorously, and glancing up now and again at the serene blue sky overhead.

'Supposing—you—you, in fact, made the remark to me,'

burst forth the German suddenly, 'that you were looking for a situation.'

Bonaparte opened his mouth wide, and sent a stream of smoke through his lips.

'Now supposing,' said the German,—'merely supposing, of course,—that someone, someone in fact, should make an offer to you, say, to become schoolmaster on their farm and teach two children, two little girls, perhaps, and would give you forty pounds a year, would you accept it?—Just supposing, of course.'

'Well, my dear friend,' said Bonaparte, 'that would depend on circumstances. Money is no consideration with me. For my wife I have made provision for the next year. My health is broken. Could I meet a place where a gentleman would be treated as a gentleman I would accept it, however small the remuneration. With me,' said Bonaparte, 'money is no consideration.'

'Well,' said the German, when he had taken a whiff or two more from his pipe. 'I think I shall go up and see Tant' Sannie a little. I go up often on Sunday afternoon to have a general conversation, to see her, you know. Nothing—nothing particular, you know.'

The old man put his book into his pocket, and walked up to the farmhouse with a peculiarly knowing and delighted expression of countenance.

'He doesn't suspect what I'm going to do,' soliloquized the German; 'hasn't the least idea. A nice surprise for him.'

The man whom he had left at his doorway winked at the retreating figure with a wink that was not to be described.

CHAPTER VI
Bonaparte Blenkins makes his Nest

'AH, what is the matter?' asked Waldo, stopping at the foot of the ladder with a load of skins on his back that he was carrying up to the loft. Through the open door in the gable little Em was visible, her feet dangling from the high bench on which she sat. The room, once a store-room, had been divided by a row of 'mealie' bags into two parts—the back being Bonaparte's bedroom, the front his schoolroom.

'Lyndall made him angry,' said the girl tearfully; 'and he has given me the fourteenth of John* to learn. He says he will teach me to behave myself, when Lyndall troubles him.'

'What did she do?' asked the boy.

'You see,' said Em, hopelessly turning the leaves, 'whenever he talks she looks out at the door, as though she did not hear him. To-day she asked him what the signs of the Zodiac were, and he said he was surprised that she should ask him; it was not a fit and proper thing for little girls to talk about. Then she asked him who Copernicus* was; and he said he was one of the Emperors of Rome, who burned the Christians in a golden pig, and the worms ate him up while he was still alive. I don't know why,' said Em plaintively, 'but she just put her books under her arm and walked out; and she will never come to his school again, she says, and she *always* does what she says. And now I must sit here every day alone,' said Em, the great tears dropping softly.

'Perhaps Tant' Sannie will send him away,' said the boy, in his mumbling way, trying to comfort her.

'No,' said Em, shaking her head; 'no. Last night when the little Hottentot maid was washing her feet, he told her he liked such feet, and that fat women were so nice to him; and she said I must always put him pure cream in his coffee now. No; he'll never go away,' said Em dolorously.

The boy put down his skins and fumbled in his pocket, and

produced a small piece of paper containing something. He stuck it out towards her.

'There, take it for you,' he said. This was by way of comfort.

Em opened it and found a small bit of gum, a commodity prized by the children; but the great tears dropped down slowly on to it.

Waldo was distressed. He had cried so much in his morsel of life that tears in another seemed to burn him.

'If,' he said, stepping in awkwardly and standing by the table, 'if you will not cry I will tell you something—a secret.'

'What is that?' asked Em, instantly becoming decidedly better.

'You will tell it to no human being?'

'No.'

He bent nearer to her, and with deep solemnity said,

'*I have made a machine!*'

Em opened her eyes.

'Yes; a machine for shearing sheep. It is almost done,' said the boy. 'There is only one thing that is not right yet; but it will be soon. When you think, and think, and think, all night and all day, it comes at last,' he added mysteriously.

'Where is it?'

'Here! I always carry it here,' said the boy, putting his hand to his breast, where a bulging-out was visible. 'This is a model. When it is done they will have to make a large one.'

'Show it me.'

The boy shook his head.

'No, not till it is done. I cannot let any human being see it till then.'

'It is a beautiful secret,' said Em; and the boy shuffled out to pick up his skins.

That evening father and son sat in the cabin eating their supper. The father sighed deeply sometimes. Perhaps he thought how long a time it was since Bonaparte had visited the cabin; but his son was in that land in which signs have no part. It is a question whether it were not better to be the shabbiest of fools, and know the way up the little stair of imagination to the land of dreams, than the wisest of men, who see nothing that the eyes do not show, and feel nothing that the hands do not touch. The boy chewed his brown bread and drank his coffee; but in truth he saw only his machine finished—that last something found out and added. He saw it as it worked with beautiful smoothness; and over and above, as he chewed his bread and drank his coffee, there was that delightful conscious-ness of something bending over him and loving him. It would not have been better in one of the courts of heaven, where the walls are set with rows of the King of Glory's amethysts and milk-white pearls, than there, eating his supper in that little room.

As they sat in silence there was a knock at the door. When it was opened the small woolly head of a little nigger showed itself. She was a messenger from Tant' Sannie; the German was wanted at once at the homestead. Putting on his hat with both hands, he hurried off. The kitchen was in darkness, but in the pantry beyond, Tant' Sannie and her maids were assembled.

A Kaffir girl, who had been grinding pepper between two stones, knelt on the floor, the lean Hottentot stood with a brass candlestick in her hand, and Tant' Sannie, near the shelf, with a hand on each hip, was evidently listening intently, as were her companions.

'What may it be?' cried the old German in astonishment.

The room beyond the pantry was the store-room. Through the thin wooden partition there arose at that instant, evidently from some creature ensconced there, a prolonged and prodi-gious howl, followed by a succession of violent blows against the partition wall.

The German seized the churn-stick, and was about to rush round the house, when the Boer-woman impressively held her hand upon his arm.

'That is his head,' said Tant' Sannie, 'that is his head.'

'But what might it be?' asked the German, looking from one to the other, churn-stick in hand.

A low hollow bellow prevented reply, and the voice of Bonaparte lifted itself on high.

'Mary Ann! my angel! my wife!'

'Isn't it dreadful?' said Tant' Sannie, as the blows were repeated fiercely. 'He has got a letter: his wife is dead. You must go and comfort him,' said Tant' Sannie at last, 'and I will go with you. It would not be the thing for me to go alone—me, who am only thirty-three, and he an unmarried man now,' said Tant' Sannie, blushing and smoothing out her apron.

Upon this they all trudged round the house in company—the Hottentot maid carrying the light, Tant' Sannie and the German following, and the Kaffir girl bringing up the rear.

'Oh,' said Tant' Sannie, 'I see now it wasn't wickedness made him do without his wife so long—only necessity.'

At the door she motioned to the German to enter, and followed him closely. On the stretcher behind the sacks Bonaparte lay on his face, his head pressed into a pillow, his legs kicking gently. The Boer-woman sat down on a box at the foot of the bed. The German stood with folded hands looking on.

'We must all die,' said Tant' Sannie at last; 'it is the dear Lord's will.'

Hearing her voice, Bonaparte turned himself on to his back.

'It's very hard,' said Tant' Sannie, 'I know, for I've lost two husbands.'

Bonaparte looked up into the German's face.

'Oh, what does she say? Speak to me words of comfort!'

The German repeated Tant' Sannie's remark.

'Ah, I—I also! Two dear, dear wives, whom I shall never see any more!' cried Bonaparte, flinging himself back upon the bed.

He howled, till the tarantulas, who lived between the rafters and the zinc roof, felt the unusual vibration, and looked out with their wicked bright eyes, to see what was going on.

Tant' Sannie sighed, the Hottentot maid sighed, the Kaffir girl who looked in at the door put her hand over her mouth and said 'Mow-wah!'

'You must trust in the Lord,' said Tant' Sannie. 'He can give you more than you have lost.'

'I do, I do!' he cried; 'but oh, I have no wife! I have no wife!'

Tant' Sannie was much affected, and came and stood near the bed.

'Ask him if he won't have a little pap*—nice, fine, flour pap. There is some boiling on the kitchen fire.'

The German made the proposal, but the widower waved his hand.

'No, nothing shall pass my lips. I should be suffocated. No, no! Speak not of food to me!'

'Pap, and a little brandy in,' said Tant' Sannie coaxingly.

Bonaparte caught the word.

'Perhaps, perhaps—if I struggled with myself—for the sake of my duties I might imbibe a few drops,' he said, looking with quivering lip up into the German's face. 'I must do my duty, must I not?'

Tant' Sannie gave the order, and the girl went for the pap.

'I know how it was when my first husband died. They could do nothing with me,' the Boer-woman said, 'till I had eaten a sheep's trotter, and honey, and a little roaster-cake. *I* know.'

Bonaparte sat up on the bed with his legs stretched out in front of him, and a hand on each knee, blubbering softly.

'Oh, she was a woman! You are very kind to try and comfort me, but she was my wife. For a woman that is my wife I could live; for the woman that is my wife I could die! For a woman that is my wife I could—Ah! that sweet word *wife;* when will it rest upon my lips again?'

When his feelings had subsided a little he raised the corners of his turned-down mouth, and spoke to the German with flabby lips.

'Do you think she understands me? Oh, tell her every word, that she may think I thank her.'

At that instant the girl reappeared with a basin of steaming gruel and a black bottle.

Tant' Sannie poured some of its contents into the basin, stirred it well, and came to the bed.

'Oh, I can't, I can't! I shall die! I shall die!' said Bonaparte, putting his hands to his side.

'Come, just a little,' said Tant' Sannie coaxingly; 'just a drop.'

'It's too thick, it's too thick. I should choke.'

Tant' Sannie added from the contents of the bottle and held out a spoonful; Bonaparte opened his mouth like a little bird waiting for a worm, and held it open, as she dipped again and again into the pap.

'Ah, this will do your heart good,' said Tant' Sannie, in whose mind the relative functions of heart and stomach were exceedingly ill-defined.

When the basin was emptied the violence of his grief was much assuaged; he looked at Tant' Sannie with gentle tears.

'Tell him,' said the Boer-woman, 'that I hope he will sleep well, and that the Lord will comfort him, as the Lord only can.'

'Bless you, dear friend, God bless you,' said Bonaparte.

When the door was safely shut on the German, the Hottentot, and the Dutch-woman, he got off the bed and washed away the soap he had rubbed on his eyelids.

'Bon,' he said, slapping his leg, 'you're the 'cutest lad I ever came across. If you don't turn out the old Hymns-and-prayers, and pummel the Ragged coat, and get your arms round the fat's one's waist and a wedding-ring on her finger, then you are not Bonaparte. But you *are* Bonaparte. Bon, you're a fine boy!'

Making which pleasing reflection, he pulled off his trousers and got into bed cheerfully.

CHAPTER VII
He sets his Trap

'MAY I come in? I hope I do not disturb you, my dear friend,' said Bonaparte, late one evening, putting his nose in at the cabin door, where the German and his son sat finishing their supper.

It was now two months since he had been installed as schoolmaster in Tant' Sannie's household, and he had grown mighty and more mighty day by day. He visited the cabin no more, sat close to Tant' Sannie drinking coffee all the evening, and walked about loftily with his hands under the coat-tails of the German's black cloth, and failed to see even a nigger who wished him a deferential good-morning. It was therefore with no small surprise that the German perceived Bonaparte's red nose at his door.

'Walk in, walk in,' he said joyfully. 'Boy, boy, see if there is coffee left. Well, none. Make a fire. We have done supper, but——'

'My dear friend,' said Bonaparte, taking off his hat, 'I came not to sup, not for mere creature comforts, but for an hour of brotherly intercourse with a kindred spirit. The press of business and the weight of thought, but they alone, may sometimes prevent me from sharing the secrets of my bosom with him for whom I have so great a sympathy. You perhaps wonder when I shall return the two pounds——'

'Oh, no, no! Make a fire, make a fire, boy. We will have a pot of hot coffee presently,' said the German, rubbing his hands and looking about, not knowing how best to show his pleasure at the unexpected visit.

For three weeks the German's diffident 'Good evening' had met with a stately bow; the chin of Bonaparte lifting itself higher daily; and his shadow had not darkened the cabin doorway since he came to borrow the two pounds. The German walked to the head of the bed and took down a blue bag that hung there. Blue bags were a speciality of the German's. He kept above fifty stowed away in different corners of his room— some filled with curious stones, some with seeds that had been in his possession fifteen years, some with rusty nails, and bits of old harness—in all, a wonderful assortment, but highly prized.

'We have something here not so bad,' said the German, smiling knowingly, as he dived his hand into the bag and took out a handful of almonds and raisins; 'I buy these for my chickens. They increase in size, but they still think the old man must have something nice for them. And the old man— well, a big boy may have a sweet tooth sometimes, may he not? Ha, ha!' said the German, chuckling at his own joke, as he heaped the plate with almonds. 'Here is a stone—two stones to crack them—no late patent improvement—well, Adam's nut-cracker; ha, ha! But I think we shall do. We will not leave them uncracked. We will consume a few without fashionable improvements.'

Here the German sat down on one side of the table, Bonaparte on the other; each one with a couple of flat stones before him, and the plate between them.

'Do not be afraid,' said the German, 'do not be afraid. I do not forget the boy at the fire; I crack for him. The bag is full. Why, this is strange,' he said suddenly, cracking open a large nut; 'three kernels! I have not observed that before. This must be retained. This is valuable.' He wrapped the nut gravely in paper, and put it carefully in his waistcoat pocket. 'Valuable, very valuable!' he said, shaking his head.

'Ah, my friend,' said Bonaparte, 'what joy it is to be once more in your society.'

The German's eye glistened, and Bonaparte seized his hand and squeezed it warmly. They then proceeded to crack and eat. After a while Bonapart said, stuffing a handful of raisins into his mouth—

'I was so deeply grieved, my dear friend, that you and Tant' Sannie had some slight unpleasantness this evening.'

'Oh, no, no,' said the German; 'it is all right now. A few sheep missing; but I make it good myself. I give my twelve sheep, and work in the other eight.'

'It is rather hard that you should have to make good the lost sheep,' said Bonaparte; 'it is no fault of yours.'

'Well,' said the German, 'this is the case. Last evening I count the sheep at the kraal—twenty are missing. I ask the herd; he tells me they are with the other flock; he tells me so *distinctly*; how can I think he lies? This afternoon I count the other flock. The sheep are not there. I come back here: the herd is gone; the sheep are gone. But I cannot—no, I will not—believe he stole them,' said the German, growing suddenly excited. 'Someone else, but not he. I know that boy; I knew him three years. He is a good boy. I have seen him deeply affected on account of his soul. And she would send the police after him! I say I would rather make the loss good myself. I will not have it; he has fled in fear. I know his heart. It was,' said the German, with a little gentle hesitation, 'under my words that he first felt his need of a Saviour.'

Bonaparte cracked some more almonds, then said, yawning, and more as though he asked for the sake of having something to converse about than from any interest he felt in the subject—

'And what has become of the herd's wife?'

The German was alight again in a moment.

'Yes; his wife. She has a child six days old, and Tant' Sannie would turn her out into the fields this night. That,' said the German, rising, 'that is what I call cruelty—diabolical cruelty. My soul abhors that deed. The man that could do such a thing I could run him through with a knife!' said the German, his grey eyes flashing, and his bushy black beard adding to the murderous fury of his aspect. Then suddenly subsiding, he said,—'But all is now well; Tant' Sannie gives her word that the maid shall remain for some days. I go to Oom Muller's to-morrow to learn if the sheep may not be there. If they are not, then I return. They are gone; that is all. I make it good.'

'Tant' Sannie is a singular woman,' said Bonaparte, taking the tobacco bag the German passed to him.

'Singular! Yes,' said the German; 'but her heart is on her right side. I have lived long years with her, and I may say, I have for her an affection, which she returns. I may say,' added the German with warmth, 'I may say, that there is not one soul on this farm for whom I have *not* an affection.'

'Ah, my friend,' said Bonaparte, 'when the grace of God is in our hearts, is it not so with us all? Do we not love the very worm we tread upon, and as we tread upon it? Do we know distinctions of race, or of sex, or of colour? *No!*

> '"Love so amazing, so divine,
> It fills my soul, my life, my all."'*

After a time he sank into a less fervent mood, and remarked,—

'The coloured female who waits upon Tant' Sannie appears to be of a virtuous disposition, an individual who——'

'Virtuous!' said the German; 'I have confidence in her. There is that in her which is pure, that which is noble. The rich and high that walk this earth with lofty eyelids might exchange with her.'

The German here got up to bring a coal for Bonaparte's pipe, and they sat together talking for a while. At length Bonparte knocked the ashes out of his pipe.

'It is time that I took my departure, dear friend,' he said; 'but, before I do so, shall we not close this evening of sweet communion and brotherly intercourse by a few words of prayer? Oh, how good and how pleasant a thing it is for brethren to dwell together in unity! It is like the dew upon the mountains of Hermon;* for there the Lord bestowed a blessing, even life for evermore.'

'Stay and drink some coffee,' said the German.

'No, thank you, my friend; I have business that must be done to-night,' said Bonaparte. 'Your dear son appears to have gone to sleep. He is going to take the waggon to the mill to-morrow! What a little *man* he is.'

'A fine boy.'

But though the boy nodded before the fire he was not asleep; and they all knelt down to pray.

When they rose from their knees Bonaparte extended his hand to Waldo, and patted him on the head.

'Good-night, my lad,' he said. 'As you go to the mill to-morrow, we shall not see you for some days. Good-night!

Good-bye! The Lord bless and guide you; and may He bring you back to us in safety to find us all *as you have left us!*' He laid some emphasis on the last words. 'And you, my dear friend,' he added, turning with redoubled warmth to the German, 'long, long shall I look back to this evening as a time of refreshing from the presence of the Lord, as an hour of blessed intercourse with a brother in Jesus. May such often return. The Lord, bless you!' he added, with yet deeper fervour, 'richly, richly.'

Then he opened the door and vanished out into the darkness.

'He, he, he!' laughed Bonaparte as he stumbled over the stones. 'If there isn't the rarest lot of fools on this farm that ever God Almighty stuck legs to. He, he he! When the worms come out then the blackbirds feed. Ha, ha, ha!' Then he drew himself up: even when alone he liked to pose with a certain dignity; it was second nature to him.

He looked in at the kitchen door. The Hottentot maid who acted as interpreter between Tant' Sannie and himself was gone, and Tant' Sannie herself was in bed.

'Never mind, Bon, my boy,' he said, as he walked round to his own room, 'to-morrow will do. He, he, he!'

CHAPTER VIII

He Catches the Old Bird

AT four o'clock the next afternoon the German rode across the plain, returning from his search for the lost sheep. He rode slowly, for he had been in the saddle since sunrise and was somewhat weary, and the heat of the afternoon made his horse sleepy as it picked its way slowly along the sandy road. Every now and then a great red spider would start out of the karroo on one side of the path and run across to the other, but nothing else broke the still monotony. Presently, behind one of the highest of the milk-bushes that dotted the roadside, the German caught sight of a Kaffir woman, seated there evidently for such shadow as the milk-bush might afford from the sloping rays of the sun. The German turned the horse's head out of the road. It was not his way to pass a living creature without a word of greeting. Coming nearer, he found it was no other than the wife of the absconding Kaffir herd. She had a baby tied on her back by a dirty strip of red blanket; another strip hardly larger was twisted round her waist, for the rest her black body was naked. She was a sullen, ill-looking woman, with lips hideously protruding.

The German questioned her as to how she came there. She muttered in broken Dutch that she had been turned away. Had she done evil? She shook her head sullenly. Had she had food given her? She grunted a negative, and fanned the flies from her baby. Telling the woman to remain where she was, he turned his horse's head to the road and rode off at a furious pace.

'Hard-hearted! cruel! Oh, my God! Is this the way? Is this charity?'

'Yes, yes, yes,' ejaculated the old man as he rode on; but, presently, his anger began to evaporate, his horse's pace slackened, and by the time he had reached his own door he was nodding and smiling.

Dismounting quickly, he went to the great chest where his provisions were kept. Here he got out a little meal, a little mealies, a few roaster-cakes. These he tied up in three blue handkerchiefs, and putting them into a sail-cloth bag, he strung them over his shoulders. Then he looked circumspectly out at the door. It was very bad to be discovered in the act of giving; it made him red up to the roots of his old grizzled hair. No one was about, however, so he rode off again. Beside the milk-bush sat the Kaffir woman still—like Hagar,* he thought, thrust out by her mistress in the wilderness to die. Telling her to loosen the handkerchief from her head, he poured into it the contents of his bag. The woman tied it up in sullen silence.

'You must try and get to the next farm,' said the German.

The woman shook her head; she would sleep in the field.

The German reflected. Kaffir women were accustomed to sleep in the open air; but then, the child was small, and after so hot a day the night might be chilly. That she would creep back to the huts at the homestead when the darkness favoured her, the German's sagacity did not make evident to him. He took off his old brown salt-and-pepper coat, and held it out to her. The woman received it in silence, and laid it across her knee. 'With that they will sleep warmly; not so bad. Ha, ha!' said the German. And he rode home, nodding his head in a manner that would have made any other man dizzy.

'I wish he would not come back to-night,' said Em, her face wet with tears.

'It will be just the same if he comes back to-morrow,' said Lyndall.

The two girls sat on the step of the cabin waiting for the German's return. Lyndall shaded her eyes with her hand from the sunset light.

'There he comes,' she said, 'whistling "Ach Jerusalem du schöne"* so loud I can hear him here.'

'Perhaps he has found the sheep.'

'Found them!' said Lyndall. 'He would whistle just so if he knew he had to die to-night.'

'You look at the sunset, eh, chickens?' the German said, as he came up at a smart canter. 'Ah, yes, that *is* beautiful!' he added, as he dismounted, pausing for a moment with his hand on the saddle to look at the evening sky, where the sun shot up long flaming streaks, between which and the eye thin yellow clouds floated. 'Ei! you weep?' said the German, as the girls ran up to him.

Before they had time to reply the voice of Tant' Sannie was heard.

'You child, of the child, of the child of a Kaffir's dog, come here!'

The German looked up. He thought the Dutch-woman, come out to cool herself in the yard, called to some misbehaving servant. The old man looked round to see who it might be.

'You old vagabond of a praying German, are you deaf?'

Tant' Sannie stood before the steps of the kitchen; upon them sat the lean Hottentot, upon the highest stood Bonaparte Blenkins, both hands folded under the tails of his coat, and his eyes fixed on the sunset sky.

The German dropped the saddle on the ground.

'Bish, bish, bish! what may *this* be?' he said, and walked toward the house. 'Very strange!'

The girls followed him: Em still weeping; Lyndall with her face rather white and her eyes wide open.

'And I have the heart of a devil, did you say? You could run me through with a knife, could you?' cried the Dutch-woman. 'I could not drive the Kaffir maid away because I was afraid of *you*, was I? Oh, you miserable rag! I loved you, did I? I would have liked to marry you, would I? *would* I? WOULD I?' cried the Boer-woman; 'you cat's tail, you dog's paw! Be near my house to-morrow morning when the sun rises,' she gasped, 'my Kaffirs will drag you through the sand. They would do it gladly, any of them, for a bit of tobacco, for all your prayings with them.'

'I am bewildered, I am bewildered,' said the German, standing before her and raising his hand to his forehead; 'I—I do not understand.'

'Ask him, ask him!' cried Tant' Sannie, pointing to Bonaparte; 'he knows. You thought he could not make me understand, but he did, he did, you old fool! I know enough English for that. You be here,' shouted the Dutch-woman, 'when the morning star rises, and I will let my Kaffirs take you out and drag you, till there is not one bone left in your old body that is not broken as fine as bobootie-meat,* you old beggar! All your rags are not worth that they should be thrown out on to the ash-heap,' cried the Boer-woman; 'but I will have them for my sheep. Not one rotten hoof of your old mare do you take with you; I will have her—all, all for my sheep that you have lost, you godless thing!'

The Boer-woman wiped the moisture from her mouth with the palm of her hand.

The German turned to Bonaparte, who still stood on the step absorbed in the beauty of the sunset.

'Do not address me; do not approach me, lost man,' said Bonaparte, not moving his eye nor lowering his chin. 'There is a crime from which all nature revolts; there is a crime whose name is loathsome to the human ear—that crime is yours; that crime is ingratitude. This woman has been your benefactress; on her farm you have lived; after her sheep you have looked; into her house you have been allowed to enter and hold Divine service—an honour of which you were never worthy; and how have you rewarded her?—Basely, basely, basely!'

'But it is all false, lies and falsehoods. I must, I will speak,' said the German, suddenly looking round bewildered. 'Do I dream? Are you mad? What may it be?'

'Go, dog,' cried the Dutch-woman; 'I would have been a rich woman this day if it had not been for your laziness. Praying with the Kaffirs behind the kraal walls. Go, you Kaffir's dog!'

'But what then is the matter? What may have happened since I left?' said the German, turning to the Hottentot woman who sat upon the step.

She was his friend; she would tell him kindly the truth. The woman answered by a loud, ringing laugh.

'Give it him, old missis! Give it him!'

It was so nice to see the white man who had been master hunted down. The coloured woman laughed, and threw a dozen mealie grains into her mouth to chew.

All anger and excitement faded away from the old man's face. He turned slowly away and walked down the little path to his cabin, with his shoulders bent; it was all dark before him. He stumbled over the threshold of his own well-known door.

Em, sobbing bitterly, would have followed him; but the Boer-woman prevented her by a flood of speech which convulsed the Hottentot, so low were its images.

'Come, Em,' said Lyndall, lifting her small, proud head, 'let us go in. We will not stay to hear such language.'

She looked into the Boer-woman's eyes. Tant' Sannie understood the meaning of the look if not the words. She waddled after them, and caught Em by the arm. She had struck Lyndall once years before, and had never done it again, so she took Em.

'So you will defy me too, will you, you Englishman's ugliness!' she cried, as with one hand she forced the child down, and held her head tightly against her knee; with the other she beat her first upon one cheek, and then upon the other.

For one instant Lyndall looked on, then she laid her small fingers on the Boer-woman's arm. With the exertion of half its strength Tant' Sannie might have flung the girl back upon the stones. It was not the power of the slight fingers, tightly though they clenched her broad wrist—so tightly that at bedtime the marks were still there; but the Boer-woman looked into the clear eyes and at the quivering white lips, and with a half-surprised curse relaxed her hold. The girl drew Em's arm through her own.

'Move!' she said to Bonaparte, who stood in the door; and he, Bonaparte the invincible, in the hour of his triumph, moved to give her place.

The Hottentot ceased to laugh, and an uncomfortable silence fell on all the three in the doorway.

Once in their room, Em sat down on the floor and wailed bitterly. Lyndall lay on the bed with her arm drawn across her eyes, very white and still.

'Hoo, hoo!' cried Em; 'and they won't let him take the grey mare; and Waldo has gone to the mill. Hoo, hoo! And perhaps they won't let us go and say good-bye to him. Hoo, hoo, hoo!'

'I wish you would be quiet,' said Lyndall, without moving.

'Does it give you such felicity to let Bonaparte know he is hurting you? We will ask no one. It will be supper time soon. Listen—and when you hear the chink of the knives and forks we will go out and see him.'

Em suppressed her sobs and listened intently, kneeling at the door. Suddenly someone came to the window and put the shutter up.

'Who was that?' said Lyndall, starting.

'The girl, I suppose,' said Em. 'How early she is this evening!'

But Lyndall sprang from the bed and seized the handle of the door, shaking it fiercely. The door was locked on the outside. She ground her teeth.

'What is the matter?' asked Em.

The room was in perfect darkness now.

'Nothing,' said Lyndall quietly; 'only they have locked us in.'

She turned, and went back to bed again. But ere long Em heard a sound of movement. Lyndall had climbed up into the window, and with her fingers felt the wood-work that surrounded the panes. Slipping down, the girl loosened the iron knob from the foot of the bedstead, and climbing up again she broke with it every pane of glass in the window, beginning at the top and ending at the bottom.

'What are you doing?' asked Em, who heard the falling fragments.

Her companion made her no reply; but leaned on every little cross-bar, which cracked and gave way beneath her. Then she pressed with all her strength against the shutter. She had thought the wooden buttons would give way, but by the clinking sound she knew that the iron bar had been put across. She was quite quiet for a time. Clambering down, she took from the table a small one-bladed pen-knife, with which she began to peck at the hard wood of the shutter.

'What are you doing now?' asked Em, who had ceased crying in her wonder, and had drawn near.

'Trying to make a hole,' was the short reply.

'Do you think you will be able to?'

'No; but I am trying.'

In an agony of suspense Em waited. For ten minutes Lyndall pecked. The hole was three-eighths of an inch deep—then the blade sprang into ten pieces.

'What has happened now?' asked Em, blubbering afresh.

'Nothing,' said Lyndall. 'Bring me my night-gown, a piece of paper, and the matches.

Wondering, Em fumbled about till she found them.

'What are you going to do with them?' she whispered.

'Burn down the window.'

'But won't the whole house take fire and burn down too?'

'Yes.'

'But will it not be very wicked?'

'Yes, very. And I do not care.'

She arranged the night-gown carefully in the corner of the window, with the chips of the frame about it. There was only one match in the box. She drew it carefully along the wall. For a moment it burnt up blue, and showed the tiny face with its glistening eyes. She held it carefully to the paper. For an instant it burnt up brightly, then flickered and went out. She blew the spark, but it died also. Then she threw the paper on to the ground, trod on it, and went to her bed, and began to undress.

Em rushed to the door, knocking against it wildly.

'Oh, Tant' Sannie! Tant' Sannie! Oh, let us out!' she cried. 'Oh, Lyndall, what are we to do?'

Lyndall wiped a drop of blood off the lip she had bitten.

'I am going to sleep,' she said. 'If you like to sit there and howl till the morning, do. Perhaps you will find that it helps; I never heard that howling helped anyone.'

Long after, when Em herself had gone to bed and was almost asleep, Lyndall came and stood at her bedside.

'Here,' she said, slipping a little pot of powder into her hand; 'rub some on to your face. Does it not burn where she struck you?'

Then she crept back to her own bed. Long, long after, when Em was really asleep, she lay still awake, and folded her hands on her little breast, and muttered,—

'When that day comes, and I am strong, I will hate

everything that has power, and help everything that is weak.'
And she bit her lip again.

The German looked out at the cabin door for the last time
that night. Then he paced the room slowly and sighed. Then
he drew out pen and paper, and sat down to write, rubbing his
old grey eyes with his knuckles before he began.

'MY CHICKENS,

'You did not come to say good-bye to the old man. Might
you? Ah, well, there is a land where they part no more, where
saints immortal reign.

'I sit here alone, and I think of you. Will you forget the old
man? When you wake to-morrow he will be far away. The old
horse is lazy, but he has his stick to help him; that is three
legs. He comes back one day with gold and diamonds. Will
you welcome him? Well, we shall see. I go to meet Waldo. He
comes back with the waggon; then he follows me. Poor boy!
God knows. There is a land where all things are made right,
but that land is not here.

'My little children, serve the Saviour; give your hearts to
Him while you are yet young. Life is short.

'Nothing is mine, otherwise I would say, Lyndall, take my
books, Em my stones. Now I say nothing. The things are
mine; it is not righteous, God knows! But I am silent. Let it
be. But I feel it, I must say I feel it.

'Do not cry too much for the old man. He goes out to seek
his fortune, and comes back with it in a bag, it may be.

'I love my children. Do they think of me? I am Old Otto,
who goes out to seek his fortune.'—'O. F.'

Having concluded this quaint production, he put it where
the children would find it the next morning, and proceeded to
prepare his bundle. He never thought of entering a protest
against the loss of his goods: like a child he submitted, and
wept. He had been there eleven years, and it was hard to go
away. He spread open on the bed a blue handkerchief and on
it put one by one the things he thought most necessary and
important: a little bag of curious seeds, which he meant to
plant some day, an old German hymn-book, three misshapen

stones that he greatly valued, a Bible, a shirt, and two
handkerchiefs; then there was room for nothing more. He tied
up the bundle tightly and put it on a chair by his bed-side.

'That is not much; they cannot say I take much,' he said,
looking at it.

He put his knotted stick beside it, his blue tobacco bag and
his short pipe, and then inspected his coats. He had two left—
a moth-eaten overcoat and a black alpaca out at the elbows.
He decided for the overcoat: it was warm certainly, but then
he could carry it over his arm, and only put it on when he met
someone along the road. It was more respectable than the
black alpaca. He hung the great-coat over the back of the
chair, and stuffed a hard bit of roaster-cake under the knot of
the bundle, and then his preparations were completed. The
German stood contemplating them with much satisfaction. He
had almost forgotten his sorrow at leaving, in his pleasure at
preparing. Suddenly he started; an expression of intense pain
passed over his face. He drew back his left arm quickly, and
then pressed his right hand upon his breast.

'Ah, the sudden pang again,' he said.

His face was white, but it quickly regained its colour. Then
the old man busied himself in putting everything right.

'I will leave it neat. They shall not say I did not leave it
neat,' he said. Even the little bags of seeds on the mantelpiece
he put in rows and dusted. Then he undressed and got into
bed. Under his pillow was a little story-book. He drew it forth.
To the old German a story was no story. Its events were as real
and as important to himself as the matters of his own life. He
could not go away without knowing whether that wicked Earl
relented, and whether the Baron married Emilina. So he
adjusted his spectacles and began to read. Occasionally, as his
feelings became too strongly moved, he ejaculated, 'Ah, I
thought so!—That was a rogue!—I saw it before!—I knew it
from the beginning!' More than half an hour had passed when
he looked up to the silver watch at the top of his bed.

'The march is long to-morrow; this will not do,' he said,
taking off his spectacles and putting them carefully into the
book to mark the place. 'This will be good reading as I walk
along to-morrow,' he added, as he stuffed the book into the

pocket of the great-coat; 'very good reading.' He nodded his
head and lay down. He thought a little of his own troubles, a
good deal of the two little girls he was leaving, of the Earl, of
Emilina, of the Baron; but he was soon asleep—sleeping as
peacefully as a little child upon whose innocent soul sorrow
and care cannot rest.

It was very quiet in the room. The coals in the fireplace
threw a dull red light across the floor upon the red lions on the
quilt. Eleven o'clock came, and the room was very still. One
o'clock came. The glimmer had died out, though the ashes
were still warm, and the room was very dark. The grey mouse,
who had its hole under the tool-box, came out and sat on the
sacks in the corner; then, growing bolder, the room was so
dark, it climbed the chair at the bedside, nibbled at the roaster-
cake, took one bite quickly at the candle, and then sat on its
haunches listening. It heard the even breathing of the old man,
and the steps of the hungry Kaffir dog going his last round in
search of a bone or a skin that had been forgotten; and it heard
the white hen call out as the wild cat ran away with one of her
brood, and it heard the chicken cry. Then the grey mouse
went back to its hole under the tool-box, and the room was
quiet. And two o'clock came. By that time the night was grown
dull and cloudy. The wild cat had gone to its home on the
'kopje:' the Kaffir dog had found a bone, and lay gnawing it.

An intense quiet reigned everywhere. Only in her room the
Boer-woman tossed her great arms in her sleep; for she
dreamed that a dark shadow with outstretched wings fled
slowly over her house, and she moaned and shivered. And the
night was very still.

But, quiet as all places were, there was a quite peculiar quiet
in the German's room. Though you strained your ear most
carefully you caught no sound of breathing.

He was not gone, for the old coat still hung on the chair—
the coat that was to be put on when he met anyone; and the
bundle and stick were ready for to-morrow's long march. The
old German himself lay there, his wavy black hair just touched
with grey thrown back upon the pillow. The old face was lying
there alone in the dark, smiling like a little child's—oh, so
peacefully. There is a stranger whose coming, they say, is

worse than all the ills of life, from whose presence we flee away trembling; but he comes very tenderly sometimes. And it seemed almost as though Death had known and loved the old man, so gently it touched him. And how could it deal hardly with him—the loving, simple, childlike old man?

So it smoothed out the wrinkles that were in the old forehead, and fixed the passing smile, and sealed the eyes that they might not weep again; and then the short sleep of time was melted into the long, long sleep of eternity.

'How has he grown so young in this one night?' they said when they found him in the morning.

Yes, dear old man; to such as you time brings no age. You die, with the purity and innocence of your childhood upon you, though you die in your grey hairs.

CHAPTER IX

He sees a Ghost

BONAPARTE stood on the ash-heap. He espied across the plain a moving speck, and he chucked his coat-tails up and down in expectancy of a scene.

The waggon came on slowly. Waldo lay curled among the sacks at the back of the waggon, the hand in his breast resting on the sheep-shearing machine. It was finished now. The right thought had struck him the day before, as he sat, half asleep, watching the water go over the mill-wheel. He muttered to himself with half-closed eyes,—

'To-morrow smooth the cogs—tighten the screws a little—show it to them.' Then after a pause—'Over the whole world—the whole world—mine, that I have made!' He pressed the little wheels and pulleys in his pocket till they cracked. Presently his muttering became louder—'And fifty pounds—a black hat for my dadda—for Lyndall a blue silk, very light; and one purple like the earth-bells, and white shoes.' He muttered on—'A box full, full of books. They shall tell me all, all, all,' he added, moving his fingers desiringly: 'why the crystals grow in such beautiful shapes; why lightning runs to the iron; why black people are black; why the sunlight makes things warm. I shall read, read, read,' he muttered slowly. Then came over him suddenly what he called 'The presence of God;' a sense of a good, strong something folding him round. He smiled through his half-shut eyes. 'Ah, Father, my own Father, it is so sweet to feel you, like the warm sunshine. The Bibles and books cannot tell of you and all I feel you. They are mixed with men's words; but you——'

His muttering sank into inaudible confusion, till opening his eyes wide, it struck him that the brown plain he looked at was the old home farm. For half an hour they had been riding in it, and he had not known it. He roused the leader, who sat nodding on the front of the waggon in the early morning sunlight. They were within half a mile of the homestead. It seemed to him that he had been gone from them all a year. He fancied he could see Lyndall standing on the brick wall to watch for him; his father, passing from one house to the other, stopping to look.

He called aloud to the oxen. For each one at home he had brought something. For his father a piece of tobacco, bought at the shop by the mill; for Em a thimble; for Lyndall a beautiful flower dug out by the roots, at a place where they had 'out-spanned;'* for Tant' Sannie a handkerchief. When they drew near the house he threw the whip to the Kaffir leader, and sprang from the side of the waggon to run on. Bonaparte stopped him as he ran past the ash-heap.

'Good-morning, my dear boy. Where are you running to so fast with your rosy cheeks?'

The boy looked up at him, glad even to see Bonaparte.

'I am going to the cabin,' he said, out of breath.

'You won't find them in just now—not your good old father,' said Bonaparte.

'Where is he?' asked the lad.

'There beyond the camps,' said Bonaparte, waving his hand oratorically towards the stone-walled ostrich-camps.

'What is he doing there?' asked the boy.

Bonaparte patted him on the cheek kindly.

'We could not keep him any more, it was too hot. We've buried him, my boy,' said Bonaparte, touching with his finger the boy's cheek. 'We couldn't keep him any more. He, he, he!' laughed Bonaparte, as the boy fled away along the low stone wall, almost furtively, as one in fear.

At five o'clock Bonaparte knelt before a box in the German's room. He was busily unpacking it.

It had been agreed upon between Tant' Sannie and himself, that now the German was gone he, Bonaparte, was to be no longer schoolmaster, but overseer of the farm. In return for his past scholastic labours he had expressed himself willing to take possession of the dead man's goods and room. Tant' Sannie hardly liked the arrangement. She had a great deal more respect for the German dead than the German living, and would rather his goods had been allowed to descend peacefully to his son. For she was a firm believer in the chinks in the world above, where not only ears, but eyes might be applied to see how things went on in this world below. She never felt sure how far the spirit-world might overlap this world of sense, and, as a rule, prudently abstained from doing anything which might offend unseen auditors. For this reason she abstained from ill-using the dead Englishman's daughter and niece, and for this reason she would rather the boy had had his father's goods. But it was hard to refuse Bonaparte anything when she and he sat so happily together in the evening drinking coffee, Bonaparte telling her in the broken Dutch he was fast learning how he adored fat women, and what a splendid farmer he was.

So at five o'clock on this afternoon Bonaparte knelt in the German's room.

'Somewhere here it is,' he said, as he packed the old clothes carefully out of the box, and, finding nothing, packed them in again. 'Somewhere in this room it is; and if it's here Bonaparte finds it,' he repeated. 'You didn't stay here all these years without making a little pile somewhere, my lamb. You weren't such a fool as you looked. Oh, no!' said Bonaparte.

He now walked about the room, diving his fingers in everywhere: sticking them into the great crevices in the wall and frightening out the spiders; rapping them against the old plaster till it cracked and fell in pieces; peering up the chimney, till the soot dropped on his bald head and blackened it. He felt in little blue bags; he tried to raise the hearthstone; he shook each book, till the old leaves fell down in showers on the floor.

It was getting dark, and Bonaparte stood with his finger on his nose reflecting. Finally he walked to the door, behind which hung the trousers and waistcoat the dead man had last worn. He had felt in them, but hurriedly, just after the funeral the day before; he would examine them again. Sticking his fingers into the waistcoat pockets, he found in one corner a hole. Pressing his hand through it, between the lining and the cloth, he presently came into contact with something. Bonaparte drew it forth—a small, square parcel, sewed up in sail-cloth. He gazed at it, squeezed it; it cracked, as though full of bank notes. He put it quickly into his own waistcoat pocket, and peeped over the half-door to see if there was anyone coming. There was nothing to be seen but the last rays of yellow sunset light, painting the karroo bushes in the plain, and shining on the ash-heap, where the fowls were pecking. He turned and sat down on the nearest chair, and, taking out his pen-knife, ripped the parcel open. The first thing that fell was a shower of yellow faded papers. Bonaparte opened them carefully one by one, and smoothed them out on his knee. There was something very valuable to be hidden so carefully, though the German characters he could not decipher. When he came to the last one, he felt there was something hard in it.

'You've got it, Bon, my boy! you've got it!' he cried, slapping his leg hard. Edging nearer to the door, for the light was fading he opened the paper carefully. There was nothing inside but a plain gold wedding-ring.

'Better than nothing!' said Bonaparte, trying to put it on his little finger, which, however, proved too fat.

He took it off and set it down on the table before him, and looked at it with his cross-wise eyes.

'When that auspicious hour, Sannie,' he said, 'shall have arrived, when, panting, I shall lead thee, lighted by Hymen's torch, to the connubial altar, upon thy fair amaranthine finger, my joyous bride, shall this ring repose.

> '"Thy fair body, oh, my girl,
> Shall Bonaparte possess;
> His fingers in thy money-bags,
> He therein, too, shall mess.'

Having given utterance to this flood of poesy, he sat lost in joyous reflection.

'He therein, too, *shall* mess,' he repeated, meditatively.

At this instant, as Bonaparte swore, and swore truly to the end of his life, a slow and distinct rap was given on the crown of his bald head.

Bonaparte started and looked up. No 'reim,' or strap, hung down from the rafters above, and not a human creature was near the door. It was growing dark; he did not like it. He began to fold up the papers expeditiously. He stretched out his hand for the ring. The ring was gone! Gone, although no human creature had entered the room; gone, although no form had crossed the doorway. Gone!

He would not sleep there, that was certain.

He stuffed the papers into his pocket. As he did so, three slow and distinct taps were given on the crown of his head. Bonaparte's jaw fell: each separate joint lost its power; he could not move; he dared not rise; his tongue lay loose in his mouth.

'Take all, take all!' he gurgled in his throat. 'I—I do not want them. Take——'

Here a resolute tug at the grey curls at the back of his head, caused him to leap up, yelling wildly. Was he to sit still paralysed, to be dragged away *bodily* to the devil? With terrific shrieks he fled, casting no glance behind.

When the dew was falling, and the evening was dark, a small figure moved towards the gate at the farthest ostrich-camp, driving a bird before it. When the gate was opened and the bird driven in and the gate fastened, it turned away, but then suddenly paused near the stone wall.

'Is that you, Waldo?' said Lyndall, hearing a sound.

The boy was sitting on the damp ground with his back to the wall. He gave her no answer.

'Come,' she said, bending over him, 'I have been looking for you all day.'

He mumbled something.

'You have had nothing to eat. I have put some supper in your room. You must come home with me, Waldo.'

She took his hand, and the boy rose slowly.

She made him take her arm, and twisted her small fingers among his.

'You must forget,' she whispered. 'Since it happened, I walk, I talk, I never sit still. If we remember, we cannot bring back the dead.' She knit her little fingers closer among his. 'Forgetting is the best thing. He did not watch it coming,' she whispered presently. 'That is the dreadful thing, to *see* it coming!' She shuddered. 'I want it to come so to me too. Why do you think I was driving that bird?' she added quickly. 'That was Hans, the bird that hates Bonaparte. I let him out this afternoon; I thought he would chase him and perhaps kill him.'

The boy showed no sign of interest.

'He did not catch him; but he put his head over the half-door of your cabin and frightened him horribly. He was there, busy stealing your things. Perhaps he will leave them alone now; but I wish the bird had trodden on him.'

They said no more till they reached the door of the cabin.

'There is a candle and supper on the table. You must eat,' she said authoritatively. 'I cannot stay with you now, lest they find out about the bird.'

He grasped her arm and brought his mouth close to her ear.

'There is no God!' he almost hissed; 'no God; not anywhere!'

She started.

'*Not anywhere!*'

He ground it out between his teeth, and she felt his hot breath on her cheek.

'Waldo, you are mad,' she said, drawing herself from him instinctively.

He loosened his grasp and turned away from her also.

In truth, is it not life's way? We fight our little battles alone; you yours, I mine. We must not help or find help.

When your life is most real, to me you are mad; when your agony is blackest I look at you and wonder. Friendship is good, a strong stick; but when the hour comes to lean hard, it gives. In the day of their bitterest need all souls are alone.

Lyndall stood by him in the dark, pityingly, wonderingly. As he walked to the door she came after him.

'Eat your supper; it will do you good,' she said.

She rubbed her cheek against his shoulder and then ran away.

In the front room the little woolly Kaffir girl was washing Tant' Sannie's feet in a small tub, and Bonaparte, who sat on the wooden sofa, was pulling off his shoes and stockings that his own feet might be washed also. There were three candles burning in the room, and he and Tant' Sannie sat close together, with the lean Hottentot not far off; for when ghosts are about much light is needed, there is great strength in numbers. Bonaparte had completely recovered from the effects of his fright in the afternoon, and the numerous doses of brandy that it had been necessary to administer to him to effect his restoration had put him into a singularly pleasant and amiable mood.

'That boy Waldo,' said Bonaparte, rubbing his toes, 'took himself off coolly this morning as soon as the waggon came, and has not done a stiver* of work all day. *I'll* not have that kind of thing now I'm master of this farm.'

The Hottentot maid translated.

'Ah, I expect he's sorry that his father's dead,' said Tant' Sannie. 'It's nature, you know. I cried the whole morning when my father died. One can always get another husband, but one can't get another father,' said Tant' Sannie, casting a sidelong glance at Bonaparte.

Bonaparte expressed a wish to give Waldo his orders for the next day's work, and accordingly the little woolly-headed Kaffir was sent to call him. After a considerable time the boy appeared, and stood in the doorway.

If they had dressed him in one of the swallow-tailed coats, and oiled his hair till the drops fell from it, and it lay as smooth as an elder's on sacrament Sunday, there would still have been something unanointed in the aspect of the fellow. As it was, standing there in his strange old costume, his head presenting much the appearance of having been deeply rolled in sand, his eyelids swollen, the hair hanging over his forehead, and a dogged sullenness on his features, he presented most the appearance of an ill-conditioned young buffalo.

'Beloved Lord,' cried Tant' Sannie, 'how he looks! Come in, boy. Couldn't you come and say good-day to me? Don't you want some supper?'

He said he wanted nothing, and turned his heavy eyes away from her.

'There's a ghost been seen in your father's room,' said Tant' Sannie. 'If you're afraid you can sleep in the kitchen.'

'I will sleep in our room,' said the boy slowly.

'Well, you can go now,' she said; 'but be up early to take the sheep. The herd——'

'Yes, be up early, my boy,' interrupted Bonaparte, smiling.

'I am to be master of this farm now; and we shall be good friends, I trust, very good friends, if you try to do your duty, my dear boy.'

Waldo turned to go, and Bonaparte, looking benignly at the candle, stretched out one unstockinged foot, over which Waldo, looking at nothing in particular, fell with a heavy thud upon the floor.

'Dear me! I hope you are not hurt, my boy,' said Bonaparte. 'You'll have many a harder thing than that though, before you've gone through life,' he added consolingly, as Waldo picked himself up.

The lean Hottentot laughed till the room rang again; and Tant' Sannie tittered till her sides ached.

When he had gone the little maid began to wash Bonaparte's feet.

'Oh, Lord, beloved Lord, how he did fall! I can't think of it,' cried Tant' Sannie, and she laughed again. 'I always did know he was not right; but this evening anyone could see it,' she added, wiping the tears of mirth from her face. 'His eyes are as wild as if the devil was in them. He never *was* like other children. The dear Lord knows, if he doesn't walk along for hours talking to himself. If you sit in the room with him you can see his lips moving the whole time; and if you talk to him twenty times he doesn't hear you. Daft-eyes; he's as mad as mad can be.'

The repetition of the word mad conveyed meaning to Bonaparte's mind. He left off paddling his toes in the water.

'Mad, mad? *I* know that kind of mad,' said Bonaparte, 'and I know the thing to give for it. The front end of a little horsewhip, the tip! Nice thing; takes it out,' said Bonaparte.

The Hottentot laughed, and translated.

'No more walking about and talking to themselves on this farm now,' said Bonaparte: 'no more minding of sheep and reading of books at the same time. The point of a horsewhip is a little thing, but I think he'll have a taste of it before long.' Bonaparte rubbed his hands and looked pleasantly across his nose; and then the three laughed together grimly.

And Waldo in his cabin crouched in the dark in a corner, with his knees drawn up to his chin.

CHAPTER X
He shows his Teeth

DOSS sat among the karroo bushes, one yellow ear drawn over his wicked little eye, ready to flap away any adventurous fly that might settle on his nose. Around him in the morning sunlight fed the sheep; behind him lay his master polishing his machine. He found much comfort in handling it that morning. A dozen philosophical essays, or angelically attuned songs for the consolation of the bereaved, could never have been to him what that little sheep-shearing machine was that day.

After struggling to see the unseeable, growing drunk with the endeavour to span the infinite, and writhing before the inscrutable mystery, it is a renovating relief to turn to some simple, feelable, weighable substance; to something which has a smell and colour, which may be handled and turned over this way and that. Whether there be or be not a hereafter, whether there be any use in calling aloud to the Unseen power, whether there be an Unseen power to call to, whatever be the true nature of the *I* who call and of the objects around me, whatever be our meaning, our internal essence, our cause (and in a certain order of minds death and the agony of loss inevitably awaken the wild desire, at other times smothered, to look into these things), whatever be the nature of that which the limits of the human intellect build up on every hand, this thing is certain—a knife will cut wood, and one cogged wheel will turn another. This is sure.

Waldo found an immeasurable satisfaction in the handling of his machine; but Doss winked and blinked, and thought it all frightfully monotonous out there on the flat, and presently dropped asleep, sitting bolt upright. Suddenly his eyes opened wide; something was coming from the direction of the home-stead. Winking his eyes and looking intently, he perceived it was the grey mare. Now Doss had wondered much of late what had become of her master. Seeing she carried someone on her back, he now came to his own conclusion, and began to move his tail violently up and down. Presently he pricked up one ear and let the other hang; his tail became motionless, and the expression of his mouth was one of decided disapproval bordering on scorn. He wrinkled his lips up on each side into little lines.

The sand was soft, and the grey mare came on so noiselessly that the boy heard nothing till Bonaparte dismounted. Then Doss got up and moved back a step. He did not approve of Bonaparte's appearance. His costume, in truth, was of a unique kind. It was a combination of the town and country. The tails of his black cloth coat were pinned up behind to keep them from rubbing; he had on a pair of moleskin trousers and leather gaiters, and in his hand he carried a little whip of rhinoceros hide.

Waldo started and looked up. Had there been a moment's time he would have dug a hole in the sand with his hands and buried his treasure. It was only a toy of wood, but he loved it, as one of necessity loves what has been born of him, whether of the flesh or spirit. When cold eyes have looked at it, the feathers are rubbed off our butterfly's wing for ever.

'What have you here, my lad?' said Bonaparte, standing by him, and pointing with the end of his whip to the medley of wheels and hinges.

The boy muttered something inaudible, and half-spread his hand over the thing.

'But this seems to be a very ingenious little machine,' said Bonaparte, seating himself on the ant-heap, and bending down over it with deep interest. 'What is it for, my lad?'

'Shearing sheep.'

'It is a very nice little machine,' said Bonaparte. 'How does it work, now? I have never seen anything so ingenious!'

There was never a parent who heard deception in the voice that praised his child—his first-born. Here was one who liked the thing that had been created in him. He forgot everything. He showed how the shears would work with a little guidance, how the sheep would be held, and the wool fall into the trough. A flush burst over his face as he spoke.

'I tell you what, my lad,' said Bonaparte emphatically, when the explanation was finished, 'we must get you a patent. Your fortune is made. In three years' time there'll not be a farm in this colony where it isn't working. You're a genius, that's what *you* are!' said Bonaparte, rising.

'If it were made larger,' said the boy, raising his eyes, 'it would work more smoothly. Do you think there would be anyone in this colony would be able to make it?'

'I'm sure they could,' said Bonaparte; 'and if not, why I'll do my best for you. I'll send it to England. It must be done somehow. How long have you worked at it?'

'Nine months,' said the boy.

'Oh, it is such a nice little machine,' said Bonaparte, 'one can't help feeling an interest in it. There is only *one* little improvement, one very little improvement, I should like to make.'

Bonaparte put his foot on the machine and crushed it into the sand. The boy looked up into his face.

'Looks better now,' said Bonaparte, 'doesn't it? If we can't have it made in England we'll send it to America. Good-bye; ta-ta,' he added. 'You're a great genius, a born genius, my dear boy, there's no doubt about it.'

He mounted the grey mare and rode off. The dog watched his retreat with cynical satisfaction; but his master lay on the ground with his head on his arms in the sand, and the little wheels and chips of wood lay on the ground around him. The dog jumped on to his back and snapped at the black curls, till, finding that no notice was taken, he walked off to play with a black beetle. The beetle was hard at work trying to roll home a great ball of dung it had been collecting all the morning; but Doss broke the ball, and ate the beetle's hind legs, and then bit off its head. And it was all play, and no one could tell what it had lived and worked for. A striving, and a striving, and an ending in nothing.

CHAPTER XI
He Snaps

'I HAVE found something in the loft,' said Em to Waldo, who was listlessly piling cakes of fuel on the kraal wall, a week after. 'It is a box of books that belonged to my father. We thought Tant' Sannie had burnt them.'

The boy put down the cake he was raising and looked at her.

'I don't think they are very nice, not stories,' she added, 'but you can go and take any you like.'

So saying, she took up the plate in which she had brought his breakfast, and walked off to the house.

After that the boy worked quickly. The pile of fuel Bonaparte had ordered him to pack was on the wall in half an hour. He then went to throw salt on the skins laid out to dry. Finding the pot empty, he went to the loft to refill it.

Bonaparte Blenkins, whose door opened at the foot of the ladder, saw the boy go up, and stood in the doorway waiting for his return. He wanted his boots blacked. Doss, finding he could not follow his master up the round bars, sat patiently at the foot of the ladder. Presently he looked up longingly, but no one appeared. Then Bonaparte looked up also, and began to call; but there was no answer. What could the boy be doing? The loft was an unknown land to Bonaparte. He had often wondered what was up there; he liked to know what was in all locked-up places and out-of-the-way corners, but he was afraid to climb the ladder. So Bonaparte looked up, and, in the name of all that was tantalizing, questioned what the boy did up there. The loft was used only as a lumber-room. What could the fellow find up there to keep him so long?

Could the Boer-woman have beheld Waldo at that instant, any lingering doubt which might have remained in her mind as to the boy's insanity would instantly have vanished. For, having filled the salt-pot, he proceeded to look for the box of books among the rubbish that filled the loft. Under a pile of sacks he found it—a rough packing-case, nailed up, but with one loose plank. He lifted that, and saw the even backs of a row of books. He knelt down before the box, and ran his hand along its rough edges, as if to assure himself of its existence. He stuck his hand in among the books, and pulled out two. He felt them, thrust his fingers in among the leaves, and crumpled them a little, as a lover feels the hair of his mistress. The fellow gloated over his treasure. He had had a dozen books in the course of his life; now here was a mine of them opened at his feet. After a while he began to read the titles, and now and again opened a book and read a sentence; but he was too excited to catch the meanings distinctly. At last he came to a dull, brown volume. He read the name, opened it in the centre, and where he opened began to read. 'Twas a chapter on property that he fell upon—Communism, Fourier-ism, St Simonism* in a work on Political Economy. He read down one page and turned over to the next; he read down that without changing his posture by an inch; he read the next, and the next, kneeling up all the while with the book in his hand, and his lips parted.

All he read he did not fully understand; the thoughts were new to him; but this was the fellow's startled joy in the book—the thoughts were his, they belonged to him. He had never thought them before, but they were his.

He laughed silently and internally, with the still intensity of triumphant joy.

So, then, all thinking creatures did not send up the one cry—'As thou, dear Lord, hast created things in the beginning, so are they now, so ought they to be, so will they be, world without end; and it doesn't concern us what they are. Amen.' There were men to whom not only kopjes and stones were calling out imperatively, 'What are we, and how came we here? Understand us, and know us;' but to whom even the old, old relations between man and man, and the customs of the ages called, and could not be made still and forgotten.

The boy's heavy body quivered with excitement. So he was not alone, not alone. He could not quite have told anyone why he was so glad, and this warmth had come to him. His cheeks were burning. No wonder that Bonaparte called in vain, and Doss put his paws on the ladder, and whined till three-quarters of an hour had passed. At last the boy put the book in his breast and buttoned it tightly to him. He took up the salt-pot, and went to the top of the ladder. Bonaparte, with his hands folded under his coat-tails, looked up when he appeared, and accosted him.

'You've been rather a long time up there, my lad,' he said, as the boy descended with a tremulous haste, most unlike his ordinary slow movements. 'You didn't hear me calling, I suppose?'

Bonaparte whisked the tails of his coat up and down as he looked at him. He, Bonaparte Blenkins, had eyes which were very far-seeing. He looked at the pot. It was rather a small pot to have taken three-quarters of an hour in the filling. He looked at the face. It was flushed. And yet, Tant' Sannie kept no wine—he had not been drinking; his eyes were wide open and bright—he had not been sleeping; there was no girl up there—he had not been making love. Bonaparte looked at him sagaciously. What would account for the marvellous change in the boy coming down the ladder from the boy going up the ladder? *One* thing there was. Did not Tant' Sannie keep in the loft 'Bultongs,'* and nice smoked sausages? There must be something nice to *eat* up there! Aha! that was it!

Bonaparte was so interested in carrying out this chain of inductive reasoning that he quite forgot to have his boots blacked.

He watched the boy shuffle off with the salt-pot under his arm; then he stood in his doorway, and raised his eyes to the quiet blue sky, and audibly propounded this riddle to himself.

'What is the connection between the naked back of a certain boy with a great-coat on and a salt-pot under his arm, and the tip of a horsewhip? Answer: No connection at present, but there will be soon.'

Bonaparte was so pleased with this sally of his wit that he chuckled a little, and went to lie down on his bed.

There was bread-baking that afternoon, and there was a fire lighted in the brick oven behind the house, and Tant' Sannie had left the great wooden-elbowed chair in which she passed her life, and waddled out to look at it. Not far off was Waldo, who, having thrown a pail of food into the pig-sty, now leaned over the sod-wall looking at the pigs. Half of the sty was dry, but the lower half was a pool of mud, on the edge of which the mother sow lay with closed eyes, her ten little ones sucking; the father pig, knee-deep in the mud, stood running his snout into a rotten pumpkin and wriggling his curled tail.

Waldo wondered dreamily as he stared why they were pleasant to look at. Taken singly they were not beautiful; taken together they were. Was it not because there was a certain harmony about them? The old sow was suited to the little pigs, and the little pigs to their mother; the old boar to the rotten pumpkin, and all to the mud. They suggested the thought of nothing that should be added, of nothing that should be taken away. And, he wondered on vaguely, was not *that* the secret of all beauty, that you who look on—— So he stood dreaming, and leaned further and further over the sod-wall, and looked at the pigs.

All this time Bonaparte Blenkins was sloping down from the house in an aimless sort of way; but he kept one eye fixed on the pig-sty, and each gyration brought him nearer to it. Waldo stood like a thing asleep when Bonaparte came close up to him.

In old days, when a small boy, playing in an Irish street gutter, he, Bonaparte, had been familiarly known among his comrades under the title of Tripping Ben; this, from the rare ease and dexterity with which, by merely projecting his foot, he could precipitate any unfortunate companion on to the crown of his head. Years had elapsed, and Tripping Ben had become Bonaparte; but the old gift was in him still. He came close to the pig-sty. All the defunct memories of his boyhood returned to him in a flood, as with an adroit movement he inserted his leg between Waldo and the wall, and sent him over into the pig-sty.

The little pigs were startled at the strange intruder, and ran behind their mother, who sniffed at him. Tant' Sannie smote her hands together and laughed; but Bonaparte was far from joining her. Lost in reverie, he gazed at the distant horizon.

The sudden reversal of head and feet had thrown out the

volume that Waldo carried in his breast. Bonaparte picked it up, and began to inspect it, as the boy climbed slowly over the wall. He would have walked off sullenly, but he wanted his book, and waited till it should be given him.

'Ha!' said Bonaparte, raising his eyes from the leaves of the book which he was examining. 'I hope your coat has not been injured; it is of an elegant cut. An heirloom, I presume, from your paternal grandfather? It looks nice now.'

'Oh, Lord! oh, Lord!' cried Tant' Sannie, laughing and holding her sides; 'how the child looks—as though he thought the mud would never wash off. Oh, Lord, I shall die! You, Bonaparte, are the funniest man I ever saw.'

Bonaparte Blenkins was now carefully inspecting the volume he had picked up. Among the subjects on which the darkness of his understanding had been enlightened during his youth, Political Economy had not been one. He was not, therefore, very clear as to what the nature of the book might be; and as the name of the writer, J. S. Mill, might, for anything he knew to the contrary, have belonged to a venerable member of the British and Foreign Bible Society, it by no means threw light upon the question. He was not in any way sure that Political Economy had nothing to do with the cheapest way of procuring clothing for the army and navy, which would be, certainly, both a political and economical subject.

But Bonaparte soon came to a conclusion as to the nature of the book and its contents, by the application of a simple rule now largely acted upon, but which, becoming universal, would save much thought and valuable time. It is of marvellous simplicity, of infinite utility, of universal applicability. It may easily be committed to memory, and runs thus:-

Whenever you come into contact with any book, person, or opinion of which you absolutely comprehend nothing, declare that book, person, or opinion to be immoral. Bespatter it, vituperate against it, strongly insist that any man or woman harbouring it is a fool or a knave, or both. Carefully abstain from studying it. Do all that in you lies to annihilate that book, person, or opinion.

Acting on this rule, so wide in its comprehensiveness, so beautifully simple in its working, Bonaparte approached Tant'

Sannie with the book in his hand. Waldo came a step nearer, eyeing it like a dog whose young has fallen into evil hands.

'This book,' said Bonaparte, 'it not a fit and proper study for a young and immature mind.'

Tant' Sannie did not understand a word, and said, 'What?'

'This book,' said Bonaparte, bringing down his finger with energy on the cover, 'this book is *sleg, sleg, Davel, Davel!*'★

Tant' Sannie perceived from the gravity of his countenance that it was no laughing matter. From the words *sleg* and *Davel* she understood that the book was evil, and had some connection with the prince who pulls the wires of evil over the whole earth.

'Where did you get this book?' she asked, turning her twinkling little eyes on Waldo. 'I wish that my legs may be as thin as an Englishman's if it isn't one of your father's. He had more sins than all the Kaffirs in Kaffirland, for all that he pretended to be so good all those years, and to live without a wife because he was thinking of the one that was dead! As though ten dead wives could make up for one fat one with arms and legs!' cried Tant' Sannie, snorting.

'It was not my father's book,' said the boy savagely. 'I got it from your loft.'

'My loft! my book! How dare you?' cried Tant' Sannie.

'It was Em's father's. She gave it me,' he muttered more sullenly.

'Give it here. What is the name of it? What is it about?' she asked, putting her finger upon the title.

Bonaparte understood.

'Political Economy,' he said slowly.

'Dear Lord!' said Tant' Sannie, 'cannot one hear from the very sound what an ungodly book it is! One can hardly say the name. Haven't we got curses enough on this farm?' cried Tant' Sannie, eloquently: 'my best imported Merino ram dying of nobody knows what, and the short-horn cow casting her two calves, and the sheep eaten up with the scab and the drought? And is *this* a time to bring ungodly things about the place, to call down the vengeance of Almighty God to punish us more? Didn't the minister tell me when I was confirmed not to read any book except my Bible and hymn-book, that the Devil was in all the rest? And I never have read any other book,' said Tant' Sannie with virtuous energy, 'and I never will!'

Waldo saw that the fate of his book was sealed, and turned sullenly on his heel.

'So you will not stay to hear what I say!' cried Tant' Sannie. 'There, take your Polity-gollity-gominy, your devil's book!' she cried, flinging the book at his head with much energy.

It merely touched his forehead on one side and fell to the ground.

'Go on,' she cried; 'I know you are going to talk to yourself. People who talk to themselves always talk to the Devil. Go and tell him all about it. Go, go! run!' cried Tant' Sannie.

But the boy neither quickened nor slackened his pace, and passed sullenly round the back of the waggon-house.

Books have been thrown at other heads before and since that summer afternoon, by hands more white and delicate than those of the Boer-woman; but whether the result of the process has been in any case wholly satisfactory, may be questioned. We love that with a peculiar tenderness, we treasure it with a peculiar care, it has for us quite a fictitious value, for which we have suffered. If we may not carry it anywhere else we will carry it in our hearts, and always to the end.

Bonaparte Blenkins went to pick up the volume, now loosened from its cover, while Tant' Sannie pushed the stumps of wood farther into the oven. Bonaparte came close to her, tapped the book knowingly, nodded, and looked at the fire. Tant' Sannie comprehended, and, taking the volume from his hand, threw it into the back of the oven. It lay upon the heap of coals, smoked, flared, and blazed, and the 'Political Economy' was no more—gone out of existence, like many another poor heretic of flesh and blood.

Bonaparte grinned, and to watch the process brought his face so near the oven door that the white hair on his eyebrows got singed. He then inquired if there were any more books in the loft.

Learning that there were, he made signs indicative of taking up armfuls and flinging them into the fire. But Tant' Sannie was dubious. The deceased Englishman had left all his personal effects specially to his child. It was all very well for Bonaparte to talk of burning the books. He had had his hair spiritually pulled, and she had no wish to repeat his experience.

She shook her head. Bonaparte was displeased. But then a happy thought occurred to him. He suggested that the key of the loft should henceforth be put into his own safe care and keeping—no one gaining possession of it without his permission. To this Tant' Sannie readily assented, and the two walked lovingly to the house to look for it.

CHAPTER XII

He Bites

BONAPARTE BLENKINS was riding home on the grey mare. He had ridden out that afternoon, partly for the benefit of his health, partly to maintain his character as overseer of the farm. As he rode on slowly, he thoughtfully touched the ears of the grey mare with his whip.

'No, Bon, my boy,' he addressed himself, 'don't propose! You can't marry for four years, on account of the will; then why propose? Wheedle her, tweedle her, teedle her, but *don't* let her make sure of you. When a woman,' said Bonaparte, sagely resting his finger against the side of his nose, 'when a woman is sure of you she does what she likes with you; but when she isn't, you do what you like with her. And I—' said Bonaparte.

Here he drew the horse up suddenly and looked. He was now close to the house, and leaning over the pig-sty wall, in company with Em, who was showing her the pigs, was a strange female figure. It was the first visitor that had appeared on the farm since his arrival, and he looked at her with interest. She was a tall, pudgy girl of fifteen, weighing a hundred and fifty pounds, with baggy, pendulous cheeks and up-turned nose. She strikingly resembled Tant' Sannie, in form and feature, but her sleepy good eyes lacked the twinkle that dwelt in the Boer-woman's small orbs. She was attired in a bright green print, wore brass rings in her ears, and glass beads round her neck, and was sucking the tip of her large finger as she looked at the pigs.

'Who is it that has come?' asked Bonaparte, when he stood drinking his coffee in the front room.

'Why, my niece, to be sure,' said Tant' Sannie, the Hottentot maid translating. 'She's the only daughter of my only brother Paul, and she's come to visit me. She'll be a nice mouthful to the man that can get her,' added Tant' Sannie.

'Her father's got two thousand pounds in the green waggon box under his bed, and a farm, and five thousand sheep, and God Almighty knows how many goats and horses. They milk ten cow in mid-winter, and the young men are after her like flies about a bowl of milk. She says she means to get married in four months, but she doesn't yet know to whom. It was so with me when I was young,' said Tant' Sannie: 'I've sat up with the young men four and five nights a week. And they will come riding again, as soon as ever they know that the time's up that the Englishman made me agree not to marry in.'

The Boer-woman smirked complacently.

'Where are you going to?' asked Tant' Sannie presently, seeing that Bonaparte rose.

'Ha! I'm just going to the kraals; I'll be in to supper,' said Bonaparte.

Nevertheless, when he reached his own door he stopped and turned in there. Soon after he stood before the little glass, arrayed in his best white shirt with the little tucks, and shaving himself. He had on his very best trousers, and had heavily oiled the little fringe at the back of his head, which, however, refused to become darker. But what distressed him most was his nose—it was very red. He rubbed his finger and thumb on the wall, and put a little whitewash on it; but, finding it rather made matters worse, he rubbed it off again. Then he looked carefully into his own eyes. They certainly were a little pulled down at the outer corners, which gave them the appearance of looking cross-wise; but then they were a nice blue. So he put on his best coat, took up his stick, and went out to supper, feeling on the whole well satisfied.

'Aunt,' said Trana to Tant' Sannie, when that night they lay together in the great wooden bed, 'why does the Englishman sigh so when he looks at me?'

'Ha!' said Tant' Sannie, who was half asleep, but suddenly started, wide awake. 'It's because he thinks you look like me. I tell you, Trana,' said Tant' Sannie, 'the man is mad with love of me. I told him the other night I couldn't marry till Em was sixteen, or I'd lose all the sheep her father left me. And he talked about Jacob working seven years and seven years again for his wife.* And of course he meant me,' said Tant' Sannie pompously. 'But he won't get me so easily as he thinks; he'll have to ask more than once.'

'Oh!' said Trana, who was a lumpish girl and not much given to talking; but presently she added, 'Aunt, why does the Englishman always knock against a person when he passes them?'

'That's because you are always in the way,' said Tant' Sannie.

'But, Aunt,' said Trana, presently, 'I think he is very ugly.'

'Phugh!' said Tant' Sannie. 'It's only because we're not accustomed to such noses in this country. In his country he says all the people have such noses, and the redder your nose is the higher you are. He's of the family of the Queen Victoria, you know,' said Tant' Sannie, wakening up with her subject: 'and he doesn't think anything of governors and Church elders, and such people; they are nothing to him. When his aunt with the dropsy dies he'll have money enough to buy all the farms in this district!'

'Oh!' said Trana. That certainly made a difference.

'Yes,' said Tant' Sannie; 'and he's only forty-one, though you'd take him to be sixty. And he told me last night the real reason for his baldness.'

Tant' Sannie then proceeded to relate how, at eighteen years of age, Bonaparte had courted a fair young lady. How a deadly rival jealous of his verdant locks, his golden flowing hair, had, with a damnable and insinuating deception, made him a present of a pot of pomatum. How, applying it in the evening, on rising in the morning he found his pillow strewn with the golden locks, and looking into the glass, beheld the shining and smooth expanse which henceforth he must bear. The few remaining hairs, were turned to a silvery whiteness and the young lady married his rival.

'And,' said Tant' Sannie solemnly, 'if it had not been for the grace of God, and reading of the psalms, he says he would have killed himself. He says he could kill himself quite easily if he wants to marry a woman and she won't.'

'A le wereld,'* said Trana: and then they went to sleep.

Everyone was lost in sleep soon; but from the window of the cabin the light streamed forth. It came from a dung fire, over which Waldo sat brooding. Hour after hour he sat there, now and again throwing a fresh lump of fuel on to the fire, which burnt up bravely, and then sank into a great bed of red coals, which reflected themselves in the boy's eyes as he sat there brooding, brooding, brooding. At last, when the fire was blazing at its brightest, he rose suddenly and walked slowly to a beam from which an ox 'reim' hung. Loosening it, he ran a noose in one end and then doubled it round his arm.

'Mine, mine! I have a right,' he muttered; and then something louder, 'if I fall and am killed, so much the better!'

He opened the door and went out into the starlight.

He walked with his eyes bent upon the ground, but overhead it was one of those brilliant southern nights when every space so small that your hand might cover it shows fifty cold white points, and the Milky Way is a belt of sharp frosted silver. He passed the door where Bonaparte lay dreaming of Trana and her wealth, and he mounted the ladder steps. From those he clambered with some difficulty on to the roof of the house. It was of old rotten thatch with a ridge of white plaster, and it crumbled away under his feet at every step. He trod as heavily as he could. So much the better if he fell.

He knelt down when he got to the far gable, and began to fasten his 'reim' to the crumbling bricks. Below was the little window of the loft. With one end of the 'reim' tied round the gable, the other end round his waist, how easy to slide down to it, and to open it, through one of the broken panes, and to go in, and to fill his arms with books, and to clamber up again! They had burnt one book—he would have twenty. Every man's hand was against his—his should be against every man's. No one would help him—he would help himself.

He lifted the black damp hair from his knit forehead, and looked round to cool his hot face. Then he saw what a regal night it was. He knelt silently and looked up. A thousand eyes were looking down at him, bright, and so cold. There was a laughing irony in them.

'So hot, so bitter, so angry? Poor little mortal!'

He was ashamed. He folded his arms, and sat on the ridge of the roof looking up at them.

'*So* hot, *so* bitter, *so* angry?'

It was as though a cold hand had been laid upon his throbbing forehead, and slowly they began to fade and grow dim. Tant' Sannie and the burnt book, Bonaparte and the broken machine, the box in the loft, he himself sitting here— how small they all became! Even the grave over yonder. Those stars that shone on up above so quietly, they had seen a thousand such little existences, a thousand such little existences fight just so fiercely, flare up just so brightly, and go out; and they, the old, old stars, shone on for ever.

'So hot, so angry, poor little soul?' they said.

The 'reim' slipped from his fingers; he sat with his arms folded, looking up.

'We,' said the stars, 'have seen the earth when it was young. We have seen small things creep out upon its surface—small things that prayed and loved and cried very loudly, and then crept under it again. But we,' said the stars, 'are as old as the Unknown.'

He leaned his chin against the palm of his hand and looked up at them. So long he sat there that bright stars set and new ones rose, and yet he sat on.

Then at last he stood up, and began to loosen the 'reim' from the gable.

What did it matter about the books? The lust and the desire for them had died out. If they pleased to keep them from him they might. What matter? It was a very little thing. Why hate, and struggle, and fight? Let it be as it would.

He twisted the 'reim' round his arm and walked back along the ridge of the house.

By this time Bonaparte Blenkins had finished his dream of Trana, and as he turned himself round for a fresh doze he heard the steps descending the ladder. His first impulse was to draw the blanket over his head and his legs under him, and to shout; but, recollecting that the door was locked and the window carefully bolted, he allowed his head slowly to crop out among the blankets, and listened intently. Whosoever it might be, there was no danger of their getting at *him*; so he clambered out of bed, and going on tiptoe to the door, applied his eye to the keyhole. There was nothing to be seen; so walking to the window, he brought his face as close to the glass as his nose would allow. There was a figure just discernible. The lad was not trying to walk softly, and the heavy shuffling of the well-known 'vel-schoens' could be clearly heard through the closed window as they crossed the stones in the yard. Bonaparte listened till they had died away round the corner of the waggon-house; and, feeling that his bare legs were getting cold, he jumped back into bed again.

'What do you keep up in your loft?' enquired Bonaparte of the Boer-woman the next evening, pointing upwards, and elucidating his meaning by the addition of such Dutch words as he knew, for the lean Hottentot was gone home.

'Dried skins,' said the Boer-woman, 'and empty bottles, and boxes, and sacks, and soap.'

'You don't keep any of your provisions there—sugar, now?' said Bonaparte, pointing to the sugar-basin and then up at the loft.

Tant' Sannie shook her head.

'Only salt, and dried peaches.'

'Dried peaches! Eh?' said Bonaparte. 'Shut the door, my dear child, shut it tight,' he called out to Em, who stood in the dining-room. Then he leaned over the elbow of the sofa and brought his face as close as possible to the Boer-woman's, and made signs of eating. Then he said something she did not comprehend; then said, 'Waldo, Waldo, Waldo,' pointed up to the loft, and made signs of eating again.

Now an inkling of his meaning dawned on the Boer-woman's mind. To make it clearer, he moved his legs afer the manner of one going up a ladder, appeared to be opening a door, masticated vigorously, said, 'Peaches, peaches, peaches,' and appeared to be coming down the ladder.

It was now evident to Tant' Sannie that Waldo had been in her loft and eaten her peaches.

To exemplify his own share in the proceedings, Bonaparte lay down on the sofa, and shutting his eyes tightly, said, 'Night, night, night!' Then he sat up wildly, appearing to be intently listening, mimicked with his feet the coming down a ladder, and looked at Tant' Sannie. This clearly showed how, roused in the night, he had discovered the theft.

'He must have been a great fool to eat my peaches,' said Tant' Sannie. 'They are full of mites as a sheepskin, and as hard as stones.'

Bonaparte, fumbling in his pocket, did not even hear her remark, and took out from his coat-tail a little horsewhip, nicely rolled up. Bonaparte winked at the little rhinoceros horsewhip, at the Boer-woman, and then at the door.

'Shall we call him—Waldo, Waldo?' he said.

Tant' Sannie nodded, and giggled. There was something so exceedingly humorous in the idea that he was going to beat the boy, though for her own part she did not see that the peaches were worth it. When the Kaffir maid came with the wash-tub she was sent to summon Waldo; and Bonaparte doubled up the little whip and put it in his pocket. Then he drew himself up, and prepared to act his important part with becoming gravity. Soon Waldo stood in the door, and took off his hat.

'Come in, come in, my lad,' said Bonaparte, 'and shut the door behind.'

The boy came in and stood before them.

'You need not be so afraid, child,' said Tant' Sannie. 'I was a child myself once. It's no great harm if you have taken a few.'

Bonaparte perceived that her remark was not in keeping with the nature of the proceedings, and of the little drama he intended to act. Pursing out his lips, and waving his hand, he solemnly addressed the boy.

'Waldo, it grieves me beyond expression to have to summon you for so painful a purpose; but it is at the imperative call of duty, which I dare not evade. I do not state that frank and unreserved confession will obviate the necessity of chastisement, which if requisite shall be fully administered; but the nature of that chastisement may be mitigated by free and humble confession. Waldo, answer me as you would your own father, in whose place I now stand to you: have you, or have you not, did you, or did you not, eat of the peaches in the loft?'

'Say you took them, boy, say you took them, then he won't

beat you much,' said the Dutch-woman good-naturedly, getting a little sorry for him.

The boy raised his eyes slowly and fixed them vacantly upon her, then suddenly his grew dark with blood.

'*So*, you haven't got anything to say to us, my lad?' said Bonaparte, momentarily forgetting his dignity, and bending forward with a little snarl. 'But what I mean is just this, my lad—when it takes a boy three-quarters of an hour to fill a salt-pot, and when at three o'clock in the morning he goes knocking about the doors of a loft, it's natural to suppose there's mischief in it. It's certain there *is* mischief in it; and where there's mischief *in* it must be taken *out*,' said Bonaparte, grinning into the boy's face. Then, feeling that he had fallen from that high gravity which was as spice to the pudding, and the flavour of the whole little tragedy, he drew himself up. 'Waldo,' he said, 'confess to me instantly, and without reserve, that you ate the peaches.'

The boy's face was white now. His eyes were on the ground, his hands doggedly clasped before him.

'What, you do not intend to answer?'

The boy looked up at them once from under his bent eyebrows, and then looked down again.

'The creature looks as if all the devils in hell were in it,' cried Tant' Sannie. 'Say you took them, boy. Young things will be young things; I was older than you when I used to eat "bultong" in my mother's loft, and get the little niggers whipped for it. Say you took them.'

But the boy said nothing.

'I think a little solitary confinement might perhaps be beneficial' said Bonaparte. 'It will enable you, Waldo, to reflect on the enormity of the sin you have committed against our Father in heaven. And you may also think of the submission you owe to those who are older and wiser than you are, and whose duty it is to check and correct you.'

Saying this, Bonaparte stood up and took down the key of the fuel-house, which hung on a nail against the wall.

'Walk on, my boy,' said Bonaparte, pointing to the door; and as he followed him out he drew his mouth expressively on one side, and made the lash of the little horsewhip stick out of his pocket and shake up and down.

Tant' Sannie felt half sorry for the lad; but she could not help laughing, it was always so funny when one was going to have a whipping, and it would do him good. Anyhow he would forget all about it when the places were healed. Had not she been beaten many times and been all the better for it?

Bonaparte took up a lighted candle that had been left burning on the kitchen table, and told the boy to walk before him. They went to the fuel-house. It was a little stone erection that jutted out from the side of the waggon-house. It was low, and without a window; and the dried dung was piled in one corner, and the coffee-mill stood in another, fastened on the top of a short post about three feet high. Bonaparte took the padlock off the rough door.

'Walk in, my lad,' he said.

Waldo obeyed sullenly; one place to him was much the same as another. He had no objection to being locked up.

Bonaparte followed him in, and closed the door carefully.

He put the light down on the heap of dung in the corner, and quietly introduced his hand under his coat-tails and drew slowly from his pocket the end of a rope which he concealed behind him.

'I'm very sorry, exceedingly sorry, Waldo, my lad, that you should have acted in this manner. It grieves me,' said Bonaparte.

He moved round towards the boy's back. He hardly liked the look in the fellow's eyes, though he stood there motionless. If he should spring on him!

So he drew the rope out very carefully, and shifted round to the wooden post. There was a slip-knot in one end of the rope, and a sudden movement drew the boy's hands to his back and passed it round them. It was an instant's work to drag it twice round the wooden post: then Bonaparte was safe.

For a moment the boy struggled to free himself; then he knew that he was powerless, and stood still.

'Horses that kick must have their legs tied,' said Bonaparte, as he passed the other end of the rope round the boy's knees.

'And now, my dear Waldo,' taking the whip out of his pocket, 'I am going to beat you.'

He paused for a moment. It was perfectly quiet; they could hear each other's breath.

'"Chasten thy son while there is hope,"' said Bonaparte, '"and let not thy soul spare for his crying." Those are God's words. I shall act as a father to you, Waldo. I think we had better have your naked back.'

He took out his pen-knife, and slit the shirt down from the shoulder to the waist.

'Now,' said Bonaparte, 'I hope the Lord will bless and sanctify to you what I am going to do to you.'

The first cut ran from the shoulder across the middle of the back; the second fell exactly in the same place. A shudder passed through the boy's frame.

'Nice, eh?' said Bonaparte, peeping round into his face, speaking with a lisp, as though to a very little child. '*Nith, eh?*'

But the eyes were black and lustreless, and seemed not to see him. When he had given sixteen Bonaparte paused in his work to wipe a little drop of blood from his whip.

'Cold, eh? What makes you shiver so? Perhaps you would like to pull up your shirt? But I've not quite done yet.'

When he had finished he wiped the whip again, and put it back in his pocket. He cut the rope through with his penknife, and then took up the light.

'You don't seem to have found your tongue yet. Forgotten how to cry?' said Bonaparte, patting him on the cheek.

The boy looked up at him—not sullenly, not angrily. There was a wild, fitful terror in the eyes. Bonaparte made haste to go out and shut the door, and leave him alone in the darkness. He himself was afraid of that look.

It was almost morning. Waldo lay with his face upon the ground at the foot of the fuel-heap. There was a round hole near the top of the door, where a knot of wood had fallen out, and a stream of grey light came in through it.

Ah, it was going to end at last! Nothing lasts for ever, not even the night. How was it he had never thought of that before? For in all that long dark night he had been very strong, had never been tired, never felt pain, had run on and on, up and down, up and down; he had not dared to stand still, and he had not known it would end. He had been so strong, that when he struck his head with all his force upon the stone wall it did not stun him nor pain him—only made him laugh. That was a dreadful night. When he clasped his hands frantically and prayed—'O God, my beautiful God, my sweet God, once, only once, let me feel you near me to-night!' he could not feel Him. He prayed aloud, very loud, and he got no answer; when he listened it was all quite quiet—like when the priests of Baal cried aloud to their god—'Oh, Baal,* hear us! Oh, Baal, hear us!' but Baal was gone a-hunting.

That was a long wild night, and wild thoughts came and went in it; but they left their marks behind them for ever: for, as years cannot pass without leaving their traces behind them, neither can nights into which are forced the thoughts and sufferings of years. And now the dawn was coming, and at last he was very tired. He shivered, and tried to draw the shirt up over his shoulders. They were getting stiff. He had never known they were cut in the night. He looked up at the white light that came in through the hole at the top of the door and shuddered. Then he turned his face back to the ground and slept again.

Some hours later Bonaparte came towards the fuel-house with a lump of bread in his hand. He opened the door and peered in; then entered, and touched the fellow with his boot. Seeing that he breathed heavily, though he did not rouse, Bonaparte threw the bread down on the ground. He was alive, that was one thing. He bent over him, and carefully scratched open one of the cuts with the nail of his forefinger, examining with much interest his last night's work. He would have to count his sheep himself that day; the boy was literally cut up. He locked the door and went away again.

'Oh, Lyndall,' said Em, entering the dining-room, and bathed in tears, that afternoon, 'I have been begging Bonaparte to let him out, and he won't.

'The more you beg the more he will not,' said Lyndall. She was cutting out aprons on the table.

'Oh, but it's late, and I think they want to kill him,' said Em, weeping bitterly; and finding that no more consolation was to be gained from her cousin, she went off blubbering—'I wonder you can cut out aprons when Waldo is shut up like that.'

For ten minutes after she was gone Lyndall worked on quietly; then she folded up her stuff, rolled it tightly together, and stood before the closed door of the sitting-room with her hands closely clasped. A flush rose to her face; she opened the door quickly, and walked in, went to the nail on which the key of the fuel-room hung. Bonaparte and Tant' Sannie sat there and saw her.

'What do you want?' they asked together.

'This key,' she said, holding it up, and looking at them.

'Do you mean her to have it?' said Tant' Sannie in Dutch.

'Why don't you stop her?' asked Bonaparte in English.

'Why don't you take it from her?' said Tant' Sannie.

So they looked at each other, talking, while Lyndall walked to the fuel-house with the key, her underlip bitten in.

'Waldo,' she said, as she helped him to stand up, and twisted his arm about her waist to support him, 'we will not be children always; we shall have the power too, some day.' She kissed his naked shoulder with her soft little mouth. It was all the comfort her young soul could give him.

CHAPTER XIII
He Makes Love

'HERE,' said Tant' Sannie to her Hottentot maid, 'I have been in this house four years, and never been up in the loft. Fatter women than I go up ladders; I will go up to-day and see what it is like, and put it to rights up there. You bring the little ladder, and stand at the bottom.'

'There's one would be sorry if you were to fall,' said the Hottentot maid, leering at Bonaparte's pipe, that lay on the table.

'Hold your tongue, jade,' said her mistress, trying to conceal a pleased smile, 'and go and fetch the ladder.'

There was a never-used trap-door at one end of the sitting-room; this the Hottentot maid pushed open, and setting the ladder against it, the Boer-woman with some danger and difficulty climbed into the loft. Then the Hottentot maid took the ladder away, as her husband was mending the waggon-house, and needed it; but the trap-door was left open.

For a little while Tant' Sannie poked about among the empty bottles and skins, and looked at the bag of peaches that Waldo was supposed to have liked so; then she sat down near the trap-door beside a barrel of salt mutton. She found that the pieces of meat were much too large, and took out her clasp-knife to divide them.

That was always the way when one left things to servants, she grumbled to herself; but when once she was married to her husband Bonaparte it would not matter whether a sheep spoiled or no—when once his rich aunt with the dropsy was dead. She smiled as she dived her hand into the pickle-water.

At that instant her niece entered the room below, closely followed by Bonaparte, with his head on one side, smiling mawkishly. Had Tant' Sannie spoken at that moment the life of Bonaparte Blenkins would have run a wholly different course; as it was, she remained silent, and neither noticed the open trap-door above their heads.

'Sit there, my love,' said Bonaparte, motioning Trana into her aunt's elbow-chair, and drawing another close up in front of it, in which he seated himself. 'There, put your feet upon the stove too. Your aunt has gone out somewhere. Long have I waited for this auspicious event!'

Trana, who understood not one word of English, sat down in the chair and wondered if this was one of the strange customs of other lands, that an old gentleman may bring his chair up to yours, and sit with his knees touching you. She had been five days in Bonaparte's company, and feared the old man, and disliked his nose.

'How long have I desired this moment!' said Bonaparte. 'But that aged relative of thine is always casting her unhallowed shadow upon us. Look into my eyes, Trana.'

Bonaparte knew that she comprehended not a syllable; but he understood that it is the eye, the tone, the action, and not at all the rational word, that touches the love-chords. He saw she changed colour.

'All night,' said Bonaparte, 'I lie awake; I see naught but thy angelic countenance. I open my arms to receive thee—where art thou, where? Thou art not there!' said Bonaparte, suiting the action to the words, and spreading out his arms and drawing them to his breast.

'Oh, please, I don't understand,' said Trana, 'I want to go away.'

'Yes, yes,' said Bonaparte, leaning back in his chair, to her great relief, and pressing his hands on his heart, 'since first thy amethystine countenance was impressed *here*—what have I not suffered, what have I not felt? Oh, the pangs unspoken, burning as an ardent coal in a fiery and uncontaminated bosom!' said Bonaparte, bending forward again.

'Dear Lord!' said Trana to herself, 'how foolish I have been! The old man has a pain in his stomach, and now, as my aunt is out, he has come to me to help him.'

She smiled kindly at Bonaparte, and pushing past him, went to the bedroom, quickly returning with a bottle of red drops in her hand.

'They are very good for "benaawdheit;"* my mother always drinks them,' she said, holding the bottle out.

The face in the trap-door was a fiery red. Like a tiger-cat ready to spring, Tant' Sannie crouched, with the shoulder of mutton in her hand. Exactly beneath her stood Bonaparte. She rose and clasped with both arms the barrel of salt meat.

'What, rose of the desert, nightingale of the colony, that with thine amorous lay whilest the lonesome night!' cried Bonaparte, seizing the hand that held the 'vonlicsense.'* 'Nay, struggle not! Fly as a stricken fawn into the arms that would embrace thee, then——'

Here a stream of cold pickle-water, heavy with ribs and shoulders, descending on his head abruptly terminated his speech. Half-blinded, Bonaparte looked up through the drops that hung from his eye-lids, and saw the red face that looked down at him. With one wild cry he fled. As he passed out at the front door a shoulder of mutton, well-directed, struck the black coat in the small of the back.

'Bring the ladder! bring the ladder! I will go after him!' cried the Boer-woman, as Bonaparte Blenkins, wildly fled into the fields.

Late in the evening of the same day Waldo knelt on the floor of his cabin. He bathed the foot of his dog which had been pierced by a thorn. The bruises on his own back had had five days to heal in, and except a little stiffness in his movements, there was nothing remarkable about the boy.

The troubles of the young are soon over; they leave no external mark. If you wound the tree in its youth the bark will quickly cover the gash; but when the tree is very old, peeling the bark off, and looking carefully, you will see the scar there still. All that is buried is not dead.

Waldo poured the warm milk over the little swollen foot; Doss lay very quiet, with tears in his eyes. Then there was a tap at the door. In an instant Doss looked wide awake, and winked the tears out from between his little lids.

'Come in,' said Waldo, intent on his work; and slowly and cautiously the door opened.

'Good-evening, Waldo, my boy,' said Bonaparte Blenkins in a mild voice, not venturing more than his nose within the door. 'How are you this evening?'

Doss growled and showed his little teeth, and tried to rise, but his paw hurt him, so he whined.

'I'm very tired, Waldo, my boy,' said Bonaparte plaintively.

Doss showed his little white teeth again. His master went on with his work without looking round. There are some people at whose hands it is best not to look. At last he said.

'Come in.'

Bonaparte stepped cautiously a little way into the room, and left the door open behind him. He looked at the boy's supper on the table.

'Waldo, I've had nothing to eat all day—I'm very hungry,' he said.

'Eat!' said Waldo after a moment, bending lower over his dog.

'You won't go and tell her that I am here, will you, Waldo?' said Bonaparte most uneasily. 'You've heard how she used me, Waldo? I've been *badly* treated; you'll know yourself what it is some day when you can't carry on a little conversation with a lady without having salt meat and pickle-water thrown at you. Waldo, look at me; do I look as a gentleman should?'

But the boy neither looked up nor answered, and Bonaparte grew more uneasy.

'You wouldn't go and tell her that I am here, would you?' said Bonaparte, whiningly. 'There's no knowing what she would to do me. I've such trust in you, Waldo; I've always thought you such a promising lad, though you mayn't have known it, Waldo.'

'Eat,' said the boy, 'I shall say nothing.'

Bonaparte, who knew the truth when another spoke it, closed the door, carefully putting on the button. Then he looked to see that the curtain of the window was closely pulled down, and seated himself at the table. He was soon munching the cold meat and bread. Waldo knelt on the floor, bathing the foot with hands which the dog licked lovingly. Once only he glanced at the table, and turned away quickly.

'Ah, yes! I don't wonder that you can't look at me, Waldo,'

said Bonaparte: 'my condition would touch any heart. You see, the water was fatty, and that has made all the sand stick to me; and my hair,' said Bonaparte, tenderly touching the little fringe at the back of his head, 'is all caked over like a little plank: you wouldn't think it was hair at all,' said Bonaparte plaintively. 'I had to creep all along the stone walls for fear she'd see me, and with nothing on my head but a red handkerchief tied under my chin, Waldo; and to hide in a "sloot" the whole day, with not a mouthful of food, Waldo. And she gave me such a blow, just here,' said Bonaparte.

He had cleared the plate of the last morsel, when Waldo rose and walked to the door.

'Oh, Waldo, my dear boy, you are not going to call her,' said Bonaparte, rising anxiously.

'I am going to sleep in the waggon,' said the boy, opening the door.

'Oh, we can both sleep in this bed: there's plenty of room. Do stay, my boy, please.'

But Waldo stepped out.

'It was such a little whip, Waldo,' said Bonaparte, following him deprecatingly. 'I didn't think it would hurt you so much. It was such a *little* whip. I'm *sure* you didn't take the peaches. You aren't going to call her, Waldo, are you?'

But the boy walked off.

Bonaparte waited till his figure had passed round the front of the waggon-house, and then slipped out. He hid himself round the corner, but kept peeping out to see who was coming. He felt sure the boy was gone to call Tant' Sannie. His teeth chattered with inward cold as he looked round into the darkness, and thought of the snakes that might bite him, and the dreadful things that might attack him, and the dead that might arise out of their graves if he slept out in the field all night. But more than an hour passed, and no footstep approached.

Then Bonaparte made his way back to the cabin. He buttoned the door and put the table against it, and, giving the dog a kick to silence his whining when the foot throbbed, he climbed into bed. He did not put out the light for fear of the ghost, but, worn out with the sorrows of the day, was soon asleep himself.

About four o'clock Waldo, lying between the seats of the horse-waggon, was awakened by a gentle touch on his head.

Sitting up, he espied Bonaparte looking through one of the windows with a lighted candle in his hand.

'I'm about to depart, my dear boy, before my enemies arise; and I could not leave without coming to bid you farewell,' said Bonaparte.

Waldo looked at him.

'I shall always think of you with affection' said Bonaparte. 'And there's that old hat of yours, if you could let me have it for a keepsake——'

'Take it,' said Waldo.

'I thought you would say so, so I brought it with me,' said Bonaparte, putting it on. 'The Lord bless you, my dear boy. You haven't a few shillings,—just a trifle you don't need,— have you?'

'Take the two shillings that are in the broken vase.'

'May the blessing of my God rest upon you, my dear child,' said Bonaparte; 'may He guide and bless you. Give me your hand.'

Waldo folded his arms closely, and lay down.

'Farewell, adieu!' said Bonaparte. 'May the blessing of my God and my father's God rest on you, now and evermore.'

With these words the head and nose withdrew themselves, and the light vanished from the window.

After a few moments the boy, lying in the waggon, heard stealthy footsteps as they passed the waggon-house and made their way down the road. He listened as they grew fainter and fainter, and at last died away altogether! and from that night the footstep of Bonaparte Blenkins was heard no more at the old farm.

PART II

'And it was all play, and no one could tell what it had lived and worked for. A striving, and a striving, and an ending in nothing.'

CHAPTER I
Times and Seasons

WALDO lay on his stomach on the sand. Since he prayed and howled to his God in the fuel-house three years had passed.

They say that in the world to come time is not measured out by months and years. Neither is it here. The soul's life has seasons of its own;* periods not found in any calendar, times that years and months will not scan, but which are as deftly and sharply cut off from one another as the smoothly-arranged years which the earth's motion yields us.

To stranger eyes these divisions are not evident; but each, looking back at the little track his consciousness illuminates, sees it cut into distinct portions, whose boundaries are the termination of mental states.

As man differs from man, so differ these souls' years. The most material life is not devoid of them; the story of the most spiritual is told in them. And it may chance that some, looking back, see the past cut out after this fashion:-

I

The year of infancy, where from the shadowy background of forgetfulness start out pictures of startling clearness, disconnected, but brightly coloured, and indelibly printed in the mind. Much that follows fades, but the colours of those baby-pictures are permanent.

There rises, perhaps, a warm summer's evening; we are

seated on the door-step; we have yet the taste of the bread and milk in our mouth, and the red sunset is reflected in our basin.

Then there is a dark night, where, waking with a fear that there is some great being in the room, we run from our own bed to another, creep close to some large figure, and are comforted.

Then there is remembrance of the pride when, on someone's shoulder, with our arms around their head, we ride to see the little pigs, the new little pigs with their curled tails and tiny snouts—where do they come from?

Remembrance of delight in the feel and smell of the first orange we ever see; of sorrow which makes us put up our lip, and cry hard, when one morning we run out to try and catch the dew-drops, and they melt and wet our little fingers; of almighty and despairing sorrow when we are lost behind the kraals, and cannot see the house anywhere.

And then one picture starts out more vividly than any.

There has been a thunder-storm; the ground, as far as the eye can reach, is covered with white hail; the clouds are gone, and overhead a deep blue sky is showing; far off a great rainbow rests on the white earth. We, standing in a window to look, feel the cool, unspeakably sweet wind blowing in on us, and a feeling of longing comes over us—unutterable longing, we cannot tell for what. We are so small, our head only reaches as high as the first three panes. We look at the white earth, and the rainbow, and the blue sky; and oh, we want it, we want—we do not know what. We cry as though our heart was broken. When one lifts our little body from the window we cannot tell what ails us. We run away to play.

So looks the first year.

II

Now the pictures become continuous and connected. Material things still rule, but the spiritual and intellectual take their places.

In the dark night, when we are afraid, we pray and shut our eyes. We press our fingers very hard upon the lids, and see dark spots moving round and round, and we know they are heads and wings of angels sent to take care of us, seen dimly in the dark as they move round our bed. It is very consoling.

In the day we learn our letters, and are troubled because we cannot see why k-n-o-w should be know, and p-s-a-l-m psalm. They tell us it is so because it *is* so. We are not satisfied; we hate to learn; we like better to build little stone houses. We can build them as we please, and know the reason for them.

Other joys too we have, incomparably greater than even the building of stone houses.

We are run through with a shudder of delight when in the red sand we come on one of those white wax flowers that lie between their two green leaves flat on the sand. We hardly dare pick them, but we feel compelled to do so; and we smell and smell till the delight becomes almost pain. Afterwards we pull the green leaves softly into pieces to see the silk threads run across.

Beyond the 'kopje' grow some pale-green, hairy-leaved bushes. We are so small, they meet over our head; and we sit among them, and kiss them, and they love us back: it seems as though they were alive.

One day we sit there and look up at the blue sky, and down at our fat little knees; and suddenly it strikes us, Who are we? This *I*, what is it? We try to look in upon ourself, and ourself beats back upon ourself. Then we get up in great fear and run home as hard as we can. We can't tell anyone what frightened us. We never quite lose that feeling of *self* again.

III

And then a new time rises. We are seven years old. We can read now—read the Bible. Best of all we like the story of Elijah in his cave at Horeb,* and the still, small voice.

One day, a notable one, we read on the 'kopje,' and discover the fifth chapter of Matthew,* and read it all through. It is a new gold-mine. Then we tuck the Bible under our arm and rush home. They didn't know it was wicked to take your things again if someone took them, wicked to go to law, wicked to—! We are quite breathless when we get to the house; we tell them we have discovered a chapter they never heard of; we tell them what it says. The old wise people tell us they knew all about it. Our discovery is a mare's-nest to them; but to us it is very real. The ten commandments and the old 'Thou shalt' we have heard about long enough, and don't care about it; but this new law sets us on fire. We will deny ourself. Our little waggon that we have made, we give to the little Kaffirs. We keep quiet when they throw sand at us (feeling, oh, so happy). We conscientiously put the cracked teacup for ourselves at breakfast, and take the burnt roaster-cake. We save our money, and buy three pence worth of tobacco for the Hottentot maid who calls us names. We are exotically virtuous. At night we are profoundly religious; even the ticking watch says, 'Eternity, eternity! hell, hell, hell!' and the silence talks of God, and the things that shall be.

Occasionally, also, unpleasantly shrewd questions begin to be asked by someone, we know not who, who sits somewhere behind our shoulder. We get to know him better afterwards. Now we carry the questions to the grown-up people, and they give us answers. We are more or less satisfied for the time. The grown-up people are very wise, and they say it was kind of God to make hell, and very loving of Him to send men there; and besides He couldn't help Himself; and they are very wise, we think, so we believe them—more or less.

IV

Then a new time comes, of which the leading feature is, that the shrewd questions are asked louder. We carry them to the grown-up people; they answer us, and we are *not* satisfied.

And now between us and the dear old world of the senses the spirit-world begins to peep in, and wholly clouds it over. What are the flowers to us? They are fuel waiting for the great burning. We look at the walls of the farm-house and the matter-of-fact sheep-kraals, with the merry sunshine playing over all; and do not see it. But we see a great white throne, and Him that sits on it. Around Him stand a great multitude that no man can number, harpers harping with their harps, a thousand times ten thousand, and thousands of thousands. How white are their robes, washed in the blood of the Lamb!

And the music rises higher, and rends the vault of heaven with its unutterable sweetness. And we, as we listen, ever and anon, as it sinks on the sweetest, lowest note, hear a groan of the damned from below. We shudder in the sunlight.

'The torment,' says Jeremy Taylor, whose sermons our father reads aloud in the evening, 'comprises as many torments as the body of man has joints, sinews, arteries, &c., being caused by that penetrating and real fire of which this temporal fire is but a painted fire. What comparison will there be between burning for a hundred years' space and to be burning without intermission as long as God is God!'*

We remember the sermon there in the sunlight. One comes and asks why we sit there nodding so moodily. Ah, they do not see what we see.

> 'A moment's time, a narrow space,
> Divides me from that heavenly place,
>   Or shuts me up in hell.'

So says Wesley's hymn,* which we sing evening by evening. What matter sunshine and walls, men and sheep?

'The things which are seen are temporal, but the things which are not seen are eternal.' They are real.

The Bible we bear always in our breast; its pages are our food; we learn to repeat it; we weep much, for in sunshine and in shade, in the early morning or the late evening, in the field or in the house, the Devil walks with us. He comes to us a real person, copper-coloured face, head a little on one side, forehead knit, asking questions. Believe me, it were better to be followed by three deadly diseases than by him. He is never silenced—without mercy. Though the drops of blood stand out on your heart he will put his question. Softly he comes up (we are only a wee bit child); 'Is it good of God to make hell? Was it kind of Him to let no one be forgiven unless Jesus Christ died?'

Then he goes off, and leaves us writhing. Presently he comes back.

'Do you love Him?'—waits a little. 'Do you love Him? You will be lost if you don't.'

We say we try to.

'But do you?' Then he goes off.

It is nothing to him if we go quite mad with fear at our own wickedness. He asks on, the questioning Devil; he cares nothing what he says. We long to tell someone, that they may share our pain. We do not yet know that the cup of affliction is made with such a narrow mouth that only one lip can drink at a time, and that each man's cup is made to match his lip.

One day we try to tell someone. Then a grave head is shaken solemnly at us. We are wicked, very wicked, they say; we ought not to have such thoughts. God is good, very good. We are wicked, very wicked. That is the comfort we get. Wicked! Oh, Lord! do we not know it? Is it not the sense of our own exceeding wickedness that is drying up our young heart, filling it with sand, making all life a dust-bin for us?

Wicked? We know it! Too vile to live, too vile to die, too vile to creep over this, God's earth, and move among His believing men. Hell is the one place for him who hates his master, and there we do not want to go. This is the comfort we get from the old.

And once again we try to seek for comfort. This time great eyes look at us wondering, and lovely little lips say,—

'If it makes you so unhappy to think of these things, why do you not think of something else, and forget?'

Forget! We turn away and shrink into ourself. Forget and think of other things! Oh, God! do they not understand that the material world is but a film, through every pore of which God's awful spirit-world is shining through on us? We keep as far from others as we can.

One night, a rare, clear moonlight night, we kneel in the window; everyone else is asleep, but we kneel reading by the moonlight. It is a chapter in the prophets,* telling how the chosen people of God shall be carried on the Gentiles' shoulders. Surely the Devil might leave us alone; there is not much handle for him there. But presently he comes.

'Is it right there should be a chosen people? To Him, who is father to all, should not all be dear?'

How can we answer him? We were feeling so good till he came. We put our head down on the Bible and blister it with tears. Then we fold our hands over our head and pray, till our teeth grind together. Oh, that from that spirit-world, so real and yet so silent, that surrounds us, one word would come to guide us! We are left alone with this devil; and God does not whisper to us. Suddenly we seize the Bible, turning it round and round, and say hurriedly,—

'It will be God's voice speaking to us; His voice as though we heard it.'

We yearn for a token from the inexorably Silent One.

We turn the book, put our finger down on a page, and bend to read by the moonlight. It is God's answer. We tremble.

'Then fourteen years after I went up again to Jerusalem with Barnabas, and took Titus* with me also.'

For an instant our imagination seizes it; we are twisting, twirling, trying to make an allegory. The fourteen years are fourteen months; we are Paul and the devil is Barnabas, Titus is—— Then a sudden loathing comes to us: we are liars and hypocrites, we are trying to deceive ourselves. What is Paul to us—and Jerusalem? Who are Barnabas and Titus? We know not the men. Before we know we seize the book, swing it round our head, and fling it with all our might to the farther end of the room. We put down our head again and weep. Youth and ignorance; is there anything else that can weep so? It is as though the tears were drops of blood congealed beneath the eyelids; nothing else is like those tears. After a long time we are weak with crying, and lie silent, and by chance we knock against the wood that stops the broken pane. It falls. Upon our hot stiff face a sweet breath of wind blows. We raise our head, and with our swollen eyes look out at the beautiful still world, and the sweet night-wind blows in upon us, holy and gentle, like a loving breath from the lips of God. Over us a deep peace comes, a calm, still joy; the tears now flow readily and softly. Oh, the unutterable gladness! At last, at last we have found it! *'The peace with God.' 'The sense of sins forgiven.'* All doubt vanished, God's voice in the soul, the Holy Spirit filling us! We feel Him! we feel Him! Oh, Jesus Christ! through you, through you this joy! We press our hands upon our breast and look upward with adoring gladness. Soft waves of bliss break through us. *'The peace with God.' 'The sense of sins forgiven.'* Methodists and Revivalists say the words, and the mocking world shoots out its lip, and walks by smiling— 'Hypocrite!'

There are more fools and fewer hypocrites than the wise world dreams of. The hypocrite is rare as icebergs in the tropics; the fool common as butter-cups beside a water-furrow: Whether you go this way or that you tread on him; you dare not look at your own reflection in the water but you see one. There is no cant phrase, rotten with age, but it was the dress of a living body; none but at heart it signifies a real bodily or mental condition which some have passed through.

After hours and nights of frenzied fear of the supernatural desire to appease the power above, a fierce quivering excitement in every inch of nerve and blood-vessel, there comes a time when nature cannot endure longer, and the spring long bent recoils. We sink down emasculated. Up creeps the deadly delicious calm.

'I have blotted out as a cloud thy sins, and as a thick cloud thy trespasses, and will remember them no more for ever.' We weep with soft transporting joy.

A few experience this; many imagine they experience it; one here and there lies about it. In the main, 'The peace with God; a sense of sins forgiven,' stands for a certain mental and physical reaction. Its reality those know who have felt it.

And we, on that moonlight night, put down our head on the window, 'Oh, God! we are happy, happy; thy child for ever. Oh, thank you, God!' and we drop asleep.

Next morning the Bible we kiss. We are God's for ever. We go out to work, and it goes happily all day, happy all night; but hardly so happily, not happily at all, the next day; and the next night the Devil asks us, 'Where is your Holy Spirit?'

We cannot tell.

So month by month, summer and winter, the old life goes on—reading, praying, weeping, praying. They tell us we become utterly stupid. We know it. Even the multiplication table we learnt with so much care we forget The physical world recedes further and further from us. Truly we love not the world, neither the things that are in it. Across the bounds of sleep our grief follows us. When we wake in the night we are sitting up in bed weeping bitterly, or find ourselves outside in the moonlight, dressed, and walking up and down, and wringing our hands, and we cannot tell how we came there. so pass two years, as men reckon them.

V

Then a new time.

Before us there were three courses possible—to go mad, to die, to sleep.

We take the later course; or nature takes it for us.

All things take rest in sleep; the beasts, birds, the very flowers close their eyes, and the streams are still in winter; all things take rest; then why not the human reason also? So the questioning Devil in us drops asleep; and in that sleep a beautiful dream rises for us. Though you hear all the dreams of men, you will hardly find a prettier one than ours. It ran so:

In the centre of all things is a Mighty Heart, which, having begotten all things, loves them; and, having born them into life, beats with great throbs of love towards them. No death for His dear insects, no hell for His dear men, no burning up for His dear world—His own, own world that He has made. In the end all will be beautiful. Do not ask us how we make our dream tally with facts; the glory of a dream is this—that it despises facts, and makes its own. Our dream saves us from going mad; that is enough.

Its peculiar point of sweetness lay here. When the Mighty Heart's yearning of love became too great for other expression, it shaped itself into the sweet Rose of heaven, the beloved Man-god.

Jesus! you Jesus of our dream! how we loved you; no Bible tells of you as we knew you. Your sweet hands held ours fast; your sweet voice said always, 'I am here, my loved one, not far off; put your arms about Me, and hold fast.'

We find Him in everything in those days. When the little weary lamb we drive home drags its feet, we seize on it, and carry it with its head against our face. His little lamb! We feel we have got Him.

When the drunken Kaffir lies by the road in the sun we

draw his blanket over his head, and put green branches of milk-bush on it. His Kaffir; why should the sun hurt him?

In the evening, when the clouds lift themselves like gates, and the red lights shine through them, we cry; for in such glory He will come, and the hands that ache to touch Him will hold Him, and we shall see the beautiful hair and eyes of our God. 'Lift up your heads, O ye gates;* and be ye lifted up, ye everlasting doors, and our King of glory shall come in!'

The purple flowers, the little purple flowers, are His eyes looking at us. We kiss them, and kneel alone on the flat, rejoicing over them. And the wilderness and the solitary place shall be glad for Him, and the desert shall rejoice and blossom as a rose.

If ever in our tearful, joyful ecstasy the poor sleepy, half-dead Devil should raise his head, we laugh at him. It is not his hour now.

'If there should be a hell, after all!' he mutters. 'If your God should be cruel! If there should be no God! If you should find out it is all imagination! If——'

We laugh at him. When a man sits in the warm sunshine, do you ask him for proof of it? He feels—that is all. And we feel—that is all. We want no proof of our God. We feel, we feel!

We do not believe in our God because the Bible tells us of Him. We believe in the Bible because He tells us of it. We feel Him, we feel Him, we feel—that is all! And the poor half-swamped Devil mutters—

'But if the day should come when you do not feel?'

And we laugh, and cry him down.

'It will never come—never,' and the poor Devil slinks to sleep again, with his tail between his legs. Fierce assertion many times repeated is hard to stand against; only time separates the truth from the lie. So we dream on.

One day we go with our father to town, to church. The townspeople rustle in their silks, and the men in their sleek cloth, and settle themselves in their pews, and the light shines in through the windows on the artificial flowers in the women's bonnets. We have the same miserable feeling that we have in a shop where all the clerks are very smart. We wish our father hadn't brought us to town, and we were out on the karroo. Then the man in the pulpit begins to preach. His text is 'He that believeth not shall be damned.'*

The day before, the magistrate's clerk, who was an atheist, has died in the street, struck by lightning.

The man in the pulpit mentions no name; but he talks of 'The hand of God made visible among us.' He tells us how, when the white stroke fell, quivering and naked, the soul fled, robbed of his earthly filament, and lay at the footstool of God; how over its head has been poured out the wrath of the Mighty One, whose existence it has denied; and, quivering and terrified, it has fled to the everlasting shade.

We, as we listen, half start up; every drop of blood in our body has rushed to our head. He lies! he lies! he lies! That man in the pulpit lies! Will no one stop him? Have none of them heard—do none of them know, that when the poor dark soul shut its eyes on earth it opened them in the still light of heaven? that there is no wrath where God's face is? that if one could once creep to the footstool of God, there is everlasting peace there? like the fresh stillness of the early morning. While the atheist lay wondering and afraid, God bent down and said, 'My child *here* I am—I, whom you have not known; I, whom you have not believed in; I am here. I sent My messenger, the white sheet lightning, to call you home. I am here.'

Then the poor soul turned to the light,—its weakness and pain were gone for ever.

Have they not known, have they not heard, who it is rules?

'For a little moment have I hidden my face from thee; but with everlasting kindness will I have mercy upon thee, saith the Lord thy Redeemer.'

We mutter on to ourselves, till someone pulls us violently by the arm to remind us we are in church. We see nothing but our own ideas.

Presently everyone turns to pray. There are six hundred souls lifting themselves to the Everlasting light.

Behind us sit two pretty ladies; one hands her scent-bottle softly to the other, and a mother pulls down her little girl's frock. One lady drops her handkerchief; a gentleman picks it up; she blushes. The women in the choir turn softly the leaves of their tune-books, to be ready when the praying is done. It is as though they thought more of the singing than the Everlasting Father. Oh, would it not be more worship of Him to sit alone in the karroo and kiss one little purple flower that He had made? Is it not mockery? Then the thought comes, '*What doest thou here, Elijah?*'* We who judge, what are we better than they?—rather worse. Is it any excuse to say, 'I am but a child, and must come?' Does God allow any soul to step in between the spirit He made and Himself? What do we there in that place, where all the words are lies against the All Father? Filled with horror, we turn and flee out of the place. On the pavement we smite our foot, and swear in our child's soul never again to enter those places where men come to sing and pray. We are questioned afterwards. Why was it we went out of the church?

How can we explain?—we stand silent. Then we are pressed further, and we try to tell. Then a head is shaken solemnly at us. No one *can* think it wrong to go to the house of the Lord; it is the idle excuse of a wicked boy. When will we think seriously of our souls, and love going to church? We are wicked, very wicked. And we—we slink away and go alone to cry. Will it be always so? Whether we hate and doubt, or whether we believe and love, to our dearest, are we to seem always wicked?

We do not yet know that in the soul's search for truth the bitterness lies here, the striving cannot always hide itself among the thoughts; sooner or later it will clothe itself in outward action; then it steps in and divides between the soul and what it loves. All things on earth have their price; and for truth we pay the dearest. We barter it for love and sympathy. The road to honour is paved with thorns; but on the path to truth, at every step you set your foot down on your own heart.

VI

Then at last a new time—the time of waking: short, sharp, and not pleasant, as wakings often are.

Sleep and dreams exist on this condition—that no one wake the dreamer.

And now life takes us up between her finger and thumb, shakes us furiously, till our poor nodding head is well-nigh rolled from our shoulders, and she sets us down a little hardly on the bare earth, bruised and sore, but preternaturally wide awake.

We have said in our days of dreaming, 'Injustice and wrong are a seeming; pain is a shadow. Our God, He is real; He who made all things, and He only, is Love.'

Now life takes us by the neck and shows us a few other things,—new-made graves with the red sand flying about them; eyes that we love with the worms eating them; evil men walking sleek and fat, the whole terrible hurly-burly of the thing called life,—and she says, 'What do you think of these?' We dare not say, 'Nothing.' We feel them; they are very real. But we try to lay our hands about and feel that other thing we felt before. In the dark night in the fuel-room we cry to our Beautiful dream-god—'Oh, let us come near you, and lay our head against your feet. Now in our hour of need be near us.' But He is not there; He is gone away. The old questioning Devil is there.

We must have been awakened sooner or later. The imagination cannot always triumph over reality, the desire over truth. We must have been awakened. If it was done a little sharply, what matter? It was done thoroughly, and it had to be done.

VII

And a new life begins for us—a new time, a life as cold as that of a man who sits on the pinnacle of an iceberg and sees the glittering crystals all about him. The old looks indeed like a long hot delirium, peopled with phantasies. The new is cold enough.

Now we have no God. We have had two: the old God that our fathers handed down to us, that we hated, and never liked; the new one that we made for ourselves, that we loved; but now he has flitted away from us, and we see what he was made of—the shadow of our highest ideal, crowned and throned. Now we have no God.

'The fool hath said in his heart, There is no God.' It may be so. Most things said or written have been the work of fools.

This thing is certain—he is a fool who says, 'No man hath said in his heart, There is no God.'

It has been said many thousand times in hearts with profound bitterness of earnest faith.

We do not cry and weep; we sit down with cold eyes and look at the world. We are not miserable. Why should we be? We eat and drink, and sleep all night; but the dead are not colder.

And, we say it slowly, but without sighing, 'Yes, we see it now: there is no God.'

And, we add, growing a little colder yet, 'There is no justice. The ox dies in the yoke, beneath its master's whip; it turns its anguish-filled eyes on the sunlight, but there is no sign of recompense to be made it. The black man is shot like a dog, and it goes well with the shooter. The innocent are accused, and the accuser triumphs. If you will take the trouble to scratch the surface anywhere, you will see under the skin a sentient being writhing in impotent anguish.'

And, we say further, and our heart is as the heart of the dead for coldness, 'There is no order: all things are driven about by a blind chance.'

What a soul drinks in with its mother's milk will not leave it in a day. From our earliest hour we have been taught that the thought of the heart, the shaping of the rain-cloud, the amount of wool that grows on a sheep's back, the length of a drought, and the growing of the corn, depend on nothing that moves immutable, at the heart of all things; but on the changeable will of a changeable being, whom our prayers can alter. To us, from the beginning, nature has been but a poor plastic thing, to be toyed with this way or that, as man happens to please his deity or not; to go to church or not; to say his prayers right or not; to travel on a Sunday or not. Was it possible for us in an instant to see Nature as she is—the flowing vestment of an unchanging reality? When a soul breaks free from the arms of a superstition, bits of the claws and talons break themselves off in him. It is not the work of a day to squeeze them out.

And so, for us, the human-like driver and guide being gone,

all existence, as we look out at it with our chilled, wondering eyes, is an aimless rise and swell of shifting waters. In all that weltering chaos we can see no spot so large as a man's hand on which we may plant our foot.

Whether a man believes in a human-like God or no is a small thing. Whether he looks into the mental and physical world and sees no relation between cause and effect, no order, but a blind chance sporting, this is the mightiest fact that can be recorded in any spiritual existence. It were almost a mercy to cut his throat, if indeed he does not do it for himself.

We, however, do not cut our throats. To do so would imply some desire and feeling, and we have no desire and no feeling; we are only cold. We do not wish to live, and we do not wish to die. One day a snake curls itself round the waist of a Kaffir woman. We take it in our hand, swing it round and round, and fling it on the ground—dead. Everyone looks at us with eyes of admiration. We almost laugh. Is it wonderful to risk that for which we care nothing?

In truth, nothing matters. This dirty little world full of confusion, and the blue rag, stretched overhead for a sky, is so low we could touch it with our hand.

Existence is a great pot, and the old Fate who stirs it round cares nothing what rises to the top and what goes down, and laughs when the bubbles burst. And we do not care. Let it boil about. Why should we trouble ourselves? Nevertheless the physical sensations are real. Hunger hurts, and thirst, therefore we eat and drink: inaction pains us, therefore we work like galley-slaves. No one demands it, but we set ourselves to build a great dam in red sand beyond the graves. In the grey dawn, before the sheep are let out, we work at it. All day, while the young ostriches we tend feed about us, we work on through the fiercest heat. The people wonder what new spirit has seized us now. They do not know we are working for life. We bear the greatest stones, and feel a satisfaction when we stagger under them, and are hurt by a pang that shoots through our chest. While we eat our dinner we carry on baskets full of earth, as though the Devil drove us. The Kaffir servants have a story that at night a witch and two white oxen come to us. No wall, they say, could grow so quickly under one man's hands.

At night, alone in our cabin, we sit no more brooding over the fire. What should we think of now? All is emptiness. So we take the old arithmetic; and the multiplication table, which with so much pains we learnt long ago and forgot directly, we learn now in a few hours and never forget again. We take a strange satisfaction in working arithmetical problems. We pause in our building to cover the stones with figures and calculations. We save money for a Latin Grammar and an Algebra, and carry them about in our pockets, poring over them as over our Bible of old. We have thought we were utterly stupid, incapable of remembering anything, of learning anything. Now we find that all is easy. Has a new soul crept into this old body, that even our intellectual faculties are changed? We marvel; not perceiving that what a man expends in prayer and ecstasy he cannot have over for acquiring knowledge. You never shed a tear or create a beautiful image, or quiver with emotion, but you pay for it at the practical, calculating end of your nature. You have just so much force: when the one channel runs over the other runs dry.

And now we turn to Nature. All these years we have lived beside her, and we have never seen her; now we open our eyes and look at her.

The rocks have been to us a blur of brown; we bend over them, and the disorganized masses dissolve into a many-coloured, many-shaped, carefully-arranged form of existence. Here masses of rainbow-tinted crystals, half-fused together; there bands of smooth grey and red, methodically overlying each other. This rock here is covered with a delicate silver tracery, in some mineral, resembling leaves and branches; there on the flat stone, on which we so often have sat to weep and pray, we look down, and see it covered with the fossil footprints of great birds, and the beautiful skeleton of a fish. We have often tried to picture in our mind what the fossiled remains of creatures must be like, and all the while we sat on them. We have been so blinded by thinking and feeling that we have never seen the world.

The flat plain has been to us a reach of monotonous red. We look at it, and every handful of sand starts into life. That wonderful people, the ants, we learn to know; see them make war and peace, play and work, and build their huge palaces. And that smaller people we make acquaintance with, who live in the flowers. The bitto flower has been for us a mere blur of yellow; we find its heart composed of a hundred perfect flowers, the homes of the tiny black people with red stripes, who move in and out in that little yellow city. Every bluebell has its inhabitant. Every day the karroo shows us a new wonder sleeping in its teeming bosom. On our way to work we pause and stand to see the ground-spider make its trap, bury itself in the sand, and then wait for the falling in of its enemy. Farther on walks a horned beetle, and near him starts open the door of a spider, who peeps out carefully, and quickly pulls it down again. On a karroo-bush a green fly is laying her silver eggs. We carry them home, and see the shells pierced, the spotted grub come out, turn to a green fly, and flit away. We are not satisfied with what Nature shows us, and will see something for ourselves. Under the white hen we put a dozen eggs, and break one daily, to see the white spot wax into the chicken. We are not excited or enthusiastic about it; but a man is not to lay his throat open, he must think of something. So we plant seeds in rows on our dam-wall, and pull one up daily to see how it goes with them. Alladeen* buried her wonderful stone, and a gold palace sprang up at her feet. We do far more. We put a brown seed in the earth, and a living thing starts out—starts upwards—why, no more than Alladeen can we say—starts upwards, and does not desist till it is higher than our heads, sparkling with dew in the early morning, glittering with yellow blossoms, shaking brown seeds with little embryo souls on to the ground. We look at it solemnly, from the time it consists of two leaves peeping above the ground and a soft white root, till we have to raise our faces to look at it; but we find no reason for that upward starting.

We look into dead ducks and lambs. In the evening we carry them home, spread newspapers on the floor, and lie working with them till midnight. With a startled feeling near akin to ecstasy we open the lump of flesh called a heart, and find little doors and strings inside. We feel them, and put the heart away; but every now and then return to look, and to feel them again. Why we like them so we can hardly tell.

A gander drowns itself in our dam. We take it out, and open it on the bank, and kneel, looking at it. Above are the organs divided by delicate tissues; below are the intestines artistically curved in a spiral form, and each tier covered by a delicate network of blood-vessels standing out red against the faint blue background. Each branch of the blood-vessels is comprised of a trunk, bifurcating and rebifurcating into the most delicate, hair-like threads, symmetrically arranged. We are struck with its singular beauty. And, moreover—and here we drop from our kneeling into a sitting posture—this also we remark: of that same exact shape and outline is our thorn-tree seen against the sky in mid-winter: of that shape also is delicate metallic tracery between our rocks; in that exact path does our water flow when without a furrow we lead it from the dam; so shaped are the antlers of the horned beetle. How are these things related that such deep union should exist between them all? Is it chance? Or, are they not all the fine branches of one trunk, whose sap flows through us all? That would explain it. We nod over the gander's inside.

This thing we call existence; is it not a something which has its roots far down below in the dark, and its branches stretching out into the immensity above, which we among the branches cannot see? Not a chance jumble; a living thing, a *One*. The thought gives us intense satisfaction, we cannot tell why.

We nod over the gander; then start up suddenly, look into the blue sky, throw the dead gander and the refuse into the damn, and go to work again.

And so, it comes to pass in time, that the earth ceases for us to be a weltering chaos. We walk in the great hall of life, looking up and round reverentially. Nothing is despicable—all is meaning-full; nothing is small—all is part of a whole, whose beginning and end we know not. The life that throbs in us is a pulsation from it; too mighty for our comprehension, not too small.

And so, it comes to pass at last, that whereas the sky was at first a small blue rag stretched out over us, and so low that our hands might touch it, pressing down on us, it raises itself into an immeasurable blue arch over our heads, and we begin to live again.

CHAPTER II
Waldo's Stranger

WALDO lay on his stomach on the red sand. The small ostriches he herded wandered about him, pecking at the food he had cut, or at pebbles and dry sticks. On his right lay the graves; to his left the dam; in his hand was a large wooden post covered with carvings, at which he worked. Doss lay before him basking in the winter sunshine, and now and again casting an expectant glance at the corner of the nearest ostrich-camp. The scrubby thorn-trees under which they lay yielded no shade, but none was needed in that glorious June weather, when in the hottest part of the afternoon the sun was but pleasantly warm; and the boy carved on, not looking up, yet conscious of the brown serene earth about him and the intensely blue sky above.

Presently, at the corner of the camp, Em appeared, bearing a covered saucer in one hand, and in the other a jug with a cup in the top. She was grown into a premature little old woman of sixteen, ridiculously fat. The jug and saucer she put down on the ground before the dog and his master, and dropped down beside them herself, panting and out of breath.

'Waldo, as I came up the camps I met someone on horse-back; and I do believe it must be the new man that is coming.'

The new man was an Englishman to whom the Boer-woman had hired half the farm.

'Hum!' said Waldo.

'He is quite young,' said Em, holding her side, 'and he has brown hair, and beard curling close to his face, and such dark blue eyes. And, Waldo, I was so ashamed! I was just looking back to see, you know, and he happened just to be looking back too, and we looked right into each other's faces; and he got red, and I got so red. I believe he is the new man.'

'Yes,' said Waldo.

'I must go now. Perhaps he has brought us letters from the

post from Lyndall. You know she can't stay at school much longer, she must come back soon. And the new man will have to stay with us till his house is built. I must get his room ready. Good-bye!'

She tripped off again, and Waldo carved on at his post. Doss lay with his nose close to the covered saucer, and smelt that someone had made nice little fat cakes that afternoon. Both were so intent on their occupation that not till a horse's hoofs beat beside them in the sand did they look up to see a rider drawing in his steed.

He was certainly not the stranger whom Em had described. A dark, somewhat French-looking little man of eight-and-twenty, rather stout, with heavy, cloudy eyes and pointed moustaches. His horse was a fiery creature, well caparisoned; a highly-finished saddle-bag hung from the saddle; the man's hands were gloved, and he presented the appearance—an appearance rare on that farm—of a well-dressed gentleman.

In an uncommonly melodious voice he inquired whether he might be allowed to remain there for an hour. Waldo directed him to the farm-house, but the stranger declined. He would merely rest under the trees, and give his horse water. He removed the saddle, and Waldo led the animal away to the dam. When he returned, the stranger had settled himself under the trees, with his back against the saddle. The boy offered him of the cakes. He declined, but took a draught from the jug; and Waldo lay down not far off, and fell to work again. It mattered nothing if cold eyes saw it. It was not his sheep-shearing machine. With material loves, as with human, we go mad once, love out, and have done. We never get up the true enthusiasm a second time. This was but a thing he had made, laboured over, loved and liked—nothing more—not his machine.

The stranger forced himself lower down in the saddle and yawned. It was a drowsy afternoon, and he objected to travel in these out-of-the-world parts. He liked better civilized life, where at every hour of the day a man may look for his glass of wine, and his easy-chair, and paper; where at night he may lock himself into his room with his books and a bottle of brandy, and taste joys mental and physical. The world said of him—the all-knowing, omnipotent world, whom no locks can bar, who has the cat-like propensity of seeing best in the dark—the world said, that better than the books he loved the brandy, and better than books or brandy that which it had been better had he loved less. But for the world he cared nothing; he smiled blandly in its teeth. All life is a dream; if wine and philosophy and women keep the dream from becoming a nightmare, so much the better. It is all they are fit for, all they can be used for. There was another side to his life and thought; but of that the world knew nothing, and said nothing, as the way of the wise world is.

The stranger looked from beneath his sleepy eyelids at the brown earth that stretched away, beautiful in spite of itself in that June sunshine; looked at the graves, the gables of the farm-house showing over the stone walls of the camps, at the clownish fellow at his feet, and yawned. But he had drunk of the hind's tea, and must say something.

'Your father's place, I presume?' he inquired sleepily.

'No; I am only a servant.'

'Dutch people?'

'Yes.'

'And you like the life?'

The boy hesitated.

'On days like these.'

'And why on these?'

The boy waited.

'They are very beautiful.'

The stranger looked at him. It seemed that as the fellow's dark eyes looked across the brown earth they kindled with an intense satisfaction; then they looked back at the carving.

What had that creature, so coarse-clad and clownish, to do with the subtle joys of the weather? Himself, white-handed and delicate, *he* might hear the music which shimmering sunshine and solitude play on the finely-strung chords of nature; but that fellow! Was not the ear in that great body too gross for such delicate mutterings?

Presently he said,

'May I see what you work at?'

The fellow handed his wooden post. It was by no means

lovely. The men and birds were almost grotesque in their laboured resemblance to nature, and bore signs of patient thought. The stranger turned the thing over on his knee.

'Where did you learn this work?'

'I taught myself.'

'And these zigzag lines represent——'

'A mountain.'

The stranger looked.

'It has some meaning, has it not?'

The boy muttered confusedly.

'Only things.'

The questioner looked down at him—the huge, unwieldy figure, in size a man's, in right of its childlike features and curling hair a child's; and it hurt him—it attracted him and it hurt him. It was something between pity and sympathy.

'How long have you worked at this?'

'Nine months.'

From his pocket the stranger drew his pocket-book, and took something from it. He could fasten the post to his horse in some way, and throw it away in the sand when at a safe distance.

'Will you take this for your carving?'

The boy glanced at the five-pound note and shook his head.

'No; I cannot.'

'You think it is worth more?' asked the stranger with a little sneer.

He pointed with his thumb to a grave.

'No; it is for him.'

'And who is there?' asked the stranger.

'My father.'

The man silently returned the note to his pocket-book, and gave the carving to the boy; and, drawing his hat over his eyes, composed himself to sleep. Not being able to do so, after a while he glanced over the fellow's shoulder to watch him work. The boy carved letters into the back.

'If,' said the stranger, with his melodious voice, rich with a sweetness that never showed itself in the clouded eyes—for sweetness will linger on in the voice long after it has died out in the eyes—'if for such a purpose, why write that upon it?'

The boy glanced round at him, but made no answer. He had almost forgotten his presence.

'You surely believe,' said the stranger, 'that some day, sooner or later, these graves will open, and those Boer-uncles with their wives walk about here in the red sand, with the very fleshly legs with which they went to sleep? Then why say, "He sleeps for ever?" You believe he will stand up again?'

'Do you?' asked the boy, lifting for an instant his heavy eyes to the stranger's face.

Half taken aback, the stranger laughed. It was as though a curious little tadpole which he held under his glass should suddenly lift its tail and begin to question him.

'I?—no.' He laughed his short thick laugh. 'I am a man who believes nothing, hopes nothing, fears nothing, feels nothing. I am beyond the pale of humanity; no criterion of what you should be who live here among your ostriches and bushes.'

The next moment the stranger was surprised by a sudden movement on the part of the fellow, which brought him close to the stranger's feet. Soon after, he raised his carving and laid it across the man's knee.

'Yes, I will tell you,' he muttered; 'I will tell you all about it.'

He put his finger on the grotesque little mannikin at the bottom (Ah! that man who believed nothing, hoped nothing, felt nothing; *how he loved him!*), and with eager finger the fellow moved upwards, explaining over fantastic figures and mountains, to the crowning bird from whose wing dropped a feather. At the end he spoke with broken breath—short words, like one who utters things of mighty import.

The stranger watched more the face than the carving; and there was now and then a show of white teeth beneath the moustaches as he listened.

'I think,' he said blandly, when the boy had done, 'that I partly understand you. It is something after this fashion, is it not?' (He smiled.) 'In certain valleys there was a hunter.'* (He touched the grotesque little figure at the bottom.) 'Day by day he went to hunt for wild-fowl in the woods; and it chanced that once he stood on the shores of a large lake. While he stood waiting in the rushes for the coming of the birds, a great

shadow fell on him, and in the water he saw a reflection. He
looked up to the sky; but the thing was gone. Then a burning
desire came over him to see once again that reflection in the
water, and all day he watched and waited; but night came, and
it had not returned. Then he went home with his empty bag,
moody and silent. His comrades came questioning about him
to know the reason, but he answered them nothing; he sat
alone and brooded. Then his friend came to him, and to him
he spoke.

"'I have seen to-day,' he said, 'that I which I never saw
before—a vast white bird, with silver wings outstretched,
sailing in the everlasting blue. And now it is as though a great
fire burnt within my breast. It was but a sheen, a shimmer, a
reflection in the water; but now I desire nothing more on earth
than to hold her.'

'His friend laughed.

"'It was but a beam playing on the water, or the shadow of
your own head. To-morrow you will forget her,' he said.

'But to-morrow, and to-morrow, and to-morrow the hunter
walked alone. He sought in the forest and in the woods, by the
lakes and among the rushes, but he could not find her. He shot
no more wild-fowl; what were they to him?

"'What ails him?' said his comrades.

"'He is mad,' said one.

"'No; but he is worse,' said another; 'he would see that
which none of us have seen, and make himself a wonder.'

"'Come, let us forswear his company,' said all.

'So the hunter walked alone.

'One night, as he wandered in the shade, very heartsore and
weeping, an old man stood before him, grander and taller than
the sons of men.

"'Who are you?' asked the hunter.

"'I am Wisdom,' answered the old man; 'but some men
called me Knowledge. All my life I have grown in these
valleys; but no man sees me till he has sorrowed much. The
eyes must be washed with tears that are to behold me; and,
according as a man has suffered, I speak.'

'And the hunter cried—

"'Oh, you who have lived here so long, tell me, what is that

great wild bird I have seen sailing in the blue? They would
have me believe she is a dream; the shadow of my own head."

'The old man smiled.

'"Her name is Truth. He who has once seen her never rests
again. Till death he desires her."

'And the hunter cried—

'"Oh, tell me where I may find her."

'But the man said,

'"You have not suffered enough," and went.

'Then the hunter took from his breast the shuttle of Imagination, and wound on it the thread of his Wishes; and all night
he sat and wove a net.

'In the morning he spread the gold net open on the ground,
and into it he threw a few grains of credulity, which his father
had left him, and which he kept in his breast-pocket. They
were like white puff-balls, and when you trod on them a brown
dust flew out. Then he sat by to see what would happen. The
first that came into the net was a snow-white bird, with dove's
eyes, and he sang a beautiful song—"A human-God! a human-
God! a human-God!" it sang. The second that came was black
and mystical, with dark, lovely eyes, that looked into the
depths of your soul, and he sang only this—"Immortality!"

'And the hunter took them both in his arms, for he said—

'"They are surely of the beautiful family of Truth."

'Then came another, green and gold, who sang in a shrill
voice, like one crying in the market-place,—"Reward after
Death! Reward after Death!"

'And he said—

'"You are not so fair; but you are fair too," and he took it.

'And others came, brightly coloured, singing pleasant songs,
till the grains were finished. And the hunter gathered all his
birds together, and built a strong iron cage called a new creed,
and put all his birds in it.

'Then the people came about dancing and singing.

'"Oh, happy hunter!" they cried. "Oh, wonderful man! Oh,
delightful birds! Oh, lovely songs!"

'No one asked where the birds had come from, nor how they
had been caught; but they danced and sang before them. And
the hunter too was glad, for he said—

'"Surely Truth is among them. In time she will moult her feathers, and I shall see her snow-white form."'

'But the time passed, and the people sang and danced; but the hunter's heart grew heavy. He crept alone, as of old, to weep; the terrible desire had awakened again in his breast. One day, as he sat alone weeping, it chanced that Wisdom met him. He told the old man what he had done.

'And Wisdom smiled sadly.

'"Many men," he said, "have spread that net for Truth; but they have never found her. On the grains of credulity she will not feed; in the net of wishes her feet cannot be held; in the air of these valleys she will not breathe. The birds you have caught are of the brood of Lies. Lovely and beautiful, but still lies; Truth knows them not."

'And the hunter cried out in bitterness—

'"And must I then sit still, to be devoured of this great burning?"

'And the old man said,

'"Listen, and in that you have suffered much and wept much, I will tell you what I know. He who sets out to search for Truth must leave these valleys of superstition for ever, taking with him not one shred that has belonged to them. Alone he must wander down into the Land of Absolute Negation and Denial; he must abide there; he must resist temptation; when the light breaks he must arise and follow it into the country of dry sunshine. The mountains of stern reality will rise before him: he must climb them: *beyond* them lies Truth."

'"And he will hold her fast! he will hold her in his hands!" the hunter cried.

'Wisdom shook his head.

'"He will never see her, never hold her. The time is not yet."

'"Then there is no hope?" cried the hunter.

'"There is this,' said Wisdom. "Some men have climbed on those mountains; circle above circle of bare rock they have scaled; and, wandering there, in those high regions, some have chanced to pick up on the ground, one white silver feather, dropped from the wing of Truth. And it shall come to pass," said the old man, raising himself prophetically, and pointing with his finger to the sky, "it shall come to pass, that, when enough of those silver feathers shall have been gathered by the hands of men, and shall have been woven into a cord, and the cord into a net, that in *that* net Truth may be captured. *Nothing but Truth can hold Truth.*"

'The hunter arose. "I will go," he said.

'But Wisdom detained him.

'"Mark you well—who leaves these valleys *never* returns to them. Though he should weep tears of blood seven days and nights upon the confines, he can never put his foot across them. Left—they are left for ever. Upon the road which you would travel there is no reward offered. Who goes, goes freely—for the great love that is in him. The work is his reward."

'"I go," said the hunter: "but upon the mountains, tell me, which path shall I take?"

'"I am the child of The-Accumulated-Knowledge-of-Ages," said the man; "I can walk only where many men have trodden. On those mountains few feet have passed; each man strikes out a path for himself. He goes at his own peril: my voice he hears no more. I may follow after him, but I cannot go before him.'

'Then Knowledge vanished.

'And the hunter turned. He went to his cage, and with his hands broke down the bars, and the jagged iron tore his flesh. It is sometimes easier to build than to break.

'One by one he took his plumed birds and let them fly. But, when he came to his dark-plumed bird, he held it, and looked into its beautiful eyes, and the bird uttered its low deep cry— "Immortality!"

'And he said quickly, "I cannot part with it. It is not heavy; it eats no food. I will hide it in my breast; I will take it with me." And he buried it there, and covered it over with his cloak.

'But the thing he had hidden grew heavier, heavier, heavier—till it lay on his breast like lead. He could not move with it. He could not leave those valleys with it. Then again he took it out and looked at it.

'"Oh, my beautiful, my heart's own!' he cried, "may I not keep you?"'

'He opened his hands sadly.

'"Go," he said. "It may happen that in Truth's song one note is like to yours; but *I* shall never hear it."

'Sadly he opened his hand, and the bird flew from him for ever.

'Then from the shuttle of imagination he took the thread of his wishes, and threw it on the ground; and the empty shuttle he put into his breast, for the thread was made in those valleys, but the shuttle came from an unknown country. He turned to go, but now the people came about him, howling.

'"Fool, hound, demented lunatic!" they cried. "How dared you break your cage and let the birds fly?"

'The hunter spoke; but they would not hear him.

'"Truth! who is she? Can you eat her? can you drink her? Who has ever seen her? Your birds were real: all could hear them sing! Oh, fool! vile reptile! atheist!" they cried, "you pollute the air."

'"Come, let us take up stones and stone him," cried some.

'"What affair is it of ours?" said others. "Let the idiot go," and went away. But the rest gathered up stones and mud and threw at him. At last, when he was bruised and cut, the hunter crept away into the woods. And it was evening about him.'

At every word the stranger spoke the fellow's eyes flashed back on him—yes, and yes, and yes! The stranger smiled. It was almost worth the trouble of exerting oneself, even on a lazy afternoon, to win those passionate flashes, more thirsty and desiring than the love-glances of a woman.

'He wandered on and on,' said the stranger, 'and the shade grew deeper. He was on the borders now of the land where it is always night. Then he stepped into it, and there was no light there. With his hands he groped; but each branch as he touched it broke off, and the earth was covered with cinders. At every step his foot sank in, and a fine cloud of impalpable ashes flew up into his face; and it was dark. So he sat down upon a stone and buried his face in his hands, to wait in that Land of Negation and Denial till the light came.

'And it was night in his heart also.

'Then from the marshes to his right and left cold mists arose and closed about him. A fine, imperceptible rain fell in the dark, and great drops gathered on his hair and clothes. His heart beat slowly, and a numbness crept through all his limbs. Then, looking up, two merry whisp lights came dancing. He lifted his head to look at them. Nearer, nearer they came. So warm, so bright, they danced like stars of fire. They stood before him at last. From the centre of the radiating flame in one looked out a woman's face, laughing, dimpled, with streaming yellow hair. In the centre of the other were merry laughing ripples, like the bubbles on a glass of wine. They danced before him.

'"Who are you," asked the hunter, "who alone come to me in my solitude and darkness?"

'"We are the twins Sensuality," they cried, "Our father's name is Human-Nature, and our mother's name is Excess. We are as old as the hills and rivers, as old as the first man; but we never die," they laughed.

'"Oh, let me wrap my arms about you!" cried the first: "they are soft and warm. Your heart is frozen now, but I will make it beat. Oh, come to me!"

'"I will pour my hot life into you," said the second; "your brain is numb, and your limbs are dead now; but they shall live with a fierce free life. Oh, let me pour it in!"

'"Oh, follow us," they cried, "and live with us. Nobler hearts than yours have sat here in this darkness to wait, and they have come to us and we to them; and they have never left us, never. All else is a delusion, but *we* are real, we are real. Truth is a shadow; the valleys of superstition are a farce; the earth is of ashes, the trees all rotten; but we—feel us—we live! You cannot doubt us. Feel us, how warm we are! Oh, come to us! Come with us!"

'Nearer and nearer round his head they hovered, and the cold drops melted on his forehead. The bright light shot into his eyes, dazzling him, and the frozen blood began to run. And he said—

'"Yes; why should I die here in this awful darkness? They are warm, they melt my frozen blood!" and he stretched out his hands to take them.

'Then in a moment there arose before him the image of the thing he had loved, and his hand dropped to his side.

'"Oh, come to us!" they cried.

'But he buried his face.

'"You dazzle my eyes," he cried, "you make my heart warm; but you cannot give me what I desire. I will wait here—wait till I die. Go!"

'He covered his face with his hands and would not listen; and when he looked up again they were two twinkling stars, that vanished in the distance.

'And the long, long night rolled on.

'All who leave the valley of superstition pass through that dark land; but some go through it in a few days, some linger there for months, some for years, and some die there.'

The boy had crept closer; his hot breath almost touched the stranger's hand; a mystic wonder filled his eyes.

'At last for the hunter a faint light played along the horizon and he rose to follow it; and he reached that light at last, and stepped into the broad sunshine. Then before him rose the almighty mountains of Dry-facts and Realities. The clear sunshine played on them, and the tops were lost in the clouds. At the foot many paths ran up. An exultant cry burst from the hunter. He chose the straightest and began to climb; and the rocks and ridges resounded with his song. They had exaggerated; after all, it was not so high, nor was the road so steep! A few days, a few weeks, a few months at most, and then the top! Not one feather only would he pick up; he would gather all that other men had found—weave the net—capture Truth—hold her fast—touch her with his hands—clasp her!

'He laughed in the merry sunshine, and sang loud. Victory was very near. Nevertheless, after a while the path grew steeper. He needed all his breath for climbing, and the singing died away. On the right and left rose huge rocks, devoid of lichen or moss, and in the lava-like earth chasms yawned. Here and there he saw a sheen of white bones. Now, too, the path began to grow less and less marked; then it became a mere trace, with a footmark here and there; then it ceased altogether. He sang no more, but struck forth a path for himself, until he reached a mighty wall of rock, smooth and without break, stretching as far as the eye could see. "I will rear a stair against it; and, once this wall climbed, I shall be almost there," he said bravely; and worked. With his shuttle of imagination he dug out stones; but half of them would not fit, and half a month's work would roll down because those below were ill chosen. But the hunter worked on, saying always to himself, "Once this wall climbed, I shall be almost there. This great work ended!"

'At last he came out upon the top, and he looked about him. Far below rolled the white mist over the valleys of superstition, and above him towered the mountains. They had seemed low before; they were of an immeasurable height now, from crown to foundation surrounded by walls of rock, that rose tier above tier in mighty circles. Upon them played the eternal sunshine. He uttered a wild cry. He bowed himself on to the earth, and when he rose his face was white. In absolute silence he walked on. He was very silent now. In those high regions the rarefied air is hard to breath by those born in the valleys; every breath he drew hurt him, and the blood oozed out from the tips of his fingers. Before the next wall of rock he began to work. The height of this seemed infinite, and he said nothing. The sound of his tool rang night and day upon the iron rocks into which he cut steps. Years passed over him, yet he worked on; but the wall towered up always above him to heaven. Sometimes he prayed that a little moss or lichen might spring up on those bare walls to be a companion to him; but it never came.' The stranger watched the boy's face.

'And the years rolled on: he counted them by the steps he had cut—a few for a year—only a few. He sang no more; he said no more, "I will do this or that"—he only worked. And at night, when the twilight settled down, there looked out at him from the holes and crevices in the rocks strange wild faces.

'"Stop your work, you lonely man, and speak to us," they cried.

'"My salvation is in work. If I should stop but for one moment you would creep down upon me," he replied. And they put out their long necks further.

'"Look down into the crevice at your feet," they said. "See what lie there—white bones! As brave and strong a man as you climbed to these rocks. And he looked up. He saw there was no use in striving; he would never hold Truth, never see her, never find her. So he lay down here, for he was very tired. He went to sleep for ever. He put himself to sleep. Sleep is very tranquil. You are not lonely when you are asleep, neither do you hands ache, nor your heart." And the hunter laughed between his teeth.

"'Have I torn from my heart all that was dearest; have I wandered alone in the land of night; have I resisted temptation; have I dwelt where the voice of my kind is never heard, and laboured alone, to lie down and be food for you, ye harpies?"

'He laughed fiercely; and the Echoes of Despair slunk away, for the laugh of a brave, strong heart is as a death-blow to them.

'Nevertheless they crept out again and looked at him.

"'Do you know that your hair is white?" they said, "that your hands begin to tremble like a child's? Do you see that the point of your shuttle is gone?—it is cracked already. If you should ever climb this stair," they said, "it will be your last. You will never climb another."

'And he answered, "*I know it!*" and worked on.

'The old, thin hands cut the stones ill and jaggedly, for the fingers were stiff and bent. The beauty and the strength of the man was gone.

'At last, an old, wizened, shrunken face looked out above the rocks. It saw the eternal mountains rise with walls to the white clouds; but its work was done.

'The old hunter folded his tired hands and lay down by the precipice where he had worked away his life. It was the sleeping time at last. Below him over the valleys rolled the thick white mist. Once it broke; and through the gap the dying eyes looked down on the trees and fields of their childhood. From afar seemed borne to him the cry of his own wild birds, and he heard the noise of people singing as they danced. And he thought he heard among them the voices of his old comrades; and he saw far off the sunlight shine on his early home. And great tears gathered in the hunter's eyes.

"'Ah! they who die there do not die alone," he cried.

'Then the mists rolled together again; and he turned his eyes away.

'"I have sought," he said, "for long years I have laboured; but I have not found her. I have not rested, I have not repined, and I have not seen her; now my strength is gone. Where I lie down worn out other men will stand, young and fresh. By the steps that I have cut they will climb; by the stairs that I have built they will mount. They will never know the name of the man who made them. At the clumsy work they will laugh; when the stones roll they will curse me. But they will mount, and on *my* work; they will climb, and by *my* stair! They will find her, and through me! And no man liveth to himself, and no man dieth to himself."

'The tears rolled from beneath the shrivelled eyelids. If Truth had appeared above him in the clouds now he could not have seen her, the mist of death was in his eyes.

'"My soul hears their glad step coming," he said; "and they shall mount! they shall mount! He raised his shrivelled hand to his eyes.

'Then slowly from the white sky above, through the still air, came something falling, falling, falling. Softly it fluttered down, and dropped on to the breast of the dying man. He felt it with his hands. It was a feather. He died holding it.'

The boy had shaded his eyes with his hand. On the wood of the carving great drops fell. The stranger must have laughed at him, or remained silent. He did so.

'How did you know it?' the boy whispered at last. 'It is not written there—not on that wood. How did you know it?'

'Certainly,' said the stranger, 'the whole of the story is not written here, but it is suggested. And the attribute of all true art, the highest and the lowest, is this—that it says more than it says, and takes you away from itself. It is a little door that opens into an infinite hall where you may find what you please. Men, thinking to detract, say, "People read more in this or that work of genius than was ever written in it," not perceiving that they pay the highest compliment. If we pick up the finger and nail of a real man, we can decipher a whole story—could almost reconstruct the creature again, from head to foot. But half the body of a Mumboo-jumbow* idol leaves us utterly in the dark as to what the rest was like. We see what we see, but nothing more. There is nothing so universally intelligible as truth. It has a thousand meanings, and suggests a thousand more.' He turned over the wooden thing. 'Though a man should carve it into matter with the least possible manipulative skill, it will yet find interpreters. It is the soul that looks out with burning eyes through the most gross fleshly filament. Whosoever should portray truly the life and death of a little flower—its birth, sucking in of nourishment, reproduction of its kind, withering and vanishing—would have shaped a symbol of all existence. All true facts of nature or the mind are related. Your little carving represents some mental facts as they really are, therefore fifty different true stories might be read from it. What your work wants is not truth, but beauty of external form, the other half of art.' He leaned almost gently towards the boy. 'Skill may come in time, but you will have to work hard. The love of beauty and the desire for it must be born in a man; the skill to reproduce it he must make. He must work hard.'

'All my life I have longed to see you,' the boy said.

The stranger broke off the end of his cigar, and lit it. The boy lifted the heavy wood from the stranger's knee and drew yet nearer him. In the dog-like manner of his drawing near there was something superbly ridiculous, unless one chanced to view it in another light. Presently the stranger said, whiffing, 'Do something for me.'

The boy started up.

'No; stay where you are. I don't want you to go anywhere; I want you to talk to me. Tell me what you have been doing all your life.'

The boy slunk down again. Would that the man had asked him to root up bushes with his hands for his horse to feed on; or to run to the far end of the plain for the fossils that lay there; or to gather the flowers that grew on the hills at the edge of the plain; he would have run and been back quickly—but now!

'I have never done anything,' he said.

'Then tell me of that nothing. I like to know what other

folks have been doing whose word I can believe. It is interesting. What was the first thing you ever wanted very much?'

The boy waited to remember, then began hesitatingly; but
soon the words flowed. In the smallest past we find an
inexhaustible mine when once we begin to dig at it.

A confused, disordered story—the little made large and the
large small, and nothing showing its inward meaning. It is not
till the past has receded many steps that before the clearest
eyes it falls into co-ordinate pictures. It is not till the "I" we
tell of has ceased to exist that it takes its place among other
objective realities, and finds its true niche in the picture. The
present and the near past is a confusion, whose meaning flashes
on us as it slinks away into the distance.

The stranger lit one cigar from the end of another, and
puffed and listened with half-closed eyes.

'I will remember more to tell you if you like,' said the fellow.

He spoke with that extreme gravity common to all very
young things who feel deeply. It is not till twenty that we learn
to be in deadly earnest and to laugh. The stranger nodded,
while the fellow sought for something more to relate. He would
tell all to this man of his—all that he knew, all that he had felt,
his most inmost sorest thought. Suddenly the stranger turned
upon him.

'Boy,' he said, 'you are happy to be here.'

Waldo looked at him. Was his delightful one ridiculing him?
Here, with this brown earth and these low hills, while the rare
wonderful world lay all beyond. Fortunate to be here!

The stranger read his glance.

'Yes,' he said, 'here with the karroo-bushes and red sand.
Do you wonder what I mean? To all who have been born in
the old faith there comes a time of danger, when the old slips
from us, and we have not yet planted our feet on the new. We
hear the voice from Sinai* thundering no more, and the still
small voice of reason is not yet heard. We have proved the
religion our mothers fed us on to be a delusion; in our
bewilderment we see no rule by which to guide our steps day
by day; and yet every day we must step somewhere.' The
stranger leaned forward and spoke more quickly, 'We have
never once been taught by word or act to distinguish between

religion and the moral laws on which it has artfully fastened itself, and from which it has sucked its vitality. When we have dragged down the weeds and creepers that covered the solid wall and have found them to be rotten wood, we imagine the wall itself to be rotten wood too. We find it is solid and standing only when we fall headlong against it. We have been taught that all right and wrong originate in the will of an irresponsible being. It is some time before we see how the inexorable "Thou shalt and shalt not," are carved into the nature of things. This is the time of danger.'

His dark, misty eyes looked into the boy's.

'In the end experience will inevitably teach us that the laws for a wise and noble life have a foundation infinitely deeper than the fiat of any being, God or man, even in the groundwork of human nature. She will teach us that whoso sheddeth man's blood, though by man his blood be not shed, though no man avenge and no hell await, yet every drop shall blister on his soul and eat in the name of the dead. She will teach that whoso takes a love not lawfully his own, gathers a flower with a poison on its petals; that whoso revenges, strikes with a sword that has two edges—one for his adversary, one for himself; that who lives to himself is dead, though the ground is not yet on him; that who wrongs another clouds his own sun; and that who sins in secret stands accused and condemned before the one Judge who deals eternal justice—his own all-knowing self.

'Experience *will* teach us this, and reason will show us why it *must* be so; but at first the world swings before our eyes, and no voice cries out, "This is the way, walk ye in it!" You are happy to be here, boy! When the suspense fills you with pain you build stone walls and dig earth for relief. Others have stood where you stand to-day, and have felt as you feel; and another relief has been offered them, and they have taken it.

'When the day has come when they have seen the path in which they might walk, they have not the strength to follow it. Habits have fastened on them from which nothing but death can free them; which cling closer than his sacerdotal sanctimony to a priest; which feed on the intellect like a worm sapping energy, hope, creative power, all that makes a man higher than a beast—leaving only the power to yearn, to regret, and to sink lower in abyss.

'Boy,' he said, and the listener was not more unsmiling now than the speaker, 'you are happy to be here! Stay where you are. If you ever pray, let it be only the one old prayer—"Lead us not into temptation." Live on here quietly. The time may yet come when you will be that which older men have hoped to be and never will be now.'

The stranger rose, shook the dust from his sleeve, and, ashamed at his own earnestness, looked across the bushes for his horse.

'We should have been on our way already,' he said. 'We shall have a long ride in the dark to-night.'

Waldo hastened to fetch the animal; but he returned leading it slowly. The sooner it came the sooner would its rider be gone.

The stranger was opening his saddle-bag, in which were a bright French novel and an old brown volume. He took the last and held it out to the boy.

'It may be of some help to you,' he said carelessly. 'It was a gospel to me when I first fell on it. You must not expect too much; but it may give you a centre round which to hang your ideas, instead of letting them lie about in a confusion that makes the head ache. We of this generation are not destined to eat and be satisfied as our fathers were; we must be content to go hungry.'

He smiled his automaton smile, and rebuttoned the bag. Waldo thrust the book into his breast, and while he saddled the horse the stranger made inquiries as to the nature of the road and the distance to the next farm.

When the bags were fixed Waldo took up his wood post and began to fasten it on to the saddle, tying it with the little blue cotton handkerchief from his neck. The stranger looked on in silence. When it was done the boy held the stirrup for him to mount.

'What is your name?' he inquired, ungloving his right hand when he was in the saddle.

The boy replied.

'Well, I trust we shall meet again some day, sooner or later.'

He shook hands with the ungloved hand; then drew on the glove, and touched his horse, and rode slowly away. The boy stood to watch him.

Once when the stranger had gone half across the plain he looked back.

'Poor devil,' he said, smiling and stroking his moustache. Then he looked to see if the little blue handkerchief were still safely knotted. 'Poor devil!'

He smiled, and then he sighed wearily, very wearily.

And Waldo waited till the moving speck had disappeared on the horizon; then he stooped and kissed passionately a hoof-mark in the sand. Then he called his young birds together, and put his book under his arm, and walked home along the stone wall. There was a rare beauty to him in the sunshine that evening.

CHAPTER III

Gregory Rose finds his Affinity

THE new man, Gregory Rose, sat at the door of his dwelling, his arms folded, his legs crossed, and a profound melancholy seeming to rest over his soul. His house was a little square daub-and-wattle building, far out in the 'karroo,' two miles from the homestead. It was covered outside with a sombre coating of brown mud, two little panes being let into the walls for windows. Behind it were the 'sheep-kraals,' and to the right a large dam, now principally containing baked mud. Far off, the little 'kopje' concealed the homestead, and was not itself an object conspicuous enough to relieve the dreary monotony of the landscape.

Before the door sat Gregory Rose in his shirt-sleeves, on a camp-stool, and ever and anon he sighed deeply. There was that in his countenance for which even his depressing circumstances failed to account. Again and again he looked at the little 'kopje,' at the milk-pail at his side, and at the brown pony, who a short way off cropped the dry bushes—and sighed.

Presently he rose and went into his house. It was one tiny room, the whitewashed walls profusely covered with prints cut from the 'Illustrated London News,' and in which there was a noticeable preponderance of female faces and figures. A stretcher filled one end of the hut, and a rack for a gun and a little hanging looking-glass diversified the gable opposite, while in the centre stood a chair and table. All was scrupulously neat and clean, for Gregory kept a little duster folded in the corner of his table-drawer, just as he had seen his mother do, and every morning before he went out he said his prayers, and made his bed, and dusted the table and the legs of the chairs, and even the pictures on the wall and the gun-rack.

On this hot afternoon he took from beneath his pillow a watch-bag made by his sister Jemima, and took out the watch.

Only half-past four! With a suppressed groan he dropped it back and sat down beside the table. Half-past four! Presently he roused himself. He would write to his sister Jemima. He always wrote to her when he was miserable. She was his safety-valve. He forgot her when he was happy; but he used her when he was wretched.

He took out ink and paper. There was a family crest and motto on the latter, for the Roses since coming to the colony had discovered that they were of distinguished lineage. Old Rose himself, an honest English farmer, knew nothing of his noble descent; but his wife and daughter knew—especially his daughter. There were Roses in England who kept a park and dated from the Conquest. So the colonial 'Rose Farm' became 'Rose Manor,' in remembrance of the ancestral domain, and the claim of the Roses to noble blood was established—in their own minds, at least.

Gregory took up one of the white, crested sheets; but on deeper reflection he determined to take a pink one, as more suitable to the state of his feelings. He began—

> 'Kopje Alone
> 'Monday Afternoon.

'MY DEAR JEMIMA,—'

Then he looked up into the little glass opposite. It was a youthful face reflected there, with curling brown beard and hair; but in the dark blue eyes there was a look of languid longing that touched him. He re-dipped his pen and wrote,—
— 'When I look up into the little glass that hangs opposite me, I wonder if that changed and sad face—'

Here he sat still and reflected. It sounded almost as if he might be conceited or unmanly to be looking at his own face in the glass. No, that would not do. So he looked for another pink sheet and began again.

> 'Kopje Alone,
> 'Monday Afternoon.

'DEAR SISTER,

'It is hardly six months since I left you to come to this spot, yet could you now see me I know what you would say, I know what mother would say—"Can that be our Greg—that thing with the strange look in his eyes?"

'Yes, Jemima, it is your Greg, and the change has been coming over me ever since I came here; but it is greatest since yesterday. You know what sorrows I have passed through Jemima: how unjustly I was always treated at school, the masters keeping me back and calling me a blockhead, though, as they themselves allowed, I had the best memory of any boy in the school, and could repeat whole books from beginning to end. You know how cruelly father always used me, calling me a noodle and a milksop, just because he couldn't understand my fine nature. You know how he has made a farmer of me instead of a minister, as I ought to have been; you know it all, Jemima; and how I have borne it all, not as a woman, who whines for every touch, but as a man should—in silence.

'But there are things, there is *a* thing, which the soul longs to pour forth into a kindred ear.

'Dear sister, have you ever known what it is to keep wanting and wanting and wanting to kiss someone's mouth, and you may not; to touch someone's hand, and you cannot? I am in love, Jemima.

'The old Dutch-woman from whom I hire this place has a little step-daughter, and her name begins with *E*.

'She is English. I do not know how her father came to marry a Boer-woman. It makes me feel so strange to put down that letter, that I can hardly go on writing—*E*. I've loved her ever since I came here. For weeks I have not been able to eat or drink; my very tobacco, when I smoke, has no taste; and I can remain for no more than five minutes in one place, and sometimes feel as though I were really going mad.

'Every evening I go there to fetch my milk. Yesterday she gave me some coffee. The spoon fell on the ground. She picked it up; when she gave it me her finger touched mine. Jemima, I do not know if I fancied it—I shivered hot, and she shivered too! I thought, "It is all right; she will be mine; she loves me!" Just then, Jemima, in came a fellow, a great, coarse fellow, a German—a ridiculous fellow, with curls right down to his shoulders; it makes one *sick* to look at him. He's only a servant of the Boer-woman's, and a low, vulgar, uneducated thing, that's never been to boarding-school in his life. He had been to the next farm seeking sheep. When he came in she said, "Good evening, Waldo. Have some coffee!" *and she kissed him.*

'All last night I heard nothing else but "Have some coffee; have some coffee." If I went to sleep for a moment I dreamed that her finger was pressing mine; but when I woke with a start I heard her say, "Good evening, Waldo. Have some coffee!"

'Is this madness?

'I have not eaten a mouthful to-day. This evening I go and propose to her. If she refuses me I shall go and kill myself to-morrow. There is a dam of water close by. The sheep have drunk most of it up, but there is still enough if I tie a stone to my neck.

'It is a choice between death and madness. I can endure no more. If this should be the last letter you ever get from me, think of me tenderly, and forgive me. Without her, life would be a howling wilderness, a long tribulation. She is my affinity; the one love of my youth, of my manhood; my sunshine; my God-given blossom.

'"They never loved who dreamed that they loved once,
And who saith, "I loved once"?——
Not angels, whose deep eyes look down through realms of light!*

'Your disconsolate brother, on what is, in all probability, the last and distracted night of his life,

GREGORY NAZIANZEN* ROSE.

'P.S.—Tell mother to take care of my pearl studs. I left them in the washhand-stand drawer. Don't let the children get hold of them.

'P.P.S.—I shall take this letter with me to the farm. If I turn down one corner you may know I have been accepted; if not, you may know it is all up with your heart-broken brother,

'G. N. R.'

Gregory having finished this letter, read it over with much approval, put it in an envelope, addressed it, and sat contemplating the ink-pot, somewhat relieved in mind.

The evening turned out chilly and very windy after the day's heat. From afar off, as Gregory neared the homestead on the brown pony, he could distinguish a little figure in a little red cloak at the door of the cow-kraal. Em leaned over the poles that barred the gate, and watched the frothing milk run through the black fingers of the herdsman, while the unwilling cows stood with tethered heads by the milking poles. She had thrown the red cloak over her own head, and held it under her chin with a little hand, to keep from her ears the wind, that playfully shook it, and tossed the little fringe of yellow hair into her eyes.

'Is it not too cold for you to be standing here?' said Gregory, coming softly close to her.

'Oh, no; it is so nice. I always come to watch the milking. That red cow with the short horns is bringing up the calf of the white cow that died. She loves it so—just as if it were her own. It is so nice to see her lick its little ears. Just look!'

'The clouds are black. I think it is going to rain to-night,' said Gregory.

'Yes,' answered Em, looking up as well as she could for the little yellow fringe.

'But I'm sure you must be cold,' said Gregory, and put his hand under the cloak, and found there a small fist doubled up, soft, and very warm. He held it fast in his hand.

'Oh, Em, I love you better than all the world besides! Tell me, *do* you love me a little?'

'Yes, I do,' said Em hesitating, and trying softly to free her hand.

'Better than everything; better than all the world, darling?' he asked, bending down so low that the yellow hair was blown into his eyes.

'I don't know,' said Em gravely. 'I do love you very much; but I love my cousin who is at school, and Waldo, very much. You see I have known them so long!'

'Oh, Em, do not talk to me so coldly,' Gregory cried, seizing the little arm that rested on the gate, and pressing it till she was half afraid. The herdsman had moved away to the other end of the 'kraal' now, and the cows, busy with their calves, took no notice of the little human farce. 'Em, if you talk so to me I will go mad! You must love me, love me better than all! You must give yourself to me. I have loved you since that first moment when I saw you walking by the stone wall with the jug in your hands. You were made for me, created for me! I will love you till I die! Oh, Em, do not be so cold, so cruel to me!'

He held her arm so tightly that her fingers relaxed their hold, and the cloak fluttered down on to the ground, and the wind played more roughly than ever with the little yellow head.

'I do love you very much,' she said; 'but I do not know if I want to marry you. I love you better than Waldo, but I can't tell if I love you better than Lyndall. If you would let me wait for a week, I think perhaps I could tell you.'

Gregory picked up the cloak and wrapped it round her.

'If you could but love me as I love you,' he said; 'but no woman *can* love as a man can. I will wait till next Saturday. I will not once come near you till then. Good-bye! Oh, Em,' he said, turning again, and twining his arm about her, and kissing her surprised little mouth, 'if you are not my wife I cannot live. I have never loved another woman, and I never shall!— never, never!'

'You make me afraid,' said Em. 'Come, let us go, and I will fill your pail.'

'I want no milk.—Good-bye! You will not see me again till Saturday.'

Late that night, when everyone else had gone to bed, the yellow-haired little woman stood alone in the kitchen. She had come to fill the kettle for the next morning's coffee, and now stood before the fire. The warm reflection lit the grave old-womanish little face, that was so unusually thoughtful this evening.

'Better than all the world; better than everything; he loves me better than everything!' She said the words aloud, as if they were more easy to believe if she spoke them so. She had given out so much love in her little life, and had got none of it back with interest. Now one said, 'I love you better than all the world.' One loved her better than she loved him. How suddenly rich she was. She kept clasping and unclasping her hands. So a beggar feels who falls asleep on the pavement wet and hungry, and who wakes in a palace-hall with servants and lights, and a feast before him. Of course the beggar's is only a dream, and he wakes from it; and this was real.

Gregory had said to her, 'I will love you as long as I live.' She said the words over and over to herself like a song.

'I will send for him to-morrow, and I will tell him how I love him back,' she said.

But Em needed not to send for him. Gregory discovered on reaching home that Jemima's letter was still in his pocket. And, therefore, much as he disliked the appearance of vacillation and weakness, he was obliged to be at the farmhouse before sunrise to post it.

'If I see her,' Gregory said, 'I shall only bow to her. She shall see that I am a man, one who keeps his word.'

As to Jemima's letter, he had turned down one corner of the page, and then turned it back, leaving a deep crease. That would show that he was neither accepted nor rejected, but that matters were in an intermediate condition. It was a more poetical way than putting it in plain words.

Gregory was barely in time with his letter, for Waldo was starting when he reached the homestead, and Em was on the door-step to see him off. When he had given the letter, and Waldo had gone, Gregory bowed stiffly and prepared to remount his own pony, but somewhat slowly. It was still early; none of the servants were about. Em came up close to him and put her little hand softly on his arm as he stood by his horse.

'I do love you best of all,' she said. She was not frightened now, however much he kissed her. 'I wish I was beautiful and nice,' she added, looking up into his eyes as he held her against his breast.

'My darling, to me you are more beautiful than all the women in the world; dearer to me than everything it holds. If you were in hell I would go after you to find you there! If you were dead, though my body moved, my soul would be under

the ground with you. All life as I pass it with you in my arms
will be perfect to me. It will pass like a ray of sunshine.'

Em thought how beautiful and grand his face was as she
looked up into it. She raised her hand gently and put it on his
forehead.

'You are so silent, so cold, my Em,' he cried. 'Have you
nothing to say to me?'

A little shade of wonder filled her eyes.

'I will do everything you tell me,' she said.

What else could she say? Her idea of love was only service.

'Then, my own precious one, promise never to kiss that
fellow again. I cannot bear that you should love anyone but
me. You must not! I will not have it! If every relation I had in
the world were to die to-morrow, I would be quite happy if I
still only had you! My darling, my love, why are you so cold?
Promise me not to love him any more. If you asked *me* to do
anything for *you*, I would do it, though it cost my life.'

Em put her hand very gravely round his neck.

'I will never kiss him,' she said, 'and I will try not to love
anyone else. But I do not know if I will be able.'

'Oh, my darling, I think of *you* all night, all day. I think of
nothing else, love, nothing else,' he said, folding his arms
about her.

Em was a little conscience-stricken; even that morning she
had found time to remember that in six months her cousin
would come back from school, and she had thought to remind
Waldo of the lozenges for his cough, even when she saw
Gregory coming.

'I do not know how it is,' she said humbly, nestling to him,
'but I cannot love you so much as you love me. Perhaps it is
because I am only a woman; but I *do* love you as much as I
can.'

Now the Kaffir maids were coming from the huts. He kissed
her again, eyes and mouth and hands, and left her.

Tant' Sannie was well satisfied when told of the betroth-
ment. She herself contemplated marriage within the year with
one or other of her numerous 'vrijers,'* and she suggested that
the weddings might take place together.

Em set to work busily to prepare her own household linen

and wedding garments. Gregory was with her daily, almost hourly, and the six months which elapsed before Lyndall's return passed, as he felicitously phrased it, 'like a summer night, when you are dreaming of someone you love.'

Late one evening, Gregory sat by his little love, turning the handle of her machine as she drew her work through it, and they talked of the changes they would make when the Boer-woman was gone, and the farm belonged to them alone. There should be a new room here, and a kraal there. So they chatted on. Suddenly Gregory dropped the handle, and impressed a fervent kiss on the fat hand that guided the linen.

'You are so beautiful, Em,' said the lover. 'It comes over me in a flood suddenly, how I love you.'

Em smiled.

'Tant' Sannie says when I am her age no one will look at me; and it is true. My hands are as short and broad as a duck's foot, and my forehead is so low, and I haven't any nose. I *can't* be pretty.'

She laughed softly. It was so nice to think he should be so blind.

'When my cousin comes to-morrow you will see a beautiful woman, Gregory,' she added presently. 'She is like a little queen: her shoulders are so upright, and her head looks as though it ought to have a little crown upon it. You must come to see her to-morrow as soon as she comes. I am sure you will love her.'

'Of course I shall come to see her, since she is your cousin; but do you think I could *ever* think any woman as lovely as I think you?'

He fixed his seething eyes upon her.

'You could not help seeing that she is prettier,' said Em, slipping her right hand into his; 'but you will never be able to like anyone so much as you like me.'

Afterwards, when she wished her lover good-night, she stood upon the doorstep to call a greeting after him; and she waited, as she always did, till the brown pony's hoofs became inaudible behind the 'kopje'.

Then she passed through the room where Tant' Sannie lay

snoring, and, through the little room that was all draped in white, waiting for her cousin's return, on to her own room.

She went to the chest of drawers to put away the work she had finished, and sat down on the floor before the lowest drawer. In it were the things she was preparing for her marriage. Piles of white linen, and some aprons and quilts; and in the little box in the corner a spray of orange-blossom which she had brought from a smouse. There too was a ring Gregory had given her, and a veil his sister had sent, and there was a little roll of fine embroidered work which Trana had given her. It was too fine and good even for Gregory's wife— just right for something very small and soft. She would keep it. And she touched it gently with her forefinger, smiling; and then she blushed and hid it far behind the other things. She knew so well all that was in that drawer, and yet she turned them all over as though she saw them for the first time, packed them all out, and packed them all in, without one fold or crumple; and then sat down and looked at them.

To-morrow evening when Lyndall came she would bring her here, and show it her all. Lyndall would so like to see it— the little wreath, and the ring, and the white veil! It would be so nice! Then Em fell to seeing pictures. Lyndall should live with them till she herself got married some day.

Every day when Gregory came home, tired from his work, he would look about and say, 'Where is my wife? Has no one seen my wife? Wife, some coffee!' and she would give him some.

Em's little face grew very grave at last, and she knelt up and extended her hands over the drawer of linen.

'Oh, God!' she said, 'I am so glad! I do not know what I have done that I should be so glad. Thank you!'

CHAPTER IV
Lyndall

SHE was more like a princess, yes, far more like a princess, than the lady who still hung on the wall in Tant' Sannie's bedroom. So Em thought. She leaned back in the little armchair; she wore a grey dressing-gown, and her long hair was combed out and hung to the ground. Em, sitting before her, looked up with mingled respect and admiration.

Lyndall was tired after her long journey, and had come to her room early. Her eyes ran over the familiar objects. Strange to go away for four years, and come back, and find that the candle standing on the dressing-table still cast the shadow of an old crone's head in the corner beyond the clothes-horse. Strange that even a shadow should last longer than man! She looked about among the old familiar objects; all was there, but the old self was gone.

'What are you noticing?' asked Em.

'Nothing and everything. I thought the windows were higher. If I were you, when I get this place I should raise the walls. There is not room to breathe here; one suffocates.'

'Gregory is going to make many alterations,' said Em; and drawing nearer to the grey dressing-gown respectfully. 'Do you like him, Lyndall? Is he not handsome?'

'He must have been a fine baby,' said Lyndall, looking at the white dimity curtain that hung above the window.

Em was puzzled.

'There are some men,' said Lyndall, 'whom you never can believe were babies at all; and others you never see without thinking how very nice they must have looked when they wore socks and pink sashes.'

Em remained silent; then she said with a little dignity, 'When you know him you will love him as I do. When I compare other people with him, they seem so weak and little. *Our* hearts are so cold, our loves are mixed up with so many other things. But he—no one is worthy of his love. I am not. It is so great and pure.'

'You need not make yourself unhappy on that point—your poor return for his love, my dear,' said Lyndall. 'A man's love is a fire of olive-wood. It leaps higher every moment; it roars, it blazes, it shoots out red flames; it threatens to wrap you round and devour you—you who stand by like an icicle in the glow of its fierce warmth. You are self-reproached at your own chilliness and want of reciprocity. The next day, when you go to warm your hands a little, you find a few ashes! 'Tis a long love and cool against a short love and hot; men, at all events, have nothing to complain of.'

'You speak so because you do not know men,' said Em, instantly assuming the dignity of superior knowledge so universally affected by affianced and married women in discussing man's nature with their uncontracted sisters.

'You will know them too some day, and then you will think differently,' said Em, with the condescending magnanimity which superior knowledge can always afford to show to ignorance.

Lyndall's little lip quivered in a manner indicative of intense amusement. She twirled a massive ring upon her forefinger—a ring more suitable for the hand of a man, and noticeable in design—a diamond cross let into gold, with the initials 'R. R.' below it.

'Ah, Lyndall,' Em cried, 'perhaps you are engaged yourself—that is why you smile. Yes; I am sure you are. Look at this ring!'

Lyndall drew the hand quickly from her.

'I am not in so great a hurry to put my neck beneath any man's foot; and I do not so greatly admire the crying of babies,' she said, as she closed her eyes half wearily and leaned back in the chair. 'There are other women glad of such work.'

Em felt rebuked and ashamed. How could she take Lyndall and show her the white linen, and the wreath, and the embroidery? She was quiet for a little while, and then began to talk about Trana and the old farm-servants, till she saw her companion was weary; then she rose and left her for the night. But after Em was gone Lyndall sat on, watching the old crone's face in the corner, and with a weary look, as though the whole world's weight rested on these frail young shoulders.

The next morning, Waldo, starting off before breakfast with a bag of mealies slung over his shoulder to feed the ostriches, heard a little step behind him.

'Wait for me; I am coming with you,' said Lyndall, adding as she came up to him, 'If I had not gone to look for you yesterday you would not have come to greet me till now. Do you not like me any longer, Waldo?'

'Yes—but—you are changed.'

It was the old clumsy, hesitating mode of speech.

'You liked the pinafores better?' she said quickly. She wore a dress of a simple cotton fabric, but very fashionably made, and on her head was a broad white hat. To Waldo she seemed superbly attired. She saw it. 'My dress has changed a little,' she said, 'and I also; but not to you. Hang the bag over your other shoulder, that I may see your face. You say so little that if one does not look at you you are an uncomprehended cipher.' Waldo changed the bag, and they walked on side by side. 'You have improved,' she said. 'Do you know that I have sometimes wished to see you while I was away; not often, but still sometimes.'

They were at the gate of the first camp now. Waldo threw over a bag of mealies, and they walked on over the dewy ground.

'Have you learnt much?' he asked her simply, remembering how she had once said, 'When I come back again I shall know everything that a human being can.'

She laughed.

'Are you thinking of my old boast? Yes; I have learnt something, though hardly what I expected, and not *quite* so much. In the first place, I have learnt that one of my ancestors must have been a very great fool; for they say nothing comes out in a man but one of his forefathers possessed it before him. In the second place, I have discovered that of all cursed places under the sun, where the hungriest soul can hardly pick up a few grains of knowledge, a girls' boarding-school is the worst. They are called finishing schools, and the name tells accurately what they are. They finish everything but imbecility and weakness, and that they cultivate. They are nicely adapted machines for experimenting on the question, "Into how little space a human soul can be crushed?" I have seen some souls so compressed that they would have fitted into a small thimble, and found room to move there—wide room. A woman who has been for many years at one of those places carries the mark of the beast on her till she dies, though she may expand a little afterwards, when she breathes in the free world.'

'Were you miserable?' he asked, looking at her with quick anxiety.

'I?—no. I am never miserable and never happy. I wish I were. But I should have run away from the place on the fourth day, and hired myself to the first Boer-woman whose farm I came to, to make fire under her soap-pot, if I had to live as the rest of the drove did. Can you form an idea, Waldo, of what it must be to be shut up with crackling old women, who are without knowledge of life, without love of the beautiful, without strength, to have your soul cultured by them? It is suffocation only to breathe the air they breathe; but I made them give me a room. I told them I should leave, and they knew I came there on my own account; so they gave me a bedroom without the companionship of one of those things that were having their brains slowly diluted and squeezed out of them. I did not learn music, because I had no talent; and when the drove made cushions and hideous flowers that the roses laugh at, and a footstool in six weeks that a machine would have made better in five minutes, I went to my room. With the money saved from such work I bought books and newspapers, and at night I sat up. I read, and epitomized what I read; and I found time to write some plays, and find out how hard it is to make your thoughts look anything but imbecile fools when you paint them with ink on paper. In the holidays I learnt a great deal more. I made acquaintances, saw a few places, and many people, and some different ways of living, which is more than any books can show one. On the whole, I am not dissatisfied with my four years. I have not learnt what I expected; but I have learnt something else. What have you been doing?'

'Nothing.'

'That is not possible. I shall find out by-and-by.'

They still stepped on side by side over the dewy bushes. Then suddenly she turned on him.

'Don't you wish you were a woman, Waldo?'

'No,' he answered readily.

She laughed.

'I thought not. Even you are too worldly-wise for that. I never met a man who did. This is a pretty ring,' she said, holding out her little hand, that the morning sun might make the diamonds sparkle. 'Worth fifty pounds at least. I will give it to the first man who tells me he would like to be a woman. There might be one on Robbin Island[1] who would win it perhaps, but I doubt it even there. It is delightful to be a woman; but every man thanks the Lord devoutly that he isn't one.'

She drew her hat to one side to keep the sun out of her eyes as she walked. Waldo looked at her so intently that he stumbled over the bushes. Yes, this was his little Lyndall who had worn the check pinafores; he saw it now, and he walked closer beside her. They reached the next camp.

'Let us wait at this camp and watch the birds,' she said, as an ostrich hen came bounding towards them, with velvety wings outstretched, while far away over the bushes the head of the cock was visible as he sat brooding on the eggs.

Lyndall folded her arms on the gate bar, and Waldo threw his empty bag on the wall and leaned beside her.

'I like these birds,' she said; 'they share each other's work, and are companions. Do you take an interest in the position of women, Waldo?'

'No.'

'I thought not. No one does, unless they are in need of a subject upon which to show their wit. And as for you, from of old you can see nothing that is not separated from you by a few millions of miles, and strewed over with mystery. If women were the inhabitants of Jupiter, of whom you had happened to hear something, you would pore over us and our condition night and day; but because we are before your eyes

---

[1] Lunatics at the Cape are sent to Robbin Island.

you never look at us. You care nothing that *this* is ragged and ugly,' she said, putting her little finger on his sleeve; 'but you strive mightily to make an imaginary leaf on an old stick beautiful. I'm sorry you don't care for the position of women: I should have liked us to be friends; and it is the only thing about which I think much or feel much—if, indeed, I have any feeling about anything,' she added flippantly, readjusting her dainty little arms. 'When I was a baby, I fancy my parents left me out in the frost one night, and I got nipped internally—it feels so!'

'I have only a few old thoughts,' he said, 'and I think them over and over again; always beginning where I left off. I never get any further. I am weary of them.'

'Like an old hen that sits on its eggs month after month and they never come out?' she said quickly. 'I am so pressed in upon by new things that, lest they should trip one another up, I have to keep forcing them back. My head swings sometimes. But this one thought stands, never goes—if I might but be one of those born in the future; then, perhaps, to be born a woman will not be to be born branded.'

Waldo looked at her. It was hard to say whether she were in earnest or mocking.

'I know it is foolish. Wisdom never kicks at the iron walls it can't bring down,' she said. 'But we are cursed, Waldo, born cursed from the time our mothers bring us into the world till the shrouds are put on us. Do not look at me as though I were talking nonsense. Everything has two sides—the outside that is ridiculous, and the inside that is solemn.'

'I am not laughing,' said the boy sedately enough; 'but what curses you?'

He thought she would not reply to him, she waited so long.

'It is not what is done to us, but what is made of us,' she said at last, 'that wrongs us. No man can be really injured but by what modifies himself. We all enter the world little plastic beings, with so much natural force, perhaps, but for the rest—blank; and the world tells us what we are to be, and shapes us by the ends it sets before us. To you it says—*Work*; and to us it says—*Seem*! To you it says—As you approximate to man's highest ideal of God, as your arm is strong and your knowledge great, and the power to labour is with you, so you shall gain all that human heart desires. To us it says—Strength shall not help you, nor knowledge, nor labour. You shall gain what men gain, but by other means. And so the world makes men and women.

'Look at this little chin of mine, Waldo, with the dimple in it. It is but a small part of my person; but though I had a knowledge of all things under the sun, and the wisdom to use it, and the deep loving heart of an angel, it would not stead me through life like this little chin. I can win money with it, I can win love; I can win power with it, I can win fame. What would knowledge help me? The less a woman has in her head the lighter she is for climbing. I once heard an old man say, that he never saw intellect help a woman so much as a pretty ankle; and it was the truth. They begin to shape us to our cursed end,' she said, with her lips drawn in to look as though they smiled, 'when we are tiny things in shoes and socks. We sit with our little feet drawn up under us in the window, and look out at the boys in their happy play. We want to go. Then a loving hand is laid on us: "Little one, you cannot go," they say; "your little face will burn, and your nice white dress be spoiled." We feel it must be for our good, it is so lovingly said; but we cannot understand; and we kneel still with one little cheek wistfully pressed against the pane. Afterwards we go and thread blue beads, and make a string for our neck; and we go and stand before the glass. We see the complexion we were not to spoil, and the white frock, and we look into our own great eyes. Then the curse begins to act on us. It finishes its work when we are grown women, who no more look out wistfully at a more healthy life; we are contented. We fit our sphere as a Chinese woman's foot fits her shoe, exactly, as though God had made both—and yet He knows nothing of either. In some of us the shaping to our end has been quite completed. The parts we are not to use have been quite atrophied, and have even dropped off; but in others, and we are not less to be pitied, they have been weakened and left. We wear the bandages, but our limbs have not grown to them; we know that we are compressed, and chafe against them.

'But what does it help? A little bitterness, a little longing when we are young, a little futile searching for work, a little passionate striving for room for the exercise of our powers,— and then we go with the drove. A woman must march with her regiment. In the end she must be trodden down or go with it; and if she is wise she goes.

'I see in your great eyes what you are thinking,' she said, glancing at him; 'I always know what the person I am talking to is thinking of. How is this woman who makes such a fuss worse off than I? I will show you by a very little example. We stand here at this gate this morning, both poor, both young, both friendless; there is not much to choose between us. Let us turn away just as we are, to make our way in life. This evening you will come to a farmer's house. The farmer, albeit you come alone and on foot, will give you a pipe of tobacco and a cup of coffee and a bed. If he has no dam to build and no child to teach, to-morrow you can go on your way with a friendly greeting of the hand. I, if I come to the same place to-night, will have strange questions asked me, strange glances cast on me. The Boer-wife will shake her head and give me food to eat with the Kaffirs, and a right to sleep with the dogs. That would be the first step in our progress—a very little one, but every step to the end would repeat it. We were equals once when we lay new-born babes on our nurse's knees. We will be equals again when they tie up our jaws for the last sleep.'

Waldo looked in wonder at the little quivering face; it was a glimpse into a world of passion and feeling wholly new to him.

'Mark you,' she said, 'we have always this advantage over you—we can at any time step into ease and competence, where you must labour patiently for it. A little weeping, a little wheedling, a little self-degradation, a little careful use of our advantages, and then some man will say—"Come, be my wife!" With good looks and youth marriage is easy to attain. There are men enough; but a woman who has sold herself, even for a ring and a new name, need hold her skirt aside for no creature in the street. They both earn their bread in one way. Marriage for love is the beautifullest external symbol of the union of souls; marriage without it is the uncleanliest traffic that defiles the world.' She ran her little finger savagely along the topmost bar, shaking off the dozen little dew-drops that still hung there. 'And they tell us we have men's chivalrous attention!' she cried. 'When we ask to be doctors, lawyers, law-makers, anything but ill-paid drudges, they say,—No; but you have men's chivalrous attention; now think of that and be satisfied! What would you do without it?'

The bitter little silvery laugh, so seldom heard, rang out across the bushes. She bit her little teeth together.

'I was coming up in Cobb and Co.'s the other day. At a little wayside hotel we had to change the large coach for a small one. We were ten passengers, eight men and two women. As I sat in the house the gentlemen came and whispered to me, "There is not room for all in the new coach, take your seat quickly." We hurried out, and they gave me the best seat, and covered me with rugs, because it was drizzling. Then the last passenger came running up to the coach—an old woman with a wonderful bonnet, and a black shawl pinned with a yellow pin.

'"There is no room," they said; "you must wait till next week's coach takes you up;" but she climbed on to the step, and held on at the window with both hands.

'"My son-in-law is ill, and I must go and see him," she said.

'"My good woman," said one, "I am really exceedingly sorry that your son-in-law is ill; but there is absolutely no room for you here."

'"You had better get down," said another, "or the wheel will catch you."

'I got up to give her my place.

'"Oh, no, no!" they cried, "we will not allow that."

'"I will rather kneel," said one, and he crouched down at my feet; so the woman came in.

'There were nine of us in that coach, and only one showed chivalrous attention—and that was a woman to a woman.

'I shall be old and ugly too one day, and I shall look for men's chivalrous help, but I shall not find it.

'The bees are very attentive to the flowers till their honey is done, and then they fly over them. I don't know if the flowers feel grateful to the bees; they are great fools if they do.'

'But some women,' said Waldo, speaking as though the words forced themselves from him at that moment, 'some women have power.'

She lifted her beautiful eyes to his face.

'Power! Did you ever hear of men being asked whether other souls should have power or not? It is born in them. You may dam up the fountain of water, and make it a stagnant marsh, or you may let it run free and do its work; but *you* cannot say whether it shall be there; *it is there*. And it will act, if not openly for good, then covertly for evil; but it will act. If Goethe had been stolen away a child, and reared in a robber horde in the depths of a German forest, do you think the world would have had "Faust" and "Iphigenie"?* But he would have been Goethe still—stronger, wiser than his fellows. At night, round their watch-fire, he would have chanted wild songs of rapine and murder, till the dark faces about him were moved, and trembled. His songs would have echoed on from father to son, and nerved the heart and arm—for evil. Do you think if Napoleon had been born a woman that he would have been contented to give small tea-parties and talk small scandal? He would have risen; but the world would not have heard of him as it hears of him now—a man, great and kingly, with all his sins; he would have left one of those names that stain the leaf of every history—the names of women, who, having power, but being denied the right to exercise it openly, rule in the dark, covertly, and by stealth, through the men whose passions they feed on, and by whom they climb.

'Power!' she said suddenly, smiting her little hand upon the rail. 'Yes, we have power; and since we are not to expend it in tunneling mountains, nor healing diseases, nor making laws, nor money, not on any extraneous object, we expend it on *you*. You are our goods, our merchandise, our material for operating on; we buy you, we sell you, we make fools of you, we act the wily old Jew with you, we keep six of you crawling to our little feet, and praying only for a touch of our little hand; and they say truly, there was never an ache or a pain or a broken heart but a woman was at the bottom of it. We are not to study law, nor science, nor art; so we study you. There is never a nerve or fibre in your man's nature but we know it. We keep six of you dancing in the palm of one little hand,' she said, balancing her outstretched arm gracefully, as though tiny beings disported themselves in its palm. 'There—we throw you away, and you sink to the Devil,' she said, folding her arms composedly. 'There was never a man who said one word for woman but he said two for man, and three for the whole human race.'

She watched the bird pecking up the last yellow grains; but Waldo looked only at her.

When she spoke again it was very measuredly.

'They bring weighty arguments against us when we ask for the perfect freedom of woman,' she said; 'but, when you come to the objections, they are like pumpkin devils with candles inside; hollow, and can't bite. They say that women do not wish for the sphere and freedom we ask for them and would not use it!

'If the bird *does* like its cage, and *does* like its sugar and will not leave it, why keep the door so very carefully shut? Why not open it, only a little? Do they know there is many a bird will not break its wings against the bars, but would fly if the doors were open.' She knit her forehead, and leaned further over the bars.

'Then they say, "If the women have the liberty you ask for, they will be found in positions for which they are not fitted!" If two men climb one ladder, did you ever see the weakest anywhere but at the foot? The surest sign of fitness is success. The weakest never wins but where there is handicapping. Nature left to herself will as beautifully apportion a man's work to his capacities as long ages ago she graduated the colours on the bird's breast. If we are not fit, you give us to no purpose the right to labour; the work will fall out of our hands into those that are wiser.'

She talked more rapidly as she went on, as one talks of that over which they have brooded long, and which lies near their hearts.

Waldo watched her intently.

'They say women have one great and noble work left them, and they do it ill.—That is true; they do it execrably. It is the work that demands the broadest culture, and they have not even the narrowest. The lawyer may see no deeper than his law books, and the chemist see no further than the windows of his laboratory, and they may do their work well. But the woman who does woman's work needs a many-sided, multiform culture; the heights and depths of human life must not be beyond the reach of her vision; she must have knowledge of men and things in many states, a wide catholicity of sympathy, the strength that springs from knowledge, and the magnanimity which springs from strength. *We* bear the world, and *we* make it. The souls of little children are marvellously delicate and tender things, and keep for ever the shadow that first falls on them, and that is the mother's or at best a woman's. There was never a great man who had not a great mother—it is hardly an exaggeration. The first six years of our life makes us; all that is added later is veneer; and yet some say, if a woman can cook a dinner or dress herself well she has culture enough.

'The mightiest and noblest of human work is given to us, and we do it ill. Send a navvy to work into an artist's studio, and see what you will find there! And yet, thank God, we have this work,' she added quickly: 'it is the one window through which we see into the great world of earnest labour. The meanest girl who dances and dresses becomes something higher when her children look up into her face and ask her questions. It is the only education we have and which they cannot take from us.'

She smiled slightly; 'They say that we complain of woman's being compelled to look upon marriage as a profession; but that she is free to enter upon it or leave it as she pleases.

'Yes—and a cat set afloat in a pond is free to sit in the tub till it dies there, it is under no obligation to wet its feet; and a drowning man may catch at a straw or not, just as he likes—it is a glorious liberty! Let any man think for five minutes of what old maidenhood means to a woman—and then let him be silent. Is it easy to bear through life a name that in itself signifies defeat? to dwell, as nine out of ten unmarried women must, under the finger of another woman? Is it easy to look forward to an old age without honour, without the reward of useful labour, without love? I wonder how many men there are who would give up everything that is dear in life for the sake of maintaining a high ideal purity.'

She laughed a little laugh that was clear without being pleasant. 'And then, when they have no other argument against us, they say—"Go on; but when you have made women what you wish, and her children inherit her culture, you will defeat yourself. Man will gradually become extinct from excess of intellect, the passions which replenish the race will die." Fools!' she said, curling her pretty lip. 'A Hottentot sits at the road-side and feeds on a rotten bone he has found there, and takes out his bottle of Cape-smoke* and swills at it, and grunts with satisfaction; and the cultured child of the nineteenth century sits in his arm-chair, and sips choice wines with the lip of a connoisseur, and tastes delicate dishes with a delicate palate, and with a satisfaction of which the Hottentot knows nothing. Heavy jaw and sloping forehead—all have gone with increasing intellect; but the animal appetites are there still— refined, discriminative, but immeasurably intensified. Fools! Before men forgave or worshipped, while they still were weak on their hind legs, did they not eat, and fight for wives? When all the later additions to humanity have vanished, will not the foundation on which they are built remain?'

She was silent then for a while, and said somewhat dreamily, more as though speaking to herself than to him—

'They ask, "What will you gain, even if man does not become extinct?—you will have brought justice and equality on to the earth, and sent love from it. When men and women are equals they will love no more. Your highly-cultured women will not be lovable, will not love."

'Do they see nothing, understand nothing? It is Tant' Sannie who buries husbands one after another, and folds her hands resignedly,—"The Lord gave, and the Lord hath taken away, and blessed be the name of the Lord,"—and she looks for another. It is the hard-headed, deep thinker who, when the wife who has thought and worked with him goes, can find no rest, and lingers near her till he finds sleep beside her.

'A great soul draws and is drawn with a more fierce intensity than any small one. By every inch we grow in intellectual height our love strikes down its roots deeper, and spreads out its arms wider. It is for love's sake yet more than for any other that we look for that new time.' She had leaned her head against the stones, and watched with her sad, soft eyes the retreating bird. 'Then when that time comes,' she said slowly, 'when love is no more bought or sold, when it is not a means of making bread, when each woman's life is filled with earnest, independent labour, then love will come to her, a strange sudden sweetness breaking in upon her earnest work; not sought for, but found. Then, but not now——'

Waldo waited for her to finish the sentence, but she seemed to have forgotten him.

'Lyndall,' he said, putting his hand upon her—she started—'if you think that that new time will be so great, so good, you who speak so easily——'

She interrupted him.

'Speak! speak!' she said; 'the difficulty is not to speak; the difficulty is to keep silence.'

'But why do you not try to bring that time?' he said with pitiful simplicity. 'When you speak I believe all you say; other people would listen to you also.'

'I am not so sure of that,' she said with a smile.

Then over the small face came the weary look it had worn last night as it watched the shadow in the corner. Ah, so weary!

'I, Waldo, I?' she said. 'I will do nothing good for myself, nothing for the world, till someone wakes me. I am asleep, swathed, shut up in self; till I have been delivered I will deliver no one.'

He looked at her wondering, but she was not looking at him.

'To see the good and the beautiful,' she said, 'and to have no strength to live it, is only to be Moses on the mountain of Nebo,* with the land at your feet and no power to enter. It would be better not to see it. Come,' she said, looking up into his face, and seeing its uncomprehending expression, 'let us go, it is getting late. Doss is anxious for his breakfast also,' she added, wheeling round and calling to the dog, who was endeavouring to unearth a mole, an occupation to which he had been zealously addicted from the third month, but in which he had never on any single occasion proved successful.

Waldo shouldered his bag, and Lyndall walked on before in silence, with the dog close to her side. Perhaps she thought of the narrowness of the limits within which a human soul may speak and be understood by its nearest of mental kin, of how soon it reaches that solitary land of the individual experience, in which no fellow-footfall is ever heard. Whatever her thoughts may have been, she was soon interrupted. Waldo came close to her, and standing still, produced with awkwardness from his breastpocket a small carved box.

'I made it for you,' he said, holding it out.

'I like it,' she said, examining it carefully.

The workmanship was better than that of the grave-post. The flowers that covered it were delicate, and here and there small conical protuberances were let in among them. She turned it round critically. Waldo bent over it lovingly.

'There is one strange thing about it,' he said earnestly, putting a finger on one little pyramid. 'I made it without these, and I felt something was wrong; I tried many changes, and at last I let these in, and then it was right. But why was it? They are not beautiful in themselves.'

'They relieve the monotony of the smooth leaves, I suppose.'

He shook his head as over a weighty matter.

'The sky is monotonous,' he said, 'when it is blue, and yet it is beautiful. I have thought of that often; but it is not monotony and it is not variety makes beauty. What is it? The sky, and your face, and this box—the same thing is in them all, only more in the sky and in your face. But what is it?'

She smiled.

'So you are at your old work still. Why, why, why? What is the reason? It is enough for me,' she said, 'if I find out what is beautiful and what is ugly, what is real and what is not. Why it is there, and over the final cause of things in general, I don't trouble myself; there must be one, but what is it to me? If I howl to all eternity I shall never get hold of it; and if I did I might be no better off. But you Germans are born with an aptitude for burrowing; you can't help yourselves. You must sniff after reasons, just as that dog must after a mole. He knows perfectly well he will never catch it, but he's under the imperative necessity of digging for it.'

'But he *might* find it.'

'*Might*!—but he never has and never will. Life is too short to run after mights; we must have certainties.'

She tucked the box under her arm and was about to walk

on, when Gregory Rose, with shining spurs, an ostrich feather in his hat, and a silver-headed whip, careered past. He bowed gallantly as he went by. They waited till the dust of the horse's hoofs had laid itself.

'There,' said Lyndall, 'goes a true woman—one born for the sphere that some women have to fill without being born for it. How happy he would be sewing frills into his little girl's frocks, and how pretty he would look sitting in a parlour, with a rough man making love to him! Don't you think so?'

'I shall not stay here when he is master,' Waldo answered, not able to connect any kind of beauty with Gregory Rose.

'I should imagine not. The rule of a woman is tyranny; but the rule of a man-woman grinds fine. Where are you going?'

'Anywhere.'

'What to do?'

'See—see everything.'

'You will be disappointed.'

'And were you?'

'Yes; and you will be more so. I want some things that men and the world give, you do not. If you have a few yards of earth to stand on, and a bit of blue over you, and something that you cannot see to dream about, you have all that you need, all that you know how to use. But I like to see real men. Let them be as disagreeable as they please, they are more interesting to me than flowers, or trees, or stars, or any other thing under the sun. Sometimes,' she added, walking on, and shaking the dust daintily from her skirts, 'when I am not too busy to find a new way of doing my hair that will show my little neck to better advantage, or over other work of that kind, sometimes it amuses me intensely to trace out the resemblance between one man and another: to see how Tant' Sannie and I, you and Bonaparte, St Simon on his pillar, and the emperor dining off larks' tongues, are one and the same compound, merely mixed in different proportions. What is microscopic in one is largely developed in another; what is a rudimentary in one man is an active organ in another; but all things are in all men, and one soul is the model of all. We shall find nothing new in human nature after we have once carefully dissected and analysed the one being we ever shall truly know—ourself.

The Kaffir girl threw some coffee on my arm in bed this morning; I felt displeased, but said nothing. Tant' Sannie would have thrown the saucer at her and sworn for an hour; but the feeling would be the same irritated displeasure. If a huge animated stomach like Bonaparte were put under a glass by a skilful mental microscopist, even he would be found to have an embryonic doubling somewhere indicative of a heart, and rudimentary buddings that might have become conscience and sincerity.—Let me take your arm, Waldo. How full you are of mealie dust.—No, never mind. It will brush off.—and sometimes what is more amusing still than tracing the likeness between man and man, is to trace the analogy there always is between the progress and development of one individual and of a whole nation; or again, between a single nation and the entire human race. It is pleasant when it dawns on you that the one is just the other written out in large letters; and very odd to find all the little follies and virtues, and developments and retrogressions, written out in the big world's book that you find in your little internal self. It is the most amusing thing I know of; but of course, being a woman, I have not often time for such amusements. Professional duties always first, you know. It takes a great deal of time and thought always to look perfectly exquisite, even for a pretty woman. Is the old buggy still in existence, Waldo?'

'Yes; but the harness is broken.'

'Well, I wish you would mend it. You must teach me to drive. I must learn something while I am here. I got the Hottentot girl to show me how to make "sarsarties"* this morning; and Tant' Sannie is going to teach me to make "kapjes." I will come and sit with you this afternoon while you mend the harness.'

'Thank you.'

'No, don't thank me; I come for my own pleasure. I never find anyone I can talk to. Women bore me, and men, I talk *so* to—"Going to the ball this evening?—Nice little dog that of yours.—Pretty little ears.—So fond of pointer pups!"—And they think me fascinating, charming! Men are like the earth and we are the moon; we turn always one side to them, and they think there is no other, because they don't see it—but there is.'

They had reached the house now.

'Tell me when you set to work,' she said, and walked towards the door.

Waldo stood to look after her, and Doss stood at his side, a look of painful uncertainty depicted on his small countenance, and one little foot poised in the air. Should he stay with his master or go? He looked at the figure with the wide straw hat moving towards the house, and he looked up at his master; then he put down the little paw and went. Waldo watched them both in at the door and then walked away alone. He was satisfied that at least his dog was with her.

CHAPTER V

Tant' Sannie holds an Upsitting,* and Gregory writes a Letter

IT was just after sunset, and Lyndall had not yet returned from her first driving-lesson, when the lean coloured woman standing at the corner of the house to enjoy the evening breeze, saw coming along the road a strange horseman. Very narrowly she surveyed him, as slowly he approached. He was attired in the deepest mourning, the black cape round his tall hat totally concealing the black felt, and nothing but a dazzling shirt-front relieving the funeral tone of his attire. He rode much forward in his saddle, with his chin resting on the uppermost of his shirt-studs, and there was an air of meek subjection to the will of Heaven, and to what might be in store for him, that bespoke itself even in the way in which he gently urged his steed. He was evidently in no hurry to reach his destination, for the nearer he approached to it the slacker did his bridle hang. The coloured woman having duly inspected him, dashed into the dwelling.

'Here is another one,' she cried—'a widower; I see it by his hat.'

'Good Lord!' said Tant' Sannie; 'it's the seventh I've had this month; but the men know where sheep and good looks and money in the bank are to be found,' she added, winking knowingly. 'How does he look?'

'Nineteen, weak eyes, white hair, little round nose,' said the maid.

'Then it's he! then it's he!' said Tant' Sannie triumphantly: 'Little Piet Vander Walt, whose wife died last month—two farms, twelve thousand sheep. I've not seen him, but my sister-in-law told me about him, and I dreamed about him last night.'

Here Piet's black hat appeared in the doorway, and the Boer-woman drew herself up in dignified silence, extended the tips of her fingers, and motioned solemnly to a chair. The young man seated himself, sticking his feet as far under it as they would go, and said mildly—

'I am Little Piet Vander Walt, and my father is Big Piet Vander Walt.'

Tant' Sannie said solemnly, 'Yes.'

'Aunt,' said the young man, starting up spasmodically; 'can I off-saddle?'

'Yes.'

He seized his hat, and disappeared with a rush through the door.

'I told you so! I knew it!' said Tant' Sannie. 'The dear Lord doesn't send dreams for nothing. Didn't I tell you this morning that I dreamed of a great beast like a sheep, with red eyes, and I killed it? Wasn't the white wool his hair, and the red eyes his weak eyes, and my killing him meant marriage? Get supper ready quickly; the sheep's inside and roaster-cakes. We shall sit up to-night.'

To young Piet Vander Walt that supper was a period of intense torture. There was something overawing in that assembly of English people, with their incomprehensible speech; and moreover, it was his first courtship: his first wife had courted him, and ten months of severe domestic rule had not raised his spirit nor courage. He ate little, and when he raised a morsel to his lips glanced guiltily round to see if he were not observed. He had put three rings on his little finger, with the intention of sticking it out stiffly when he raised a coffee-cup; now the little finger was curled miserably among its fellows. It was small relief when the meal was over, and Tant' Sannie and he repaired to the front room. Once seated there, he set his knees close together, stood his black hat upon them, and wretchedly turned the brim up and down. But supper had cheered Tant' Sannie, who found it impossible longer to maintain that decorous silence, and whose heart yearned over the youth.

'I was related to your aunt Selena who died,' said Tant' Sannie. 'My mother's step-brother's child was married to her father's brother's step-nephew's niece.'

'Yes, aunt,' said the young man, 'I knew we were related.'

'It was her cousin,' said Tant' Sannie, now fairly on the

flow, 'who had the cancer cut out of her breast by the other doctor, who was not the right doctor they sent for, but who did it quite as well.'

'Yes, aunt,' said the young man.

'I've heard about it often,' said Tant' Sannie. 'And he was the son of the old doctor that they say died on Christmas day; but I don't know if that's true. People do tell such awful lies. Why should he die on Christmas day more than on any other day?'

'Yes, aunt, why?' said the young man meekly.

'Did you ever have the toothache?' asked Tant' Sannie.

'No, aunt.'

'Well, they say that doctor,—not the son of the old doctor that died on Christmas day, the other that didn't come when he was sent for,—he gave such good stuff for the toothache that if you opened the bottle in the room where anyone was bad they got better directly. You could see it was good stuff,' said Tant' Sannie; 'it tasted horrid. *That* was a real doctor! He used to give a bottle so high,' said the Boer-woman, raising her hand a foot from the table, 'you could drink at it for a month and it wouldn't get done, and the same medicine was good for all sorts of sicknesses—croup, measles, jaundice, dropsy. *Now* you have to buy a new kind for each sickness. The doctors aren't so good as they used to be.'

'No, aunt,' said the young man, who was trying to gain courage to stick out his legs and clink his spurs together. He did so at last.

Tant' Sannie had noticed the spurs before; but she thought it showed a nice manly spirit, and her heart warmed yet more to the youth.

'Did you ever have convulsions when you were a baby?' asked Tant' Sannie.

'Yes,' said the young man.'

'Strange!' said Tant' Sannie; 'I had convulsions too. Wonderful that we should be so much alike!'

'Aunt,' said the young man explosively, 'can we sit up to-night?'

Tant' Sannie hung her head and half closed her eyes; but finding that her little wiles were thrown away, the young man staring fixedly at his hat, she simpered 'Yes,' and went away to fetch candles.

In the dining-room Em worked at her machine, and Gregory sat close beside her, his great blue eyes turned to the window where Lyndall leaned out talking to Waldo.

Tant' Sannie took two candles out of the cupboard and held them up triumphantly, winking all round the room.

'He's asked for them,' she said.

'Does he want them for his horse's rubbed back?' asked Gregory, new to up-country life.

'No,' said Tant' Sannie indignantly; 'we're going to sit up!' and she walked off in triumph with the candles.

Nevertheless, when all the rest of the house had retired, when the long candle was lighted, when the coffee-kettle was filled, when she sat in the elbow-chair, with her lover on a chair close beside her, and when the vigil of the night was fairly begun, she began to find it wearisome. The young man looked chilly, and said nothing.

'Won't you put your feet on my stove?' said Tant' Sannie

'No, thank you, aunt,' said the young man, and both lapsed into silence.

At last Tant' Sannie, afraid of going to sleep, tapped a strong cup of coffee for herself, and handed another to her lover. This visibly revived both.

'How long were you married, cousin?'

'Ten months, aunt.'

'How old was your baby?'

'Three days when it died.'

'It's very hard when we must give our husbands and wives to the Lord,' said Tant' Sannie.

'Very,' said the young man; 'but it's the Lord's will.'

'Yes,' said Tant' Sannie, and sighed.

'She was such a good wife, aunt: I've known her break a churn-stick over a maid's head for only letting dust come on a milk-cloth.'

Tant' Sannie felt a twinge of jealousy. She had never broken a churn-stick over a maid's head.

'I hope your wife made a good end,' she said.

'Oh, beautiful, aunt: she said up a psalm and two hymns and a half before she died.'

'Did she leave any messages?' asked Tant' Sannie.

'No,' said the young man; 'but the night before she died I was lying at the foot of her bed; I felt her foot kick me.'

'"Piet," she said.

'"Annie, my heart," said I.

'"My little baby that died yesterday has been here, and it stood over the waggon-box," she said.

'"What did it say?" I asked.

'"It said that if I died you must marry a fat woman."

'"I will," I said, and I went to sleep again. Presently she woke me.

'"The little baby has been here again, and it says you must marry a woman over thirty, and who's had two husbands."

'I didn't go to sleep after that for a long time, aunt; but when I did she woke me.

'"The baby has been here again," she said, "and it says you mustn't marry a woman with a mole." I told her I wouldn't; and the next day she died.'

'That was a vision from the Redeemer,' said Tant' Sannie.

The young man nodded his head mournfully. He thought of a younger sister of his wife's who was not fat, and who *had* a mole, and of whom his wife had always been jealous, and he wished the little baby had liked better staying in heaven than coming and standing over the waggon-chest.

'I suppose that's why you came to me,' said Tant' Sannie.

'Yes, aunt. And pa said I ought to get married before shearing-time. It is bad if there's no one to see after things then; and the maids waste such a lot of fat.'

'When do you want to get married?'

'Next month, aunt,' said the young man in a tone of hopeless resignation. 'May I kiss you, aunt?'

'Fie! fie!' said Tant' Sannie, and then gave him a resounding kiss. 'Come, draw your chair a little closer,' she said, and, their elbows now touching, they sat on through the night.

The next morning at dawn, as Em passed through Tant' Sannie's bedroom, she found the Boer-woman pulling off her boots preparatory to climbing into bed.

'Where is Piet Vander Walt?'

'Just gone,' said Tant' Sannie; 'and I am going to marry him this day four weeks. I am dead sleepy,' she added; 'the stupid thing doesn't know how to talk love-talk at all,' and she climbed into the four-poster, clothes and all, and drew the quilt up to her chin.

On the day preceding Tant' Sannie's wedding, Gregory Rose sat in the blazing sun on the stone wall behind his daub-and-wattle house. It was warm, but he was intently watching a small buggy that was being recklessly driven over the bushes in the direction of the farmhouse. Gregory never stirred till it had vanished; then, finding the stones hot, he slipped down and walked into the house. He kicked the little pail that lay in the doorway, and sent it into one corner; that did him good. Then he sat down on the box, and began cutting letters out of a piece of newspaper. Finding that the snippings littered the floor, he picked them up and began scribbling on his blotting-paper. He tried the effect of different initials before the name Rose: G. Rose, E. Rose, L. Rose, L. Rose, L. L. L. L. Rose. When he had covered the sheet, he looked at it discontentedly a little while, then suddenly began to write a letter.

'Beloved Sister,

'It is a long while since I last wrote to you, but I have had no time. This is the first morning I have been at home since I don't know when. Em always expects me to go down to the farm-house in the morning; but I didn't feel as though I could stand the ride to-day.

'I have much news for you.

'Tant' Sannie, Em's Boer stepmother, is to be married to-morrow. She is gone to town to-day, and the wedding feast is to be at her brother's farm. Em and I are going to ride over on horseback, but her cousin is going to ride in the buggy with that German. I don't think I've written to you since she came back from school. I don't think you would like her at all, Jemima; there's something so proud about her. She thinks just because she's handsome there's nobody good enough to talk to

her, and just as if there had nobody else but her been to
boarding-school before.

'They are going to have a grand affair to-morrow: all the
Boers about are coming, and they are going to dance all night;
but I don't think I shall dance at all; for, as Em's cousin says,
these Boer dances are low things. I am sure I only danced at
the last to please Em. I don't know why she is fond of dancing.
Em talked of our being married on the same day as Tant'
Sannie; but I said it would be nicer for her if she waited till the
shearing was over, and I took her down to see you. I suppose
she will have to live with us (Em's cousin, I mean), as she has
not anything in the world but a poor fifty pounds. I don't like
her *at all*, Jemima, and I don't think you would. She's got
such queer ways: she's always driving about in a gig with that
low German; and I don't think it's at all the thing for a woman
to be going about with a man she's not engaged to. Do you? If
it was me now, of course, who am a kind of connection, it
would be different. The way she treats me, considering that I
am so soon to be her cousin, is not at all nice. I took down my
album the other day with your likenesses in it, and I told her
she could look at it, and put it down close to her; but she just
said, "Thank you," and never even touched it, as much as to
say—What are your relations to me?

'She gets the wildest horses in that buggy, and a horrid
snappish little cur belonging to the German sitting in front,
and then she drives out alone. I don't think it's at all proper
for a woman to drive out alone; I wouldn't allow it if she was
my sister. The other morning, I don't know how it happened,
I was going in the way from which she was coming, and that
little beast—they call him Doss—began to bark when he saw
me—he always does, the little wretch—and the horses began
to spring, and kicked the splash-board all to pieces. It was a
sight to see, Jemima! She has got the littlest hands I ever
saw—I could hold them both in one of mine, and not know
that I'd got anything except that they were so soft; but she
held those horses in as though they were made of iron. When
I wanted to help her she said, "No, thank you; I can manage
them myself. I've got a pair of bits that would break their jaws

if I used them well," and she laughed and drove away. It's so unwomanly.

'Tell father my hire of the ground will not be out for six months, and before that Em and I will be married. My pair of birds is breeding now, but I haven't been down to see them for three days. I don't seem to care about anything any more. I don't know what it is: I'm not well. If I go into town on Saturday I will let the doctor examine me; but perhaps she'll go in herself. It's a very strange thing, Jemima, but she never will send her letters to post by me. If I ask her she has none, and the very next day she goes in and posts them herself. You mustn't say anything about it, Jemima, but *twice* I've brought her letters from the post in a gentleman's hand, and I'm sure they were both from the same person, because I noticed every little mark, even the dotting of the *i*'s. Of course it's nothing to *me*; but for Em's sake I can't help feeling an interest in her, however much I may dislike her myself; and I hope she's up to nothing. I pity the man who marries *her*; I wouldn't be him for *anything*. If I had a wife with pride I'd make her give it up, *sharp*. I don't believe in a man who can't make a woman obey him. Now Em—I'm very fond of her, as you know—but if I tell her to put on a certain dress, that dress she puts on; and if I tell her to sit on a certain seat, on that seat she sits; and if I tell her not to speak to a certain individual, she does not speak to them. If a man lets a woman do what he doesn't like, *he's a muff*.

'Give my love to mother and the children. The "veld"* here is looking pretty good, and the sheep are better since we washed them. Tell father the dip he recommended is very good.

'Em sends her love to you. She is making me some woollen shirts; but they don't fit me so nicely as those mother made me.

'Write soon to

'Your loving brother,

'GREGORY.

'P.S.—She drove past just now; I was sitting on the kraal wall right before her eyes, and she never even bowed.

'G. N. R.'

CHAPTER VI
A Boer-wedding

'I DIDN'T know before you were so fond of riding hard,' said Gregory to his little betrothed.

They were cantering slowly on the road to Oom Muller's on the morning of the wedding.

'Do you call this riding hard?' asked Em in some astonishment.

'Of course I do! It's enough to break the horses' necks, and knock one up for the whole day besides,' he added testily; then twisted his head to look at the buggy that came on behind. 'I thought Waldo was such a mad driver; they are taking it easily enough to-day,' said Gregory. 'One would think the black stallions were lame.'

'I suppose they want to keep out of our dust,' said Em. 'See, they stand still as soon as we do.'

Perceiving this to be the case, Gregory rode on.

'It's all that horse of yours: she kicks up such a confounded dust, I can't stand it myself,' he said.

Meanwhile the cart came on slowly enough.

'Take the reins, said Lyndall, 'and make them walk. I want to rest and watch their hoofs to-day—not to be exhilarated; I am so tired.'

She leaned back in her corner, and Waldo drove on slowly in the grey dawn light along the level road. They passed the very milk-bush behind which, so many years before, the old German had found the Kaffir woman. But their thoughts were not with him that morning: they were thoughts of the young, that run out to meet the future and labour in the present. At last he touched her arm.

'What is it?'

'I feared you had gone to sleep, and might be jolted out,' he said; 'you sat so quietly.'

'No; do not talk to me; I am not asleep;' but after a time she said suddenly, 'It must be a terrible thing to bring a human being into the world.'

Waldo looked round; she sat drawn into the corner, her blue cloud wound tightly about her, and she still watched the horses' feet. Having no comment to offer on her somewhat unexpected remark, he merely touched up his horses.

'I have no conscience, none,' she added; 'but I would not like to bring a soul into this world. When it sinned and when it suffered something like a dead hand would fall on me,— "You did it, you, for your own pleasure you created this thing! See your work!" If it lived to be eighty it would always hang like a millstone round my neck, have the right to demand good from me, and curse me for its sorrow. A parent is only like to God: if his work turns out bad so much the worse for him; he *dare* not wash his hands of it. Time and years can never bring the day when you can say to your child, "Soul, what have I to do with you?"'

Waldo said dreamily,—

'It is a marvellous thing that one soul should have power to cause another.'

She heard the words as she heard the beating of the horses' hoofs; her thoughts ran on in their own line.

'They say, "God sends the little babies." Of all the dastardly revolting lies men tell to suit themselves, I hate that most. I suppose my father said so when he knew he was dying of consumption, and my mother when she knew she had nothing to support me on, and they created me to feed like a dog from stranger hands. Men do not say God sends the books, or the newspaper articles, or the machines they make; and then sigh, and shrug their shoulders, and say they can't help it. Why do they say so about other things? Liars! "God sends the little babies!"' She struck her foot fretfully against the splashboard. 'The small children say so earnestly. *They* touch the little stranger reverently who has just come from God's far country, and they peep about the room to see if not one white feather has dropped from the wing of the angel that brought him. On their lips the phrase means much; on all others it is a *deliberate lie*. Noticeable too,' she said, dropping in an instant from the passionate into a low, mocking tone, 'when people are married, though they should have sixty children, they throw the whole *onus* on God. When they are not, we hear nothing about god's having sent them. When there has been no legal contract between the parents, who sends the little children then? The Devil perhaps!' she laughed her little silvery, mocking laugh. 'Odd that some men should come from hell and some from heaven, and yet all look so much alike when they get here.'

Waldo wondered at her. He had not the key to her thoughts, and did not see the string on which they were strung. She drew her cloud tighter about her.

'It must be very nice to believe in the Devil,' she said; 'I wish I did. If it would be of any use I would pray three hours night and morning on my bare knees, "God let me believe in Satan." He is so useful to those people who do. They may be as selfish and as sensual as they please, and, between God's will and the Devil's action, always have some one to throw their sin on. But we, wretched unbelievers, we bear our own burdens; we must say, "I myself did it, *I*. Not God, not Satan; I myself!" That is the sting that strikes deep. Waldo,' she said gently, with a sudden and complete change of manner, 'I like you so much, I love you.' She rested her cheek softly against his shoulder. 'When I am with you I never know that I am a woman and you are a man; I only know that we are both things that think. Other men when I am with them, whether I love them or not, they are mere bodies to me; but you are a spirit; I like you. Look,' she said quickly, sinking back into her corner, 'what a pretty pinkness there is on all the hill-tops! The sun will rise in a moment.'

Waldo lifted his eyes to look round over the circle of golden hills; and the horses, as the first sunbeams touched them, shook their heads and champed their bright bits, till the brass settings in their harness glittered again.

It was eight o'clock when they neared the farmhouse: a red-brick building, with kraals to the right and a small orchard to the left. Already there were signs of unusual life and bustle: one cart, a waggon, and a couple of saddles against the wall betokened the arrival of a few early guests, whose numbers would soon be largely increased. To a Dutch country wedding guests start up in numbers astonishing to one who has merely ridden through the plains of sparsely-inhabited karroo.

As the morning advances, riders on many shades of steeds appear from all directions, and add their saddles to the long rows against the walls, shake hands, drink coffee, and stand about outside in groups to watch the arriving carts and ox-waggons, as they are unburdened of their heavy freight of massive Tantes and comely daughters, followed by swarms of children of all sizes, dressed in all manner of print and moleskin, who are taken care of by Hottentot, Kaffir, and half-caste nurses, whose many-shaded complexions, ranging from light yellow up to ebony black, add variety to the animated scene. Everywhere is excitement and bustle, which gradually increases as the time for the return of the wedding party approaches. Preparations for the feast are actively advancing in the kitchen; coffee is liberally handed round, and amid a profound sensation, and the firing of guns, the horse-waggon draws up, and the wedding party alight. Bride and bride-groom, with their attendants, march solemnly to the marriage-chamber, where bed and box are decked out in white, with ends of ribbon and artificial flowers, and where on a row of chairs the party solemnly seat themselves. After a time brides-maid and best man rise, and conduct in with ceremony each individual guest, to wish success and to kiss bride and bride-groom. Then the feast is set on the table, and it is almost sunset before the dishes are cleared away, and the pleasure of the day begins. Everything is removed from the great front room, and the mud floor, well rubbed with bullock's blood, glistens like polished mahogany. The female portion of the assembly flock into the side-rooms to attire themselves for the evening; and re-issue clad in white muslin, and gay with bright ribbons and brass jewellery. The dancing begins as the first tallow candles are stuck up about the walls, the music coming from a couple of fiddlers in a corner of the room. Bride and bridegroom open the ball, and the floor is soon covered with whirling couples, and every one's spirits rise. The bridal pair mingle freely in the throng, and here and there a musical man sings vigorously as he drags his partner through the Blue Water or John Speriwig;* boys shout and applaud, and the enjoyment and confusion are intense, till eleven o'clock comes. By this time the children who swarm in the side-rooms are not to be kept quiet longer, even by hunches of bread and cake; there is a general howl and wail, that rises yet higher than the scraping of fiddles, and mothers rush from their partners to knock small heads together, and cuff little nursemaids, and force the wailers down into unoccupied corners of beds, under tables, and behind boxes. In half-an-hour every variety of childish snore is heard on all sides, and it has become perilous to raise or set down a foot in any of the side-rooms lest a small head or hand should be crushed. Now, too, the busy feet have broken the solid coating of the floor, and a cloud of fine dust arises, that makes a yellow halo round the candles, and sets asthmatic people coughing, and grows denser, till to recognize any one on the opposite side of the room becomes impossible, and a partner's face is seen through a yellow mist.

At twelve o'clock the bride is led to the marriage-chamber and undressed; the lights are blown out, and the bridegroom is brought to the door by the best man, who gives him the key; then the door is shut and locked, and the revels rise higher than ever. There is no thought of sleep till morning, and no unoccupied spot where sleep may be found.

It was at this stage of the proceedings on the night of Tant' Sannie's wedding that Lyndall sat near the doorway in one of the side-rooms, to watch the dancers as they appeared and disappeared in the yellow cloud of dust. Gregory sat moodily in a corner of the large dancing-room. His little betrothed touched his arm.

'I wish you would go and ask Lyndall to dance with you,' she said; 'she must be so tired; she has sat still the whole evening.'

'I have asked her three times,' replied her lover shortly. 'I'm not going to be *her* dog, and creep to *her* feet, just to give her the pleasure of kicking me—not for you, Em, nor for anybody else.'

'Oh, I didn't know you had asked her, Greg,' said his little betrothed humbly; and she went away to pour out coffee.

Nevertheless, some time after, Gregory, found he had shifted so far round the room as to be close to the door where

Lyndall sat. After standing for some time he inquired whether he might not bring her a cup of coffee. She declined: but still he stood on (why should he not stand there as well as anywhere else?), and then he stepped into the bedroom.

'May I not bring you a stove, Miss Lyndall, to put your feet on?'

'Thank you.'

He sought for one, and put it under her feet.

'There is a draught from that broken window; shall I stuff something in the pane?'

'No; we want air.'

Gregory looked round, but, nothing else suggesting itself, he sat down on a box on the opposite side of the door. Lyndall sat before him, her chin resting in her hand; her eyes, steel-grey by day but black by night, looked through the doorway into the next room. After a time he thought she had entirely forgotten his proximity, and he dared to inspect the little hands and neck as he never dared when he was in momentary dread of the eyes being turned upon him. She was dressed in black, which seemed to take her yet further from the white-clad, gewgawed women about her; and the little hands were white, and the diamond ring glittered. Where had she got that ring? He bent forward a little and tried to decipher the letters, but the candle-light was too faint. When he looked up her eyes were fixed on him. She was looking at him—not, Gregory felt, as she had ever looked at him before; not as though he were a stump or a stone that chance had thrown in her way. To-night, whether it were critically, or kindly, or unkindly he could not tell, but she looked at him, at the man, Gregory Rose, with attention. A vague elation filled him. He clenched his fist tight to think of some good idea he might express to her; but of all those profound things he had pictured himself as saying to her, when he sat alone in the daub-and-wattle house, not one came. He said at last,

'These Boer dances are very low things;' and then, as soon as it had gone from him, he thought it was not a clever remark, and wished it back.

Before Lyndall replied Em looked in at the door.

'Oh, come,' she said; 'they are going to have the cushion-dance. I do not want to kiss any of these fellows. Take me quickly.'

She slipped her hand into Gregory's arm.

'It is so dusty, Em; do you care to dance any more?' he asked, without rising.

'Oh, I do not mind the dust, and the dancing rests me.'

But he did not move.

'I feel tired; I do not think I shall dance again,' he said.

Em withdrew her hand, and a young farmer came to the door and bore her off.

'I have often imagined,' remarked Gregory—but Lyndall had risen.

'I am tired,' she said. 'I wonder where Waldo is; he must take me home. These people will not leave off till morning, I suppose; it is three already.'

She made her way past the fiddlers, and a bench full of tired dancers, and passed out at the front door. On the 'stoep'* a group of men and boys were smoking, peeping in at the windows, and cracking coarse jokes. Waldo was certainly not among them, and she made her way to the carts and waggons drawn up at some distance from the homestead.

'Waldo,' she said, peering into a large cart, 'is that you? I am so dazed with the tallow candles, I can see nothing.'

He had made himself a place between the two seats. She climbed up and sat on the sloping floor in front.

'I thought I should find you here,' she said, drawing her skirt up about her shoulders. 'You must take me home presently, but not now.'

She leaned her head on the seat near to his, and they listened in silence to the fitful twanging of the fiddles as the night-wind bore it from the farmhouse, and to the ceaseless thud of the dancers, and the peals of gross laughter. She stretched out her little hand to feel for his.

'It is so nice to lie here and hear that noise,' she said. 'I like to feel that strange life beating up against me. I like to realize forms of life utterly unlike mine.' She drew a long breath. 'When my own life feels small, and I am oppressed with it, I like to crush together, and see it in a picture, in an instant, a multitude of disconnected unlike phases of human life—a mediæval monk with his string of beads pacing the quiet orchard, and looking up from the grass at his feet to the heavy fruit-trees; little Malay boys playing naked on a shining sea-beach; a Hindoo philosopher alone under his banyan tree, thinking, thinking, so that in the thought of God he may lose himself; a troop of Bacchanalians dressed in white, with crowns of vine-leaves, dancing along the Roman streets; a martyr on the night of his death looking through the narrow window to the sky, and feeling that already he has the wings that shall bear him up' (she moved her hand dreamily over her face); 'an epicurean discoursing at a Roman bath to a knot of his disciples on the nature of happiness; a Kaffir witch-doctor seeking for herbs by moonlight, while from the huts on the hill-side come the sound of dogs barking, and the voices of women and children; a mother giving bread and milk to her children in little wooden basins and singing the evening song. I like to see it all; I feel it run through me—that life belongs to me; it makes my little life larger; it breaks down the narrow walls that shut me in.'

She sighed, and drew a long breath.

'Have you made any plan?' she asked him presently.

'Yes,' he said, the words coming in jets, with pauses between; 'I will take the grey mare,—I will travel first—I will see the world—then I will find work.'

'What work?'

'I do not know.'

She made a little impatient movement.

'That is no plan; travel—see the world—find work! If you go into the world aimless, without a definite object, dreaming—dreaming, you will be definitely defeated, bamboozled, knocked this way and that. In the end you will stand with your beautiful life all spent, and nothing to show. They talk of genius—it is nothing but this, that a man knows what he can do best, and does it, and nothing else. Waldo,' she said, knitting her little fingers closer among his, 'I wish I could help you; I wish I could make you see that you must decide what you will be and do. It does not matter what you choose,—be a farmer, business-man, artist, what you will,—but know your aim, and live for that one thing. We have only one life. The secret of success is concentration; wherever there has been a great life, or a great work, that has gone before. Taste everything a little, look at everything a little; but live for one thing. Anything is possible to a man who knows his end and moves straight for it, and for it alone. I will show you what I mean,' she said, concisely; 'words are gas till you condense them into pictures.

'Supposing a woman, young, friendless as I am, the weakest thing on God's earth. But she must make her way through life. What she would be she cannot be because she is a woman; so she looks carefully at herself and the world about her, to see where her path must be made. There is no one to help her; she must help herself. She looks. These things she has—a sweet voice, rich in subtle intonations; a fair, very fair face, with a power of concentrating in itself, and giving expression to, feelings that otherwise must have been dissipated in words; a rare power of entering into other lives unlike her own, and intuitively reading them aright. These qualities she has. How shall she use them? A poet, a writer, needs only the mental; what use has he for a beautiful body that registers clearly mental emotions? And the painter wants an eye for form and colour, and the musician an ear for time and tune, and the mere drudge has no need for mental gifts. But there is one art in which all she has would be used, for which they are all necessary—the delicate expressive body, the rich voice, the power of mental transposition. The actor, who absorbs and then reflects from himself other human lives, needs them all, but needs not much more. This is her end; but how to reach it? Before her are endless difficulties: seas must be crossed, poverty must be endured, loneliness, want. She must be content to wait long before she can even get her feet upon the path. If she has made blunders in the past, if she has weighted herself with a burden which she must bear to the end, she must but bear the burden bravely, and labour on. There is no use in wailing and repentance here: the next world is the place for that; this life is too short. By our errors we see deeper into life. They help us.' She waited for a while. 'If she does all this,—if she waits patiently, if she is never cast down, never despairs, never forgets her end, moves straight towards it, bending men and things most unlikely to her purpose,—she must succeed at last. Men and things are plastic; they part to the right and left when one comes among them moving in a straight line to one end. I know it by my own little experience,' she said. 'Long years ago I resolved to be sent to school. It seemed a thing utterly out of my power; but I waited, I watched, I collected clothes, I wrote, took my place at the school; when all was ready I bore with my full force on the Boer-woman, and she sent me at last. It was a small thing; but life is made up of small things, as a body is built up of cells. What has been done in small things can be done in large. Shall be,' she said softly.

Waldo listened. To him the words were no confession, no glimpse into the strong, proud, restless heart of the woman. They were general words with a general application. He looked up into the sparkling sky with dull eyes.

'Yes,' he said; 'but when we lie and think, and think, we see that there is nothing worth doing. The universe is so large, and the man is so small——'

She shook her head quickly.

'But we must not think so far; it is madness, it is a disease. We know that no man's work is great, and stands for ever. Moses is dead, and the prophets, and the books that our grandmothers fed on the mould is eating. Your poet and painter and actor,—before the shouts that applaud them have died their names grow strange, they are milestones that the world has passed. Men have set their mark on mankind for ever, as they thought; but time has washed it out as it has washed out mountains and continents.' She raised herself on her elbow. 'And what, if we *could* help mankind, and leave the traces of our work upon it to the end? Mankind is only an ephemeral blossom on the tree of time; there were others before it opened; there will be others after it has fallen. Where was man in the time of the dicynodont,* and when hoary monsters wallowed in the mud? Will he be found in the æons that are to come? We are sparks, we are shadows, we are pollen, which the next wind will carry away. We are dying already; it is all a dream.

'I know that thought. When the fever of living is on us,

when the desire to become, to know, to do, is driving us mad, we can use it as an anodyne, to still the fever and cool our beating pulses. But it is a poison, not a food. If we live on it it will turn our blood to ice; we might as well be dead. We must not, Waldo; I want your life to be beautiful, to end in something. You are nobler and stronger than I,' she said; 'and as much better as one of God's great angels is better than a sinning man. Your life must go for something.'

'Yes, we will work,' he said.

She moved closer to him and lay still, his black curls touching her smooth little head.

Doss, who had lain at his master's side, climbed over the bench, and curled himself up in her lap. She drew her skirt up over him, and the three sat motionless for a long time.

'Waldo,' she said, suddenly, 'they are laughing at us.'

'Who?' he asked, starting up.

'They—the stars!' she said, softly. 'Do you not see? there is a little, white, mocking finger pointing down at us from each one of them! We are talking of to-morrow, and to-morrow, and our hearts are so strong; we are not thinking of something that can touch us softly in the dark, and make us still for ever. They are laughing at us, Waldo.'

Both sat looking upwards.

'Do you ever pray?' he asked her in a low voice.

'No.'

'I never do; but I might when I look up there. I will tell you,' he added, in a still lower voice, 'where I could pray. If there were a wall of rock on the edge of a world, and one rock stretched out far, far into space, and I stood alone upon it, alone, with stars above me, and stars below me,—I would not say anything; but the feeling would be prayer.'

There was an end to their conversation after that, and Doss fell asleep on her knee. At last the night-wind grew very chilly.

'Ah,' she said, shivering, and drawing the skirt about her shoulders, 'I am cold. Span-in the horses, and call me when you are ready.'

She slipped down and walked towards the house, Doss stiffly following her, not pleased at being roused. At the door she met Gregory.

'I have been looking for you everywhere; may I not drive you home?' he said.

'Waldo drives me,' she replied, passing on; and it appeared to Gregory that she looked at him in the old way, without seeing him. But before she had reached the door an idea had occurred to her, for she turned.

'If you wish to drive me you may.'

Gregory went to look for Em, whom he found pouring out coffee in the back room. He put his hand quickly on her shoulder.

'You must ride with Waldo: I am going to drive your cousin home.'

'But I can't come just now, Greg; I promised Tant' Annie Muller to look after the things while she went to rest a little.'

'Well, you can come presently, can't you? I didn't say you were to come now. I'm sick of this thing,' said Gregory, turning sharply on his heel. 'Why must I sit up the whole night because your step-mother chooses to get married?'

'Oh, it's all right, Greg, I only meant——'

But he did not hear her, and a man had come up to have his cup filled.

An hour after Waldo came in to look for her, and found her still busy at the table.

'The horses are ready,' he said; 'but if you would like to have one dance more I will wait.'

She shook her head wearily.

'No; I am quite ready. I want to go.'

And soon they were on the sandy road the buggy had travelled an hour before. Their horses, with heads close together, nodding sleepily as they walked in the starlight, you might have counted the rise and fall of their feet in the sand; and Waldo in his saddle nodded drowsily also. Only Em was awake, and watched the starlit road with wide-open eyes. At last she spoke.

'I wonder if all people feel so old, so very old, when they get to be seventeen?'

'Not older than before,' said Waldo sleepily, pulling at his bridle.

Presently she said again,

'I wish I could have been a little child always. You are good then. You are never selfish; you like every one to have everything; but when you are grown-up there are some things you like to have all to yourself, you don't like any one else to have any of them.'

'Yes,' said Waldo sleepily, and she did not speak again.

When they reached the farmhouse all was dark, for Lyndall had retired as soon as they got home.

Waldo lifted Em from her saddle, and for a moment she leaned her head on his shoulder and clung to him.

'You are very tired,' he said, as he walked with her to the door; 'let me go in and light a candle for you.'

'No, thank you; it is all right,' she said. 'Good-night, Waldo dear.'

But when she went in she sat long alone in the dark.

CHAPTER VII

Waldo goes out to Taste Life, and Em stays at Home and Tastes it

AT nine o'clock in the evening, packing his bundles for the next morning's start, Waldo looked up, and was surprised to see Em's yellow head peeping in at his door. It was many a month since she had been there. She said she had made him sandwiches for his journey, and she stayed a while to help him put his goods into the saddle-bags.

'You can leave the old things lying about,' she said; 'I will lock the room, and keep it waiting for you to come back some day.'

To come back some day! Would the bird ever return to its cage? But he thanked her. When she went away he stood on the doorstep holding the candle till she had almost reached the house. But Em was that evening in no hurry to enter, and, instead of going in at the back door, walked with lagging footsteps round the low brick wall that ran before the house. Opposite the open window of the parlour she stopped. The little room, kept carefully closed in Tant' Sannie's time, was well lighted by a paraffin lamp; books and work lay strewn about it, and it wore a bright, habitable aspect. Beside the lamp at the table in the corner sat Lyndall, the open letters and papers of the day's post lying scattered before her, while she perused the columns of a newspaper. At the centre table, with his arms folded on an open paper, which there was not light enough to read, sat Gregory. He was looking at her. The light from the open window fell on Em's little face under its white 'kapje' as she looked in, but no one glanced that way.

'Go and fetch me a glass of water,' Lyndall said at last.

Gregory went out to find it; when he put it down at her side he merely moved her head in recognition, and he went back to his seat and his old occupation. Then Em moved slowly away from the window, and through it came in spotted, hard-winged insects, to play round the lamp, till, one by one, they stuck to its glass, and fell at the foot dead.

Ten o'clock struck. Then Lyndall rose, gathered up her papers and letters, and wished Gregory good-night. Some time after Em entered; she had been sitting all the while on the loft ladder, and had drawn her 'kapje' down very much over her face.

Gregory was piecing together the bits of an envelope when she came in.

'I thought you were never coming,' he said, turning round quickly, and throwing the fragments on to the floor. 'You know I have been shearing all day, and it is ten o'clock already.'

'I'm sorry. I did not think you would be going so soon,' she said in a low voice.

'I can't hear what you say. What makes you mumble so? Well, good-night, Em.'

He stooped down hastily to kiss her.

'I want to talk to you, Gregory.'

'Well, make haste,' he said pettishly. 'I'm awfully tired. I've been sitting here all the evening. Why couldn't you come and talk before?'

'I will not keep you long,' she answered, very steadily now. 'I think, Gregory, it would be better if you and I were never to be married.'

'Good heavens! Em, what do you mean? I thought you were so fond of me? You always *professed* to be. What on earth have you taken into your head now?'

'I think it would be better,' she said, folding her hands over each other, very much as though she were praying.

'Better, Em! What do you mean? Even a woman can't take a freak all about nothing! You must have *some* reason for it, and I'm sure I've done nothing to offend you. I wrote only to-day to my sister to tell her to come up next month to our wedding, and I've been as affectionate and happy as possible. Come—what's the matter?'

He put his arm half round her shoulder, very loosely.

'I think it would be better,' she answered slowly.

'Oh, well,' he said, drawing himself up, 'if you won't enter into explanations, you won't; and I'm not the man to beg and pray—not to any woman, and you know that! If you don't want to marry me I can't oblige you to, of course.'

She stood quite still before him.

'You women never *do* know your own minds for two days together; and of course you know the state of your own feelings best; but it's very strange. Have you really made up your mind, Em?'

'Yes.'

'Well, I'm very sorry. I'm sure I've not been in anything to blame. A man can't always be billing and cooing; but, as you say, if your feeling for me has changed, it's much better you shouldn't marry me. There's nothing so foolish as to marry some one you don't love; and I only wish for your happiness, I'm sure. I daresay you'll find some one can make you much happier than *I* could; the first person we love is seldom the right one. You are very young; it's quite natural you should change.'

She said nothing.

'Things often seem hard at the time, but Providence makes them turn out for the best in the end,' said Gregory. 'You'll let me kiss you, Em, just for old friendship's sake.' He stooped down. 'You must look upon me as a dear brother, as a cousin at least; as long as I am on the farm I shall always be glad to help you, Em.'

Soon after, the brown pony was cantering along the footpath to the daub-and-wattle house, and his master as he rode whistled John Speriwig, and the Thorn Kloof Schottische.*

The sun had not yet touched the outstretched arms of the prickly-pear upon the 'kopje,' and the early cocks and hens still strutted about stiffly after the night's roost, when Waldo stood before the waggon-house saddling the grey mare. Every now and then he glanced up at the old familiar objects: they had a new aspect that morning. Even the cocks, seen in the light of parting, had a peculiar interest, and he listened with conscious attention while one crowed clear and loud as it stood on the pig-sty wall. He wished good-morning softly to the

Kaffir woman who was coming up from the huts to light the fire. He was leaving them all to that old life, and from his height he looked down on them pityingly. So they would keep on crowing, and coming to light fires, when for him that old colourless existence was but a dream.

He went into the house to say good-bye to Em, and then he walked to the door of Lyndall's room to wake her; but she was up, and standing in the doorway.

'So you are ready,' she said.

Waldo looked at her with sudden heaviness; the exhilaration died out of his heart. Her grey dressing-gown hung close about her, and below its edge the little bare feet were resting on the threshold.

'I wonder when we shall meet again, Waldo? What you will be, and what I?'

'Will you write to me?' he asked of her.

'Yes; and if I should not, you can still remember, wherever you are, that you are not alone.'

'I have left Doss for you,' he said.

'Will you not miss him?'

'No; I want you to have him. He loves you better than he loves me.'

'Thank you.'

They stood quiet.

'Good-bye!' she said, putting her little hand in his, and he turned away; but when he reached the door she called to him: 'Come back, I want to kiss you.' She drew his face down to hers, and held it with both hands, and kissed it on the forehead and mouth. 'Good-bye, dear!'

When he looked back the little figure with its beautiful eyes was standing in the doorway still.

CHAPTER VIII
The Kopje

'GOOD morning!'

Em, who was in the store-room measuring the Kaffirs' rations, looked up and saw her former lover standing betwixt her and the sunshine. For some days after that evening on which he had ridden home whistling he had shunned her. She might wish to enter into explanations, and he, Gregory Rose, was not the man for that kind of thing. If a woman had once thrown him overboard she must take the consequences, and stand by them. When, however, she showed no inclination to revert to the past, and shunned him more than he shunned her, Gregory softened.

'You must let me call you "Em" still, and be like a brother to you till I go,' he said; and Em thanked him so humbly that he wished she hadn't. It wasn't so easy after that to think himself an injured man.

On that morning he stood some time in the doorway switching his whip, and moving rather restlessly from one leg to the other.

'I think I'll just take a walk up to the camps and see how your birds are getting on. Now Waldo's gone you've no one to see after things. Nice morning, isn't it?' Then he added suddenly, 'I'll just go round to the house and get a drink of water first;' and somewhat awkwardly walked off. He might have found water in the kitchen, but he never glanced towards the buckets. In the front room a monkey and two tumblers stood on the centre table; but he merely looked round, peeped into the parlour, looked round again, and then walked out at the front door, and found himself again at the store-room without having satisfied his thirst. 'Awfully nice morning this,' he said, trying to pose himself in a graceful and indifferent attitude against the door. 'It isn't hot and it isn't cold. It's awfully nice.'

'Yes,' said Em.

'Your cousin, now,' said Gregory, in an aimless sort of way—'I suppose she's shut up in her room writing letters.'

'No,' said Em.

'Gone for a drive, I expect? Nice morning for a drive.'

'No.'

'Gone to see the ostriches, I suppose?'

'No.' After a little silence Em added, 'I saw her go by the kraals to the "kopje."'

Gregory crossed and uncrossed his legs.

'Well, I think I'll just go and have a look about,' he said, 'and see how things are getting on before I go to the camps. Good-bye; so long.'

Em left for a while the bags she was folding and went to the window, the same through which, years before, Bonaparte had watched the slouching figure cross the yard. Gregory walked to the pig-sty first, and contemplated the pigs for a few seconds; then turned round, and stood looking fixedly at the wall of the fuel-house as though he thought it wanted repairing; then he started off suddenly with the evident intention of going to the ostrich-camps; then paused, hesitated, and finally walked off in the direction of the 'kopje.'

Then Em went back to the corner, and folded more sacks.

On the other side of the 'kopje' Gregory caught sight of a white tail waving among the stones, and a succession of short, frantic barks told where Doss was engaged in howling imploringly to a lizard who had crept between two stones, and who had not the slightest intention of re-sunning himself at that particular moment.

The dog's mistress sat higher up, under the shelving rock, her face bent over a volume of plays upon her knee. As Gregory mounted the stones she started violently and looked up; then resumed her book.

'I hope I am not troubling you,' said Gregory, as he reached her side. 'If I am I will go away. I just——'

'No; you may stay.'

'I fear I startled you.'

'Yes; your step was firmer than it generally is. I thought it was that of some one else.'

'Who could it be but me?' asked Gregory, seating himself on a stone at her feet.

'Do you suppose you are the only man who would find anything to attract him to this "kopje"?'

'Oh, no,' said Gregory.

He was not going to argue that point with her, nor any other; but no old Boer was likely to take the trouble of climbing the 'kopje,' and who else was there?

She continued the study of her book.

'Miss Lyndall,' he said at last, 'I don't know why it is you never talk to me.'

'We had a long conversation yesterday,' she said, without looking up.

'Yes; but you ask me questions about sheep and oxen. I don't call that talking. You used to talk to Waldo, now,' he said, in an aggrieved tone of voice. 'I've heard you when I came in, and then you've just left off. You treated me like that from the first day; and you couldn't tell from just looking at me that I couldn't talk about the things you like. I'm sure I know as much about such things as Waldo does,' said Gregory, in exceeding bitterness of spirit.

'I do not know which things you refer to. If you will enlighten me I am quite prepared to speak of them,' she said, reading as she spoke.

'Oh, you never used to ask Waldo like that,' said Gregory, in a more sorely aggrieved tone than ever. 'You used just to begin.'

'Well, let me see,' she said, closing her book and folding her hands on it. 'There at the foot of the "kopje" goes a Kaffir; he has nothing on but a blanket; he is a splendid fellow—six feet high, with a magnificent pair of legs. In his leather bag he is going to fetch his rations, and I suppose to kick his wife with his beautiful legs when he gets home. He has a right to; he bought her for two oxen. There is a lean dog going after him, to whom I suppose he never gives more than a bone from which he has sucked the marrow; but his dog loves him, as his wife does. There is something of the master about him in spite of his blackness and wool. See how he brandishes his stick and holds up his head!'

'Oh, but aren't you making fun?' said Gregory, looking doubtfully from her to the Kaffir herd, who rounded the 'kopje.'

'No; I am very serious. He is the most interesting and intelligent thing I can see just now, except, perhaps, Doss. He is profoundly suggestive. Will his race melt away in the heat of a collision with a higher? Are the men of the future to see his bones only in museums—a vestige of one link that spanned between the dog and the white man? He wakes thoughts that run far out into the future and back into the past.'

Gregory was not quite sure how to take these remarks. Being about a Kaffir, they appeared to be of the nature of a joke; but, being seriously spoken, they appeared earnest: so he half laughed and half not, to be on the safe side.

'I've often thought so myself. It's funny we should both think the same; I knew we should if once we talked. But there are other things—love, now,' he added. 'I wonder if we would think alike about that. I wrote an essay on love once; the master said it was the best I ever wrote, and I can remember the first sentence still—"Love is something that you feel in your heart."'

'That was a trenchant remark. Can't you remember any more?'

'No,' said Gregory, regretfully; 'I've forgotten the rest. But tell me what do you think about love?'

A look, half of abstraction, half amusement, played on her lips.

'I don't know much about love,' she said, 'and I do not like to talk of things I do not understand; but I have heard two opinions. Some say the Devil carried the seed from hell, and planted it on the earth to plague men and make them sin; and some say, that when all the plants in the garden of Eden were pulled up by the roots, one bush that the angels had planted was left growing, and it spread its seed over the whole earth, and its name is love. I do not know which is right—perhaps both. There are different species that go under the same name. There is a love that begins in the head, and goes down to the heart, and grows slowly; but it lasts till death, and asks less than it gives. There is another love, that blots out wisdom, that is sweet with the sweetness of life and bitter with the bitterness of death, lasting for an hour; but it is worth having lived a whole life for that hour. I cannot tell: perhaps the old monks were right when they tried to root love out; perhaps the poets are right when they try to water it. It is a blood-red flower, with the colour of sin; but there is always the scent of a god about it.'

Gregory would have made a remark; but she said, without noticing,

'There are as many kinds of loves as there are flowers; everlastings that never wither; speedwells that wait for the wind to fan them out of life; blood-red mountain-lilies that pour their voluptuous sweetness out for one day, and lie in the dust at night. There is no flower has the charm of all—the speedwell's purity, the everlasting's strength, the mountain-lily's warmth; but who knows whether there is no love that holds all—friendship, passion, worship?

'Such a love,' she said, in her sweetest voice, 'will fall on the surface of strong, cold, selfish life as the sunlight falls on a torpid winter world; there, where the trees are bare, and the ground frozen, till it rings to the step like iron, and the water is solid, and the air is sharp as a two-edged knife, that cuts the unwary. But, when its sun shines on it, through its whole dead crust a throbbing yearning wakes: the trees feel him, and every knot and bud swell, aching to open to him. The brown seeds, who have slept deep under the ground, feel him, and he gives them strength, till they break through the frozen earth, and lift two tiny, trembling green hands in love to him. And he touches the water, till down to its depths it feels him and melts, and it flows, and the things, strange sweet things that were locked up in it, it sings as it runs, for love of him. Each plant tries to bear at least one fragrant little flower for him; and the world that was dead lives, and the heart that was dead and self-centred throbs, with an upward, outward yearning, and it has become that which it seemed impossible ever to become. There, does that satisfy you?' she asked, looking down at Gregory. 'Is that how you like me to talk?'

'Oh, yes,' said Gregory, 'that is what I have already thought. We have the same thoughts about everything. How strange!'

'Very,' said Lyndall, working with her little toe at a stone in the ground before her.

Gregory felt he must sustain the conversation. The only thing he could think of was to recite a piece of poetry. He knew he had learnt many about love; but the only thing that would come into his mind now was the '*Battle of Hohenlinden*'* and '*Not a drum was heard*,' neither of which seemed to bear directly on the subject on hand.

But unexpected relief came to him from Doss, who, too deeply lost in comtemplation of his crevice, was surprised by the sudden descent of the stone Lyndall's foot had loosened, which, rolling against his little front paw, carried away a piece of white skin. Doss stood on three legs, holding up the paw with an expression of extreme self-commiseration; he then proceeded to hop slowly upwards in search of sympathy.

'You have hurt that dog,' said Gregory.

'Have I?' she replied indifferently, and re-opened the book, as though to resume her study of the play.

'He's a nasty, snappish little cur!' said Gregory, calculating from her manner that the remark would be endorsed. 'He snapped at my horse's tail yesterday, and nearly made it throw me. I wonder his master didn't take him, instead of leaving him here to be a nuisance to all of us!'

Lyndall seemed absorbed in her play; but he ventured another remark.

'Do you think now, Miss Lyndall, that he'll ever have anything in the world,—that German, I mean,—money enough to support a wife on, and all that sort of thing? *I* don't. He's what *I* call a soft.'

She was spreading her skirt out softly with her left hand for the dog to lie down on it.

'I think I *should* be rather astonished if he ever became a respectable member of society,' she said. 'I don't expect to see him the possessor of bank-shares, the chairman of a divisional council, and the father of a large family; wearing a black hat, and going to church twice on a Sunday. He would rather astonish me if he came to such an end.'

'Yes; I don't expect *anything* of him either,' said Gregory, zealously.

'Well, I don't know,' said Lyndall; 'there are some small things I rather look to him for. If he were to invent wings, or carve a statue that one might look at for half-an-hour without wanting to look at something else, I should not be surprised. He may do some little thing of that kind perhaps, when he has done fermenting, and the sediment has all gone to the bottom.'

Gregory felt that what she said was not wholly intended as blame.

'Well, I don't know,' he said sulkily; 'to me he looks like a fool. To walk about always in that dead-and-alive sort of way, muttering to himself like an old Kaffir witch-doctor! He works hard enough, but it's always as though he didn't know what he was doing. You don't know how he looks to a person who sees him for the first time.'

Lyndall was softly touching the little sore foot as she read, and Doss, to show he liked it, licked her hand.

'But, Miss Lyndall,' persisted Gregory, 'what do you really think of him?'

'I think,' said Lyndall, 'that he is like a thorn-tree, which grows up very quietly, without any one's caring for it, and one day suddenly breaks out into yellow blossoms.'

'And what do you think I am like?' asked Gregory hopefully.

Lyndall looked up from her book.

'Like a little tin duck floating on a dish of water, that comes after a piece of bread stuck on a needle, and the more the needle pricks it the more it comes on.'

'Oh, you *are* making fun of me now, you really are!' said Gregory, feeling wretched. 'You *are* making fun, aren't you, now?'

'Partly. It is always diverting to make comparisons.'

'Yes; but you don't compare me to anything nice, and you do other people. What is Em like, now?'

'The accompaniment of a song. She fills up the gaps in other people's lives, and is always number two; but I think she is like many accompaniments—a great deal better than the song she is to accompany.'

'She is not half so good as you are?' said Gregory, with a burst of uncontrollable ardour.

'She is so much better than I, that her little finger has more goodness in it than my whole body. I hope you may not live to find out the truth of that fact.'

'You are like an angel,' he said, the blood rushing to his head and face.

'Yes, probably; angels are of many orders.'

'You are the one being that I love!' said Gregory, quivering; 'I thought I loved before, but I know now! Do not be angry with me. I know you could never like me; but, if I might but always be near you to serve you, I would be utterly, utterly happy. I would ask nothing in return! If you could only take everything I have and use it; I want nothing but to be of use to you.'

She looked at him for a few moments.

'How do you know,' she said slowly, 'that you could not do something to serve me? You could serve me by giving me your name.'

He started, and turned his burning face to her.

'You are very cruel; you are ridiculing me,' he said.

'No, I am not, Gregory. What I am saying is plain, matter-of-fact business. If you are willing to give me your name within three weeks' time, I am willing to marry you; if not, well. I want nothing more than your name. That is a clear proposal, is it not?'

He looked up. Was it contempt, loathing, pity, that moved in the eyes above? He could not tell; but he stooped over the little foot and kissed it.

She smiled.

'Do you really mean it?' he whispered.

'Yes. You wish to serve me, and to have nothing in return!—you shall have what you wish.' She held out her fingers for Doss to lick.—'Do you see this dog? He licks my hand because I love him; and I allow him to. Where I do not love I do not allow it. I believe you love me; I too could love so, that to lie under the foot of the thing I loved would be more heaven than to lie in the breast of another.—Come! let us go. Carry the dog,' she added; 'he will not bite you if I put him in your arms. So—do not let his foot hang down.'

They descended the 'kopje.' At the bottom he whispered,—

'Would you not take my arm, the path is very rough?'

She rested her fingers lightly on it.

'I may yet change my mind about marrying you before the time comes. It is very likely. Mark you!' she said, turning round on him; 'I remember your words:—*You will give everything, and expect nothing*. The knowledge that you are serving me is to be your reward; and you will have that. You will serve me, and greatly. The reasons I have for marrying you I need not inform you of now; you will probably discover some of them before long.'

'I only want to be of some use to you,' he said.

It seemed to Gregory that there were pulses in the soles of his feet, and the ground shimmered as on a summer's day. They walked round the foot of the 'kopje,' and past the Kaffir huts. An old Kaffir maid knelt at the door of one grinding mealies. That she should see him walking so made his heart beat so fast that the hand on his arm felt its pulsation. It seemed that she must envy him.

Just then Em looked out again at the back window and saw them coming. She cried bitterly all the while she sorted the skins.

But that night when Lyndall had blown her candle out, and half turned round to sleep, the door of Em's bedroom opened.

'I want to say good-night to you, Lyndall,' she said, coming to the bedside and kneeling down.

'I thought you were asleep,' Lyndall replied.

'Yes, I have been asleep; but I had such a vivid dream,' she said, holding the other's hands, 'and that awoke me. I never had so vivid a dream before.

'It seemed I was a little girl again, and I came somewhere into a large room. On a bed in the corner there was something lying dressed in white, and its little eyes were shut, and its little face was like wax. I thought it was a doll, and I ran forward to take it; but some one held up her finger and said, "Hush! it is a little dead baby." And I said, "Oh, I must go and call Lyndall, that she may look at it also.'

'And they put their faces close down to my ear and whispered, "It is Lyndall's baby.'

'And I said, "She cannot be grown up yet; she is only a little girl! Where is she?" And I went to look for you, but I could not find you.

'And when I came to some people who were dressed in black, I asked them where you were, and they looked down at their black clothes, and shook their heads, and said nothing; and I could not find you anywhere. And then I awoke.

'Lyndall,' she said, putting her face down upon the hands she held, 'it made me think about that time when we were little girls and used to play together, when I loved you better than anything else in the world. It isn't any one's fault that they love you, they can't help it. And it isn't your fault; you don't make them love you. I know it.'

'Thank you, dear,' Lyndall said, 'It is nice to be loved, but it would be better to be good.'

Then they wished good night, and Em went back to her room. Long after, Lyndall lay in the dark thinking, thinking; and as she turned round wearily to sleep she muttered,

'There are some wiser in their sleeping than in their waking.'

CHAPTER IX
Lyndall's Stranger

A FIRE is burning in the unused hearth of the cabin. The fuel blazes up, and lights the black rafters, and warms the faded red lions on the quilt, and fills the little room with a glow of warmth and light made brighter by contrast, for outside the night is chill and misty.

Before the open fireplace sits a stranger, his tall slight figure reposing in the broken arm-chair, his keen blue eyes studying the fire from beneath delicately pencilled, drooping eyelids. One white hand plays thoughtfully with a heavy flaxen moustache; yet once he starts, and for an instant the languid lids raise themselves: there is a keen, intent look upon the face as he listens for something. Then he leans back in his chair, fills his glass from the silver flask in his bag, and resumes his old posture.

Presently the door opens noiselessly. It is Lyndall, followed by Doss. Quietly as she enters, he hears her, and turns.

'I thought you were not coming.'

'I waited till all had gone to bed. I could not come before.'

She removed the shawl that enveloped her, and the stranger rose to offer her his chair; but she took her seat on a low pile of sacks before the window.

'I hardly see why I should be outlawed after this fashion,' he said, re-seating himself and drawing his chair a little nearer to her; 'these are hardly the quarters one expects to find after travelling a hundred miles in answer to an invitation.'

'I said, "Come if you wish."'

'And I did wish. You give me a cold reception.'

'I could not take you to the house. Questions would be asked which I could not answer without prevarication.'

'Your conscience is growing to have a certain virgin tenderness,' he said, in a low melodious voice.

'I have no conscience. I spoke one deliberate lie this evening.

I said the man who had come looked rough, we had best not have him in the house; therefore I brought him here. It was a deliberate lie, and I hate lies. I tell them if I must, but they hurt me.'

'Well, you do not tell lies to yourself, at all events. You are candid, so far.'

She interrupted him.

'You got my short letter?'

'Yes; that is why I came. You sent a very foolish reply, you must take it back. Who is this fellow you talk of marrying?'

'A young farmer.'

'Lives here?'

'Yes; he has gone to town to get things for our wedding.'

'What kind of a fellow is he?'

'A fool.'

'And you would rather marry him than me?'

'Yes; because you are not one.'

'That is a novel reason for refusing to marry a man,' he said, leaning his elbow on the table, and watching her keenly.

'It is a wise one,' she said shortly. 'If I marry him I shall shake him off my hand when it suits me. If I remained with him for twelve months he would never have dared to kiss my hand. As far as I wish he should come, he comes, and no further. Would you ask me what you might and what you might not do?'

Her companion raised the moustache with a caressing movement from his lip and smiled. It was not a question that stood in need of any answer.

'Why do you wish to enter on this semblance of marriage?'

'Because there is only one point on which I have a conscience. I have told you so.'

'Then why not marry me?'

'Because if once you have me you would hold me fast. I shall never be free again.' She drew a long low breath.

'What have you done with the ring I gave you?' he said.

'Sometimes I wear it; then I take it off and wish to throw it into the fire; the next day I put it on again, and sometimes I kiss it.'

'So you do love me a little?'

'If you were not something more to me than any other man in the world, do you think——' she paused. 'I love you when I see you; but when you are away from me I hate you.'

'Then I fear I must be singularly invisible at the present moment,' he said. 'Possibly if you were to look less fixedly into the fire you might perceive me.'

He moved his chair slightly so as to come between her and the firelight. She raised her eyes to his face.

'If you do love me,' he asked her, 'why will you not marry me?'

'Because, if I had been married to you for a year, I should have come to my senses, and seen that your hands and your voice are like the hands and the voice of any other man. I cannot quite see that now. But it is all madness. You call into activity one part of my nature; there is a higher part that you know nothing of, that you never touch. If I married you, afterwards it would arise and assert itself, and I should hate you always, as I do now sometimes.'

'I like you when you grow metaphysical and analytical,' he said, leaning his face upon his hand. 'Go a little further in your analysis; say, "I love you with the right ventricle of my heart, but not the left, and with the left auricle of my heart, but not the right; and, this being the case, my affection for you is not of a duly elevated, intellectual, and spiritual nature." I like you when you get philosophical.'

She looked quietly at him; he was trying to turn her own weapons against her.

'You are acting foolishly, Lyndall,' he said, suddenly changing his manner, and speaking earnestly, 'most foolishly. You are acting like a little child; I am surprised at you. It is all very well to have ideals and theories; but you know as well as anyone can that they must not be carried into the practical world. I love you. I do not pretend that it is in any high, superhuman sense; I do not say that I should like you as well if you were ugly and deformed, or that I should continue to prize you whatever your treatment of me might be, or to love you though you were a spirit without any body at all. That is sentimentality for beardless boys. Every one not a mere child (and you are not a child, except in years) knows what love between a man and a woman means. I love you with that love. I should not have believed it possible that I could have brought myself twice to ask of any woman to be my wife, more especially one without wealth, without position, and who——'

'Yes—go on. Do not grow sorry for me. Say what you were going to—who has put herself into my power, and who has lost the right of meeting me on equal terms.' Say what you think. At least we two may speak the truth to one another.'

Then she added after a pause,

'I believe you do love me, as much as you possibly could love anything; and I believe that when you ask me to marry you you are performing the most generous act you ever have performed in the course of your life, or ever will; but, at the same time, if I had required your generosity, it would not have been shown me. If, when I got your letter a month ago, hinting at your willingness to marry me, I had at once written, imploring you to come, you would have read the letter. "Poor little Devil!" you would have said, and torn it up. The next week you would have sailed for Europe, and have sent me a cheque for a hundred and fifty pounds (which I would have thrown in the fire), and I would have heard no more of you.' The stranger smiled. 'But because I declined your proposal, and wrote that in three weeks I should be married to another, then what you call love woke up. Your man's love is a child's love for butterflies. You follow till you have the thing, and break it. If you have broken one wing, and the things flies still, then you love it more than ever, and follow till you break both; then you are satisfied when it lies still on the ground.'

'You are profoundly wise in the ways of the world; you have seen far into life,' he said.

He might as well have sneered at the firelight.

'I have seen enough to tell me that you love me because you cannot bear to be resisted, and want to master me. You liked me at first because I treated you and all men with indifference. You resolved to have me because I seemed unattainable. That is all your love means.'

He felt a strong inclination to stoop down and kiss the little lips that defied him; but he restrained himself. He said quietly, 'And you loved me——?'

'Because you are strong. You are the first man I ever was afraid of. And'—a dreamy look came into her face—'because I like to experience, I like to try. You don't understand that.'

He smiled.

'Well, since you will not marry me, may I inquire what your intentions are, the plan you wrote of. You asked me to come and hear it, and I have come.'

'I said, "Come if you wish."—If you agree to it, well; if not, I marry on Monday.'

'Well?'

She was still looking beyond him at the fire.

'I cannot marry you,' she said slowly, 'because I cannot be tied; but, if you wish, you may take me away with you, and take care of me; then when we do not love any more we can say good-bye. I will not go down country,' she added; 'I will not go to Europe. You must take me to the Transvaal. That is out of the world. People we meet there we need not see again in our future lives.'

'Oh, my darling,' he said, bending tenderly, and holding his hand out to her, 'why will you not give yourself entirely to me? One day you will desert me and go to another.'

She shook her head without looking at him.

'No, life is too long. But I will go with you.'

'When?'

'To-morrow. I have told them that before daylight I go to the next farm. I will write from the town and tell them the facts. I do not want them to trouble me; I want to shake myself free of these old surroundings; I want them to lose sight of me. You can understand that is necessary for me.'

He seemed lost in consideration; then he said,

'It is better to have you on those conditions than not at all. If you *will* have it, let it be so.'

He sat looking at her. On her face was the weary look that rested there so often now when she sat alone. Two months had not passed since they parted; but the time had set its mark on her. He looked at her carefully, from the brown, smooth head to the little crossed feet on the floor. A worn look had grown over the little face, and it made its charm for him stronger. For pain and time, which trace deep lines and write a story on

a human face, have a strangely different effect on one face and
another. The face that is only fair, even very fair, they mar
and flaw; but to the face whose beauty is the harmony between
that which speaks from within and the form through which it
speaks, power is added by all that causes the outer man to bear
more deeply the impress of the inner. The pretty woman fades
with the roses on her cheeks, and the girlhood that lasts an
hour; the beautiful woman finds her fulness of bloom only
when a past has written itself on her, and her power is then
most irresistible when it seems going.

From under their half-closed lids the keen eyes looked down
at her. Her shoulders were bent; for a moment the little figure
had forgotten its queenly bearing, and drooped wearily; the
wide dark eyes watched the fire very softly.

It certainly was not in her power to resist him, nor any
strength in her that made his own at that moment grow soft as
he looked at her.

He touched one little hand that rested on her knee.

'Poor little thing!' he said; 'you are only a child.'

She did not draw her hand away from his, and looked up at
him.

'You are very tired?'

'Yes.'

She looked into his eyes as a little child might whom a long
day's play had saddened.

He lifted her gently up, and sat her on his knee.

'Poor little thing!' he said.

She turned her face to his shoulder, and buried it against his
neck; he wound his strong arm about her, and held her close
to him. When she had sat for a long while, he drew with his
hand the face down, and held it against his arm. He kissed it,
and then put it back in its old resting-place.

'Don't you want to talk to me?'

'No.'

'Have you forgotten the night in the avenue?'

He could feel that she shook her head.

'Do you want to be quiet now?'

'Yes.'

They sat quite still, excepting that only sometimes he raised her fingers softly to his mouth.

Doss, who had been asleep in the corner, waking suddenly, planted himself before them, his wiry legs moving nervously, his yellow eyes filled with anxiety. He was not at all sure that she was not being retained in her present position against her will, and was not a little relieved when she sat up and held out her hand for the shawl.

'I must go,' she said.

The stranger wrapped the shawl very carefully about her.

'Keep it close around your face, Lyndall; it is very damp outside. Shall I walk with you to the house?'

'No. Lie down and rest; I will come and wake you at three o'clock.'

She lifted her face that he might kiss it, and, when he had kissed it once, she still held it that he might kiss it again. Then he let her out. He had seated himself at the fire-place, when she re-opened the door.

'Have you forgotten anything?'

'No.'

She gave one long, lingering look at the old room. When she was gone, and the door shut, the stranger filled his glass, and sat at the table sipping it thoughtfully.

The night outside was misty and damp; the faint moonlight, trying to force its way through the thick air, made darkly visible the outlines of the buildings. The stones and walls were moist, and now and then a drop, slowly collecting, fell from the eaves to the ground. Doss, not liking the change from the cabin's warmth, ran quickly to the kitchen door-step; but his mistress walked slowly past him, and took her way up the winding footpath that ran beside the stone wall of the camps. When she came to the end of the last camp, she threaded her way among the stones and bushes till she reached the German's grave. Why she had come there she hardly knew; she stood looking down. Suddenly she bent and put one hand on the face of a wet stone.

'I shall never come to you again,' she said.

Then she knelt on the ground, and leaned her face upon the stones.

'Dear old man, good old man, I am so tired!' she said (for we will come to the dead to tell secrets we would never have told to the living). 'I am so tired. There is light, there is warmth,' she wailed; 'why am I alone, so hard, so cold? I am so weary of myself! It is eating my soul to its core,—self, self, self! I cannot bear this life! I cannot breathe, I cannot live! Will nothing free me from myself?' She pressed her cheek against the wooden post. 'I want to love! I want something great and pure to lift me to itself! Dear old man, I cannot bear it any more! I am so cold, so hard, so hard; will no one help me!'

The water gathered slowly on her shawl, and fell on to the wet stones; but she lay there crying bitterly. For so the living soul will cry to the dead, and the creature to its God; and of all this crying there comes nothing. The lifting up of the hands brings no salvation; redemption is from within, and neither from God nor man: it is wrought out by the soul itself, with suffering and through time.

Doss, on the kitchen door-step, shivered, and wondered where his mistress stayed so long; and once, sitting sadly there in the damp, he had dropped asleep, and dreamed that old Otto gave him a piece of bread, and patted him on the head, and when he woke his teeth chattered, and he moved to another stone to see if it was drier. At last he heard his mistress's step, and they went into the house together. She lit a candle, and walked to the Boer-woman's bed-room. On a nail under the lady in pink hung the key of the wardrobe. She took it down and opened the great press. From a little drawer she took fifty pounds (all she had in the world), relocked the door, and turned to hang up the key. Then she paused, hesitated. The marks of tears were still on her face, but she smiled.

'Fifty pounds for a lover! A noble reward!' she said, and opened the wardrobe and returned the notes to the drawer, where Em might find them.

Once in her own room, she arranged the few articles she intended to take to-morrow, burnt her old letters, and then went back to the front room to look at the time. There were two hours yet before she must call him. She sat down at the dressing-table to wait, and leaned her elbows on it, and buried her face in her hands. The glass reflected the little brown head with its even parting, and the tiny hands on which it rested. 'One day I will love something utterly, and then I will be better,' she said once. Presently she looked up. The large dark eyes from the glass looked back at her. She looked deep into them.

'We are all alone, you and I,' she whispered; 'no one helps us, no one understands us; but we will help ourselves.' The eyes looked back at her. There was a world of assurance in their still depths. So they had looked at her ever since she could remember, when it was but a small child's face above a blue pinafore. 'We shall never be quite alone, you and I,' she said; 'we shall always be together, as we were when we were little.'

The beautiful eyes looked into the depths of her soul.

'We are not afraid; we will help ourselves!' she said. She stretched out her hand and pressed it over them on the glass. 'Dear eyes! we will never be quite alone till they part us;—till then!'

CHAPTER X
Gregory Rose has an Idea

GREGORY ROSE was in the loft putting it neat. Outside the rain poured; a six months' drought had broken, and the thirsty plain was drenched with water. What it could not swallow ran off in mad rivulets to the great 'sloot' that now foamed like an angry river across the flat. Even the little furrow between the farmhouse and the kraals was now a stream, knee-deep, which almost bore away the Kaffir-women who crossed it. It had rained for twenty-four hours, and still the rain poured on. The fowls had collected—a melancholy crowd—in and about the waggon-house, and the solitary gander, who alone had survived the six months' want of water, walked hither and thither, printing his webbed foot-marks on the mud, to have them washed out the next instant by the pelting rain, which at eleven o'clock still beat on the walls and roofs with unabated ardour.

Gregory, as he worked in the loft, took no notice of it beyond stuffing a sack into the broken pane to keep it out; and, in spite of the pelt and patter, Em's clear voice might be heard through the open trap-door from the dining-room, where she sat at work, singing the 'Blue Water'—

> 'And take me away,
> And take me away,
> And take me away,
> To the Blue Water'——

that quaint, childish song of the people, that has a world of sweetness, and sad, vague yearning when sung over and over dreamily by a woman's voice as she sits alone at her work. But Gregory heard neither that nor yet the loud laughter of the Kaffir maids, that every now and again broke through from the kitchen, where they joked and worked. Of late Gregory had grown strangely impervious to the sounds and sights about him. His lease had run out, but Em had said, 'Do not renew it; I need one to help me; just stay on.' And she had added, 'You must not remain in your own little house; live with me; you can look after my ostriches better so.'

And Gregory did not thank her. What difference did it make to him, paying rent or not, living there or not? It was all one. But yet he came. Em wished that he would still sometimes talk of the strength and master-right of man; but Gregory was as one smitten on the cheek-bone. She might do what she pleased, he would find no fault, had no word to say. He had forgotten that it is man's right to rule. On that rainy morning he had lighted his pipe at the kitchen fire, and when breakfast was over stood in the front door watching the water rush down the road till the pipe died out in his mouth. Em saw she must do something for him, and found him a large calico duster. He had sometimes talked of putting the loft neat, and to-day she could find nothing else for him to do. So she had the ladder put to the trap-door that he need not go out in the wet, and Gregory with the broom and duster mounted to the loft. Once at work he worked hard. He dusted down the very rafters, and cleaned the broken candle-moulds and bent forks that had stuck in the thatch for twenty years. He placed the black bottles neatly in rows on an old box in the corner, and piled the skins on one another, and sorted the rubbish in all the boxes; and at eleven o'clock his work was almost done. He seated himself on the packing-case which had once held Waldo's books, and proceeded to examine the contents of another which he had not yet looked at. It was carelessly nailed down. He loosened one plank, and began to lift out various articles of female attire—old-fashioned caps, aprons, dresses with long pointed bodies such as he remembeed to have seen his mother wear when he was a little child. He shook them out carefully to see there were no moths, and then sat down to fold them up again one by one. They had belonged to Em's mother, and the box, as packed at her death, had stood untouched and forgotten these long years. She must have been a tall woman, that mother of Em's, for when he stood up to shake out a dress the neck was on a level with his, and the skirt touched the ground. Gregory laid a night-cap out on his knee, and began rolling up the strings; but presently his fingers moved slower and slower, then his chin rested on his breast, and finally the imploring blue eyes were fixed on the frill abstractedly. When Em's voice called to him from the foot of the ladder he started, and threw the night-cap behind him.

She was only come to tell him that his cup of soup was ready; and, when he could hear that she was gone, he picked up the night-cap again, and a great brown sun-kapje—just such a 'kapje' and such a dress as one of those he remembered to have seen a sister-of-mercy wear. Gregory's mind was very full of thought. He took down a fragment of an old looking-glass from behind a beam, and put the 'kapje' on. His beard looked somewhat grotesque under it; he put up his hand to hide it—that was better. The blue eyes looked out with the mild gentleness that became eyes looking out from under a 'kapje.' Next he took the brown dress, and, looking round furtively, slipped it over his head. He had just got his arms in the sleeves, and was trying to hook up the back, when an increase in the patter of the rain at the window made him drag it off hastily. When he perceived there was no one coming he tumbled the things back into the box, and, covering it carefully, went down the ladder.

Em was still at her work, trying to adjust a new needle in the machine. Gregory drank his soup, and then sat before her, an awful and mysterious look in his eyes.

'I am going to town to-morrow,' he said.

'I'm almost afraid you won't be able to go,' said Em, who was intent on her needle; 'I don't think it is going to leave off to-day.'

'I am going,' said Gregory.

Em looked up.

'But the "sloots" are as full as rivers—you cannot go. We can wait for the post,' she said.

'I am not going for the post,' said Gregory impressively.

Em looked for explanation; none came.

'When will you be back?'

'I am not coming back.'

'Are you going to your friends?'

Gregory waited, then caught her by the wrist.

'Look here, Em' he said between his teeth, 'I can't stand it any more. I am going to her.'

Since that day, when he had come home and found Lyndall gone, he had never talked of her; but Em knew who it was who needed to be spoken of by no name.

She said, when he had released her hand,

'But you do not know where she is?'

'Yes, I do. She was in Bloemfontein* when I heard last. I will go there, and I will find out where she went then, and then, and then! I will have her.'

Em turned the wheel quickly, and the ill-adjusted needle sprang into twenty fragments.

'Gregory,' she said, 'she does not want us; she told us so clearly in the letter she wrote.' A flush rose on her face as she spoke. 'It will only be pain to you, Gregory. Will she like to have you near her?'

There was an answer he might have made, but it was his secret, and he did not choose to share it. He said only,

'I am going.'

'Will you be gone long, Gregory?'

'I do not know; perhaps I shall never come back. Do what you please with my things. I cannot stay here!'

He rose from his seat.

'People say, forget, forget!' he cried, pacing the room. 'They are mad! they are fools! Do they say so to men who are dying of thirst—forget, forget? Why is it only to us they say so? It is a lie to say that time makes it easy; it is afterwards, afterwards that it eats in at your heart!

'All these months,' he cried bitterly, 'I have lived here quietly, day after day, as if I cared for what I ate, and what I drank, and what I did! I care for nothing! I cannot bear it! I will not! Forget! forget!' ejaculated Gregory. 'You can forget all the world, but you cannot forget yourself. When one thing is more to you than yourself, how are you to forget it?

'I read,' he said—'yes; and then I come to a word she used, and it is all back with me again! I go to count my sheep, and I see her face before me, and I stand and let the sheep run by. I look at you, and in your smile, a something at the corner of your lips, I see her. How can I forget her when, whenever I turn, she is there, and not there? I cannot, I will not, live where I do not see her.

'I know what you think,' he said, turning upon Em. 'You think I am mad; you think I am going to see whether she will not like me! I am not so foolish. I should have known at first she never could suffer me. Who am I, what am I, that she should look at me? It was right that she left me; right that she should not look at me. If any one says it is not, it is a lie! I am not going to speak to her,' he added—'only to see her; only to stand sometimes in a place where she has stood before.'

CHAPTER XI
An Unfinished Letter

GREGORY ROSE had been gone seven months. Em sat alone on a white sheepskin before the fire.

The August night-wind, weird and shrill, howled round the chimneys and through the crannies, and in walls and doors, and uttered a long low cry as it forced its way among the clefts or the stones on the 'kopje.' It was a wild night. The prickly-pear tree, stiff and upright as it held its arms, felt the wind's might, and knocked its flat leaves heavily together, till great branches broke off. The Kaffirs, as they slept in their straw huts, whispered one to another that before morning there would not be an armful of thatch left on the roofs; and the beams of the waggon-house creaked and groaned as if it were heavy work to resist the importunity of the wind.

Em had not gone to bed. Who could sleep on a night like this? So in the dining-room she had lighted a fire, and sat on the ground before it, turning the roaster-cakes that lay on the coals to bake. It would save work in the morning; and she blew out the light because the wind through the window-chinks made it flicker and run; and she sat singing to herself as she watched the cakes. They lay at one end of the wide hearth on a bed of coals, and at the other end a fire burnt up steadily, casting its amber glow over Em's light hair and black dress with the ruffle of crape about the neck, and over the white curls of the sheepskin on which she sat.

Louder and more fiercely yet howled the storm; but Em sang on, and heard nothing but the words of her song, and heard them only faintly, as something restful. It was an old, childish song she had often heard her mother sing long ago—

> Where the reeds dance by the river,
> Where the willow's song is said,

On the face of the morning water,
Is reflected a white flower's head.

She folded her hands and sang the next verse dreamily—

Where the reeds shake by the river,
Where the moonlight's sheen is shed,
On the face of the sleeping water,
Two leaves of a white flower float dead.
Dead, Dead, Dead!

She echoed the refrain softly till it died away, and then repeated it. It was as if, unknown to herself, it harmonized with the pictures and thoughts that sat with her there alone in the fire-light. She turned the cakes over, while the wind hurled down a row of bricks from the gable, and made the walls tremble.

Presently she paused and listened; there was a sound as of something knocking at the back-doorway. But the wind had raised its level higher, and she went on with her work. At last the sound was repeated. Then she rose, lit the candle at the fire, and went to see. Only to satisfy herself, she said, that nothing could be out on such a night.

She opened the door a little way, and held the light behind her to defend it from the wind. The figure of a tall man stood there, and before she could speak he had pushed his way in, and was forcing the door to close behind him.

'Waldo!' she cried in astonishment.

He had been gone more than a year and a half.

'You did not expect to see me,' he answered, as he turned towards her; 'I should have slept in the outhouse, and not troubled you to-night; but through the shutter I saw glimmerings of a light.'

'Come in to the fire,' she said; 'it is a terrific night for any creature to be out. Shall we not go and fetch your things in first?' she added.

'I have nothing but this,' he said, motioning to the little bundle in his hand.

'Your horse?'

'Is dead.'

He sat down on the bench before the fire.

'The cakes are almost ready,' she said; 'I will get you something to eat. Where have you been wandering all this while?'

'Up and down, up and down,' he answered wearily; 'and now the whim has seized me to come back here. Em,' he said, putting his hand on her arm as she passed him, 'have you heard from Lyndall lately?'

'Yes,' said Em, turning quickly from him.

'Where is she? I had one letter from her, but that is almost a year ago now—just when she left. Where is she?'

'In the Transvaal. I will go and get you some supper; we can talk afterwards.'

'Can you give me her exact address? I want to write to her.'

But Em had gone into the next room.

When food was on the table she knelt down before the fire, turning the cakes, babbling restlessly, eagerly, now of this, now of that. She was glad to see him—Tant' Sannie was coming soon to show her her new baby—he must stay on the farm now, and help her. And Waldo himself was well content to eat his meal in silence, asking no more questions.

'Gregory is coming back next week,' she said; 'he will have been gone just a hundred and three days tomorrow. I had a letter from him yesterday.'

'Where has he been?'

But his companion stooped to lift a cake from the fire.

'How the wind blows! One can hardly hear one's own voice,' she said. 'Take this warm cake; no one's cakes are like mine. Why, you have eaten nothing!'

'I am a little weary,' he said; 'the wind was mad to-night.'

He folded his arms, and rested his head against the fire-place, whilst she removed the dishes from the table. On the mantelpiece stood an ink-pot and some sheets of paper. Presently he took them down and turned up the corner of the table-cloth.

'I will write a few lines,' he said, 'till you are ready to sit down and talk.'

Em, as she shook out the table-cloth, watched him bending intently over his paper. He had changed much. His face had grown thinner; his cheeks were almost hollow, though they were covered by a dark growth of beard.

She sat down on the skin beside him, and felt the little bundle on the bench; it was painfully small and soft. Perhaps it held a shirt and a book, but nothing more. The old black hat had a piece of unhemmed muslin twisted round it, and on his elbow was a large patch so fixed on with yellow thread that her heart ached. Only his hair was not changed, and hung in silky beautiful waves almost to his shoulders. To-morrow she would take the ragged edge off his collar, and put a new band round his hat. She did not interrupt him, but she wondered how it was that he sat to write so intently after his long weary walk. He was not tired now; his pen hurried quickly and restlessly over the paper, and his eye was bright. Presently Em raised her hand to her breast, where lay the letter yesterday had brought her. Soon she had forgotten him, as entirely as he had forgotten her; each was in his own world with his own. He was writing to Lyndall. He would tell her all he had seen, all he had done, though it were nothing worth relating. He seemed to have come back to her, and to be talking to her now he sat there in the old house.

'——and then I got to the next town, and my horse was tired, so I could go no further, and looked for work. A shopkeeper agreed to hire me as salesman. He made me sign a promise to remain six months, and he gave me a little empty room at the store to sleep in. I had still three pounds of my own, and when you have just come from the country three pounds seems a great deal.

'When I had been in the shop three days I wanted to go away again. A clerk in a shop has the lowest work to do of all people. It is much better to break stones: you have the blue sky above you, and only the stones to bend to. I asked my master to let me go, and I offered to give him my two pounds, and the bag of mealies I had bought with the other pound; but he would not.

'I found out afterwards he was only giving me half as much as he gave to the others—that was why. I had fear when I looked at the other clerks that I would at last become like them. All day they were bowing and smirking to the women who came in; smiling, when all they wanted was to get their money from them. They used to run and fetch the dresses and ribbons to show them, and they seemed to me like worms with oil on. There was one respectable thing in that store—it was the Kaffir storeman. His work was to load and unload, and he never needed to smile except when he liked, and he never told lies.

'The other clerks gave me the name of Old Salvation; but there was one person I liked very much. He was clerk in another store. He often went past the door. He seemed to me not like others—his face was bright and fresh like a little child's. When he came to the shop I felt I liked him. One day I saw a book in his pocket, and that made me feel near him. I asked him if he was fond of reading, and he said yes, when there was nothing else to do. The next day he came to me, and asked me if I did not feel lonely; he never saw me going out with the other fellows; he would come and see me that evening, he said.

'I was glad, and bought some meat and flour, because the grey mare and I always ate mealies; it is the cheapest thing; when you boil it hard you can't eat much of it. I made some cakes, and I folded my great coat on the box to make it soft for him; and at last he came.

'"You've got a rummy place here," he said.

'You see there was nothing in it but packing-cases for furniture, and it was rather empty. While I was putting the food on the box he looked at my books; he read their names out aloud. "Elementary Physiology," "First Principles."*

'"Golly!" he said; "I've got a lot of dry stuff like that at home I got for Sunday school prizes; but I only keep them to light my pipe with now; they come in handy for that." Then he asked me if I had ever read a book called the "Black-eyed Creole." "That is the style for me," he said; "there where the fellow takes the nigger-girl by the arm, and the other fellow cuts off! That's what I like."

'But what he said after that I don't remember, only it made me feel as if I were having a bad dream, and I wanted to be far away.

'When he had finished eating he did not stay long: he had to go and see some girls home from a prayer-meeting; and he asked how it was he never saw me walking out with any on Sunday afternoons. He said he had lots of sweethearts, and he was going to see one the next Wednesday on a farm, and he asked me to lend my mare. I told him she was very old. But he said it didn't matter; he would come the next day to fetch her.

'After he was gone my little room got back to its old look. I loved it so; I was so glad to get into it at night, and it seemed to be reproaching me for bringing him there. The next day he took the grey mare. On Thursday he did not bring her back, and on Friday I found the saddle and bridle standing at my door.

'In the afternoon he looked into the shop, and called out, "Hope you got your saddle, Farber?* Your bag-of-bones kicked out six miles from this. I'll send you a couple of shillings to-morrow, though the old hide wasn't worth it. Good-morning."'

'But I sprang over the counter, and got him by his throat. My father was so gentle with her; he never would ride her up hill, and now this fellow had murdered her! I asked him where he had killed her, and I shook him till he slipped out of my hand. He stood in the door grinning.

'"It didn't take much to kill *that* bag-of-bones, whose master sleeps in a packing-case, and waits till his company's finished to eat on the plate. Shouldn't wonder if you fed her on sugar-bags," he said; "and, if you think I've jumped her, you'd better go and look yourself. You'll find her along the road by the 'aas-vogels' that are eating her."

'I caught him by his collar, and I lifted him from the ground, and I threw him out into the street, half-way across it. I heard the bookkeeper say to the clerk that there was always the devil in those mum fellows; but they never called me Salvation after that.

'I am writing to you of very small things, but there is nothing else to tell; it has been all small and you will like it. Whenever anything has happened I have always thought I would tell it to you. The back thought in my mind is always you. After that only one old man came to visit me. I had seen him in the streets often; he always wore very dirty black clothes, and a hat with crape round it, and he had one eye, so I noticed him. One day he came to my room with a subscription-list for a minister's salary. When I said I had nothing to give he looked at me with his one eye.

'"Young man," he said, "how is it I never see you in the house of the Lord?" I thought he was trying to do good, so I felt sorry for him, and I told him I never went to chapel. "Young man," he said, "it grieves me to hear such godless words from the lips of one so young—so far gone in the paths of destruction. Young man, if you forget God, God will forget you. There is a seat on the right-hand side as you go at the bottom door that you may get. If you are given over to the enjoyment and frivolities of this world, what will become of your never-dying soul?"

'He would not go till I gave him half-a-crown for the minister's salary. Afterwards I heard he was the man who collected the pew-rents, and got a per-centage. I didn't get to know any one else.

'When my time in that shop was done I hired myself to drive one of a transport-rider's waggons.

'That first morning, when I sat in the front and called to my oxen, and saw nothing about me but the hills with the blue coming down to them, and the karroo bushes, I was drunk; I laughed; my heart was beating till it hurt me. I shut my eyes tight, that when I opened them I might see there were no shelves about me. There must be a beauty in buying and selling if there is beauty in everything; but it is very ugly to me. My life as transport-rider would have been the best life in the world if I had had only one waggon to drive. My master told me he would drive one, I the other, and he would hire another person to drive the third. But the first day I drove two to help him, and after that he let me drive all three. Whenever we came to an hotel he stopped behind to get a drink, and when he rode up to the waggons he could never stand; the Hottentot and I used to lift him up. We always travelled all night, and used to "out-span" for five or six hours in the heat of the day to rest. I planned that I would lie under the waggon and read for an hour or two every day before I went to sleep, and I did for the first two or three; but after that I only wanted to sleep like the rest, and I packed my books away. When you have three waggons to look after all night, you are sometimes so tired you can hardly stand. At first, when I walked along driving my waggons in the night, it was glorious; the stars had never looked so beautiful to me; and on the dark nights when we rode through the bush there were will-o'-the-wisps dancing on each side of the road. I found out that even the damp and dark are beautiful. But I soon changed, and saw nothing but the road, and my oxen. I only wished for a smooth piece of road, so that I might sit at the front and doze. At the places where we "out-spanned" there were sometimes rare plants and flowers, the festoons hanging from the bush-trees, and nuts and insects, such as we never see here; but after a little while I never looked at them—I was too tired. I ate as much as I could, and then lay down on my face under the waggon till the boy came to wake me to "in-span," and then we drove on again all night; so it went, so it went. I think sometimes when we walked by my oxen I called to them in my sleep, for I know I thought of nothing; I was like an animal. My body was strong and well to work, but my brain was dead. If you have not felt it, Lyndall, you cannot understand it. You may work, and work, and work, till you are only a body, not a soul. Now, when I see one of those evil-looking men that come from Europe—navvies, with the beast-like, sunken face, different from any Kaffir's—I know what brought that look into their eyes; and if I have only one inch of tobacco I give them half. It is work, grinding, mechanical work, that they or their ancestors have done, that has made them into beasts. You may work a man's body so that his soul dies. Work is good. I have worked at the old farm from the sun's rising till its setting, but I have had time to think, and time to feel. You may work a man so that all but the animal in him is gone; and that grows stronger with physical labour. You may work a man till he is a devil. I know it, because I have felt it. You will never understand the change that came over me. No one but I will ever know how great it was. But I was never miserable; when I could keep my oxen from sticking fast, and when I could find a place to lie down in, I had all I wanted. After I had driven eight months a rainy season came. For eighteen hours out of the twenty-four we worked in the wet. The mud went up to the axles sometimes, and we had to dig the wheels out, and we never went far in a day. My master swore at me more than ever, but when he had done he always offered me his brandy-flask. When I first came he had offered it me, and I had always refused; but now I drank as my oxen did when I gave them water—without thinking. At last I bought brandy for myself whenever we passed an hotel.

'One Sunday we "out-spanned" on the banks of a swollen river to wait for its going down. It was drizzling still, so I lay under the waggon on the mud. There was no dry place anywhere; and all the dung was wet, so there was no fire to cook food. My little flask was filled with brandy, and I drank some and went to sleep. When I woke it was drizzling still, so I drank some more. I was stiff and cold; and my master, who lay by me, offered me his flask, because mine was empty. I drank some, and then I thought I would go and see if the river was going down. I remember that I walked to the road, and it seemed to be going away from me. When I woke up I was lying by a little bush on the bank of the river. It was afternoon; all the clouds had gone, and the sky was deep blue. The Bushman boy was grilling ribs at the fire. He looked at me, and grinned from ear to ear. "Master was a little nice," he said, "and lay down in the road. Something might ride over master, so I carried him there." He grinned at me again. It was as though he said, "You and I are comrades. I have lain in a road too. I know all about it." When I turned my head from him I saw the earth, so pure after the rain, so green, so fresh, so blue;—and I was a drunken carrier, whom his leader had picked up in the mud, and laid at the roadside to sleep out his drink. I remembered my old life, and I remembered you. I saw how, one day, you would read in the papers—"A German carrier, named Waldo Farber, was killed through falling from his waggon, being instantly crushed under the wheel. Deceased was supposed to have been drunk at the time of the accident." There are those notices in the paper every month. I sat up, and I took the brandy-flask out of my pocket, and I flung it as far as I could into the dark water. The Hottentot boy ran down to see if he could catch it; it had sunk to the bottom. I never drank again. But, Lyndall, sin looks much more terrible to those who look at it than to those who do it. A convict, or a man who drinks, seems something so far off and horrible when we see him; but to himself he seems quite near to us, and like us. We wonder what kind of a creature he is; but he is just we, ourselves. We are only the wood, the knife that carves on us is the circumstance.

'I do not know why I kept on working so hard for that master. I think it was as the oxen come every day and stand by the yokes; they do not know why. Perhaps I would have been with him still; but one day we started with loads for the Diamond Fields. The oxen were very thin now, and they had been standing about in the yoke all day without food while the waggons were being loaded. Not far from the town was a hill. When we came to the foot the first waggon stuck fast. I tried for a little while to urge the oxen, but I soon saw the one "span" could never pull it up. I went to the other waggon to loosen that "span" to join them on in front, but the transport-rider, who was lying at the back of the waggon, jumped out.

'"They shall bring it up the hill; and if half of them die for it they shall do it alone," he said.

'He was not drunk, but in a bad temper, for he had been drunk the night before. He swore at me, and told me to take the whip and help him. We tried for a little time, then I told him it was no use, they could never do it. He swore louder, and called to the leaders to come on with their whips, and together they lashed. There was one ox, a black ox, so thin that the ridge of his backbone almost cut through his flesh.

'"It is you, Devil, is it, that will not pull?" the transport-rider said. "I will show you something." He looked like a Devil.

'He told the boys to leave off flogging, and he held the ox by the horn, and took up a round stone and knocked its nose with it till the blood came. When he had done they called to the oxen and took up their whips again, and the oxen strained with their backs bent, but the waggon did not move an inch.

'"So you won't, won't you?" he said. "I'll help you."

'He took out his clasp-knife, and ran it into the leg of the trembling ox three times, up to the hilt. Then he put the knife in his pocket, and they took their whips. The oxen's flanks quivered, and they foamed at the mouth. Straining, they moved the waggon a few feet forward, then stood with bent backs to keep it from sliding back. From the black ox's nostril foam and blood were streaming on to the ground. It turned its head in its anguish and looked at me with its great starting eyes. It was praying for help in its agony and weakness, and they took their whips again. The creature bellowed out aloud. If there is a God, it was calling to its Maker for help. Then a stream of clear blood burst from both nostrils; it fell on to the ground, and the waggon slipped back. The man walked up to it.

'"You are going to lie down, Devil, are you? We'll see you don't take it too easy."

'The thing was just dying. He opened his clasp-knife and stooped down over it. I do not know what I did then. But afterwards I know I had him on the stones, and I was kneeling on him. The boys dragged me off. I wish they had not. I left him standing in the sand in the road, shaking himself, and I walked back to the town. I took nothing from that accursed waggon, so I had only two shillings. But it did not matter. The next day I got work at a wholesale store. My work was to pack and unpack goods, and to carry boxes, and I had only to work from six in the morning till six in the evening; so I had plenty of time. I hired a little room, and subscribed to a library, so I had everything I needed; and in the week of Christmas holidays I went to see the sea. I walked all night, Lyndall, to escape the heat, and a little after sunrise I got to the top of a high hill. Before me was a long, low, blue, monotonous mountain. I walked looking at it, but I was thinking of the sea I wanted to see. At last I wondered what that curious blue thing might be; then it struck me it was the sea! I would have turned back again, only I was too tired. I wonder if all the things we long to see—the churches, the pictures, the men in Europe—will disappoint us so! You see I had dreamed of it so long. When I was a little boy, minding sheep behind the "kopje," I used to see the waves stretching out as far as the eye could reach in the sunlight. My sea! Is the ideal always more beautiful than the real?

'I got to the beach that afternoon, and I saw the water run up and down on the sand, and I saw the white foam breakers; they were pretty, but I thought I would go back the next day. It was not my sea.

'But I began to like it when I sat by it that night in the moonlight; and the next day I liked it better; and before I left I loved it. It was not like the sky and stars, that talk of what has no beginning and no end; but it is so human. Of all the things I have ever seen, only the sea is like a human being; the sky is not, nor the earth. But the sea is always moving, always something deep in itself is stirring it. It never rests; it is always wanting, wanting, wanting. It hurries on; and then it creeps back slowly without having reached, moaning. It is always asking a question, and it never gets the answer. I can hear it in the day and in the night; the white foam breakers are saying that which I think. I walk alone with them when there is no one to see me, and I sing with them. I lie down on the sand and watch them with my eyes half shut. The sky is better, but it is so high above our heads. I love the sea. Sometimes we must look down too. After five days I went back to Grahamstown.

'I had glorious books, and in the night I could sit in my little room and read them; but I was lonely. Books are not the same things when you are living among people. I cannot tell why, but they are dead. On the farm they would have been living beings to me; but here, where there were so many people about me, I wanted some one to belong to me. I was lonely. I wanted something that was flesh and blood. Once on this farm there came a stranger: I did not ask his name, but he sat among the karroo and talked with me. Now, wherever I have travelled I have looked for him—in hotels, in streets, in passenger waggons as they rushed in, through the open windows of houses I have looked for him, but I have not found him— never heard a voice like his. One day I went to the Botanic Gardens. It was a half-holiday, and the band was to play. I stood in the long raised avenue and looked down. There were many flowers, and ladies and children were walking about beautifully dressed. At last the music began. I had not heard such music before. At first it was slow and even, like the everyday life, when we walk through it without thought or feeling; then it grew faster, then it paused, hesitated, then it was quite still for an instant, and then it burst out. Lyndall, they made heaven right when they made it all music. It takes you up and carries you away, away, till you have the things you longed for; you are up close to them. You have got out into a large, free, open place. I could not see anything while it was playing; I stood with my head against my tree; but, when it was done, I saw that there were ladies sitting close to me on a wooden bench, and the stranger who had talked to me that day in the karroo was sitting between them. The ladies were very pretty, and their dresses beautiful. I do not think they had been listening to the music, for they were talking and laughing very softly. I heard all they said, and could even smell the rose on the breast of one. I was afraid he would see me; so I went to the other side of the tree, and soon they got up and began to pace up and down in the avenue. All the time the music played they chatted, and he carried on his arm the scarf of the prettiest lady. I did not hear the music; I tried to catch the sound of his voice each time he went by. When I was listening to the music I did not know I was badly dressed; now I felt so ashamed of myself. I never knew before what a low, horrible thing I was, dressed in tancord. That day on the farm, when we sat on the ground under the thorn-trees, I thought he quite belonged to me; now, I saw he was not mine. But he was still as beautiful. His brown eyes are more beautiful than any one's eyes, except yours.

'At last they turned to go, and I walked after them. When they got out of the gate he helped the ladies into a phaeton, and stood for a moment with his foot on the step talking to them. He had a little cane in his hand, and an Italian greyhound ran after him. Just when they drove away one of the ladies dropped her whip.

'"Pick it up, fellow," she said; and when I brought it her she threw sixpence on the ground. I might have gone back to the garden then; but I did not want music; I wanted clothes, and to be fashionable and fine. I felt that my hands were coarse, and that I was vulgar. I never tried to see him again.

'I stayed in my situation four months after that, but I was

not happy. I had no rest. The people about me pressed on me, and made me dissatisfied. I could not forget them. Even when I did not see them they pressed on me, and made me miserable. I did not love books; I wanted people. When I walked home under the shady trees in the street I could not be happy, for when I passed the houses I heard music, and saw faces between the curtains. I did not want any of them, but I wanted some one for mine, for me. I could not help it. I wanted a finer life.

'Only one day something made me happy. A nurse came to the store with a little girl belonging to one of our clerks. While the maid went into the office to give a message to its father, the little child stood looking at me. Presently she came close to me and peeped up into my face.

'"Nice curls, pretty curls," she said; "I like curls."

'She felt my hair all over with her little hands. When I put out my arm she let me take her and sit her on my knee. She kissed me with her soft mouth. We were happy till the nurse-girl came and shook her, and asked her if she was not ashamed to sit on the knee of that strange man. But I do not think my little one minded. She laughed at me as she went out.

'If the world was all children I could like it; but men and women draw me so strangely, and then press me away, till I am in agony. I was not meant to live among people. Perhaps some day, when I am grown older, I will be able to go and live among them and look at them as I look at the rocks and bushes, without letting them disturb me, and take myself from me; but not now. So I grew miserable; a kind of fever seemed to eat me; I could not rest, or read, or think; so I came back here. I knew you were not here, but it seemed as though I should be nearer you; and it is you I want—you that the other people suggest to me, but cannot give.'

He had filled all the sheets he had taken, and now lifted down the last from the mantelpiece. Em had dropped asleep, and lay slumbering peacefully on the skin before the fire. Out of doors the storm still raged; but in a fitful manner, as though growing half weary of itself. He bent over his paper again, with eager flushed cheek, and wrote on.

'It has been a delightful journey, this journey home. I have walked on foot. The evening before last, when it was just sunset, I was a little footsore and thirsty, and went out of the road to look for water. I went down into a deep little "kloof." Some trees ran along the bottom, and I thought I should find water there. The sun had quite set when I got to the bottom of it. It was very still—not a leaf was stirring anywhere. In the bed of the mountain torrent I thought I might find water. I came to the bank, and leaped down into the dry bed. The floor on which I stood was of fine white sand, and the banks rose on every side like the walls of a room. Above, there was a precipice of rocks, and a tiny stream of water oozed from them and fell slowly on to the flat stone below. Each drop you could hear fall like a little silver bell. There was one among the trees on the bank that stood cut out against the white sky. All the other trees were silent; but this one shook and trembled against the sky. Everything else was still; but those leaves were quivering, quivering. I stood on the sand; I could not go away. When it was quite dark, and the stars had come, I crept out. Does it seem strange to you that it should have made me so happy? It is because I cannot tell you how near I felt to things that we cannot see but we always feel. To-night has been a wild, stormy night. I have been walking across the plain for hours in the dark. I have liked the wind, because I have seemed forcing my way through to you. I knew you were not here, but I would hear of you. When I used to sit on the transport waggon half-sleeping, I used to start awake because your hands were on me. In my lodgings, many nights I have blown the light out, and sat in the dark, that I might see your face start out more distinctly. Sometimes it was the little girl's face who used to come to me behind the "kopje" when I minded sheep, and sit by me in her blue pinafore; sometimes it was older. I love both. I am very helpless, I shall never do anything; but you will work, and I will take your work for mine. Sometimes such a sudden gladness seizes me when I remember that somewhere in the world you are living and working. You are my very own; nothing else is my own so. When I have finished I am going to look at your room door——'

He wrote; and the wind, which had spent its fury, moaned round and round the house, most like a tired child weary with crying.

Em woke up, and sat before the fire, rubbing her eyes, and listening, as it sobbed about the gables, and wandered away over the long stone walls.

'How quiet it has grown now,' she said, and sighed herself, partly from weariness and partly from sympathy with the tired wind. He did not answer her; he was lost in his letter.

She rose slowly after a time, and rested her hand on his shoulder.

'You have many letters to write,' she said.

'No,' he answered; 'it is only one to Lyndall.'

She turned away, and stood long before the fire looking into it. If you have a deadly fruit to give, it will not grow sweeter by keeping.

'Waldo, dear,' she said, putting her hand on his, 'leave off writing.'

He threw back the dark hair from his forehead and looked at her.

'It is no use writing any more,' she said.

'Why not?' he asked.

She put her hand over the papers he had written.

'Waldo,' she said, 'Lyndall is dead.'

CHAPTER XII
Gregory's Womanhood

SLOWLY over the flat came a cart. On the back seat sat Gregory, his arms folded, his hat drawn over his eyes. A Kaffir boy sat on the front seat driving, and at his feet sat Doss, who, now and again, lifted his nose and eyes above the level of the splashboard, to look at the surrounding country; and then, with an exceedingly knowing wink of his left eye, turned to his companions, thereby intimating that he clearly perceived his whereabouts. No one noticed the cart coming. Waldo, who was at work at his carpenter's table in the waggon-house, saw nothing, till, chancing to look down, he perceived Doss standing before him, the legs trembling, the little nose wrinkled, and a series of short suffocating barks giving utterance to his joy at reunion.

Em, whose eyes had ached with looking out across the plain, was now at work in a back room, and knew nothing till, looking up, she saw Gregory, with his straw hat and blue eyes, standing in the doorway. He greeted her quietly, hung his hat up in its old place behind the door, and for any change in his manner or appearance he might have been gone only the day before to fetch letters from the town. Only his beard was gone, and his face was grown thinner. He took off his leather gaiters, said the afternoon was hot and the roads dusty, and asked for some tea. They talked of wool, and the cattle, and the sheep, and Em gave him the pile of letters that had come for him during the months of absence, but of the thing that lay at their hearts neither said anything. Then he went out to look at the kraals, and at supper Em gave him hot cakes and coffee. They talked about the servants, and then ate their meal in quiet. She asked no questions. When it was ended Gregory went into the front room, and lay in the dark on the sofa.

'Do you not want a light?' Em asked, venturing to look in.

'No,' he answered; then presently called to her, 'Come and sit here; I want to talk to you.'

She came and sat on a footstool near him.

'Do you wish to hear anything?' he asked.

She whispered, 'Yes, if it does not hurt you.'

'What difference does it make to me?' he said. 'If I talk or am silent, is there any change?'

Yet he lay quiet for a long time. The light through the open door showed him to her, where he lay, with his arm thrown across his eyes. At last he spoke. Perhaps it was a relief to him to speak.

To Bloemfontein in the Free State, to which through an agent he had traced them, Gregory had gone. At the hotel where Lyndall and her stranger had stayed he put up; he was shown the very room in which they had slept. The coloured boy who had driven them to the next town told him in which house they had boarded, and Gregory went on. In that town he found they had left the cart, and bought a spider and four greys, and Gregory's heart rejoiced. Now indeed it would be easy to trace their course. And he turned his steps northwards.

At the farmhouses where he stopped the 'ooms' and 'tantes' remembered clearly the spider* with its four grey horses. At one place the Boer-wife told how the tall, blue-eyed English-man had bought milk, and asked the way to the next farm. At the next farm the Englishman had bought a bunch of flowers, and given half-a-crown for them to the little girl. It was quite true; the Boer-mother made her get it out of the box and show it. At the next place they had slept. Here they told him that the great bull-dog who hated all strangers, had walked in in the evening and laid its head on the lady's lap. So at every place he heard something, and traced them step by step.

At one desolate farm the Boer had a good deal to tell. The lady had said she liked a waggon that stood before the door. Without asking the price the Englishman had offered a hundred and fifty pounds for the old thing, and bought oxen worth ten pounds for sixteen. The Dutchman chuckled, for he had the 'Salt-reim's' money* in the box under his bed. Gregory laughed too, in silence; he could not lose sight of them now, so slowly they would have to move with that cumbrous ox-waggon. Yet, when that evening came, and he reached a little wayside inn, no one could tell him anything of the travellers.

The master, a surly creature, half-stupid with Boer-brandy, sat on the bench before the door smoking. Gregory sat beside him, questioning, but he smoked on. He remembered nothing of such strangers. How should he know who had been there months and months before? He smoked on. Gregory, very weary, tried to awake his memory, said that the lady he was seeking for was very beautiful, had a little mouth, and tiny, very tiny, feet. The man only smoked on as sullenly as at first. What were little, very little, mouths and feet to him. But his daughter leaned out in the window above. She was dirty and lazy, and liked to loll there when travellers came, to hear the men talk, but she had a soft heart. Presently a hand came out of the window, and a pair of velvet slippers touched his shoulder, tiny slippers with black flowers. He pulled them out of her hand. Only one woman's feet had worn them, he knew that.

'Left here last summer by a lady,' said the girl; 'might be the one you are looking for. Never saw any feet so small.'

Gregory rose and questioned her.

They might have come in a waggon and spider, she could not tell. But the gentleman was very handsome, tall, lovely figure, blue eyes, wore gloves always when he went out. An English officer, perhaps; no Africander, certainly.

Gregory stopped her.

The lady? Well, she was pretty, rather, the girl said; very cold, dull air, silent. They stayed for, it might be, five days; slept in the wing over against the 'stoep;' quarrelled sometimes, she thought—the lady. She had seen everything when she went in to wait. One day the gentleman touched her hair; she drew back from him as though his fingers poisoned her. Went to the other end of the room if he came to sit near her. Walked out alone. Cold wife for such a handsome husband, the girl thought; she evidently pitied him, he was such a beautiful man. They went away early one morning, how, or in which way, the girl could not tell.

Gregory inquired of the servants, but nothing more was to be learnt; so the next morning he saddled his horse and went on. At the farms he came to the good old 'ooms' and 'tantes' asked him to have coffee, and the little shoeless children peeped out at the stranger from behind ovens and gables; but no one had seen what he asked for. This way and that he rode to pick up the thread he had dropped; but the spider and the waggon, the little lady and the handsome gentleman, no one had seen. In the towns he fared yet worse.

Once indeed hope came to him. On the 'stoep' of an hotel at which he stayed the night in a certain little village, there walked a gentleman, grave and kindly-looking. It was not hard to open conversation with him about the weather, and then— Had he ever seen such and such people, a gentleman and lady, a spider and waggon, arrive at that place? The kindly gentleman shook his head. What was the lady like, he inquired.

Gregory painted. Hair like silken floss, small mouth, underlip very full and pink, upper lip pink but very thin and curled; there were four white spots on the nail of her right hand forefinger, and her eyebrows were very delicately curved.

The gentleman looked thoughtful, as trying to remember.

'Yes; and a rose-bud tinge in the cheeks; hands like lilies, and perfectly seraphic smile.'

'That is she! that is she!' cried Gregory.

Who else could it be? He asked where she had gone to. The gentleman most thoughtfully stroked his beard. He would try to remember. Were not her ears—— Here such a violent fit of coughing seized him that he ran away into the house. An ill-fed clerk and a dirty barman standing in the doorway laughed aloud. Gregory wondered if they could be laughing at the gentleman's cough, and then he heard some one laughing in the room into which the gentleman had gone. He must follow him and try to learn more; but he soon found that there was nothing more to be learnt there. Poor Gregory!

Backwards and forwards, backwards and forwards, from the dirty little hotel where he had dropped the thread, to this farm and to that, rode Gregory, till his heart was sick and tired. That from that spot the waggon might have gone its own way and the spider another was an idea that did not occur to him. At last he saw it was no use lingering in that neighbourhood, and pressed on.

One day, coming to a little town, his horses knocked up, and he resolved to rest them there. The little hotel of the town was a bright and sunny place, like the jovial face of the clean little woman who kept it, and who trotted about talking always—talking to the customers in the tap-room, and to the maids in the kitchen, and to the passers-by when she could hail them from the windows; talking, as good-natured women with large mouths and small noses always do, in season and out.

There was a little front parlour in the hotel, kept for strangers who wanted to be alone. Gregory sat there to eat his breakfast, and the landlady dusted the room and talked of the great finds at the Diamond Fields, and the badness of maid-servants, and the shameful conduct of the Dutch parson in that town to the English inhabitants. Gregory ate his breakfast and listened to nothing. He had asked his one question, had had his answer; now she might talk on.

Presently a door in the corner opened and a woman came out—a Mozambiquer, with a red handkerchief twisted round her head. She carried in her hand a tray, with a slice of toast crumbled fine, and a half-filled cup of coffee, and an egg broken open, but not eaten. Her ebony face grinned complacently as she shut the door softly and said 'Good morning.'

The landlady began to talk to her.

'You are not going to leave her really, Ayah, are you?' she said. 'The maids say so; but I'm sure you wouldn't do such a thing.'

The Mozambiquer grinned.

'Husband says I must go home.'

'But she hasn't got any one else, and won't have any one else. Come now,' said the landlady, 'I've no time to be sitting always in a sick room, not if I was paid anything for it.'

The Mozambiquer only showed her white teeth good-naturedly for answer, and went out, and the landlady followed her.

Gregory, glad to be alone, watched the sunshine as it came over the fuchsias in the window, and ran up and down on the panelled door in the corner. The Mozambiquer had closed it loosely behind her, and presently something touched it inside.

It moved a little, then it was still, then moved again; then through the gap a small nose appeared, and a yellow ear overlapping one eye; then the whole head obtruded, placed itself critically on one side, wrinkled its nose disapprovingly at Gregory, and withdrew. Through the half-open door came a faint scent of vinegar, and the room was dark and still.

Presently the landlady came back.

'Left the door open,' she said, bustling to shut it; 'but a darkey will be a darkey, and never carries a head on its shoulders like other folks. Not ill, I hope, sir?' she said, looking at Gregory when she had shut the bedroom door.

'No,' said Gregory, 'no.'

The landlady began putting the things together.

'Who,' asked Gregory, 'is in that room?'

Glad to have a little innocent piece of gossip to relate, and some one willing to hear it, the landlady made the most of a little story as she cleared the table. Six months before a lady had come alone to the hotel in a waggon, with only a coloured leader and driver. Eight days after a little baby had been born. If Gregory stood and looked out at the window he would see a blue gum-tree in the grave-yard; close by it was a little grave. The baby was buried there. A tiny thing, only lived two hours, and the mother herself almost went with it. After a while she was better; but one day she got up out of bed, dressed herself without saying a word to any one, and went out. It was a drizzly day; a little time after some one saw her sitting on the wet ground under the blue gum-tree, with the rain dripping from her hat and shawl. They went to fetch her, but she would not come until she chose. When she did she had gone to bed, and had not risen again from it; never would, the doctor said.

She was very patient, poor thing. When you went in to ask her how she was she said always 'Better,' or 'Nearly well!' and lay still in the darkened room, and never troubled any one. The Mozambiquer took care of her, and she would not allow any one else to touch her; would not so much as allow any one else to see her foot uncovered. She was strange in many ways, but she paid well, poor thing; and now the Mozambiquer was going, and she would have to take up with some one else.

The landlady prattled on pleasantly, and now carried away

the tray with the breakfast-things. When she was gone Gregory leaned his head on his hands, but he did not think long.

Before dinner he had ridden out of the town to where on a rise a number of transport-waggons were out-spanned. The Dutchman driver of one wondered at the stranger's eagerness to free himself of his horses. Stolen perhaps; but it was worth his while to buy them at so low a price. So the horses changed masters, and Gregory walked off with his saddle-bags slung across his arm. Once out of sight of the waggons he struck out of the road and walked across the 'veld,' the dry, flowering grasses waving everywhere about him; half way across the plain he came to a deep gully which the rain torrents had washed out, but which was now dry. Gregory sprang down into its red bed. It was a safe place, and quiet. When he had looked about him he sat down under the shade of an overhanging bank and fanned himself with his hat, for the afternoon was hot, and he had walked fast. At his feet the dusty ants ran about, and the high red bank before him was covered by a network of roots and fibres washed bare by the rains. Above his head rose the clear blue African sky; at his side were the saddle-bags full of woman's clothing. Gregory looked up half plaintively into the blue sky.

'Am I, am I Gregory Nazianzen Rose?' he said.

It was all so strange, he sitting there in that 'sloot' in that up-country plain!—strange as the fantastic, changing shapes in a summer cloud. At last, tired out, he fell asleep, with his head against the bank. When he woke the shadow had stretched across the 'sloot,' and the sun was on the edge of the plain. Now he must be up and doing. He drew from his breast pocket a little sixpenny looking-glass, and hung it on one of the roots that stuck out from the bank. Then he dressed himself in one of the old-fashioned gowns and a great pinked-out collar. Then he took out a razor. Tuft by tuft the soft brown beard fell down into the sand, and the little ants took it to line their nests with. Then the glass showed a face surrounded by a frilled cap, white as a woman's, with a little mouth, a very short upper lip, and a receding chin.

Presently a rather tall woman's figure was making its way across the 'veld.' As it passed a hollowed-out ant-heap it knelt down, and stuffed in the saddle-bags with the man's clothing, closing up the ant-hill with bits of ground to look as natural as possible. Like a sinner hiding his deed of sin, the hider started once and looked round, but yet there was no one near save a 'meerkat,'* who had lifted herself out of her hole and sat on her hind legs watching. He did not like that even she should see, and when he rose she dived away into her hole. Then he walked on leisurely, that the dusk might have reached the village streets before he walked there. The first house was the smith's, and before the open door two idle urchins lolled. As he hurried up the street in the gathering gloom he heard them laugh long and loudly behind him. He glanced round fearingly, and would almost have fled, but that the strange skirts clung about his legs. And after all it was only a spark that had alighted on the head of one, and not the strange figure they laughed at.

The door of the hotel stood wide open, and the light fell out into the street. He knocked, and the landlady came. She peered out to look for the cart that had brought the traveller; but Gregory's heart was brave now he was so near the quiet room. He told her he had come with the transport waggons that stood outside the town.

He had walked in, and wanted lodgings for the night.

It was a deliberate lie, glibly told; he would have told fifty, though the recording angel had stood in the next room with his pen dipped in the ink. What was it to him? He remembered that she lay there saying always, 'I am better.'

The landlady put his supper in the little parlour where he had sat in the morning. When it was on the table she sat down in the rocking-chair, as her fashion was, to knit and talk, that she might gather news for her customers in the tap-room. In the white face under the queer, deep-fringed cap she saw nothing of the morning's traveller. The new-comer was communicative. She was a nurse by profession, she said; had come to the Transvaal, hearing that good nurses were needed there. She had not yet found work. The landlady did not perhaps know whether there would be any for her in that town?

The landlady put down her knitting and smote her fat hands together.

If it wasn't the very finger of God's Providence, as though you saw it hanging out of the sky, she said. Here was a lady ill and needing a new nurse that very day, and not able to get one to her mind, and now—well, if it wasn't enough to convert all the atheists and freethinkers in the Transvaal she didn't know!

Then the landlady proceeded to detail facts.

'I'm sure you will suit her,' she added; 'you're just the kind. She has heaps of money to pay you with; has everything that money can buy. And I got a letter with a cheque in it for fifty pounds the other day from some one, who says I'm to spend it for her, and not to let her know. She is asleep now but I'll take you in to look at her.'

The landlady opened the door of the next room, and Gregory followed her. A table stood near the bed, and a lamp burning low stood on it; the bed was a great four-poster with white curtains, and the quilt was of rich crimson satin. But Gregory stood just inside the door with his head bent low, and saw no further.

'Come nearer! I'll turn the lamp up a bit, that you can have a look at her. A pretty thing, isn't it?' said the landlady.

Near the foot of the bed was a dent in the crimson quilt, and out of it Doss's small head and bright eyes looked knowingly.

'See how the lips move; she is in pain,' said the landlady.

Then Gregory looked up at what lay on the cushion. A little white, white face, transparent as an angel's, with a cloth bound round the forehead, and with soft short hair tossed about on the pillow.

'We had to cut it off,' said the woman, touching it with her fore-finger. 'Soft as silk, like a wax doll's.'

But Gregory's heart was bleeding.

'Never get up again, the doctor says,' said the landlady.

Gregory uttered one word. In an instant the beautiful eyes opened widely, looked round the room and into the dark corners.

'Who is here? Whom did I hear speak?'

Gregory had sunk back behind the curtain; the landlady drew it aside, and pulled him forward.

'Only this lady, ma'am—a nurse by profession. She is

willing to stay and take care of you, if you can come to terms
with her.'

Lyndall raised herself on her elbow, and cast one keen
scrutinizing glance over him.

'Have I never seen you before?' she asked.

'No.'

She fell back wearily.

'Perhaps you would like to arrange the terms between
yourselves,' said the landlady. 'Here is a chair. I will be back
presently.'

Gregory sat down, with bent head and quick breath. She did
not speak, and lay with half-closed eyes, seeming to have
forgotten him.

'Will you turn the lamp down a little?' she said at last; 'I
cannot bear the light.'

Then his heart grew braver in the shadow, and he spoke.
Nursing was to him, he said, his chosen life's work. He wanted
no money: if—— She stopped him.

'I take no service for which I do not pay,' she said. 'What I
gave to my last nurse I will give to you; if you do not like it
you may go.'

And Gregory muttered humbly, he would take it.

Afterwards she tried to turn herself. He lifted her. Ah! a
shrunken little body, he could feel its weakness as he touched
it. His hands were to him glorified for what they had done.

'Thank you! that is so nice. Other people hurt me when they
touch me,' she said. 'Thank you!' Then after a little while she
repeated humbly, 'Thank you; they hurt me so.'

Gregory sat down trembling. His little ewe-lamb, could they
hurt her?

The doctor said of Gregory four days after, 'She is the most
experienced nurse I ever came in contact with.'

Gregory, standing in the passage, heard it, and laughed in
his heart. What need had he of experience? Experience teaches
us in a millennium what passion teaches us in an hour. A
Kaffir studies all his life the discerning of distant sounds; but
he will never hear my step, when my love hears it, coming to
her window in the dark over the short grass.

At first Gregory's heart was sore when day by day the body

grew lighter, and the mouth he fed took less; but afterwards he grew accustomed to it, and was happy. For passion has *one* cry, one only—'Oh, to touch thee, Beloved!'

In that quiet room Lyndall lay on the bed with the dog at her feet, and Gregory sat in his dark corner watching.

She seldom slept, and through those long, long days she would lie watching the round streak of sunlight that came through the knot in the shutter, or the massive lion's paw on which the wardrobe rested. What thoughts were in those eyes? Gregory wondered; he dared not ask.

Sometimes Doss, where he lay on her feet, would dream that they two were in the cart, tearing over the 'veld,' with the black horses snorting, and the wind in their faces; and he would start up in his sleep and bark aloud. Then awaking, he would lick his mistress's hand almost remorsefully, and slink quietly down into his place.

Gregory thought she had no pain, she never groaned; only sometimes, when the light was near her, he thought he could see slight contractions about her lips and eyebrows.

He slept on the sofa outside her door.

One night he thought he heard a sound, and, opening it softly, he looked in. She was crying out aloud, as if she and her pain were alone in the world. The light fell on the red quilt, and on the little hands that were clasped over the head. The wide-open eyes were looking up, and the heavy drops fell slowly from them.

'I cannot bear any more,' she said in a deep voice. 'Oh, God, God! Have I not borne in silence? Have I not endured these long, long months? But now, now, oh God, I cannot!'

Gregory knelt in the doorway listening.

'I do not ask for wisdom, not human love, not work, not knowledge, not for all things I have longed for,' she cried; 'only a little freedom from pain! only one little hour without pain! Then I will suffer again.'

She sat up, and bit the little hand Gregory loved.

He crept away to the front door, and stood looking out at the quiet starlight. When he came back she was lying in her usual posture, the quiet eyes looking at the lion's claw. He came close to the bed.

'You have much pain to-night?' he asked her.

'No, not much.'

'Can I do anything for you?'

'No, nothing.'

She still drew her lips together, and motioned with her fingers towards the dog who lay sleeping at her feet. Gregory lifted him and laid him at her side. She made Gregory turn open the bosom of her night-dress that the dog might put his black muzzle between her breasts. She crossed her arms over him. Gregory left them lying there together.

The next day, when they asked her how she was, she answered 'Better.'

'Some one ought to tell her,' said the landlady; 'we can't let her soul go out into eternity not knowing, especially when I don't think it was all right about the child. You ought to go and tell her, Doctor.'

So, the little doctor, edged on and on, went in at last. When he came out of the room he shook his fist in the landlady's face.

'Next time you have any Devil's work to do, do it yourself,' he said, and shook his fist in her face again, and went away swearing.

When Gregory went into the bedroom he only found her moved, her body curled up, and drawn close to the wall. He dared not disturb her. At last, after a long time, she turned.

'Bring me food,' she said, 'I want to eat. Two eggs, and toast, and meat—two large slices of toast, please.'

Wondering, Gregory brought a tray with all that she had asked for.

'Sit me up, and put it close to me,' she said; 'I am going to eat it all.' She tried to draw the things near her with her fingers, and re-arranged the plates. She cut the toast into long strips, broke open both eggs, put a tiny morsel of bread into her own mouth, and fed the dog with pieces of meat put into his jaws with her fingers.

'Is it twelve o'clock yet?' she said; 'I think I do not generally eat so early. Put it away, please, *carefully*—no, do not take it away—only on the table. When the clock strikes twelve I will eat it.'

She lay down trembling. After a little while she said,

'Give me my clothes.'

He looked at her.

'Yes; I'm going to dress to-morrow. I should get up now but it is rather late. Put them on that chair. My collars are in the little box, my boots behind the door.'

Her eyes followed him intently as he collected the articles one by one, and placed them on the chair as she directed.

'Put it nearer,' she said; 'I cannot see it;' and she lay watching the clothes, with her hand under her cheek.

'Now open the shutter wide,' she said; 'I am going to read.'

The old, old tone was again in the sweet voice. He obeyed her; and opened the shutter, and raised her up among the pillows.

'Now bring my books to me,' she said, motioning eagerly with her fingers 'the large book, and the reviews, and the plays; I want them all.'

He piled them round her on the bed; she drew them greedily closer, her eyes very bright, but her face as white as a mountain lily.

'Now the big one off the drawers. No, you need not help me to hold my book,' she said; 'I can hold it for myself.'

Gregory went back to his corner, and for a little time the restless turning over of leaves was to be heard.

'Will you open the window,' she said, almost querulously, 'and throw this book out? It is so utterly foolish. I thought it was a valuable book; but the words are merely strung together, they make no sense. Yes—so!' she said with approval, seeing him fling it out into the street. 'I must have been very foolish when I thought that book good.'

Then she turned to read, and leaned her little elbows resolutely on the great volume, and knit her brows. This was Shakespeare—it must mean something.

'I wish you would take a handkerchief and tie it tight round my head, it aches so.'

He had not been long in his seat when he saw drops fall from beneath the hands that shaded the eyes, on to the page.

'I am not accustomed to so much light, it makes my head swim a little,' she said. 'Go out and close the shutter.'

When he came back, she lay shrivelled up among the pillows.

He heard no sound of weeping; but the shoulders shook. He darkened the room completely.

When Gregory went to his sofa that night, she told him to wake her early; she would be dressed before breakfast. Nevertheless, when morning came, she said it was a little cold, and lay all day watching her clothes upon the chair. Still she sent for her oxen in the country; they would start on Monday and go down to the Colony.

In the afternoon she told him to open the window wide, and draw the bed near it.

It was a leaden afternoon, the dull rain-clouds rested close to the roofs on the houses, and the little street was silent and deserted. Now and then a gust of wind eddying round caught up the dried leaves, whirled them hither and thither under the trees, and dropped them again into the gutter: then all was quiet. She lay looking out. Presently the bell of the church began to toll, and up the village street came a long procession. They were carrying an old man to his last resting-place. She followed them with her eyes till they turned in among the trees at the gate.

'Who was that?' she asked.

'An old man,' he answered, 'a very old man; they say he was ninety-four; but his name I do not know.'

She mused a while, looking out with fixed eyes.

'That is why the bell rang so cheerfully,' she said. 'When the old die it is well; they have had their time. It is when the young die that the bells weep drops of blood.'

'But the old love life?' he said; for it was sweet to hear her speak.

She raised herself on her elbow.

'They love life, they do not want to die,' she answered; 'but what of that? They have had their time. They knew that a man's life is three-score years and ten; they should have made their plans accordingly! But the young,' she said, 'the young cut down, cruelly, when they have not seen, when they have not known—when they have not found—it is for them that the bells weep blood. I heard in the ringing it was an old man.

When the old die—— Listen to the bell! It is laughing—"It is right, it is right: he has had his time." They cannot ring so for the young.'

She fell back exhausted; the hot light died from her eyes, and she lay looking out into the street. By-and-by stragglers from the funeral began to come back and disappear here and there among the houses; then all was quiet, and the night began to settle down upon the village street. Afterwards, when the room was almost dark, so that they could not see each other's faces, she said, 'It will rain to-night;' and moved restlessly on the pillows. 'How terrible when the rain falls down on you.'

He wondered what she meant, and they sat on in the still darkening room. She moved again.

'Will you presently take my cloak—the new grey cloak from behind the door—and go out with it. You will find a little grave at the foot of the tall blue gum-tree; the water drips off the long, pointed leaves; you must cover it up with that.'

She moved restlessly as though in pain.

Gregory assented, and there was silence again. It was the first time she had ever spoken of her child.

'It was so small,' she said; 'it lived such a little while—only three hours. They laid it close by me, but I never saw it; I could feel it by me.' She waited; 'Its feet were so cold; I took them in my hand to make them warm, and my hand closed right over them they were so little.' There was an uneven trembling in the voice. 'It crept close to me; it wanted to drink, it wanted to be warm.' She hardened herself—'I did not love it; its father was not my prince; I did not care for it; but it was so little.' She moved her hand. 'They might have kissed it, one of them, before they put it in. It never did any one any harm in all its little life. They might have kissed it, one of them.'

Gregory felt that some one was sobbing in the room.

Late on in the evening, when the shutter was closed and the lamp lighted, and the rain-drops beat on the roof, he took the cloak from behind the door and went away with it. On his way back he called at the village post-office and brought back a letter. In the hall he stood reading the address. How could he fail to know whose hand had written it? Had he not long ago studied those characters on the torn fragments of paper in the old parlour? A burning pain was at Gregory's heart. If now, now at the last, one should come, should step in between! He carried the letter into the bedroom and gave it her. 'Bring me the lamp nearer,' she said. When she had read it she asked for her desk.

Then Gregory sat down in the lamp-light on the other side of the curtain, and heard the pencil move on the paper. When he looked round the curtain she was lying on the pillow musing. The open letter lay at her side; she glanced at it with soft eyes. The man with the languid eyelids must have been strangely moved before his hand set down those words: 'Let me come back to you! My darling, let me put my hand round you, and guard you from all the world. As my wife they shall never touch you. I have learnt to love you more wisely, more tenderly, than of old; you shall have perfect freedom. Lyndall, grand little woman, for your own sake be my wife!

'Why did you send that money back to me? You are cruel to me; it is not rightly done.'

She rolled the little red pencil softly between her fingers, and her face grew very soft. Yet—

'It cannot be,' she wrote; 'I thank you much for the love you have shown me; but I cannot listen. You will call me mad, foolish—the world would do so; but I know what I need and the kind of path I must walk in. I cannot marry you. I will always love you for the sake of what lay by me those three hours; but there it ends. I must know and see, I cannot be bound to one whom I love as I love you. I am not afraid of the world—I will fight the world. One day—perhaps it may be far off—I shall find what I have wanted all my life; something nobler, stronger than I, before which I can kneel down. You lose nothing by not having me now; I am a weak, selfish, erring woman. One day I shall find something to worship, and then I shall be——'

'Nurse,' she said; 'take my desk away; I am suddenly so sleepy; I will write more to-morrow.' She turned her face to the pillow; it was the sudden drowsiness of great weakness. She had dropped asleep in a moment, and Gregory moved the desk softly, and then sat in the chair watching. Hour after hour passed, but he had no wish for rest, and sat on, hearing the rain cease, and the still night settle down everywhere. At a quarter past twelve he rose, and took a last look at the bed where she lay sleeping so peacefully; then he turned to go to his couch. Before he had reached the door she had started up and was calling him back.

'You are sure you have put it up?' she said, with a look of blank terror at the window. 'It will not fall open in the night, the shutter—you are sure?'

He comforted her. Yes, it was tightly fastened.

'Even if it is shut,' she said in a whisper, 'you cannot keep it out! You feel it coming in at four o'clock, creeping, creeping, up, up; deadly cold!' She shuddered.

He thought she was wandering, and laid her little trembling body down among the blankets.

'I dreamed just now that it was not put up,' she said, looking into his eyes; 'and it crept right in and I was alone with it.'

'What do you fear?' he asked tenderly.

'The Grey Dawn,' she said, glancing round at the window. 'I was never afraid of anything, never when I was a little child, but I have always been afraid of that. You will not let it come in to me?'

'No, no; I will stay with you,' he continued.

But she was growing calmer, 'No; you must go to bed. I only awoke with a start; you must be tired. I am childish, that is all;' but she shivered again.

He sat down beside her. After some time she said, 'Will you not rub my feet?'

He knelt down at the foot of the bed and took the tiny foot in his hand; it was swollen and unsightly now, but as he touched it he bent down and covered it with kisses.

'It makes it better when you kiss it; thank you. What makes you all love me so?' Then dreamily she muttered to herself: 'Not utterly bad, not quite bad—what makes them all love me so?'

Kneeling there, rubbing softly, with his cheek pressed against the little foot, Gregory dropped to sleep at last. How long he knelt there he could not tell; but when he started up awake she was not looking at him. The eyes were fixed on the far corner, gazing wide and intent, with an unearthly light.

He looked round fearfully. What did she see there? God's angels come to call her? Something fearful? *He* saw only the purple curtain with the shadows that fell from it. Softly he whispered, asking what she saw there.

And she said, in a voice strangely unlike her own, 'I see the vision of a poor weak soul striving after good. It was not cut short; and, in the end, it learnt, through tears and much pain, that holiness is an infinite compassion for others; that greatness is to take the common things of life and walk truly among them; that'—she moved her white hand and laid it on her forehead—'happiness is a great love and much serving. It was not cut short; and it loved what it had learnt—it loved—and——'

Was that all she saw in the corner?

Gregory told the landlady the next morning that she had been wandering all night. Yet, when he came in to give her her breakfast, she was sitting up against the pillows, looking as he had not seen her look before.

'Put it close to me,' she said, 'and when I have had breakfast I am going to dress.'

She finished all he had brought her eagerly.

'I am sitting up quite by myself.' she said, 'Give me his meat;' and she fed the dog herself, cutting his food small for him. She moved to the side of the bed.

'Now bring the chair near and dress me. It is being in this room so long, and looking at that miserable little bit of sunshine that comes in through the shutter, that is making me so ill. Always that lion's paw!' she said, with a look of disgust at it. 'Come and dress me.' Gregory knelt on the floor before her, and tried to draw on one stocking, but the little swollen foot refused to be covered.

'It is very funny that I should have grown so fat since I have been so ill,' she said, peering down curiously. 'Perhaps it is want of exercise?' She looked troubled and said again, 'Perhaps it is want of exercise.' She wanted Gregory to say so too. But he only found a larger pair; and then tried to force the shoes, oh so tenderly! on to her little feet.

'There,' she said, looking down at them when they were on, with the delight of a small child over its first shoes, 'I could walk far now. How nice it looks!'

'No,' she said, seeing the soft gown he had prepared for her, 'I will not put that on. Get one of my white dresses—the one with the pink bows. I do not even want to think I have been ill. It is thinking and thinking of things that makes them real,' she said. 'When you draw your mind together, and resolve that a thing shall not be, it gives way before you; it is not. Everything is possible if one is resolved,' she said. She drew in her little lips together, and Gregory obeyed her; she was so small and slight now it was like dressing a small doll. He would have lifted her down from the bed when he had finished, but she pushed him from her, laughing very softly. It was the first time she had laughed in those long dreary months.

'No, no; I can get down myself,' she said, slipping cautiously on to the floor. 'You see!' She cast a defiant glance of triumph when she stood there. 'Hold the curtain up high, I want to look at myself.'

He raised it, and stood holding it. She looked into the glass on the opposite wall. Such a queenly little figure in its pink and white. Such a transparent little face, refined by suffering into an almost angel-like beauty. The face looked at her; she looked back, laughing softly. Doss, quivering with excitement, ran round her barking. She took one step towards the door, balancing herself with outstretched hands.

'I am nearly there,' she said.

Then she groped blindly.

'Oh, I cannot see! I cannot see! Where am I?' she cried.

When Gregory reached her she had fallen with her face against the sharp foot of the wardrobe and cut her forehead. Very tenderly he raised the little crushed heap of muslin and ribbons, and laid it on the bed. Doss climbed up, and sat looking down at it. Very softly Gregory's hands disrobed her.

'You will be stronger to-morrow, and then we shall try again,' he said, but she neither looked at him nor stirred.

When he had undressed her, and laid her in bed Doss stretched himself across her feet and lay whining softly.

So she lay all that morning, and all that afternoon.

Again and again Gregory crept close to the bedside and looked at her; but she did not speak to him. Was it stupor or was it sleep that shone under those half-closed eyelids? Gregory could not tell.

At last in the evening he bent over her.

'The oxen have come,' he said; 'we can start to-morrow if you like. Shall I get the waggon ready to-night?'

Twice he repeated his question. Then she looked up at him, and Gregory saw that all hope had died out of the beautiful eyes. It was not stupor that shone there, it was despair.

'Yes, let us go,' she said.

'It makes no difference,' said the doctor; 'staying or going; it is close now.'

So the next day Gregory carried her out in his arms to the waggon which stood 'in-spanned' before the door. As he laid her down on the 'kartel'* she looked far out across the plain. For the first time she spoke that day.

'That blue mountain, far away; let us stop when we get to it, not before.' She closed her eyes again. He drew the sails down before and behind, and the waggon rolled away slowly. The landlady and the niggers stood to watch it from the 'stoep.'

Very silently the great waggon rolled along the grass-covered plain. The driver on the front box did not clap his whip or call to his oxen, and Gregory sat beside him with folded arms. Behind them, in the closed waggon, she lay with the dog at her feet, very quiet, with folded hands. He, Gregory, dared not be in there. Like Hagar, when she laid her treasure down in the wilderness, he sat afar off:—'For Hagar said, Let me not see the death of the child.'*

Evening came, and yet the blue mountain was not reached, and all the next day they rode on slowly, but still it was far off. Only at evening they reached it; not blue now, but low and brown, covered with long waving grasses and rough stones. They drew the waggon up close to its foot for the night. It was a sheltered, warm spot.

When the dark night had come, when the tired oxen were tied to the wheels, and the driver and leader had rolled themselves in their blankets before the fire, and gone to sleep,

then Gregory fastened down the sails of the waggon securely.
He fixed a long candle near the head of the bed, and lay down
himself on the floor of the waggon near the back. He leaned
his head against the 'kartel,' and listened to the chewing of the
tired oxen and to the crackling of the fire, till, overpowered by
weariness, he fell into a heavy sleep. Then all was very still in
the waggon. The dog slept on his mistress's feet, and only two
mosquitoes, creeping in through a gap in the front sail, buzzed
drearily round.

The night was grown very old when from a long, peaceful
sleep Lyndall awoke. The candle burnt at her head, the dog
lay on her feet; but he shivered; it seemed as though a coldness
struck up to him from his resting-place. She lay with folded
hands, looking upwards; and she heard the oxen chewing, and
she saw the two mosquitoes buzzing drearily round and round,
and her thoughts,—her thoughts ran far back into the past.

Through these months of anguish a mist had rested on her
mind; it was rolled together now, and the old clear intellect
awoke from its long torpor. It looked back into the past; it saw
the present; there was no future now. The old strong soul
gathered itself together for the last time; it knew where it
stood.

Slowly raising herself on her elbow, she took from the sail a
glass that hung pinned there. Her fingers were stiff and cold.
She put the pillow on her breast, and stood the glass against it.
Then the white face on the pillow looked into the white face in
the glass. They had looked at each other often so before. It
had been a child's face once, looking out above its blue
pinafore; it had been a woman's face, with a dim shadow in
the eyes, and a something which had said, 'We are not afraid,
you and I; we are together; we will fight, you and I.' Now to-
night it had come to this. The dying eyes on the pillow looked
into the dying eyes in the glass; they knew that their hour had
come. She raised one hand and pressed the stiff fingers against
the glass. They were growing very stiff. She tried to speak to
it, but she would never speak again. Only, the wonderful
yearning light was in the eyes still. The body was dead now,
but the soul, clear and unclouded, looked forth.

Then slowly, without a sound, the beautiful eyes closed.

The dead face that the glass reflected was a thing of marvellous beauty and tranquillity. The Grey Dawn crept in over it, and saw it lying there.

Had she found what she sought for—something to worship? Had she ceased from being? Who shall tell us? There is a veil of terrible mist over the face of the Hereafter.

CHAPTER XIII
Dreams

'TELL me what a soul desires, and I will tell you what it is.' So runs the phrase.

'Tell me what a man dreams, and I will tell you what he loves.' That also has its truth.

For, ever from the earliest childhood to the latest age, day by day, and step by step, the busy waking life is followed and reflected by the life of dreams—waking dreams, sleeping dreams. Weird, misty, and distorted as the inverted image of a mirage, or a figure seen through the mountain mist, they are still the reflections of a reality.

On the night when Gregory told his story, Waldo sat alone before the fire, his untasted supper before him. He was weary after his day's work—too weary to eat. He put the plate down on the floor for Doss, who licked it clean, and then went back to his corner. After a time the master threw himself across the foot of the bed without undressing, and fell asleep there. He slept so long that the candle burnt itself out, and the room was in darkness. But he dreamed a lovely dream as he lay there.

In his dream, to his right rose high mountains, their tops crowned with snow, their sides clothed with bush and bathed in the sunshine. At their feet was the sea, blue and breezy, bluer than any earthly sea, like the sea he had dreamed of in his boyhood. In the narrow forest that ran between the mountains and the sea the air was rich with the scent of the honey-creeper that hung from dark green bushes, and through the velvety grass little streams ran purling down into the sea. He sat on a high square rock among the bushes, and Lyndall sat by him and sang to him. She was only a small child, with a blue pinafore, and a grave, grave, little face. He was looking up at the mountains, then suddenly when he looked round she was gone. He slipped down from his rock, and went to look for her, but he found only her little footmarks: he found them on the bright green grass, and in the moist sand, and there where the little streams ran purling down into the sea. In and out, in and out, and among the bushes where the honey-creeper hung, he went looking for her. At last, far off, in the sunshine, he saw her gathering shells upon the sand. She was not a child now, but a woman, and the sun shone on her soft brown hair, and in her white dress she put the shells she gathered. She was stooping, but when she heared his step she stood up, holding her skirt close about her, and waited for his coming. One hand she put in his, and together they walked on over the glittering sand and pink sea-shells; and they heard the leaves talking, and they heard the waters babbling on their way to the sea, and they heard the sea singing to itself, singing, singing.

At last they came to a place where was a long reach of pure white sand: there she stood still, and dropped on to the sand one by one the shells that she had gathered. Then she looked up into his face with her beautiful eyes. She said nothing; but she lifted one hand and laid it softly on his forehead; the other she laid on his heart.

With a cry of suppressed agony Waldo sprang from the bed, flung open the upper half of the door, and leaned out, breathing heavily.

Great God! it might be only a dream, but the pain was very real, as though a knife ran through his heart, as though some treacherous murderer crept on him in the dark! The strong man drew his breath like a frightened woman.

'Only a dream, but the pain was very real,' he muttered, as he pressed his right hand upon his breast. Then he folded his arms on the door, and stood looking out into the starlight.

The dream was with him still; the woman who was his friend was not separated from him by years—only that very night he had seen her. He looked up into the night sky that all his life long had mingled itself with his existence. There were a thousand faces that he loved looking down at him, a thousand stars in their glory, in crowns, and circles, and solitary grandeur. To the man they were not less dear than to the boy they had been, not less mysterious; yet he looked up at them and shuddered; at last turned away from them with horror.

Such countless multitudes, stretching out far into space, and yet not in one of them all was she! Though he searched through them all, to the farthest, faintest point of light, nowhere should he ever say, 'She is here!' To-morrow's sun would rise and gild the world's mountains, and shine into its thousand valleys; it would set and the stars creep out again. Year after year, century after century, the old changes of nature would go on, day and night, summer and winter, seedtime and harvest; but in none of them all would she have part!

He shut the door to keep out their hideous shining, and because the dark was intolerable lit a candle, and paced the little room, faster and faster yet. He saw before him the long ages of eternity that would roll on, on, on, and never bring her. She would exist no more. A dark mist filled the little room.

'Oh, little hand! oh, little voice! oh, little form!' he cried; 'oh, little soul that walked with mine; oh, little soul, that looked so fearlessly down into the depths, do you exist no more for ever—for all time?' He cried more bitterly: 'It is for this hour—this—that men blind reason, and crush out thought! For this hour—this, this—they barter truth and knowledge, take any lie, and creed, so it does not whisper to them of the dead that they are dead! Oh, God! God! for a Hereafter!'

Pain made his soul weak; it cried for the old faith. They are the tears that fall into the new-made grave that cement the power of the priest. For the cry of the soul that loves and loses is this: 'Bridge over Death; blend the Here with the Hereafter; cause the mortal to robe himself in immortality; let me not say of my Dead that it is dead! I will believe all else, bear all else, endure all else!'

Muttering to himself, Waldo walked with bent head, the mist in his eyes.

To the soul's wild cry for its own there are many answers. He began to think of them. Was not there one of them all from which he might suck one drop of comfort?

'You shall see her again,' says the Christian, the true Bible Christian. 'Yes; you shall see her again. "*And I saw the dead, small and great,* * *stand before God. And the books were opened,* *and the dead were judged from those things which were written in the books. And whosoever was not found written in the book of life was cast into the lake of fire, which is the second death.*" Yes; you shall see her again. She died so—with her knee unbent, with her hand unraised, with a prayer unuttered, in the pride of her intellect and the strength of her youth. She loved and she was loved; but she said no prayer to God; she cried for no mercy; she repented of no sin! Yes; you *shall* see her again.'

In his bitterness Waldo laughed low:

Ah, he had long ceased to hearken to the hellish voice.

But yet another speaks.

'You shall see her again,' says the nineteenth-century Christian, deep into whose soul modern unbelief and thought have crept, though he knows it not. He it is who uses his Bible as the pearl-fishers use their shells, sorting out gems from refuse; he sets his pearls after his own fashion, and he sets them well. 'Do not fear,' he says; 'hell and judgment are not. God is love. I know that beyond this blue sky above us is a love as widespreading over all. The All-Father will show her to you again; not spirit only—the little hands, the little feet you loved, you shall lie down and kiss them if you will. Christ arose, and did eat and drink, so shall she arise. The dead, all the dead, raised incorruptible! God is love. You shall see her again.'

It is a heavenly song, this of the nineteenth-century Christian. A man might dry his tears to listen to it, but for this one thing,—Waldo muttered to himself confusedly:—

'The thing I loved was a woman proud and young; it had a mother once, who, dying, kissed her little baby, and prayed God that she might see it again. If it had lived the loved thing would itself have had a son, who, when he closed the weary eyes and smoothed the wrinkled forehead of his mother, would have prayed God to see that old face smile again in the Hereafter. To the son heaven will be no heaven if the sweet worn face is not in one of the choirs; he will look for it through the phalanx of God's glorified angels; and the youth will look for the maid, and the mother for the baby. "And whose then shall she be at the resurrection of the dead?"'

'Ah God! ah God! a beautiful dream,' he cried; 'but can any one dream it not sleeping?'

Waldo paced on, moaning in agony and longing.

He heard the Transcendentalist's high answer.*

'What have you to do with flesh, the gross and miserable garment in which spirit hides itself? You shall see her again. But the hand, the foot, the forehead you loved, you shall see no more. The loves, the fears, the frailties that are born with the flesh, with the flesh they shall die. Let them die! There is that in man that cannot die,—a seed, a germ, an embryo, a spiritual essence. Higher than she was on earth, as the tree is higher than the seed, the man than the embryo, so shall you behold her; changed, glorified!'

High words, ringing well; they are the offering of jewels to the hungry, of gold to the man who dies for bread. Bread is corruptible, gold is incorruptible; bread is light, gold is heavy; bread is common, gold is rare; but the hungry man will barter all your mines for one morsel of bread. Around God's throne there may be choirs and companies of angels, cherubim and seraphim, rising tier above tier, but not for one of them all does the soul cry aloud. Only perhaps for a little human woman full of sin, that it once loved.

'Change is death, change is death,' he cried. 'I want no angel, only she; no holier and no better, with all her sins upon her, so give her me or give me nothing!'

And, truly, does not the heart love its own with the strongest passion for their very frailties? Heaven might keep its angels if men were but left to men.

'Change is death,' he cried, 'change is death! Who dares to say the body never dies, because it turns again to grass and flowers? And yet they dare to say the spirit never dies, because in space some strange unearthly being may have sprung up upon its ruins. Leave me! Leave me!' he cried in frantic bitterness. 'Give me back what I have lost, or give me nothing.'

For the soul's fierce cry for immortality is this,—only this:— Return to me after death the thing as it was before. Leave me in the Hereafter the being that I am to-day. Rob me of the thoughts, the feelings, the desires that are my life, and you have left nothing to take. Your immortality is annihilation, your Hereafter is a lie.

Waldo flung open the door, and walked out into the

starlight, his pain-stricken thoughts ever driving him on as he paced there.

'There must be a Hereafter because man longs for it?' he whispered. 'Is not all life from the cradle to the grave one long yearning for that which we never touch? There must be a Hereafter because we cannot think of any end to life. Can we think of a beginning? Is it easier to say "I was not" than to say "I shall not be"? And yet, where were we ninety years ago? Dreams, dreams! Ah, all dreams and lies! No ground anywhere.'

He went back into the cabin and walked there. Hour after hour passed, and he was dreaming.

For, mark you, men *will* dream; the most that can be asked of them is but that the dream be not in too glaring discord with the thing they know. He walked with bent head.

All dies, all dies! The roses are red with the matter that once reddened the cheek of the child; the flowers bloom the fairest on the last year's battle-ground; the work of death's finger cunningly wreathed over is at the heart of all things, even of the living. Death's finger is everywhere. The rocks are built up of a life that was. Bodies, thoughts, and loves die: from where springs that whisper to the tiny soul of man, 'You shall not die'? Ah, is there no truth of which this dream is shadow?

He fell into perfect silence. And, at last, as he walked there with his bent head, his soul passed down the steps of contemplation into that vast land where there is always peace; that land where the soul, gazing long, loses all consciousness of its little self, and almost feels its hand on the old mystery of Universal Unity that surrounds it.

'No death, no death,' he muttered; 'there is that which never dies—which abides. It is but the individual that perishes, the whole remains. It is the organism that vanishes, the atoms are there. It is but the man that dies, the Universal Whole of which he is part reworks him into its inmost self. Ah, what matter that man's day be short!—that the sunrise sees him, and the sunset sees his grave; that of which he is but the breath has breathed him forth and drawn him back again. That abides—we abide.'

For the little soul that cries aloud for continued personal

existence for itself and its beloved, there is no help. For the soul which knows itself no more as a unit, but as a part of the Universal Unity of which the Beloved also is a part; which feels within itself the throb of the Universal Life; for that soul there is no death.

'Let us die, beloved, you and I, that we may pass on for ever through the Universal Life!' In that deep world of contemplation all fierce desires die out, and peace comes down. He, Waldo, as he walked there, saw no more the world that was about him; cried out no more for the thing that he had lost. His soul rested. Was it only John, think you, who saw the heavens open?* The dreamers see it every day.

Long years before the father had walked in the little cabin, and seen choirs of angels, and a prince like unto men, but clothed in immortality. The son's knowledge was not as the father's, therefore the dream was new-tinted, but the sweetness was all there, the infinite peace, that men find not in the little cankered kingdom of the tangible. The bars of the real are set close about us; we cannot open our wings but they are struck against them, and drop bleeding. But, when we glide between the bars into the great unknown beyond, we may sail for ever in the glorious blue, seeing nothing but our own shadows.

So age succeeds age, and dream succeeds dream, and of the joy of the dreamer no man knoweth but he who dreameth.

Our fathers had their dream; we have ours; the generation that follows will have its own. Without dreams and phantoms man cannot exist.

CHAPTER XIV

Waldo goes out to Sit in the Sunshine

IT had been a princely day. The long morning had melted slowly into a rich afternoon. Rains had covered the karroo with a heavy coat of green that hid the red earth everywhere. In the very chinks of the stone walls dark green leaves hung out, and beauty and growth had crept even into the beds of the sandy furrows and lined them with weeds. On the broken sod-walls of the old pig-sty chick-weeds flourished, and ice-plants lifted their transparent leaves. Waldo was at work in the waggon-house again. He was making a kitchen-table for Em. As the long curls gathered in heaps before his plane, he paused for an instant now and again to throw one down to a small naked nigger, who had crept from its mother, who stood churning in the sunshine, and had crawled into the waggon-house. From time to time the little animal lifted its fat hand as it expected a fresh shower of curls; till Doss, jealous of his master's noticing any other small creature but himself, would catch the curl in his mouth and roll the little Kaffir over in the sawdust, much to that small animal's contentment. It was too lazy an afternoon to be really ill-natured, so Doss satisfied himself with snapping at the little nigger's fingers, and sitting on him till he laughed. Waldo, as he worked, glanced down at them now and then, and smiled; but he never looked out across the plain. He was conscious without looking of that broad green earth; it made his work pleasant to him. Near the shadow at the gable the mother of the little nigger stood churning. Slowly she raised and let fall the stick in her hands, murmuring to herself a sleepy chant such as her people love; it sounded like the humming of far-off bees.

A different life showed itself in the front of the house, where Tant' Sannie's cart stood ready in-spanned, and the Boer-woman herself sat in the front room drinking coffee. She had come to visit her stepdaughter, probably for the last time, as she now weighed two hundred and sixty pounds, and was not easily able to move. On a chair sat her mild young husband nursing the baby—a pudding-faced, weak-eyed child.

'You take it and get into the cart with it,' said Tant' Sannie. 'What do you want here, listening to our woman's talk?'

The young man arose, and meekly went out with the baby.

'I'm very glad you are going to be married, my child,' said Tant' Sannie, as she drained the last drop from her coffee-cup. 'I wouldn't say so while that boy was here, it would make him too conceited; but marriage is the finest thing in the world. I've been at it three times, and if it pleased God to take this husband from me I should have another. There's nothing like it, my child; nothing.'

'Perhaps it might not suit all people, at all times, as well as it suits you, Tant' Sannie,' said Em. There was a little shade of weariness in the voice.

'Not suit every one!' said Tant' Sannie. 'If the beloved Redeemer didn't mean men to have wives what did He make women for? That's what I say. If a woman's old enough to marry, and doesn't, she's sinning against the Lord—it's a wanting to know better than Him. What, does she think the Lord took all that trouble in making her for nothing? It's evident He wants babies, otherwise why does He send them? Not that I've done much in that way myself,' said Tant' Sannie sorrowfully; 'but I've done my best.'

She rose with some difficulty from her chair, and began moving slowly towards the door.

'It's a strange thing,' she said, 'but you can't love a man till you've had a baby by him. Now there's that boy there,—when we were first married if he only sneezed in the night I boxed his ears; now if he lets his pipe-ash come on my milkcloths I don't think of laying a finger on him. There's nothing like being married,' said Tant' Sannie, as she puffed toward the door. 'If a woman's got a baby and a husband she's got the best things the Lord can give her; if only the baby doesn't have convulsions. As for a husband, it's very much the same who one has. Some men are fat, and some men are thin; some men drink brandy, and some men drink gin; but it all comes to the same thing in the end; it's all one. A man's a man, you know.'

Here they came upon Gregory, who was sitting in the shade before the house. Tant' Sannie shook hands with him.

'I'm glad you're going to get married,' she said. 'I hope you'll have as many children in five years as a cow has calves, and more too. I think I'll just go and have a look at your soap-pot before I start,' she said, turning to Em. 'Not that I believe in this new plan of putting soda in the pot. If the dear Father had meant soda to be put into soap what would He have made milk-bushes for, and stuck them all over the "veld" as thick as lambs in the lambing season?'

She waddled off after Em in the direction of the built-in soap-pot, leaving Gregory as they found him, with his dead pipe lying on the bench beside him, and his blue eyes gazing out far across the flat, like one who sits on the sea-shore watching that which is fading, fading from him. Against his breast was a letter found in a desk, addressed to himself, but never posted. It held only four words: 'You must marry Em.' He wore it in a black bag round his neck. It was the only letter she had ever written to him.

'You see if the sheep don't have the scab this year!' said Tant' Sannie, as she waddled after Em. 'It's with all these new inventions that the wrath of God *must* fall on us. What were the children of Israel punished for, it if wasn't for making a golden calf?* I may have my sins, but I do remember the tenth commandment: "Honour thy father and thy mother that it may be well with thee, and that thou mayst live long in the land which the Lord they God giveth thee!" It's all very well to say we honour them, and then to be finding out things that they never knew, and doing things in a way that they never did them! *My* mother boiled soap with bushes, and I will boil soap with bushes. If the wrath of God is to fall upon this land,' said Tant' Sannie, with the serenity of conscious virtue, 'it shall not be through me. Let them make their steam-waggons and their fire-carriages; let them go on as though the dear Lord didn't know what he was about when He gave horses and oxen legs,—the destruction of the Lord will follow them. I don't know how such people read their Bibles. When do we hear of

Moses or Noah riding in a railway? The Lord sent fire-carriages out of heaven in those days: there's no chance of His sending them for us if we go on in this way,' said Tant' Sannie sorrowfully, thinking of the splendid chance which this generation had lost.

Arrived at the soap-pot she looked over into it thoughtfully.

'Depend upon it you'll get the itch, or some other disease; the blessing of the Lord'll never rest upon it,' said the Boer-woman. Then suddenly she broke forth. 'And she eighty-two, and goats, and rams, and eight thousand morgen,* and the rams real angora, and two thousand sheep, and a shorthorn bull,' said Tant' Sannie, standing upright and planting a hand on each hip.

Em looked at her in silent wonder. Had connubial bliss and the joys of motherhood really turned the old Boer-woman's head?

'Yes,' said Tant' Sannie; 'I had almost forgotten to tell you. By the Lord if I had him here! We were walking to church last Sacrament Sunday, Piet and I. Close in front of us was old Tant' Trana, with dropsy and cancer, and can't live eight months. Walking by her was something with its hands under its coat-tails, flap, flap, flap; and its chin in the air, and a stick-up collar, and the black hat on the very back of the head. I knew him! "Who's that?" I asked. "The rich Englishman that Tant' Trana married last week." "Rich Englishman! I'll rich Englishman him," I said; "I'll tell Tant' Trana a thing or two." My fingers were just in his little white curls. If it hadn't been the blessed Sacrament, he wouldn't have walked so "sourka, sourka, sourka,"* any more. But I thought, Wait till I've had it, and then—— But he, sly fox, son of Satan, seed of the Amalekite,* he saw me looking at him in the church. The blessed Sacrament wasn't half over when he takes Tant' Trana by the arm, and out they go. I clap my baby down to its father, and I go after them. But,' said Tant' Sannie, regretfully, 'I couldn't get up to them; I am too fat. When I got to the corner he was pulling Tant' Trana up into the cart. "Tant' Trana," I said, 'you've married a Kaffir's dog, a Hottentot's "brakje."* I hadn't any more breath. He winked at me; he winked at *me*,' said Tant' Sannie, her sides shaking with indignation, 'first with one eye, and then with the other, and then drove away. Child of the Amalekite!' said Tant' Sannie, 'if it hadn't been the blessed Sacrament. Lord, Lord, Lord!'

Here the little Bush-girl came running to say that the horses would stand no longer, and still breathing out vengeance against her old adversary she laboured towards the cart. Shaking hands and affectionately kissing Em, she was with some difficulty drawn up. Then slowly the cart rolled away, the good Boer-woman putting her head out between the sails to smile and nod. Em stood watching it for a time, then as the sun dazzled her eyes she turned away. There was no use in going to sit with Gregory: he liked best sitting there alone, staring across the green karroo; and till the maid had done churning there was nothing to do; so Em walked away to the waggon-house, and climbed on to the end of Waldo's table, and sat there, swinging one little foot slowly to and fro, while the wooden curls from the plane heaped themselves up against her black print dress.

'Waldo,' she said at last, 'Gregory has given me the money he got for the waggon and oxen, and I have fifty pounds besides that once belonged to some one. I know what they would have liked to have done with it. You must take it and go to some place and study for a year or two.'

'No, little one, I will not take it,' he said, as he planed slowly away; 'the time was when I would have been very grateful to any one who would have given me a little money, a little help, a little power of gaining knowledge. But now, I have gone so far alone I may go on to the end. I don't want it, little one.'

She did not seem pained at his refusal, but swung her foot to and fro, the little old wrinkled forehead more wrinkled up than ever.

'Why is it always so, Waldo, always so?' she said; 'we long for things, and long for them, and pray for them; we would give all we have to come near to them, but we never reach them. Then at last, too late, just when we don't want them any more, when all the sweetness is taken out of them, then they come. We don't want them then,' she said, folding her hands resignedly on her little apron. After a while she added; 'I

remember once, very long ago, when I was a very little girl,
my mother had a work-box full of coloured reels. I always
wanted to play with them, but she would never let me. At last
one day she said I might take the box. I was so glad I hardly
knew what to do. I ran round the house, and sat down with it
on the back steps. But when I opened the box all the cottons
were taken out.'

She sat for a while longer, till the Kaffir maid had finished
churning, and was carrying the butter towards the house. Then
Em prepared to slip off the table, but first she laid her little
hand on Waldo's. He stopped his planing and looked up.

'Gregory is going to the town to-morrow. He is going to give
in our banns to the minister; we are going to be married in
three weeks.'

Waldo lifted her very gently from the table. He did not
congratulate her; perhaps he thought of the empty box, but he
kissed her forehead gravely.

She walked away towards the house, but stopped when she
had got half-way. 'I will bring you a glass of buttermilk when
it is cool,' she called out; and soon her clear voice came ringing
out through the back windows as she sang the 'Blue Water' to
herself, and washed the butter.

Waldo did not wait till she returned. Perhaps he had at last
really grown weary of work; perhaps he felt the waggon-house
chilly (for he had shuddered two or three times), though that
was hardly likely in that warm summer weather; or, perhaps,
and most probably, one of his old dreaming fits had come upon
him suddenly. He put his tools carefully together, ready for
to-morrow, and walked slowly out. At the side of the waggon-
house there was a world of bright sunshine, and a hen with her
chickens was scratching among the gravel. Waldo seated
himself near them with his back against the red-brick wall.
The long afternoon was half spent, and the 'kopje' was just
beginning to cast its shadow over the round-headed yellow
flowers that grew between it and the farmhouse. Among the
flowers the white butterflies hovered, and on the old 'kraal'
mounds three white kids gambolled, and at the door of one of
the huts an old grey-headed Kaffir-woman sat on the ground
mending her mats. A balmy, restful, peacefulness seemed to

reign everywhere. Even the old hen seemed well satisfied. She scratched among the stones and called to her chickens when she found a treasure; and all the while tucked to herself with intense inward satisfaction. Waldo, as he sat with his knees drawn up to his chin and his arms folded on them, looked at it all and smiled. An evil world, a deceitful, treacherous, mirage-like world, it might be; but a lovely world for all that, and to sit there gloating in the sunlight was perfect. It was worth having been a little child, and having cried and prayed, so one might sit there. He moved his hands as though he were washing them in the sunshine. There will always be something worth living for while there are shimmery afternoons. Waldo chuckled with intense inward satisfaction as the old hen had done; she, over the insects and the warmth; he, over the old brick-walls, and the haze, and the little bushes. Beauty is God's wine, with which he recompenses the souls that love him; he makes them drunk.

The fellow looked, and at last stretched out one hand to a little ice-plant that grew on the sod-wall of the sty; not as though he would have picked it, but as it were in a friendly greeting. He loved it. One little leaf of the ice-plant stood upright, and the sun shone through it. He could see every little crystal cell like a drop of ice in the transparent green, and it thrilled him.

There are only rare times when a man's soul can see Nature. So long as any passion holds its revel there, the eyes are holden that they should not see her.

Go out if you will, and walk alone on the hill-side in the evening, but if your favourite child lies ill at home, or your lover comes to-morrow, or at your heart there lies a scheme for the holding of wealth, then you will return as you went out; you will have seen nothing. For Nature, ever, like the old Hebrew God, cries out, 'Thou shalt have no other gods before me.'* Only then, when there comes a pause, a blank in your life, when the old idol is broken, when the old hope is dead, when the old desire is crushed, then the Divine compensation of Nature is made manifest. She shows herself to you. So near she draws you, that the blood seems to flow from her to you, through a still uncut cord: you feel the throb of her life.

When that day comes, that you sit down broken, without one human creature to whom you cling, with your loves the dead and the living-dead; when the very thirst for knowledge through long-continued thwarting has grown dull; when in the present there is no craving, and in the future no hope, then, oh, with a beneficent tenderness, Nature enfolds you.

Then the large white snowflakes as they flutter down, softly, one by one, whisper soothingly, 'Rest, poor heart, rest!' It is as though our mother smoothed our hair, and we are comforted.

And yellow-legged bees as they hum make a dreamy lyric; and the light on the brown stone wall is a great work of art; and the glitter through the leaves makes the pulses beat.

Well to die then; for, if you live, so surely as the years come, so surely as the spring succeeds the winter, so surely will passions arise. They will creep back, one by one, into the bosom that has cast them forth, and fasten there again, and peace will go. Desire, ambition, and the fierce agonizing flood of love for the living—they will spring again. Then Nature will draw down her veil: with all your longing you shall not be able to raise one corner; you cannot bring back those peaceful days. Well to die then!

Sitting there with his arms folded on his knees, and his hat slouched down over his face, Waldo looked out into the yellow sunshine that tinted even the very air with the colour of ripe corn, and was happy.

He was an uncouth creature with small learning, and no prospect in the future but that of making endless tables and stone walls, yet it seemed to him as he sat there that life was a rare and very rich thing. He rubbed his hands in the sunshine. Ah, to live on so, year after year, how well! Always in the present; letting each day glide, bringing its own labour, and its own beauty; the gradual lighting up of the hills, night and the stars, firelight and the coals! To live on so, calmly, far from the paths of men; and to look at the lives of clouds and insects; to look deep into the heart of flowers, and see how lovingly the pistil and the stamens nestle there together; and to see in the thorn-pods how the little seeds suck their life through the delicate curled-up string, and how the little embryo sleeps inside! Well, how well, to sit so on one side, taking no part in the world's life; but when great men blossom into books looking into those flowers also, to see how the world of men too opens beautifully, leaf after leaf. Ah! life is delicious; well to live long, and see the darkness breaking, and the day coming! The day when soul shall not thrust back soul that would come to it; when men shall not be driven to seek solitude, because of the crying-out of their hearts for love and sympathy. Well to live long and see the new time breaking. Well to live long; life is sweet, sweet, sweet! In his breast pocket, where of old the broken slate used to be, there was now a little dancing-shoe of his friend who was sleeping. He could feel it when he folded his arm tight against his breast; and that was well also. He drew his hat lower over his eyes, and sat so motionless that the chickens thought he was asleep, and gathered closer around him. One even ventured to peck at his boot; but he ran away quickly. Tiny yellow fellow that he was, he knew that men were dangerous; even sleeping they might awake. But Waldo did not sleep, and coming back from his sunshiny dream, stretched out his hand for the tiny thing to mount. But the chicken eyed the hand askance, and then ran off to hide under its mother's wing, and from beneath it it sometimes put out its round head to peep at the great figure sitting there. Presently its brothers ran off after a little white moth, and it ran out to join them; and when the moth fluttered away over their heads they stood looking up disappointed, and then ran back to their mother.

Waldo through his half-closed eyes looked at them. Thinking, fearing, craving, those tiny sparks of brother life, what were they, so real there in that old yard on that sunshiny afternoon? A few years—where would they be? Strange little brother spirits! He stretched his hand towards them, for his heart went out to them; but not one of the little creatures came nearer him, and he watched them gravely for a time; then he smiled, and began muttering to himself after his old fashion. Afterwards he folded his arms upon his knees, and rested his forehead on them. And so he sat there in the yellow sunshine, muttering, muttering, muttering to himself.

It was not very long after when Em came out at the back-door with a towel thrown across her head, and in her hand a cup of milk.

'Ah,' she said, coming close to him, 'he is sleeping now. He will find it when he wakes, and be glad of it.'

She put it down upon the ground beside him. The mother-hen was at work still among the stones, but the chickens had climbed about him, and were perching on him. One stood upon his shoulder, and rubbed its little head softly against his black curls; another tried to balance itself on the very edge of the old felt hat. One tiny fellow stood upon his hand, and tried to crow; another had nestled itself down comfortably on the old coat-sleeve, and gone to sleep there.

Em did not drive them away; but she covered the glass softly at his side. 'He will wake soon,' she said, 'and be glad of it.'

But the chickens were wiser.

EXPLANATORY NOTES

The following abbreviations are used in the notes:

Clayton	Cherry Clayton (ed.), *Olive Schreiner* (Johannesburg: McGraw-Hill, 1983).
Cronwright-Schreiner	*The Letters of Olive Schreiner, 1876–1920*, ed. S. C. Cronwright-Schreiner (London: T. Fisher Unwin, 1924).
Dreams	Olive Schreiner, Dreams (London: T. Fisher Unwin, 1891).
First and Scott	Ruth First and Ann Scott, *Olive Schreiner: A Biography* (London: André Deutsch, 1980; repr. with an introduction by Nadine Gordimer, London: The Women's Press, 1989).
From Man to Man	Olive Schreiner, *From Man to Man, or Perhaps Only* . . . (London: T. Fisher Unwin, 1926).
Rive	*Olive Schreiner: Letters, i, 1871–1889*, ed. Richard Rive with historical research by Russell Martin (Oxford: Oxford University Press, 1988).

All biblical quotations are taken from the Authorized Version.

Schreiner included a reasonably comprehensive glossary of 'Dutch and Colonial' words in all editions of her novel (reproduced on p. xli), and these have been included, often with some modification, in the notes. Many of these terms are taken from Taal, the dialect of Dutch spoken by Boer (Afrikaner) settlers. Modern Afrikaans, formalized in the 1920s, brings together elements of Taal and High Dutch.

DEDICATION *Mrs John Brown*: Schreiner first met Mary Brown (1847–1935) in Fraserburg, Eastern Cape, in 1873, where her husband John Brown was district surgeon. Three years later the Browns moved to Edinburgh so that he could improve his medical qualifications. Schreiner maintained a lively correspondence with them, eventually gaining sufficient funds as a governess to fulfil the 'English plan' the Browns had devised for her in Fraserburg. Recognizing Schreiner's intellectual abilities, the Browns helped her to apply for nursing training at the Royal Infirmary in Edinburgh. They also sought a British publisher for *The Story of an African Farm* in early 1880, although it was Schreiner herself who finally secured a deal with Chapman and Hall. Shortly after arriving in Britain in 1881, Schreiner visited the Browns in Burnley, Lancashire, and discussed the possibility of registering to study as a doctor rather than a nurse. Costs encouraged Schreiner to take the latter course but bad health prevented her from staying in Edinburgh for more than three days. The relationship between the Browns and Schreiner is recorded in Mrs John Brown, *Memories of a Friendship* (Cape Town, 1923).

EPIGRAPH *Alexis de Tocqueville* (1805–59) stands among the most eminent French historians of the nineteenth century. His best-known work in English-speaking contexts is *Democracy in America* (2 vols., 1835–40). Schreiner's epigraph is taken from the beginning of ch. 2 in the 2nd volume. This quotation continues: 'The growth of nations presents something analogous to this; they all bear some marks of their origin. The circumstances that accompanied their birth and contributed to their development affected the whole germ of their being.' In this context, de Tocqueville's words suggest that *African Farm* just as much concerns the development of the South African nation as it does the histories of Schreiner's characters.

PART I

1 *karroo*: high arid plains of semi-desert in the Eastern Cape located behind the coastal mountain ranges. Given the lack of permanent water supplies, the Karoo proved extremely inhospitable to early settlers in the colony. Schreiner's writings repeatedly celebrate its boundlessness and stark beauty.

kopje: meaning 'small head', a Dutch word for hillock.

sheep kraals: a pen for sheep or cattle made of stone walls and thorn bushes. The word kraal may refer to either a pen for keeping herded animals or a black-African encampment.

Kaffir: a black African. The word comes from the Arabic, and means infidel. As this etymology indicates, the term has always been pejorative. Since Schreiner's writing often makes clear gestures against the racial subordination of native Africans (see *From Man to Man*, 417–38), her employment of this derogatory name may appear surprisingly insensitive. The abusive word Kaffir generically refers to the Bantu-speaking peoples of the Cape.

2 *Boer*: farmer (Dutch).

3 *For wide is the gate . . . Because strait is the gate*: Matthew 7: 13–14.

6 *Ye shall receive*: 'For every one that asketh receiveth; and he that seeketh findeth': Matthew 7: 8.

7 *'I am like Cain'*: 'Abel was a keeper of sheep, but Cain was a tiller of the ground. And in process of time it came to pass, that Cain brought of the fruit of the ground an offering unto the Lord. And Abel, he also brought of the firstlings of his flock and of the fat thereof. And the Lord had respect unto Abel and to his offering: but unto Cain and to his offering he had not respect. And Cain was very wroth, and his countenance fell': Genesis 4: 2–5.

coop: hide-and-seek.

10 *vel-schoen*: shoes made of raw hide.

11 *kappje*: a long cap to prevent sunburn.

Hottentot: a Taal onomatopoeia for the sounds that Boer settlers thought most characterized the language of the Khoi people.

16 *sloots*: dry watercourses, often with very deep sides.

17 *'I was a stranger, and ye took me in'*: Matthew 25: 35.

mealies: maize, corn-meal.

20 *reims*: raw hide thongs.

23 *Emmaus*: the village where Jesus Christ, after he was resurrected, appeared to two of his disciples: see Luke 24: 13–35.

28 *the angel opened the prison door for Peter*: see Acts 12: 17.

32 *nachtmaal*: the Lord's Supper.

33 *Why did the women in Mark see only one angel and the women in Luke two?*: see Mark 16: 5 and Luke 24: 4.

Jael the wife of Heber the Kenite: Jael, wife of Heber the Kenite, killed Sisera, the representative of the Israelites' enemy, Jabin, King of Canaan: see Judges 4: 17–24.

34 *Beulah*: the Hebrew word means 'married', and in Isaiah 62: 4 it stands as the name Israel will bear in future times of prosperity.

35 *predikant*: parson.

37 *meiboss*: salted and sugared apricot confectionary cut in slices.

38 *Jeremiah . . . Ezekiel . . . Hosea*: Old Testament prophets.

39 *'A charge to keep I have . . . And fit it for the sky'*: hymn by Charles Wesley (1707–88).

42 *the fourteenth of John*: this chapter teaches the well-known lesson of Jesus Christ: 'In my Father's house are many mansions . . .'.

Copernicus: Nicolaus Copernicus (1473–1543), proponent of the view that the Earth revolved around the Sun. His study, *On the Revolutions of the Celestial Spheres*, was published in 1543.

46 *pap*: porridge.

51 *Love so amazing . . . my life, my all*: from *'When I Survey the Wondrous Cross'*, a hymn by Isaac Watts (1674–1748), first collected in *Hymns and Spiritual Songs* (1707).

51 *mountains of Hermon*: a metaphor for God's blessing in Psalms 133: 3.

54 *Hagar*: in the Old Testament, Hagar was Abraham's concubine and bore him Ishmael. Sarah, Abraham's wife, banished Hagar and her child to the desert: see Genesis 21: 9–17.

'Ach Jerusalen du schone': 'Oh Jerusalem thou art beautiful', a German hymn.

56 *bobootie-meat*: curried hash.

65 *out-spanned*: unharnessed.

70 *stiver*: an infinitesimal amount; the word means a Dutch penny.

76 *Communism, Fourierism, St. Simonism*: J. S. Mill elaborates his thoughts on these revolutionary forms of social organization in his chapter 'On Property' in Book II of *Principles of Political Economy* (1848). On 29 October 1892, Schreiner wrote: 'The only man to whose moral I am conscious of owing a profound and unending debt is John Stuart Mill' (Rive, 213).

77 *bultongs*: (modern spelling: biltongs) sun-dried meat, either cut into strips or grated.

80 *sleg . . . Davel*: wicked . . . Devil.

84 *Jacob working seven years and seven years again for his wife*: the story of Jacob's labours to marry Leah and Rachel in Genesis 29: 20, 27.

85 *'A le wereld'*: an exclamation similar to the expression 'What is the world coming to?'

93 *Baal*: in the Old Testament, a heathen god worshipped by the Canaanites. Hosea brought shame upon the name of Baal.

97 *benaawdheit*: indigestion, physical discomfort.

vonlicsense: presumably the name for the red drops to cure indigestion.

PART II

101 *seasons of its own*: 'To everything there is a season, and a time to every purpose under the heaven: a time to be born, and a time to die . . .': Ecclesiastes 3: 1.

103 *Elijah in his cave at Horeb*: Elijah spent forty days and nights in the wilderness around Mount Horeb: see 1 Kings 19: 8.

the fifth chapter of Matthew: this chapter contains Christ's well-known teaching: 'Blessed are the poor in spirit: for theirs is the kingdom of heaven . . .': v.3.

105 *'The torment . . . to be burning without intermission as long as God is God'*: from one of Jeremy Taylor's sermons. Taylor (1613–51), an Anglican bishop, is celebrated for his baroque prose style. His *XXVII Sermons Preached at Golden Grove* (1651), *XXV Sermons* (1653) frequently contain, as here, physiological references.

'A moment's time . . .': from John Wesley's (1703–91), 'An Hymn for Seriousness' in *Hymns and Sacred Poems* (1749).

106 *chapter in the prophets*: presumably an allusion to Isaiah 60.

107 *Jerusalem . . . Barnabas . . . Titus*: Barnabas and Titus were among Christ's earliest disciples: see Galatians 2: 1.

110 *'Lift up your heads, O ye gates . . .'*: Psalms 24: 7.

111 *'He that believeth not shall be damned'*: Mark 16: 16.

112 *'What doest thou here, Elijah?'*: God's words to Elijah after his forty days and nights in the wilderness: 1 Kings 19: 9.

117 *Alladeen*: seemingly a confused reference to 'Aladdin, or The wonderful Lamp' from *The Arabian Nights*.

123 *'In certain valleys there was a hunter.'* Schreiner reprinted the allegory that follows in *Dreams*, 25–50.

133 *Mumboo-jumbow*: a West African god. More commonly spelled mumbo-jumbo, it is thought to be a mistranscription of the name of the Mandingo people of the Niger valley.

135 *Sinai*: God's law was handed to Moses on tablets of stone on Mount Sinai (now in modern Egypt): see Exodus 19: 1 ff.

142 *'They never loved . . . realms of light'*: quotation unidentified.

142 *Nazianzen*: St Gregory of Nazianus (329–89), a Cappadocian father; he defended the Nicene creed against Arian heresies. As Bishop of Constantinople, he was instrumental in securing the orthodox faith.

146 *vrijers*: lovers.

158 *Goethe . . . 'Faust' . . . 'Iphigenie'*: Johann Wolfgang von Goethe (1749–1832), among his many distinguished works are his verse-plays *Iphiginie auf Taurus* (1787) and *Faust* (two parts, 1808, 1832).

161 *Cape-smoke*: cheap brandy distilled in the Cape.

162 *mountain of Nebo*: worship of Nebo is denounced in Isaiah 46: 1.

165 *sasarties*: prepared meat, like kebabs.

167 *Upsitting*: An Afrikaner custom during courtship where the couple about to be married stay up all night together.

174 *veld*: open grass-country.

178 *the Blue Water . . . John Speriwig*: tunes for country dances.

181 *stoep*: a stone-flagged veranda.

184 *dicynodont*: (more usually spelt dicinodont) a fossil reptile found in red sandstone in South Africa. Schreiner mentions this creature in a letter to Havelock Ellis, 10 April 1886 about how she felt about the manuscript of her novel during her final days in the Cape: 'I sat with *The African Farm* by my stream at Lelie Kloof, at the place where I dug out my dicinodont, and such disgust came over me at the way I had expressed what was so clear to me, that I nearly threw it into the water and let it drown for ever' (Cronwright-Schreiner, 97).

190 *the Thorn Kloof Schottische*: presumably a Scottish reel. A kloof is a gorge. The farm in *From Man to Man* is called Thorn Kloof. In 1876 Schreiner's 'Ratel Hoek Journal' records that she is working on a story entitled *Thorn Kloof* (Clayton, 102).

197 *'Battle of Hohenlinden'*: a reference to 'Hohenlinden' (1824), a poem by Thomas Campbell (1777–1844), who was famed for his rousing battle songs. During his Italian campaign, Napoleon's forces, led by Jean-Victor Moreau, defeated the Austrian army at Hohenlinden, Bavaria, on 3 December 1800. 'Not a Drum was Heard', another patriotic poem, was published in *The Burial of Sir John Moore at Corunna* (1817) by the Irish poet, Charles Wolfe (1791–1823).

214 *Bloemfontein*: major city in Orange Free State, now Free State.

220 *'First Principles'*: major work by the social evolutionist, Herbert Spencer (1820–1903), published in 1862. It had a powerful impact on Schreiner, who wrote to the free-thinker, Karl Pearson, in July 1886: 'What do all the libertines in London, what do all the good husbands and wives know of happiness, compared with what I knew when I lay all night on the floor beside the fire in Dordrecht [in the Cape], and read *First Principles*, and for the first time the whole theory of evolution which I had been feeling after in the dark burst in upon my sight!' (Rive, 90).

221 *Farber*: echoing the German word for colour. This is the first time we learn of Waldo's (and Otto's) family name. It implies the quality of Otto's and Waldo's artistic natures.

233 *spider*: carriage.

'Salt-reim's' money 'Salt-reim' is a pejorative term for a native Englishman. It derives from the satirical idea that Englishmen had their bundled belongings (tied with 'reims' or rawhide thongs) covered in salty sea-spray, since they had travelled far across the ocean. It is possible that Schreiner also had the commonplace Boer insult 'salt-piel' (salty-pizzle) in mind. Since each and every Englishman was thought to have one foot in his homeland and the other in South Africa, he was known as a 'salt-piel' because his penis was left dangling in the sea beneath him. (I am grateful to Dennis Walder of the Open University for advice on this note.)

239 *meerkat*: small ground-lemur.

251 *kartel*: wooden bed inside an ox-wagon.

Let me not see the death of the child: a further reference to the plight of Hagar in the wilderness: see Genesis 21: 16.

256 *And I saw the dead, small and great* . . . : a paraphrase of Revelations 20: 12–15.

258 *the Transcendentalist's high answer*: a reference to the American transcendentalist, Ralph Waldo Emerson (1803–20), whose two series of *Essays* (1841, 1844) Schreiner knew well.

260 *Was it only John, think you, who saw the heavens open?*: see Revelations 21: 1–2.

263 *golden calf*: object of worship set up by the Israelites in Exodus 32: 2 ff.

264 *morgen*: a measurement of slightly more than two acres.

264 *sourka, sourka, sourka*: presumably meaning 'in a proud and conceited manner'.

   Amalekite: enemy tribe of the Israelites: see, for example, Numbers 14.

   brajke: cur.

267 *'Thou shalt have no other gods before me'*: Exodus 20: 3.

TROLLOPE IN OXFORD WORLD'S CLASSICS

ANTHONY TROLLOPE

An Autobiography

The American Senator

Barchester Towers

Can You Forgive Her?

The Claverings

Cousin Henry

Doctor Thorne

The Duke's Children

The Eustace Diamonds

Framley Parsonage

He Knew He Was Right

Lady Anna

The Last Chronicle of Barset

Orley Farm

Phineas Finn

Phineas Redux

The Prime Minister

Rachel Ray

The Small House at Allington

The Warden

The Way We Live Now

Émile Zola
L'Assommoir
The Attack on the Mill
La Bête humaine
La Débâde
Germinal
The Ladies' Paradise
The Masterpiece
Nana
Pot Luck
Thérèse Raquin

A SELECTION OF   **OXFORD WORLD'S CLASSICS**

The Oxford World's Classics Website

www.worldsclassics.co.uk

- Information about new titles
- Explore the full range of Oxford World's Classics
- Links to other literary sites and the main OUP webpage
- Imaginative competitions, with bookish prizes
- Peruse the Oxford World's Classics Magazine
- Articles by editors
- Extracts from Introductions
- A forum for discussion and feedback on the series
- Special information for teachers and lecturers

www.worldsclassics.co.uk

American Literature

British and Irish Literature

Children's Literature

Classics and Ancient Literature

Colonial Literature

Eastern Literature

European Literature

History

Medieval Literature

Oxford English Drama

Poetry

Philosophy

Politics

Religion

The Oxford Shakespeare

A complete list of Oxford Paperbacks, including Oxford World's Classics, Oxford Shakespeare, Oxford Drama, and Oxford Paperback Reference, is available in the UK from the Academic Division Publicity Department, Oxford University Press, Great Clarendon Street, Oxford OX2 6DP.

In the USA, complete lists are available from the Paperbacks Marketing Manager, Oxford University Press, 198 Madison Avenue, New York, NY 10016.

Oxford Paperbacks are available from all good bookshops. In case of difficulty, customers in the UK can order direct from Oxford University Press Bookshop, Freepost, 116 High Street, Oxford OX1 4BR, enclosing full payment. Please add 10 per cent of published price for postage and packing.